"You are a monster, Jack Silver."

Driven only by instinct, Elizabeth drew the black cloak from the back of the chair and held it to her breast as a shield against his still mocking gaze. Yet nothing could alleviate the feeling of nakedness, of powerlessness, that enveloped her. She raised the garment to her chin and fought the urge to bury her face in the smoky roughness of the coarse wool cloth.

He strode to her, his steps deliberate, neither slow nor rushed. Standing behind her, he parted the heavy fall of her hair and draped it over her shoulders to give him easy access to the row of buttons down her back.

She stood still, hardly daring to breathe, as she felt the deft movements of his fingers and the widening expanse of exposed flesh as the dress gaped further and further open.

"I never claimed to be anything else," he replied.

MOONSILVER

LINDA HILTON

POCKET BOOKS

New York London Toronto Sydney Tokyo Singapore

This book is a work of fiction. Names, characters, places and incidents are products of the author's imagination or are used fictitiously. Any resemblance to actual events or locales or persons, living or dead, is entirely coincidental.

An *Original* Publication of POCKET BOOKS

POCKET BOOKS, a division of Simon & Schuster Inc.
1230 Avenue of the Americas, New York, NY 10020

ISBN: 978-1-4516-7763-8

First Pocket Books printing April 1995

10 9 8 7 6 5 4 3 2 1

POCKET and colophon are registered trademarks of Simon & Schuster Inc.

Cover art by Dan Craig/Oasis Studio

Printed in the U.S.A.

Dedicated
with much love
and gratitude
to
Alexis, Brenda, Jan,
Kay, Janet, Rebecca, Coral,
Connie, Kathie, Deborah,
Kasey, Laurie, Lucy,
Penny, Sherrilyn, Sonia,
Tanya, Debra, Mary, Monique,
Jessica, and Fayrene—
the godmothers

And also to Barbara Kenshol and Shirley Stryker, who
to my good fortune married Ted and Dick Mueller to
become my aunts.

MOONSILVER

CHAPTER

1

Somerset, England
1820

He's here.

That simple thought sent a shiver of excitement down Betsy Bunch's spine. Somewhere amidst the noise and bustle, the smoke and savory aromas of the dimly lit common room of the Black Oak Inn was the man she had waited months to see.

But which of the patrons crowded into the inn this stormy January night was he? As she looked around, she felt a stab of disappointment at not immediately recognizing him. Then she scolded herself and hefted the wooden tray to her shoulder. Jack Silver would hardly frequent a public inn like the Black Oak without some kind of disguise. She was a fool to think she'd be able to spot him so easily. If an ordinary tavern maid could recognize Jack Silver, so could any thief-taker eager for the hundred-guinea reward on the highwayman's head.

Still, Betsy gazed hopefully about the room while she served plates of steaming stew and filled empty tankards. She knew more than a little about disguises herself, she thought, fingering the blond curls peeking from under her smudged white cap. To dodge a grasping young man's attempt to snare her skirt, she sidestepped nimbly, never spilling a drop of ale while she surveyed the occupants of the room.

Could he be disguised as one of the two middle-aged women who sat by the window with a young boy tucked between them? Betsy delivered their dinner and scrutinized them until there was no doubt in her mind. Neither the tall, cadaverous woman in black nor her plump companion could possibly be the dashing pirate of the road. And the boy wasn't more than nine or ten years of age.

"Here, over here!" a half-drunken voice called, gaining Betsy's attention. "We was 'ere before 'em wimmen."

"Ain'tcha never 'eard o' ladies first?" Betsy rounded on the caller, who sat at a plank table near the center of the room. "I'll get more from kitchen and bring it to you straight," she promised, taking the opportunity to study the man.

The Black Oak was built for warmth and comfort; even by day the great common room was gloomy and dark. Now, flickering candles in soot-blackened chimneys providing the only light, the place was filled with smoky, shifting shadows. Betsy had to look closely, afraid she'd mistake her own father if he sat in front of her.

Jack Silver might be a master of disguise, but no mention had ever been made of his having only half an ear, like this fellow. Nor a mouthful of rotten stumps for teeth. Disgusted, Betsy sidled between tables on her way to the kitchen. She'd seen no sign of anyone who resembled the notorious outlaw, yet she knew he had to be here. Her own clandestine trek had taken her through the woods behind the inn, where she had discovered a saddled gray stallion tethered in a secluded glade. If Jack Silver himself was variously described as either short or tall, big-boned or wiry, the reports of his escapades never failed to mention his smoke-colored steed.

Lost for a moment in her thoughts, she nearly ran into Hennie Sharpe, the innkeeper's daughter, who emerged from the kitchen with a tray balanced on each hand.

"Lor' bless you, Betsy," Hennie sighed. "'Tween this storm and the fire at the Bow and Blade last week, I never seen so much custom here. Ain't sure I ever want to again. Like to kill me, it is."

Betsy grabbed one of the trays in imminent danger of toppling from Hennie's unsteady grasp.

"I'd'a been here sooner, save Nell couldn't get word to me. Her bleedin' ladyship needed a dress mended, as if she's goin' anywheres on a night like this."

To signal her understanding of the incomprehensible ways of the gentry, Hennie rolled her eyes ceilingward and led the way back into the chaos.

Betsy allowed herself a grin. The success of her deception continued to amaze her. Hennie readily accepted that her sister Nell was unable to escape her labors as personal maid to Elizabeth Stanhope, mistress of nearby Stanhope Manor, but no one at the inn questioned that another servant like Betsy Bunch was free to come and go as she pleased.

Elizabeth's masquerade as Betsy had begun as a lighthearted challenge between mistress and maid nearly a year ago. While Nell may have doubted Elizabeth Stanhope could pass herself off as a common serving girl and not be recognized or even raise a curious eyebrow, Elizabeth found the game a welcome diversion, a chance to experience much more of life than her overprotective father would ever have allowed. Now, though an evening helping out at the inn meant a long, cold walk over snowy fields, Elizabeth enjoyed the freedom her charade gave her. And for the opportunity to see Jack Silver, who was reputed to frequent the Black Oak in search of likely victims, she would risk nearly anything.

For the next hour, she did little but serve food and clear away empty dishes and mentally tick off the impossibilities of matching each guest to the sketchy, and often contradictory, descriptions of the elusive bandit.

She recognized a pair of servants from the manor, who could be dismissed if her father learned of their absence. Others, like Harry Grove, the one-legged jockey from the earl of Kilbury's empty stables, were just as obviously erased from her list. With the common room so crowded, she had wondered if there were other patrons in the private room, but Hennie quickly assured her there were not.

"Cold as a privy in there," the exhausted Hennie explained when they had a moment to rest while young Robin Sharpe, Hennie's brother, refilled pitchers from the tap. "The old man fergot to lay a fire, and ain't nobody else had time, busy as it's been. Just afore you come, them dandies on their way to Brighton like to tear the whole place down if they couldn't have a private room. Mam showed 'em the place, said she could lock 'em in there and they'd have all the privacy they liked."

Robin deposited the last full pitcher on Hennie's tray and injected his own portion of the tale.

"She told 'em they had three choices: freeze their behinds in privacy, freeze their behinds in their coach on the road, or warm their behinds in the common room. I think they might've chose the highway, if'n she hadn't hinted it was high time old Jack Silver was ridin'. Moon's full behind them clouds."

The boy winked at Betsy, then slapped his sister on her own behind.

Hennie sighed in exasperation and pushed the half door from the taproom open, then held it for Betsy.

"Got a head full of crazy notions, that boy does,"

4

Hennie complained with a shake of her head. "I sometimes think he'd rather be out there with that bleedin' highwayman, riskin' his fool neck in a noose, than makin' an honest penny here."

Betsy bit back a retort, knowing her own notions were hardly less crazy. Jack Silver was a romantic symbol of freedom, a latter-day Robin Hood who did as he pleased and avoided all the restrictions the rest of them lived with. It made no difference that he never gave a penny to the poor; he robbed only the rich and for nearly four years had eluded both capture and the discovery of his true identity.

With Betsy leading the way, the two young women had nearly reached the center of the room when the double doors at the front entrance exploded inward.

For an instant the room lapsed into a stunned silence as all eyes turned toward the hatless, florid-faced newcomer who stood just inside the yawning doorway.

Snow swirled about him on a blast of icy wind, but something about the man's obvious rage held any complaints at bay. He surveyed the crowd, then bellowed at them in a tone that implied he held them personally responsible for his misfortune.

"I've been robbed!"

He didn't move a muscle, save for the one twitching furiously in his jaw. While Hennie gaped, as speechless as nearly everyone else, Betsy set her laden tray on the nearest available table and went to the man's assistance.

She closed the doors behind him, shutting out the bitter wind that set her teeth to chattering instantly. For a brief moment she regretted her decision to set out on such a night, for by the time she made the long trek home, the snow would be knee deep in the fields and the temperature deadly cold.

At least she had chosen freely to brave the elements; Thomas Colfax, robbed on the King's Highway, had taken his stroll through the snow and wind against his will. She ought to feel some sympathy for him, she thought with an alarming lack of guilt, but somehow she did not.

"Well, are you going to sit there and let the scoundrel get away with it?" he shrieked to his attentive audience.

"Better that than we freeze in the storm for the likes of your paltry purse," one man piped up from a back corner of the room.

Colfax turned a deeper shade of crimson as his anger mounted.

Betsy swallowed a knot of fear and took his arm to lead him none too gently toward the private room.

"This way, milord," she cajoled, keeping her face turned away from his, though she doubted he would take any notice of a common tavern maid. "Room's a bit nippy, but I'll bring some wine and Hennie'll start a blaze on the hearth. There's some nice stew left, hot in the kitchen."

He shook her off so roughly she staggered several steps before she lost her balance completely. With a little cry of surprise, she fell onto the lap of a sleepy traveler, curled beneath a heavy cloak in the cozy corner by the fireplace. The poor man grunted at the abrupt disturbing of his rest.

"Beg yer pardon, sir," she stammered as she scrambled to her feet. One hand straightened her skirts while the other made certain her cap hadn't slipped.

Then both hands stilled. A gasp rose in her throat, and a jolt of shock slammed into her heart.

Under the edge of the hood he had drawn up over his head, she saw only the flashing silver-blue of his eyes and the crooked twist of a wry smile on his lips. Yet that was enough. No matter what disguise this wayfarer may have put on, she knew for certain sure that under it all, Jack Silver moved in the flesh.

"Best see to his lordship," the cloaked gentleman

murmured as she stumbled away from his shadow-shrouded corner. "Sounds like a man with the devil's own temper."

"Aye, he has that," she mumbled in reply.

She gathered her composure quickly, though her heart continued to beat erratically and she could hardly quell the urge to look back over her shoulder and see if the stranger in the hooded cloak still lounged in his warm corner. Jack Silver could wait; there was still Thomas Colfax to be taken care of, Thomas Colfax with his temper to rival that of an angry Beelzebub.

And it was Betsy who found herself in charge of the situation. Hennie was too shocked to do anything but take orders, and none of Colfax's orders was capable of fulfillment, not when one contradicted the next.

"Get these wet boots off before my feet freeze solid!" he demanded. Then, the instant Hennie had dropped to her knees to remove the threatening footwear, Colfax barked, "I thought you were bringing me hot wine?"

Hennie struggled to her feet but had taken no more than two steps when Colfax halted her again.

"Weren't you going to lay a fire? Or do you expect me to warm my toes on yesterday's ashes?"

Thomas Colfax was, Betsy knew only too well, an arrogant bully who loved to push around those unwilling or unable to stand up for themselves. But if Hennie Sharpe dared not face the man squarely for fear of retribution, Betsy Bunch had no such worries.

"I'll go t'the kitchen and fetch his lordship's wine and supper," she told Hennie without once looking at their furious guest. "You take care o' the fire, and I'll send Robin wi' dry slippers and a robe."

That left Colfax temporarily without demands, and Betsy took the opportunity to escape, hoping Hennie could cope until he came up with more. Robin was waiting when she slipped out of the private room and shut the door carefully behind her. A broad grin lit the boy's face.

"I told ye it were a night for Jack Silver to ride," he boasted. "Did he say 'twas Jack for sure what robbed him?"

"He said nothing," she answered, "'cept to bellow like a stuck pig that he wants wine and supper and a big fire. Now, there's enough wood 'n' kindling so I told Hennie to—"

A gruff voice shouted an interruption. "It's my inn, and I'll be givin' the orders in it!"

She turned to see Ned Sharpe push his way through the knot of curious onlookers that had gathered around the door to the private chamber. And when he reached her, he planted his pudgy hands on his hips and glared at her, eye to eye.

"Well, now, if it isn't Betsy Bunch, me now-and-then servingmaid," Ned snorted. "What brings you down from yon castle on a night like this?"

Robin, head and shoulders taller, laid a restraining hand on his father's arm.

"Not now," the boy warned. "Thomas Colfax is in there, sayin' he's been robbed. Hennie was on the point of blubberin' like a babe, an' Betsy just put things to rights. You can go back to the taproom."

But Ned was not so easily turned from his anger.

"No, *you* go back to the taproom," he ordered his son. "And as for you, Betsy Bunch of Stanhope Manor—"

"I came," she interrupted just as grandly as Ned himself had, "because Hennie sent word to Nell that you needed help. Nell couldn't get away, so I come in her place, like I do whenever she can't."

Ned had never made any secret of his dislike for her, despite her offering her services in his daughter's place and never asking a farthing in pay. Perhaps, she thought in a moment of doubt, he might not have been so suspicious had she taken the miserly coin he once offered.

But she could afford neither doubts nor second thoughts now. Thomas Colfax fumed in the private room, and Jack Silver lounged in the common.

She swallowed her temper but not her pride.

"If you like, I'll not come here again," she suggested in compromise, "but for tonight ye've got trouble on yer hands." She placed one arm around Ned's ample shoulders and explained, "Mr. Thomas, now, he spends a good deal of time at the manor, bein' Miss Elizabeth's betrothed and all, and whiles I don't exactly sit in the drawin' room with him, I know what pleases him and keeps the common folk like you an' me in his good graces. It could mean something to you to please him tonight."

To emphasize, she raised her free hand and rubbed her thumb across the tips of her fingers.

Leaving Ned to contemplate that possibility, she withdrew her conspiratorial arm and marched off to the kitchen.

The room warmed slowly, but with the table pulled close to the fire, Thomas Colfax devoured his late supper in comfort. An obsequious Ned stood by, twisting his hands as he begged to be of further service and listened avidly while Jack Silver's latest victim described in minute detail the events that brought him to the Black Oak Inn.

"I set forth from Stanhope at something just after three o'clock, well before sundown," Thomas explained between mouthfuls of stew and gulps of hot, spiced wine.

With Hennie and Robin busy preparing a room for their guest to spend the night, there was no one left to wait on Colfax besides a very reluctant Betsy Bunch. She took care to draw as little attention to herself as possible while she, like Ned, took in every word of the man's elaborate narrative.

"Even with the snow, I expected to reach Kilbury in an hour, two at the very most. And who ever heard of a highwayman striking in the middle of the day?

"Besides, I always carry a pistol," Colfax assured his small but rapt audience. "One would certainly expect a highwayman to make his presence known by blocking one's path. A single shot at close range would be enough to end the fellow's raids once and for all."

How ungentlemanly, then, of the rogue to sneak up on his victim from behind and order him to halt, under threat of a pistol ball in the back, and throw down his purse. Betsy refilled Colfax's goblet without letting him see the flicker of a smile that twitched her lips. She knew better than most that Thomas Colfax had little right to accuse anyone of ungentlemanly actions.

"Then, when I had dropped the purse on the ground, he ordered me to dismount. Said there was an inn not two miles distant and bade me walk."

But Betsy, remembering the teasing voice that had reminded her of Colfax's temper, could easily imagine the way Jack Silver had taunted his victim.

The hour was growing late, much later than she had ever stayed at the inn before. Thomas continued to ramble after Hennie returned to announce that a chamber had been readied upstairs, but Betsy did not stay. She slipped out and tiptoed into the common room, now darkened and almost silent, save for the snores and shifting of those who had fallen asleep.

The old women and the boy had long since taken themselves upstairs, as had the Brighton-bound dandies. The single candle left burning on the mantel shed just enough light for Betsy to identify those who remained. The two men from Stanhope were gone; she hoped they had made their way safely home before being discovered.

Harry Grove lay on a hard bench by the great hearth, his arm for a pillow. At least he'd not be missed, for the earl of Kilbury who graciously kept the old jockey employed no longer had a stableful of racehorses for him to ride. She shook her head with a slight smile, wondering again if there were something wrong with a penniless aristocrat who refused to dismiss a useless servant.

She did not see the man in the black cloak. Whether he had retired to an upstairs room or left the inn altogether, she had no way of knowing, and she dared not ask. But she felt a sharp stab of disappointment, as sharp as the thrill of looking up into those glittering eyes of his.

Shaking off such useless sentiments, she made her way to the kitchen door. Robin sat at the long, scarred trestle table with a plate of stew and two crusts of bread.

"Ye'd best not go now," he warned, offering her a morsel of his bread and a place beside him. "Wait 'til daylight, else you'll get lost in the snow."

"They'd miss me up at the manor. I can't lose my place there."

"Mam'd give ye work here," Hennie suggested, a note of bitterness in her voice, as she walked into the room almost on Betsy's heels. She sank wearily to the bench beside her brother and snatched the bread from his hand.

"Aye, that I would," Mary Sharpe interjected as she entered the kitchen from the taproom.

Like Hennie and Robin, Mary was slender almost to gauntness, in contrast to her roly-poly husband. She wiped her work-chapped hands on her apron then turned to warm them at the kitchen hearth.

"Don't take it so hard, child," the mother soothed. "I only meant that Betsy seemed to know what she was doin' around the likes of Mister Colfax."

There was no argument Betsy could make, one way

or the other. So she took her cloak from a peg by the door and without another word stepped out into the night.

The cold took her breath away, and when she dared to exhale, a thick cloud formed before her face. It hung in the air, for there was no wind. Only snow. Soft, fat flakes filled the darkness, and already a thick carpet of them blanketed the ground.

Perhaps Robin was right. She knew her way between the Black Oak and Stanhope Manor as well as she knew her way from the dining room to the drawing room. But could she negotiate that distance blind and hobbled by the snow? Here, in the enclosed innyard, there was no more than an inch or two of newfallen snow. But the fields she had to cross were likely knee-deep with the stuff, and the stubble underneath made the footing uneven and dangerous.

The road, though it might be easier to travel, also meant near double the journey. Stanhope lay three long miles across country from the Black Oak, but by the King's Highway—which Jack Silver had once again claimed as his own—the distance was nearer to six. But after a long night's work, she doubted she had the stamina to trudge through the snowy fields.

Braced against the cold, she hunched her shoulders and pulled the cloak's hood over her cap and set off down the road. She had no choice but to follow it all those long miles home.

The moon rode high overhead, a pale glimmer behind the snow. It cast an eerie luminescence, sufficient for seeing one's way but not enough to reveal the details of a robber's face and form. Oh, yes, Jack Silver was clever and aptly named, for he rode only on those nights when the moon was just thus.

A shiver made its way down her back. She paused midstride, breath held as she listened. Only the almost silent drifting of snowflakes in the winter-leafed oaks reached her ears. She pressed on, until the cluster of trees that gave the inn its name thinned and she passed into open country once more.

She strode on, counting her footsteps until she reached a hundred. The exertion kept her comfortably warm, and though the snow continued to fall, the road was not too thickly covered to hamper her way home.

"'Twould serve me right if I did freeze," she muttered in mock chastisement, turning up the corners of her mouth in a slow, rueful smile. She lifted her face to catch the delicate kisses of snowflakes on her cheeks. "I have seen him," she whispered to the winter darkness. "At long last, I have seen him, and he spoke to me!"

With her eyes closed, she hugged the knowledge more tightly to her.

When she opened her eyes once more, a phantasm appeared in front of her, forming from the moonglow and drifting snow. Had it not snorted and stamped its foot in warning, she might have walked right into the great gray stallion who blocked the road.

"It's not wise to talk to yourself," the beast's rider advised. "You might be thought mad and packed off to Bedlam."

As a cloaked figure dismounted, the stallion snorted again and shook its heavily maned head. Elizabeth did not move, not out of fear but out of anticipation. For the voice was now a familiar one, one she had never expected to hear again so soon.

He held the reins loosely as he approached her, visible as only a dark shape in the formless shadowworld of the snowy night.

"Has fear frozen your tongue?" he asked, concern evident in his tone. "Perhaps talking to yourself is not your only symptom of an unbalanced mind. Surely anyone who ventures out on a night like this must not—"

"I'm not mad," she managed to blurt out. "I'm on me way home, late though it is. So if you'll kindly let me by, I'll forget I ever laid me eyes on ye."

Where were these words coming from? Not her brain, surely, for she could not remember thinking them before they tripped off her tongue. Good God, she had just told the man she knew who he was and where he had been! Was he not likely to do something to ensure her silence?

Then fear did take hold of her. Notions of excitement and adventure all fled when she found herself staring face to chin with Jack Silver.

"You wound me, milady," he whispered in that teasing, taunting voice. "I was about to offer you a ride on this noble steed in hopes that you remember me all your days."

CHAPTER

2

She rode awkwardly in front of him until she became accustomed to the horse's steady, rocking gait. The highwayman chuckled as she fell back against him.

"Have you never ridden on the front of a man's saddle before?"

"Never," she answered truthfully. His arm had gone around her waist with such easy intimacy that she had no chance to protest. She doubted he would have paid the slightest attention anyway.

He drew his hooded cloak around the both of them, adding to the warmth she could not reject but also adding to the unease she could not ignore.

"And certainly not on the front of a highway-man's," she muttered to herself.

Encountering the legendary Jack Silver at the Black Oak was all she had dreamed of doing. She wanted to see him, with her own eyes, perhaps exchange a smile, a laugh, a brief bit of friendly banter. That was all. Never in her wildest imaginings had she envisioned herself hoisted onto the gray stallion, the high-wayman's cloak enshrouding her with intimate warmth. No longer was she in command of the situation, able to control her own moves in what had begun as nothing more than a game.

She felt the subtle shift of the man's weight behind her as the wind picked up and swirled the snow angrily about them. Instinctively, she tucked her head down toward her shoulder, away from the sting of the wind and the icy bite of snowflakes on her skin.

At almost that same moment, he leaned forward. With his chin on her shoulder and only the wet wool of her hood separating his cheek from her hair, he asked, "Am I taking you somewhere in particular, milady, or do you accompany me on my own road?"

The enormity of her predicament came instantly clear, much more so than before. The mockery in that low, velvety voice a scant inch from her ear set her blood pounding in her veins. No, she had never counted on this, and all she could think of now was escape.

But when she struggled to be free of the highwayman's embrace, he only tightened his grip and pulled her closer against the hard warmth of his body.

He chuckled to himself as she settled more easily against him. The girl was slighter in his arms than he had expected, which probably meant she was younger than she looked, too. He had little enough experience with peasant girls, like this one who was probably some tenant farmer's daughter.

At first he had thought her older, for the figure that filled out her loosely gathered blouse was certainly that of a woman grown. But he found now, with his arm around her, that despite the generous bosom so enticingly displayed at the inn, she was slim, almost delicate.

She struggled again, and a tremor ran through her that he could not mistake.

"Don't worry, love," he reassured her, "I won't let you fall. Tell me where you need to be and we'll have you there in a trice."

"Stanhope," she said hastily as though she had just remembered her destination. "But take me 'round t'the back, so's no one sees me."

She, of course, could not see how his eyebrow raised in surprise, but she must have felt that odd tensing of his body, because she quickly added an explanation.

"Nell Sharpe, the innkeeper's daughter, she's in service to Elizabeth Stanhope. Nell's sister, Hennie, sent word they was busy at the inn an' needed Nell's help, but Her Precious Ladyship needed Nell more, to mend a dress she couldn't even wear. So I slipped out to help in Nell's place."

He chuckled again and made sure once more that he held tightly to the girl before he nudged the stallion to a brisk trot and then to a smooth, rolling canter. She let out a cry, short and sharp, then grasped the arm that kept her from losing her seat.

"Stanhope Manor it is," he called above the whistle of the midnight wind and the snow-muffled thud of his steed's great hooves.

The sky was nearly clear when they reached the gate to Edward Stanhope's kitchen garden. Moonlight streamed from the velvet darkness and turned the fresh cold snow to powdered diamonds dancing in the wind. The highwayman nudged the girl curled against him.

"See, I've brought you straight home," he whispered gently. "And sooner than if you'd walked all the way, though it's still late."

He smiled ruefully. She was a pretty wench, one he'd not mind sharing his bed with on a bitter night like this. He remembered the way she had smiled while dodging unwelcome pinches; hers was a mouth he could easily imagine kissing long and slowly.

To still the desire such musings produced, he shook her again and insisted, "You must go, milady, and I, too."

He opened his cloak to let the night air rouse her, and that did the trick.

"Oh, goodness, I am home."

She seemed surprised and even a bit bewildered. Her voice was soft with sleep, and she wriggled unconsciously against him in search of warmth.

"You did say Stanhope Manor, did you not?" he asked, a bit confused himself. If he had taken her to the wrong place . . .

"Aye, Stanhope. And by the back way, too. I left the gate unlocked."

"Then you'd best squeeze through while there's still wind to cover your tracks," he suggested. "And my own."

She braced herself as though about to drop to the ground, then at the last moment turned to face him. "Thank you," she whispered.

The moon was behind her, casting her face into deep shadow beneath the overhanging hood of her cloak. He could see nothing of her features, yet he felt as though that smile was carved into his brain. He had no idea what color her eyes were, only that they had sparkled brilliantly in the smoky lantern light at the inn. Now they were but pools of darkness reflecting pinpricks of moonlight on newfallen snow.

"Jack Silver demands more than thanks."

He found her mouth by instinct as he pulled her backward over his arm, then twisted his body over hers.

Her lips were cold but supple, and warmth flooded to them the instant he touched her. He had hoped the moment's contact would startle her into sliding timorously from the saddle; he never expected her to accept and then return the kiss.

Despite her fear, despite her thrill, the warmth of his cloak and gentle embrace coupled with the smooth gait of the stallion had lulled her almost to sleep. Awakened by the cold, her only thought was to escape, to return to the safety of the world she had fled. But now, as his lips touched hers, all conscious thought fled, leaving her with only a firestorm of sensations burning through her. No man had ever kissed her before; she had no idea how exciting yet terrifying it could be to have other lips pressed to hers, seeking, caressing, demanding, delighting.

A sigh rose within her to become a quiet moan of deep pleasure that escaped only when she felt the rasp of his tongue across the line of her lips. The sensation sent a tremor through her. She was his to do with as he would; she knew it, and she was not completely afraid.

When she opened her eyes next, she stood in the deep drifted snow outside the garden gate, and there was no sign of Jack Silver or the gray stallion. Only the remains of hoofprints in the snow gave evidence to their having brought her home, and the rising wind slowly erased even those traces.

But there was another reminder. The flush of barely aroused passion still warmed her. She remembered the texture of his mouth, the strength of his arms, the press of his body against hers. She drew that memory deep inside her and turned to slide through the narrow opening of the unlocked gate. Then, silent as Jack Silver himself, she crossed the kitchen garden and slipped through the door so that she was once again locked within the walls of Stanhope Manor.

Elizabeth slowly descended the marble staircase from the long gallery to the great hall of Stanhope Manor. At the landing where the two flights joined, she paused to sleek back a stray tendril of hair—her own dark hair, she thought, remembering the yellow curls sewn to Betsy Bunch's cap. She felt an uneasy reluctance to join the man waiting for her, as though he could see through her calm exterior to the nervousness dancing within.

"Good morning, Elizabeth," Edward Stanhope

greeted rather sharply. He had difficulty hiding his emotions, which this morning ran to impatience and frustration, exactly as Elizabeth expected. "Did you not sleep well?"

Worried that such a comment hinted at suspicion, she redoubled her efforts to maintain a controlled facade. "The wind kept me awake until long past midnight, and my room was cold. I am sorry I overslept."

She walked down the last of the stairs, aware of her father's scrutiny, aware that her hand trembled on the railing. Tardiness for breakfast was a minor infraction, one that might arouse her father's temper but would soon be forgotten. Today, however, she wanted to draw no attention at all, neither his nor anyone else's. More than anything, she wished to be alone with the thoughts that had kept her awake all night. The wind had whined around her windows, and the room had been cold when she returned to it, but it was the indelible memory of Jack Silver that left her lying wide-eyed and restless in the darkness.

Her father brought her out of her musings with an accusatory, "Mr. Colfax has been here over two hours."

"Whatever for?" Elizabeth asked, suddenly worried that last night's adventure had been discovered.

"Have you forgotten?"

"Obviously I have, Father, or I would not have asked."

Elizabeth bit her tongue; such waspishness startled her. Had the chance encounter with Jack Silver addled her to the point that she could no longer hide her feelings? Or had she played Betsy Bunch so long that the free-speaking tavern maid had taken over her personality? Perhaps, Elizabeth worried, she had less control over her masquerade than she thought.

Her father kept his voice down, though his anger

was readily apparent. "Thomas has brought with him Mr. Brinslow Copperstith, the renowned artist from London, for the purpose of painting your wedding portrait," he said icily, leading her to the breakfast room. "This sitting was scheduled weeks ago, and, Elizabeth, I distinctly remember discussing it with you. You asked if Mr. Copperstith had done Eleanor Eastman's coming out portrait."

"I remember now. I said he must be a brilliant portraitist because he had so cleverly improved Eleanor's horse face and pig's-snout nose."

Feeling a twinge of guilt at such cruelty to the homely Miss Eastman but relieved that her own clandestine activities remained undetected, Elizabeth swept into the breakfast room, which smelled deliciously of bacon and ham and salmon and eggs and fresh hot toast.

She almost ignored the two men already seated at the table, but when they hurried to rise at her entrance, she gave each of them a graceful nod and said simply, "Mr. Colfax. Mr. Copperstith," before proceeding to the sideboard where a minor feast had been laid out.

Above the sideboard hung a huge mirror, which gave Elizabeth a view of the entire room. Her father finally moved away from the door to take his place at the head of the table. A footman appeared to pour Edward another cup of coffee. To her father's left, across from the vacant place left for Elizabeth, sat Thomas Colfax. There was no hiding the fact that Thomas had not spent a pleasant night.

"You look as though you are not feeling well, Mr. Colfax," Elizabeth addressed the reflection while she heaped her plate high. "I do hope you have not caught something contagious."

His color flared, first a bright pink suffusing his cheeks, then an angry crimson that settled in his nose.

At the age of forty-two, Thomas Colfax had not lost the habit of blushing like a girl when embarrassed.

"Thomas was set upon by a highwayman yesterday evening," Edward announced.

Thomas shot his host a daggerlike glance. The blush deepened to an ugly purple.

"How horrible!" Elizabeth remarked with what she hoped was appropriate surprise and concern.

"I was forced to spend the night at a most disreputable posting inn, then rose before dawn to fetch Mr. Copperstith from Kilbury and bring him here."

As she took her seat at the table, Elizabeth knew Thomas's tale was expected to elicit her sympathy, but she could not find the proper words even when the man she had agreed to marry stared at her in anticipation. She turned away from that intense gaze and tried to concentrate on her meal.

She was saved the disaster of a stammered, insincere reply by the arrival of yet another gentleman.

Breathless, disheveled, still sporting traces of melting snow on the collar of his rumpled greatcoat, the earl of Kilbury clutched the doorframe for support as he gasped, "My God, Thomas, why didn't you tell me?"

The elder Colfax looked up from his empty plate, his pale eyes first catching Elizabeth's, then meeting his nephew's.

"It was nothing to fret over, John," Thomas assured the newcomer. The earlier embarrassment gave way to cold disdain. "I wasn't injured, and my horse returned of its own accord. As for the money the miscreant got, it was a small sum I shall hardly miss."

Elizabeth did not turn, though watching the drama from the corner of her eye left her curiosity unsatisfied. "Have you eaten, my lord?" she offered, pushing a bit of salmon around her plate.

"No, bless you, Elizabeth, I did not have time to eat before I set out," he replied as a servant rushed to take his coat, then waited while he struggled to remove his gloves.

Now Elizabeth fought to restrain other emotions. She did not love Thomas Colfax and made no secret of the fact. Their marriage was to be one of other considerations, which she had accepted and agreed to because it was expected of her. In her small circle of acquaintances, including the unattractive Miss Eleanor Eastman, arrangements made between fathers and prospective bridegrooms without consulting the bride were more common than not.

But just as Elizabeth harbored no affection for her betrothed, she resisted the warming of her heart toward Thomas's nephew. It did not matter that her father had deemed the earl of Kilbury an unsuitable match, despite his title. Her feelings, oddly stronger this morning than ever before, would not be disciplined.

She would have closed her eyes, but even blindness could not erase the mental image of John Colfax's painful clumsiness. When he finally pulled his thumb free of the second glove, he dropped the worn bit of wet leather to the floor and nearly bumped heads with the footman in an effort to retrieve it.

With a heavenward roll of his eyes, Edward Stanhope signaled to another servant to bring the earl a plate. Elizabeth bit back a remark, but it was not one of sarcasm or cruelty; she would not, however, let her father use her concern as another excuse to make malicious sport of John's awkwardness.

More often than not, she suffered painful embarrassment on John's behalf, though he acted as if he were utterly unaware of how others, particularly his uncle and Edward Stanhope, saw him. He was tall and thin and habitually wore clothes that seemed chosen to accentuate rather than disguise his physical attributes, and he often displayed a lack of coordination, such as the incident with the gloves. Elizabeth winced at the image in such marked contrast to the smooth grace of the highwayman. John was as unlike Jack Silver as she was unlike Betsy Bunch.

She found her discomfort intensified as John added his own details to Thomas's tale while reaching for a hastily filled coffee cup with one hand and trying to adjust his pince-nez with the other.

"Harry Grove told me this morning. It was Jack Silver, wasn't it, Thomas? And he held a gun on you and made you walk all the way to the Black Oak."

Elizabeth suppressed a shudder at the childlike horror in John's tone. It was hard to believe, at moments like this, that John was only ten years younger than his uncle; his innocence, his insouciance, even his tremulous voice belonged to a boy, not a man. As well as the title to the ancient seat of Kilbury, John had inherited his father's complete lack of guile, quite the opposite of his uncle, which was, she reminded herself, the reason the earl lived in genteel poverty, surrounded by crumbling memorials to past glories. Thomas, on the other hand, bragged of his growing wealth gained through nothing more glamorous than hard work and a keen mind for business.

Exactly like her father, which was a good part of the reason Edward had pushed her into agreeing to marry Thomas. They were two of a kind, caring only about their investments and incomes, percents, and profits. She had much more in common with John, whose scholarly pursuits had been interrupted by his father's untimely death. Had she not been warned of the unsuitability of the relationship, she would eagerly have cultivated the friendship the earl offered. Perhaps it was the denial of that friendship that drove her to the playful masquerade as Betsy Bunch.

Bringing her out of her speculations and back to the present, John asked his uncle with characteristic bluntness, "Were you frightened, Thomas? I know I should have been."

Elizabeth risked a sidelong glance at him, and her heart rose painfully to her throat.

How easily she could have fallen in love with him at that moment or during any of the others they had shared over the past few years since his return to Kilbury. Despite his boyish demeanor, he was fine-featured, almost handsome, with soft hazel eyes the same color as Thomas's and yet so different. Was it because John always looked at her straight on, over the lenses of his perpetually crooked spectacles? John Colfax was the embodiment of warmth and honesty. Not the brusque distance that existed between herself and her father nor the cold formality that character-ized her relationship with Thomas; with John there was always the open offer of simple companionship.

As though aware of her scrutiny, the earl turned to his left and caught her in midstare.

"Did I frighten you, Elizabeth? If I did, I am most sorry," he apologized at once. Then a most unex-pected flash of anger lit his hazel eyes behind the lop-sided spectacles. "Something must be done," he insisted. "This outlaw Jack Silver must not be allowed to continue to prey upon innocent travelers. Good heavens, think of all the times you and I have ridden that same road through the woods between here and Kilbury! It is a wonder we haven't been attacked ourselves!"

He looked so terrified at the prospect that Elizabeth was almost overcome by an urge to comfort him as she would a child. Yet the image her mind conjured was not of her holding him to her breast and kissing away his fear.

Why did John Colfax's uncomplicated gaze sudden-ly bring to mind the glittering hard brilliance of Jack Silver's eyes as he lowered his head to kiss her in the midnight darkness? Her heart began to pound in her breast, and she licked her lips, as though to bring back the taste of his. Tears, not of fear but of something else, something totally unknown to her, burned the back of her eyes.

Elizabeth had never experienced such panic before in her life. The risks she faced when she donned her disguise to take Nell Sharpe's place at the Black Oak brought her exhilaration and eagerness. Betsy Bunch was only a game, a diversion from the restrictions of life as the pampered daughter of Edward Stanhope. When that game turned more serious last night, Elizabeth had tasted fear for the first time, but fear was not at all the same as the confusion she felt now.

She could not think here, with all the sources of her confusion—save one—surrounding her. Her father scowled at her; Thomas ignored her. John returned to his breakfast as though he only just realized how cowardly his outburst made him seem. Unable to bear or to break the silence that followed, Elizabeth seized upon the only excuse she could think of to escape.

"I must change my clothes for the sitting," she announced and ran from the room and the men who stared at her.

CHAPTER

3

Nell Sharpe pulled the pins free of Elizabeth's hair and let the black tresses fall where they would. Elizabeth shook her head to ease the pain brought on by tension, lack of sleep, and the discomfort of a fashionable coiffure. Her mad flight from the breakfast room had left her breathless, but at least she was once more in control of her emotions.

"I laid out the blue gown, and Mr. Colfax sent up the sapphires," Nell explained as she began to draw a silver-handled brush through Elizabeth's hair.

"A bit presumptuous of him, don't you think? Thomas is neither my husband nor the earl of Kilbury —yet."

She had quickly stripped out of her lavender morning gown and now sat at the dressing table with a quilted robe wrapped around her against the chill that never seemed to leave this room.

Nell responded with philosophical frankness.

"I suppose it is, but it isn't likely his lordship will ever wed and get an heir. Isn't that why you're to marry his uncle? Might as well be you wearing the Kilbury jewels as anyone."

The idea of marrying Thomas so that her father's grandson would inherit the title suddenly struck Elizabeth as calculated and mercenary, as cold and emotionless as the necklace reflected in her dressing table mirror. A rueful smile crossed her face as she thought of how often she viewed the world second-hand, either through someone else's eyes or by means of surreptitious glances in a mirror.

She said wearily, "Please bring them here, Nell. I want to see them for myself."

The maid set down the brush and walked to the bed, where a profusion of blue satin and white lace lay draped on the counterpane. Nestled within the curve of the gown's neckline was a flat ebony box, its lid opened to expose a flamboyant example of the jeweler's art spread out on black velvet. Careful not to disturb the precise lay of the necklace, Nell carried the box almost ceremoniously to Elizabeth.

She took it from the maidservant and set it on the dressing table in front of her, where the candles at either side of the mirror shed even, unflickering light.

There were eight oval sapphires each the size of her thumbnail, set in a gold so pale as to be almost silver. A dozen small diamonds surrounded each blue stone, and from the center of this garish chain hung a ninth sapphire, perfectly round, as big as a penny coin. Elizabeth lifted the necklace from its bed and lay the center stone on the palm of her hand.

"Did you know, Nell, that no one has worn the Kilbury sapphires since the countess died ten years ago? Thomas said they were thought to be lost or sold by John's father to cover his debts."

Nell made an exaggerated shiver. "It'd give me the creeps to wear something a dead woman wore," she said. "And if I was his lordship, I'd be selling the thing and putting Kilbury back on its feet, not lettin' it run down the way he has."

"I suppose there's little he can do. His father had no

head for business except horses, and when the Kilbury stable no longer won races, he continued to live as if they did."

Thomas, her father had told her, tried to save the estate from financial ruin, but he was powerless in the face of his brother's demands. And John, the scholar who had spent half his life at Oxford before he inherited the bankrupt title four years ago, was no better than his father. Despite Thomas's efforts at managing the remaining Kilbury assets for his nephew, the debts mounted and the earl faced imminent financial ruin.

A single sapphire necklace could hardly change all that or even change Edward Stanhope's intentions for his daughter. He had, he told Elizabeth firmly and often, made his money in trade, one guinea at a time, and he was not about to see it wasted by a bookish fool. She had agreed with his logic, just as she had agreed not to give John any encouragement that might lead him to believe he had any chance to acquire the Stanhope fortune. Just as she had agreed to wed Thomas, who understood finances and who would in time undoubtedly inherit the Kilbury title.

And the Kilbury sapphires.

The glittering opulence held no fascination for her. "It might as well be a millstone," she murmured, giving voice to thoughts better kept private.

But she continued to stare at the thing, mesmerized by the play of light on the facets of the stones. Each flash of fire from the encircling diamond brilliants reminded her of the sparkle of moonlight on falling flakes of snow; the blue glimmer in the seductive depths of the great sapphire recalled the bitter cold of the night and the sensuous warmth of the man's cloak draped around her. She closed her hand around the stones, letting the sharp edges bite painfully into her flesh. Her eyes closed, too, as she struggled to hold back unwelcome and unexplained tears.

Then, with a sigh, she clasped the gaudy thing around her throat. She no longer had time for tears. "I might as well get used to it."

She rose without another glance in the mirror for she could not bear to look at herself and untied the sash of her dressing gown.

"But your hair, Miss Elizabeth. I haven't even started it," Nell protested.

Elizabeth replied very softly, "I have wasted enough time already today." The sapphires around her neck served as a glittering reminder that she had promised to wed Thomas Colfax—but never promised to love him. There was no room in her future for foolish dreams of romance. "Help me to dress, Nell, and I will try to make up for being so late this morning. Thomas is waiting for me."

The library afforded the best light for the painting of a portrait, so it was to that grandiose chamber that the four gentlemen retired. Copperstith immediately set to work arranging his easel and canvases, his sketchpads and charcoal.

With the practiced awkwardness that had come to typify the inept earl of Kilbury, John lowered himself into a comfortable leather wing chair by the fire, where he could observe his companions. He took particular interest in his uncle, who looked none the worse for a night at the Black Oak. Yet Thomas paced impatiently between the two windows that would give Copperstith his northerly light. Outside, the lawns of Stanhope Manor stretched away in uninterrupted white. Even the sky seemed a similar color, with a thin layer of clouds obscuring the low winter sun.

All that pale coldness contrasted with the white-hot fury Thomas Colfax tried in vain to hide. John saw the cracks in the mask of calm, faint traces of the anger bubbling beneath the surface with each sharply punctuated stride. Last night, in contrast, the mask had shattered completely. The robbery allowed Thomas an opportunity to vent some of that anger. He could blame the ignorant clods at what he no doubt considered a pathetic excuse for an inn for much of his inconvenience, and they would never dream of arguing.

He had not been able to take such liberties when Jack Silver relieved him of his purse.

John allowed himself a small smile and opened the book on his lap. Thomas had told only one lie in his recounting of the robbery this morning. Not that John was surprised; he had in fact expected Thomas to embellish the tale further. The purse Jack Silver picked off the ground on the point of his sword contained nearly three hundred pounds, an interest payment on one of the many Kilbury mortgages. Hardly a small sum.

Large or small, however, it could be replaced. Perhaps that thought comforted Thomas as he erased his scowl and turned to greet his intended bride on her reappearance.

But it was not Thomas who gasped at Elizabeth's entrance. John scrambled to his feet with such haste that the book crashed to the floor and bounced perilously close to the flames.

"Oh, Elizabeth!" he exclaimed in his overexcited voice. She had the dignity to blush, a pleasant color rising from the lace-trimmed décolletage to her throat and finally her cheeks, which had seemed in the morning light almost too pale.

He wanted her blush to mean that she was touched by his compliment, perhaps a bit embarrassed that his admiration was expressed so publicly when she would have preferred it more private. Instead, he knew she found his forthrightness gauche and unwelcome. He had been foolish to expect affection from a wealthy heiress; her betrothal to a man old enough to be her father was proof of where her desires lay.

And yet, though he had never set out to woo or win Elizabeth Stanhope and had indeed established himself as the kind of man a woman in her position was least likely to desire, he found her rejection most difficult to accept.

"Ah, my dear Miss Stanhope," Brinslow Copperstith burbled to break a sudden tension. "Come, this way. What a stunning gown you have chosen to match these marvelous gems so perfectly. I will endeavor to do my best, though with such an exquisite subject, I can hardly fail to create a masterpiece!"

Then John noticed the sapphires, and he wondered why he had not seen them immediately. No matter; the sight of them around her delicate throat, with the great single stone lying just above the shadowed valley between her breasts, sent a bolt of pain through him like stormy lightning.

It scorched his heart, then went racing along his nerves until his fingers and toes were atingle with it. He wanted to wrap the chain around his hand and jerk it from her, and if *she* suffered some hurt in the process, he would not have cared.

Yet the rapt expression on his face never changed. He gave no one any clue to his pain, his sorrow, his anger, his grief, his hatred. It was a skill, like many others, he had cultivated over the years.

"You must do me a miniature!" he begged of the artist, needing some outlet for the molten emotions surging through him. "Miss Stanhope is to be my aunt, and I must have her portrait, too." It was just the impulsive sort of thing a penniless nobleman would ask, never giving a thought to the expense. He must continue to play the role, no matter what his true thoughts and feelings.

Thomas, as John expected, was not so unrecognizant of the finances involved.

"You will have to discuss that with Mr. Copperstith

later, John. He will expect to be paid for his commission."

Turning to Elizabeth, John had a ready answer.

"You could lend me the money," he suggested. "Surely it couldn't be much for one small painting."

Something tightened in Elizabeth's throat. For the first time she became aware of how much attention was riveted on the jewels at her neck. That Thomas should stare at them was to be expected; he had sent them to her for the portrait, though they were not his to give. If and when something happened to John and Thomas came into the title, then and only then would she have any right to wear them as countess of Kilbury.

It was a thought she could not dwell upon.

Yet was that why John seemed unable to take his eyes from them? He had never shown such intense emotion before. That he did so now frightened her all over again, as if he were suddenly someone else, someone she did not know at all.

And what could she say to him? Though a date had not been set for the wedding, before summer was over she would be Thomas Colfax's wife, as her father wished, and John's aunt by marriage. She could hardly bestow the miniature as a gift upon him without arousing suspicions as to their relationship, a relationship that would never, and could never, exist beyond the formal bounds of family.

That same panic of conflicting emotions that had sent her scurrying to her bedroom earlier threatened once again to envelope her. She sought relief this time in the routine of obligation and precision that were the hallmark of her life as Edward Stanhope's daughter and mistress of his household.

"I'm sure Thomas would be pleased to make arrangements," she suggested with what she hoped was a not insincere smile. Then, turning to the artist she said, "Shall we proceed, Mr. Copperstith? I was unforgivably late this morning, so we have much time to make up for."

The earl did not blush, but he did hang his head in embarrassed shame. With a mumbled apology, he slunk back to his corner by the fire and retrieved his book. Once again, Elizabeth shared his humiliation. And she despised Thomas for doing nothing to relieve it. Surely *he* could have offered the miniature as a gift. It was, as John said, a small thing.

Perhaps, she thought as she took her seat and allowed Copperstith to pose her, she would talk to Thomas later. Or perhaps it would be better to let the matter die exactly as she had let so many of her dreams die.

While Elizabeth submitted to the artistic talents of Brinslow Copperstith, John Colfax returned to the comfort of his chair by the fire. He forced a mental wave of cold water over his anger and resumed the charade that had sustained him through the long years since his father's death. But if he found it easy to shake off the reality of his hatred in favor of a comfortable mask, he could not so easily shake off the memory that the sight of Elizabeth Stanhope in her glory aroused.

She was so cold, so perfect, with waves of blue-black hair frothing around her ivory face rather than curled and combed and pinned into some artificial precision. As much as he loved those outrageously ostentatious sapphires, he could learn to hate them with little effort, for they now put a seal on the betrayal of the woman he once thought of as his friend, a woman who, under different circumstances, he might have loved. He saw her now for a glittering creature as hard and cold as the stones themselves.

It was as if by agreeing to wed his uncle, Elizabeth Stanhope had surrendered her soul.

Why, John wondered with a silent groan, could not

the beautiful Elizabeth have one shred of the warmth and spontaneity, the laughter and liveliness, that sparkled in the eyes and burned in the lips of the tavern wench he had held in his arms last night?

"Good God, Harry, he robbed my mother's *grave!*"

John ran the fingers of both hands through his hair but never once stopped his pacing.

"I put the necklace on her so Thomas couldn't talk Father into selling it, too, but somehow that thieving reptile who calls himself my uncle took it from her!"

He had been ranting like this for almost an hour while the old jockey bustled about the Dower House's ancient hall to lay out a plain if ample repast of venison, crusty bread, and boiled turnips. If the local countryfolk ate as well, it was only because they knew the earl let them get away with poaching on the Kilbury demesne. At Kilbury Hall, half a mile up the hill from the Dower House, the fare was little better.

"And then to give them to *her,* to that cold, greedy little bitch, as if they were even his to give!"

Harry poured wine into a plain goblet. "Yer supper's ready, milord. Best eat it while it's hot."

John spun around and faced the little man with a quizzical look, as though he had hitherto been completely unaware of his companion's presence. And in a way that was true. Lost in his thoughts, he had been shouting out his feelings, not caring that there was anyone to hear.

With a long, heartfelt sigh, he walked to the table and the chair Harry held out for him. The gesture brought a ghost of a smile to his lips. Once seated, he reached for the wine and raised the goblet in salute.

"To old times, happier times, Harry," he whispered.

"What's done is done," the old man groused, limping around the table to take his own place across from John. "Best be lookin' to the future, not the past. It's time for Jack Silver to finish his work and be laid to rest."

As though the wine had an instantaneous effect, John grinned broadly and leaned forward, elbows on the bare plank table.

"You're quite right, my friend. Not tonight, but soon, Jack Silver will ride the moonlit highway for the last time. And when he does, he will take the greatest prize of his career."

This time he lifted his glass silently and without another word drained the tart red wine in a single gulp.

"Ye mean to rob yer uncle o' the sapphires?" Harry asked, this time quietly, as though afraid the very walls could hear.

"No, my friend, not the sapphires. Though it's tempting." He paused, thinking while he cut a chunk from the slab of meat Harry had put on his plate. "If there were a way I could take them as well, I would do it, for the sheer satisfaction of stealing the stones back from that filthy piece of scum. But when Thomas loses the showcase for his stolen treasure, I'll have even greater satisfaction."

John dove into his meal with enthusiasm, but his mind was not on the turnips and venison and stale bread; his thoughts instead centered on the plan, so long contemplated, that must soon come to fruition.

There were a thousand details yet to be attended to if the scheme were to succeed. Nothing at all could be left to chance. Jack Silver was often credited with uncanny luck, but in truth the highwayman's good fortune resulted from meticulous planning.

John smiled to himself with enormous satisfaction. Four years ago he would never have imagined himself in this role. He was a scholar first, comfortable in his rooms at Oxford with his books and studies, and only second did he consider himself the heir to the ancient earldom of Kilbury. The untimely death of his father, and the discovery that Thomas had looted the once-wealthy estate for his own ends, sent John back to the Somerset countryside, to Kilbury Hall, and the task of restoring dignity and honor to the Colfax name.

The intellectual challenge had intrigued him at first until he discovered how simple Thomas's scheme had been: He lent his own money to his friends, who in turn took the mortgages on the Kilbury properties, at far less than their actual value. He then collected the interest that would eventually bankrupt the estate he envisioned inheriting. Unless, of course, someone relieved him of those payments, as Jack Silver had done last night.

But while John had the utmost confidence in his plans, their execution often left him in grave doubt. In fact, he recalled with a flush of embarrassment, he had gone on that very first midnight escapade with more fear in his own heart than he expected to strike in the hearts of his victims.

Much had changed since then. He himself had changed in ways too numerous to count. Little more than a shell remained of the naive, emotional youth whose experience in life was limited to the serenity of university halls and scholarly pursuits. The heart and soul of that innocent had given way to the cunning bitterness of a man bent on revenge.

He leaned against the elaborately carved back of his chair with a sigh. "Another excellent meal, Harry," he complimented sardonically. "I expect you will be able to provide similarly sumptuous repasts when our 'guest' arrives?"

The old man raised an eyebrow, a sure sign of concern. "Aye, if the turnips hold out."

Silence hung for a bare second, then John tilted his head back and laughed. The sound, full of life and enjoyment, echoed eerily in the vaulted space, as though the very walls threw back the unfamiliar pleasure, echoes of the man he once was.

When the last chuckle had faded, he leaned forward again and pushed away his empty plate to rest his forearms comfortably on the table.

"I joined the Stanhopes and Thomas for breakfast this morning, you know," he said with a strange wistfulness in his voice. "It was positively medieval, a feast set out for five or six people at most. And they let what was left go cold and stale until it was unfit for anything but the swine. It should be interesting to see how the pampered princess fares on turnips and venison."

Harry gave his master a rather amused look, though it was short of smile. "Can't see where it's hurt you much," he observed.

This time John just nodded in acknowledgment and raised his goblet to salute Harry's astuteness.

The old jockey was only partly right, of course. The transformation of John Colfax into Jack Silver had taken more than plain food. He had been born to his height and breadth of shoulder, but only hours of physical labor had developed the musculature that was now so difficult to conceal, even beneath loose, ill-fitting clothes. Nights of riding or stalking or simply lying in wait for his prey had sharpened his eyesight and his powers of concentration. Even his hearing had become more sensitive as he learned to distinguish the sounds natural to a woodland midnight and those caused by men.

He drained the last drops of wine from the goblet and then twirled it by the stem between the fingers of his left hand.

"I've a question for you, Harry," he said slowly, weighing not only the words but the wisdom of asking.

"'Twouldn't be the first time."

"No, but this one is a bit different. As important as any before but different." He drew in a deep breath and let it out slowly before asking "What do you know of the folk who run the Black Oak?"

Harry shrugged and reached for the decanter to pour himself more wine. He offered some to John, who refused it with a small shake of his head.

"Well, far as I know, it's been in the Sharpe family one way or 'nother since before these German Georges mounted the throne. Ned and Mary took it over when Ned's uncle died maybe fifteen year ago."

"Are they the parents of the girls who work there, or are the girls hired help?"

If Harry tried to hide his surprise, he did so too late. John noticed how the old man brought the goblet to his lips to drink and then stopped, his eyes suddenly narrowed and his brows drawn together.

"They got two girls and the boy, Robin. Oldest girl, Nell, is lady's maid to the Stanhope heiress. The younger, Hennie, she works at the inn, waits tables, cleans the rooms." When John waited for him to continue, Harry added, "It ain't that busy a place most times."

A log popped in the fire, and a tiny draft sent the flames of the candles dancing, but John's gaze was fixed upon the plain crystal goblet he twisted first one way then the other, over and over.

"There were two girls there last night," he said, his voice barely above a whisper. "The slender, quiet one, she'd be Hennie Sharpe no doubt. Who's the other, the blonde who kept tugging her cap back on like she was afraid to let her hair show?"

He knew by Harry's hesitation that the old man didn't like this curiosity. Harry had been more than like a father to him these past years, and John had had too many occasions to be grateful for the experience and wisdom he learned from Harry. For a moment, however, he resented the old man's unspoken warning. John Colfax was no infant, unable to take care of himself where a woman was concerned. And yet, in those few seconds of silence, he knew Harry was right to warn him.

"That'd be Betsy Bunch. Like Nell, she's a maid up at the manor, and every now and then she comes to the Black Oak to help out. She's the one who handled Thomas last night—"

"I know who she is," John interrupted. "I encountered her on the road after I'd left the inn. She had a long, cold walk back to Stanhope, so I took her home."

He felt Harry's assessing eyes on him but said nothing more. If the old man wished to ask questions of his own, let him.

But apparently Harry had no questions. After a few moments of silence, he pushed his chair back and stood, unsteadily at first, and then proceeded to collect the dishes. The clatter of china and crystal and silver was the only sound above the steady crackle of the fire. John set down the empty goblet for Harry to take, and by then he had finally made up his mind.

"She's not likely to be there tonight," Harry said as if he had read John's thoughts. "She don't come often, and it'd be riskin' her place to sneak away two nights in a row. And you'd be riskin' even more, all for a tumble with a tavern wench."

"I know it's dangerous, Nell, but I must go."

Elizabeth surveyed her appearance in the mirror one more time. Nothing, she was certain, remained of Elizabeth Stanhope. No powder toned down the blush of excitement in her cheeks; no corsets restrained her figure. The cap with its fringe of golden ringlets covered her own dark hair.

She could see Nell's reflection as well, her face stern, her arms crossed forbiddingly as she leaned against the doorframe.

"He ain't likely to be there, not two nights in a row. No doubt he was a traveler, just passin' through."

Elizabeth bit her lip and drew a deep breath. She had told Nell nothing about the ride home with Jack

Silver, only that she had seen a man who she was certain was the notorious outlaw.

"Then if he's just a traveler and not there tonight, there's nothing at all to worry about. Besides, Hennie and the others will be grateful for my help." She gave the cap one last adjustment, then turned away from the mirror and headed toward the door.

"I oughtn't let you go," Nell admonished once more.

"And I oughtn't want to," Elizabeth admitted, "but after an entire day in Thomas's company, while we sat for that portrait, I must get out."

"You'd do better to stay home and get used to Mr. Thomas. He's to be your husband soon enough, not some handsome stranger at the Black Oak."

Was he indeed handsome? Elizabeth reluctantly admitted to herself that she had seen little of his face save those bright silver eyes.

"I'll have years and years to get used to Thomas," she said, shrugging off the thought. "For now I have only tonight." She placed her hands on Nell's sagging shoulders and knew the maid had given in again.

"Then be careful. *Extra* careful."

Nell was barely older than Elizabeth herself, and yet Elizabeth often thought of her as the mother she had never known. She planted a smacking kiss on Nell's cheek and then gently pushed past her to grasp the door handle.

"I'm always careful, Nell. Always."

Last night's storm had blown through, leaving stark white fields and a clear, star-glittered sky. A magnificent ring circled the moon, now full and bright as it hung just above the horizon. On the snow, it shed nearly as much light as day. Elizabeth had no difficulty making her way toward the Black Oak.

But the weather was also colder than the night before. By the time she reached the clearing in the woods where the inn's windows glowed with welcome yellow light, Elizabeth's feet were numb, and her shoulders ached from being hunched under her cloak. She dared not even think about the walk home.

When she reached the half-timbered building, however, she knew she would have to give the matter serious thought.

The place was almost deserted. The Sharpes had no need of her services tonight and would no doubt wonder why she came unasked. Her decision had been pure folly, and she faced the prospect of returning home in the cold without so much as a mug of hot rum beforehand.

The sound of an approaching horse startled her. She backed away from the window, out of the circle of light it spilled on the trampled snow. Leaning against the bole of an ancient oak tree, she tucked her head closer within the shelter of her cloak's hood and stomped her feet quietly in an attempt to warm them. It did no good.

Then into that halo of candlelight trotted a familiar gray stallion. Elizabeth's heart froze colder than her toes.

She had not truly seen the man himself last night, save for falling onto his lap and then riding in front of him. Yet she recognized the effortless grace as he dismounted, the silent strides he took toward the door, the elegant silhouette he cast against the lighted window.

She took a step forward, away from the sheltering shadows then held back, puzzled.

The man she knew was Jack Silver repeated her own earlier actions. Like her, he avoided the door and went instead to one of the diamond-paned windows flanking it. Keeping out of sight, he peered into the Black Oak's common room.

Of course he would check to see if it were safe to enter first, she told herself. *Just as I did.*

Unlike Elizabeth, however, he entered the cozy confines of the inn.

He had seen her; he knew he had. No one else would be fool enough to be running across snow-covered fields on a night like this. But when John strode into the almost deserted common room at the Black Oak, he saw no sign of Betsy Bunch.

Only tired-looking Hennie Sharpe greeted him.

"Ye be wantin' a room?" she asked in a weary voice. "Place be damn near empty tonight."

She yawned, though it could hardly be past seven o'clock.

"No, not a room. Just a mug of hot rum and a spot by the fire for an hour or two."

It was difficult to pay any attention to the girl; he wanted only to search every nook and cranny until he found the bright-eyed blonde with the infinitely kissable mouth. And he dared not ask about her. To do so might call too much attention to his own presence, and he preferred to remain anonymous and forgettable.

Hennie waved her arm to encompass the whole of the big room.

"Take yer pick. Last night there wasn't room fer a mouse to sit down."

She continued to mutter as she moved off to the kitchen to find a mug and the rum. He shook his head and made his way to the same secluded corner where he had sat last night, almost invisible among the crowd. Then just as he was about to sit down and soak up the warmth, he turned abruptly in the opposite direction.

A backless bench offered considerably less comfort than the cozy inglenook, but it also offered less chance of triggering a memory in Hennie's sleepy brain. She had been there when Thomas Colfax knocked Betsy onto Jack's lap; she just might remember too much if he took the same place. With a disguise as simple as black clothes that did not hide his size, a concealing hood to his cloak, loosening his hair, and taking off those damned pinching spectacles, he could not risk recognition.

She brought him his rum, and for a moment he thought she stared at him, as though struggling to recall something. But when she walked back toward the kitchen, he relaxed, certain that she had made no connection.

He sipped the drink slowly, tasting nothing, barely feeling the warmth it spread through him after the cold ride from the Dower House. One by one the other occupants of the room departed, mounting the creaking stairs to the chambers they had rented for the night. None ventured outdoors. Soon only one other patron remained, a sallow-faced parson reading his Bible by flickering candlelight. John recognized him as Simon Horne, the recently appointed vicar of St. Edwald's in the village of Kilbury.

Hardly the kind of man who would have noticed a laughing tavern maid. John muttered a bitter curse at his bad luck and let the rest of the hot rum slide down his throat.

He set the mug down with a thump and pulled a coin from a pocket. A tuppenny piece, it was more than he could afford for a farthing's worth of rum and butter, but he threw it on the scarred table all the same.

"G'night to ye," he called to the vicar, careful to keep his face in shadow, then strode to the door.

An hour, maybe a bit more, had passed, long enough for him to warm his frozen limbs and return whence he had come. The parson had heard him tell the girl he did not intend to stay; there would be too much risk in remaining longer than necessary, not the least of which would be that Horne, though he had never looked up from his reading, might remember an unusual patron. Yet he hated to go: What if she arrived later? What if she were in the kitchen, cleaning up the night's dishes, and came out to sweep the floor just moments after he had left?

But he would have to wait all night to see if any of those things happened, and he did not have all night.

The cold air seared his lungs, and another thought knifed through him. What if she were out here alone, hurt perhaps, and freezing in the bitter dark? If she came from Stanhope, it would be no difficult matter to trace her path. In the moonlight, her tracks would be plain with no wind to erase them as last night.

He had just taken hold of the gray stallion's bridle when a movement in the mottled shadows of the trees drew his attention.

In an instant, his hand was curled around the primed pistol tucked into his belt and all his senses were alert.

"Who goes there?" he whispered.

Only silence replied.

Then, daring everything, he said, "Betsy? Is it you?"

A hundred desperate thoughts clicked through his mind as he took a soundless step in her direction. Had she been discovered last night and turned out? He did not want to believe Elizabeth would be so cruel, but Edward was another matter, and since Thomas had so intimately entered their lives, anything was possible.

Or had the girl taken such a fancy to him, to the romantic notion of Jack Silver, that she risked all to come looking for him? Had the foolish wench no idea what could happen to her?

Worse yet, she could be the instrument of his downfall, sent by any one of his numerous enemies. He had learned that suspicion could be little more than caution and he trusted to both. Had she spoken of her encounter to anyone at Stanhope? God, the possibilities were endless! Yet still he walked slowly toward the shadows, knowing it could be a decoy, knowing even more certainly that it was not.

"Betsy?" he whispered once again.

She nodded weakly, and then it came to him that while he had been warming himself by the fire with a mug of rum to add to his comfort, this girl had stood in the dark and cold.

"Sweet Jesus!" he breathed as he strode to her and spun her into the shelter of his arms. Would a volley of pistol fire follow, ending once and for all the career of Jack Silver—and the dreams of John Colfax?

There was, as always, only the silence of the winter night and the gentle sigh of the frozen girl as she tumbled into his embrace.

CHAPTER

The ladder to the stable's loft creaked beneath the highwayman's boots. Elizabeth insisted she was capable of walking, only to have Jack Silver insist even more strongly that he was quite capable of carrying her.

A narrow shaft of moonlight lit the area above the stable barely enough for him to make his way to the thickest pile of hay, where he laid her down. Her teeth were still chattering.

"Stay," he ordered, "and I'll fetch you something hot from the kitchen, you little fool. You could have frozen to death, you know."

"Wait!" she cried out.

She could not let him risk his own discovery, let alone hers. Her toes and fingers might be numb, but her mind worked as nimbly as ever. "They'll ask questions," she added.

"And you'll be in trouble if you're found out. Do you think I can't sneak into a public inn and swipe a bowl of stew without being caught?"

He laughed softly and knelt once more beside her.

"I've a great deal more to lose than you, my little starlit sparrow. Now, snuggle into the hay and—"

She grabbed blindly for him when he reached to draw more of the sweet-smelling hay atop her. Her frozen fingers closed around his wrist and held tightly.

"Ye don't understand. I can't stay here. I must—"

"You've no choice, milady," he said sternly. "I'll be back."

Elizabeth stared into the darkness, fighting off the panic.

Dear God, what had she done? Why had she not minded Nell all those long hours ago and stayed home? She had no hope of escaping detection now. It would be hours before she was warm enough to contemplate the return hike to Stanhope, and then she'd be lucky to make it by dawn. Someone surely would see her, and there was neither wind nor snow to cover her tracks.

And what danger had she put Jack Silver in? He had called her a fool, but she had already berated herself with worse appellations. She could survive the scandal of being caught in a tavern wench's costume even if it became known she had spent the night in the loft of a public inn's stable. Her father would suffer extravagant humiliation and Thomas would no doubt put a substantial price on his own embarrassment at being betrothed to such a scapegrace, but in the long run their lives would continue much as they had in the past.

Jack Silver was another matter.

Elizabeth wriggled deeper into the thick hay while she wrestled with the unpleasant alternatives. She could leave now, still half frozen, and risk both death and discovery on the way home. She had no wish to die, and the more she thought about it, the less appealing was the idea of abandoning her disguise and the escape it brought. For one thing, discussion of her secret might lead to investigation, and the highwayman would once more be in danger.

Did she dare ask him to return her to Stanhope as he had done last night? It was better, she thought, than her staying here with him, but then again, if she spent the night, he was free to depart safely at any time, leaving only her to face the morning and the truth.

She was, she admitted against another stubborn rush of tears, far worse than a fool.

"Did I hear a sniffle?"

She had not heard the creak of an opening door nor the weight of his foot upon the ladder, and even the softness of his voice startled her.

"'Tis the dust from the hay," she replied. "It tickles me nose."

"Then try this."

She heard the tiny noises now, the soft clank as he lifted the lid from a crock filled with mutton stew, the tap of a spoon against the edge, the drip of broth back into the pot.

"Careful, it's hot," he warned. He blew on the spoonful of stew before bringing it to her mouth.

She wasn't hungry until the aroma stimulated her appetite, but even before that, the warmth tempted her beyond resistance. She swallowed greedily, like a starving bird.

"You'll eat and rest," the highwayman told her, "and not set out until sunup. I cannot take you home this time, but I'll not let you walk in the dark. And you must promise not to do this again."

"Never," she vowed sincerely. "I never meant any harm."

He halted any further confession with another spoonful.

"I couldn't get much," he explained. "They were still up and about, though they've few enough customers tonight. I would have—"

The sound of voices in the stableyard below cut him

off. Hardly daring to breathe, Elizabeth strained to hear, as she knew Jack Silver must be doing.

Ned Sharpe's grumble rose above the shuffle of his boots on the frozen ground. "Ye're daft, woman, draggin' me out this time o' night. There ain't no thief; ye just can't remember where ye put that crock, that's all."

"I ain't daft," Mary insisted. "I set that crock on the table so I could take it upstairs and eat some stew while it was still good 'n' hot. When I come back from droppin' the bolt, 'twere gone. Someone musta stole it."

Elizabeth's heart rose into her throat, threatening to squeeze a cry of terror from her. She choked the sound down, though she was certain the panicked thud of her pulse must give them away.

Because of the darkness and Jack Silver's silence, Elizabeth felt the movements of the highwayman that she could neither see nor hear. While Ned and Mary continued to argue, Jack slipped the cover on the little crock and set it aside, where it would not be bumped.

He cursed as he did so, making not a sound though his lips formed the words with vehement anger. He rocked back on his heels before rising slowly to a low crouch. Was the girl, after all, a convenient temptation, meant to break down his usual caution? If not, then why did she persist in wanting him to stay right where he was? He felt her grope for his hand, and her fingers closed around his wrist.

Something touched the bells of warning in his head. She *had* been a trap, he thought and cursed himself for his stupidity. And his simple lust. How many times in the past years had he forced himself to ignore temptation because his need for revenge and retribution was greater? Where had that need gone tonight?

Ned opened the door to the stable with a groan and an obscenity.

"See, there's 'is tracks," Mary said triumphantly. "'E's 'idin' in there, fillin' 'is belly wi' *my* stew."

"Anybody could've made them tracks. Might be left from when Robin brought that parson's horse."

But Mary would not be placated. She led the way into the stable, insisting they would find the thief bedded cozily in an empty stall with an empty crock. His sharp eyes straining for the merest glimmer of lantern light, John followed the sounds of their conversation to determine where Ned and Mary hunted for the elusive bandit. If the girl were in on their scheme, they should head immediately for the ladder to the loft, and he had to be prepared for that eventuality.

Quick thinking had saved his neck often enough; in the few seconds since alerted to the search, he planned three possible escape routes. Any of the three would take him to safety, but none of his plans included provisions for the girl trembling beside him.

He glanced down to where he knew she lay, nearly covered by the warming straw. Why did she not call out to her confederates, giving them the signal that she had the notorious Jack Silver in her clutches? Why did she quiver in terror and her fingers tighten in a death grip around his wrist?

Because she was not one of them. Because she was as terrified as he of being caught.

The Sharpes continued their search with an occasional grunt or grumble from Ned when they found nothing. They checked each stall, each nook and cranny, from one end of the stable to the other.

"I told ye, there weren't no thief," Ned insisted. He stood just under the edge of the loft; John could clearly see the glow from the lantern. "An' if there was, he ain't here. Not now."

Mary sniffed in anger and frustration. Next thing she'd probably declare she smelled the stolen stew!

Until she and her husband left the stable, John dared not let any feeling of relief lessen his caution.

"Mebbe 'e went up to the loft," she suggested.

The ladder was less than three feet from where she stood.

He tensed, every muscle prepared for flight. He could cover the distance from where he crouched to the narrow window in three or four strides. If he hung from his hands, the drop to the ground was no more than a few feet. Before Ned could climb the ladder or Mary sound the hue and cry, he would be out the window and sprinting to the secluded grove where the gray stallion waited.

The girl would be on her own, trapped with the evidence of her crime.

He shook his head clear of guilty feelings. She had brought this disaster on herself. Still, he reached for her. With one strong hand he lifted her, for a last silent kiss.

Ned's voice halted him.

"If he's up there, let him be. I ain't climbin' after him. That ladder don't look like it'd hold a cat."

Elizabeth's heart stopped beating. She wanted desperately to ask the man whose wrist she could not release what was going to happen to them, but she dared not move, much less make a sound.

"But he stole my stew!"

"He stole one tiny crock, not the whole pot. Come, quit yer gripin'. There's more stew."

"And what of the crock? Am I to ladle another out of the pot?"

The innkeeper let out a long sigh. Elizabeth wished she could let out a full breath. Her lungs ached, and her nose itched until she was certain she would sneeze.

"We got other crocks, woman. Tomorrow, when it's light, I'll come out here and look again. But, damn it, it's late and cold and I'm ready fer me bed."

The light from the lantern shifted, indicating that Ned had turned to head for the door and back to the inn. Mary, perhaps reluctantly, hurried after him.

One of the horses, wakened by the argument and the light, whinnied loudly.

"What was that?" Mary asked, her voice more strident that before.

"On'y a horse." They were nearly to the door when the sound came again. "See? Now what sneakthief would give himself away by makin' a noise like that when he knows we're lookin' for 'im?"

Elizabeth, hearing that comment followed by the creak and groan of the closing stable door, wanted to scream with relief. It had not been a horse making that second noise. The dust in the straw had finally forced a sneeze to the surface, one she tried mightily to suppress but could not. Though she muffled the explosion against her sleeve, the result was still deafeningly loud in the tense silence.

She froze, her face buried in the crook of her arm, and listened while Ned's grumbles and Mary's protests faded. Another door opened, no doubt to the kitchen of the inn, and then all was silent once again.

Elizabeth waited only a moment, then prepared to make good her escape. She was struggling to untangle her cloak when the highwayman hissed at her, "What are you doing?"

"Getting out of here. They could come back at any second."

His hands came to rest on her shoulders and insistently held her in a sitting position. Her feet were now more tangled than ever in her skirt as well as the cloak. If she tried to rise, she would only fall flat on her face. She had no choice but to remain still, and he probably knew it. When he spoke again, his voice was softer, more gentle.

"No, they've done with us for tonight, unless we

draw their attention by hightailing it out of here like the thieves we are."

He sat down and reached for the incriminating crock of stew. She could not get up without leaving her cloak behind because he was sitting on the end of it.

"Might as well finish this while it's hot," he suggested. "After they're all safely snoring, I'll take it to the kitchen. Tomorrow Ned will find Mary's crock on a shelf by the fire and tell her she most likely set it there to keep it warm."

Elizabeth gasped, only to learn the highwayman used her outburst to locate her mouth and fill it once more with stew. When she had swallowed, she asked, "Why not leave it here, where no one will find it?"

"Because then they'd always wonder if it really had been stolen. If I put it back, refilled with cold stew, of course, they'll think Mary forgot it, and they'll forget their imagined thief as well."

His answer made sense, she acknowledged, though she still preferred the idea of escaping now, while they had the chance. Those moments of stark terror had left her so warm she felt beads of sweat on her brow despite the freezing temperature.

Before Jack could spoon another morsel of stew into her mouth, she said, "We can't stay here long, no matter what. It's too dangerous for both of us."

"You let me worry about that," he replied. "Did that fright from Ned and Mary warm you up a bit?"

"Aye, it did indeed."

"Then you'd best lie here and cool down. You'll catch your death if you go out in a sweat."

He lapsed into silence then and fed her the rest of the stew while he tried to figure out a way to return her to Stanhope without risking his own neck. If she lived anywhere else, he could fall back on letting the kind and generous earl of Kilbury "encounter" her on the long walk, but that was too dangerous. She was a clever wench, and he could not take the chance of her putting two and two together. Not when she no doubt saw the earl frequently at Stanhope and just might recognize something familiar about him.

He scraped the last bit of stew from the pot and gave it to Betsy. A moment later, the moon moved beyond the narrow chink, and the darkness was complete.

He would, he suddenly realized, probably never see her by the light of day.

He set the empty crock aside and stretched out, careful to keep the tail of her cloak securely under the heel of his boot. Then he pulled her closer beside him beneath the hay. She probably expected a highwayman, a common thief who robbed gentlemen at the point of a gun, would be equally the rogue toward a woman who sought him out. What else was he to think of her but that she was willing to do anything he wished? And yet that was hardly the impression she gave, though he could not pinpoint what impression she *did* give.

"Don't be frightened," he pleaded in a teasing voice when she struggled to move away from him. "I only mean to keep you warm."

"Warm?" she echoed.

"Aye, milady. Warm, nothing more."

There, her struggles eased, though she lay stiff within his embrace. With the hay for a blanket, they'd be warm enough for a few hours' sleep, which was all he intended. It was all he could afford.

He settled her head against his shoulder and smoothed back the cumbersome hood and removed the untidy cap that covered her hair. The scent of lilacs assailed him, and he had to smile at the knowledge that Betsy was not above making use of her mistress's perfumed soap. Running his fingers into the tangled tresses pinned atop her head, he wished mightily for sunlight or even for the glimmer of a tiny candle. He had to make do with his imagination, picturing a thick cascade of golden ringlets. No doubt her eyes were blue, like summer skies.

Closing his own eyes and surrendering to the creep of warmth and weariness, John Colfax let his mind conjure an image of Betsy Bunch on a June morning, in the familiar garden at Stanhope, gathering mounds of fragrant purple lilacs.

Perhaps, as penniless as he was, he could aspire to the companionship of a lowly servant like her. Then again, servants were known to be as mercenary as their masters and mistresses. The earl of Kilbury was a joke at Stanhope; even a servant like Betsy Bunch would never look at him with anything but amusement or, at best, pity.

He knew that as well as anyone; he had spent four years making sure of it.

He could take no chances that she might change that perception. It meant the abandoning of the Black Oak as a place of refuge, lest they encounter one another again. It also meant he could never inquire of her at Stanhope, not even in the most subtle way. And if he should see her there, he would not acknowledge her existence, no matter how her laughing eyes and sun-kissed hair tempted him.

But in the dark of night, when he could not see her and she could not see him, he would take what he could of her pleasure.

He notched a curled finger beneath her chin and gently tilted it up.

"A kiss, milady midnight, a kiss is all I ask," he murmured when she sought to turn away. He brushed his lips across her forehead and felt the shudder that quivered through her. "Come, does a little kiss frighten you that much?"

"Aye, milord," she answered. "Who's to say you'll not want more?"

He pulled her tightly against him and chuckled.

"I *do* want more," he confessed, "but not here and not like this. A tumble in the hay on a summer's eve is pleasant enough, but on a frosty winter's night it means groping through layers of clothes or else a frozen backside. I've no desire for either."

For him it was such a light thing, a kiss, a jest, a chuckle that she felt even through those layers of clothing. For Elizabeth it was so much more, and she could not give it without thought.

Only a day ago, she had thought never to see this man. She had listened to servants' gossip for so long and had embarked on a playful masquerade in hopes of simply laying eyes on the romantic legend that was Jack Silver. In the snowy moonlight, everything had changed.

She had changed.

Now, lying beside him, she knew this last kiss was all she would ever be able to give him, and all she would have to hold in her memories for the rest of her lifetime. There would be no more Betsy Bunch at the Black Oak. The cap with the blond curls sewn to its edge, the loose-fitting blouse, the peasant's skirt she twirled so gaily as she moved between the tables, would all be consigned to the fire until not a trace remained.

She turned her face up, feeling the warmth of his breath against her cheek, then caressing her mouth. Then gently, ever so softly, his lips touched hers.

Warmth sluiced through her, liquid and sweet as molten honey. Had it been so last night, when the highwayman stole her first kiss from her? She could not remember. She could not remember anything suddenly. It was as though the past and future both had slipped away, leaving only this wondrous moment of awakening desire.

She reached up a hand to touch his face. As his mouth played upon hers, teasing her lips apart to admit his seeking tongue, she stroked his features, invisible in the deep darkness. Her touch, though she thought it gentle and innocent, seemed to arouse his passions, for his kiss became more urgent, his tongue more insistent.

He threaded the fingers of both hands into her hair and held her still while he maneuvered her onto her back, never once breaking the seal of their kiss. Cloak and skirt and petticoats offered poor protection against the heat radiating from the body slanted across hers. She felt her breasts swell, the nipples tighten in response to the pressure of his chest.

Without warning, cold rushed over her as he rolled away, depriving her of the warmth of his body.

"Enough!" he gasped into the silence. "You tempt me, wench, beyond my own common sense."

Elizabeth, too, lay breathless, pulling painful gulps of frozen air into her passion-seared lungs. She had no reply to make and feared any attempt to speak would result only in tears. So when Jack Silver laughed and once again pulled her into the comfort of his embrace, she kept her silence. And when he suggested they catch what sleep they could, she merely nodded.

She did not sleep nor, she suspected, did he, but they passed an hour or so in the cold silence of the stable. Each tiny sound, whether the snoring of a horse or the scrabbling of a mouse, made them jump. But they said nothing until he nudged her and told her it was time to leave the warmth of their bower. All was silent at the Black Oak, and its inhabitants slept soundly.

The highwayman descended the ladder first then led the way out the door and into the eerie moon-shadowed woods. Elizabeth held his hand tightly and followed him without question or resistance to the open space in the trees where his own horse waited. She kept her head down and hoped the hood of her cloak concealed any stray dark hair she had not been able to cover. When Jack let go her hand to cup the animal's nose in both of his while he spoke softly to the beast, she tried once again to secure the cap.

Elizabeth shivered as much from nervousness as the cold she had forgotten could be so piercing. There was something endearing about a man who would spend a long, affectionate moment apologizing to his horse, yet her own feet were growing numb, and she wished he would hurry.

In time he did finish with a pat to the horse's neck. After lifting her onto the saddle, he mounted behind her and turned the gray stallion toward the road.

Not a word passed between them until he reined the horse to a halt some distance down the road from Stanhope's front gate.

"I dare not go further," he said, dismounting first. "'Tis an hour or more yet 'til first light; you'll be home well before anyone stirs and finds you missing."

He raised his arms to her, and she let herself slide from the saddle. The highwayman's powerful hands clasped her about the waist and did not release her even when her feet were solidly on the frozen ground.

The moon that had offered steady light on their journey from the Black Oak was setting now behind a wooded hilltop. Elizabeth looked up, hoping to imprint a clear image of Jack Silver's face on her memory, but she saw only shadows of his features and the brilliant glitter of his eyes behind a narrow strip of black silk.

"Like a dream," she murmured. She reached a hand to touch his face; his reflexes caught her wrist quickly.

"And we must let it remain one," he answered with a touch of seriousness she had not heard earlier in his voice.

Before she could say another word, he let go her wrist and swung into the saddle. The stallion pranced several steps backward, then Jack Silver turned his mount and spurred it in the direction from which they had come. The spray of snow churned up by the stallion's hooves formed a cloud of glittering dust that stung Elizabeth's eyes, and when they had cleared, she saw only the darkness of the night.

Jack Silver was gone.

Elizabeth turned toward Stanhope and trudged the quarter mile to the gate, then made her way to the garden entrance that she knew would be left open. As she had so many times before, she slipped inside without a sound. Though she felt drained of all strength and force of will, she knew she must be more cautious this time than ever. Never had she returned so near the hour when the servants rose and run such a risk of discovery.

Exhausted, she climbed the dark stairs to her room and opened the door. Nell had left no light burning, but the banked fire shed enough for Elizabeth to find a candle. She knelt on the hearth and poked the coals to life, then touched the candle's wick to the borning flames.

She blinked at the sudden brightness and realized the crystal tears swimming in her eyes served to intensify the light all the more.

The cap was the first item consigned to the fire. Elizabeth tossed it onto the coals and let it catch before she added several sticks of fresh firewood. The blond curls sizzled and sent a foul odor into the room, but in an instant they were consumed entirely. Not even ash remained.

The ordinary brown wool cloak belonged to Nell and therefore afforded no evidence of Betsy Bunch's identity. Elizabeth draped it over a chair and promised herself to brush the remaining bits of hay from it later, before she returned it to its owner. Then she stripped off the woolen skirt and linen blouse. She was tempted to toss them, too, into the fireplace, but at the last moment thought it would be better not to waste them when there were so many in need. And who would recognize them? There must be a hundred plain brown skirts in nearby Kilbury Village alone.

The shoes, too, belonged to Nell and the stockings. Elizabeth set them beside the cloak and turned her back on them. Then she peeled off her undergarments and, naked and cold, strode to her bed. She had had her adventure, broken free of the restraints of a pampered life, if only for a while. She had been foolish to think that dreams came true. Nell was right; she should turn her attention to the reality of becoming Thomas Colfax's dutiful wife. It was what her father wanted—and what had been expected of her. She knew it and accepted it.

She climbed into the bed, her teeth chattering. There would be no heated brick to warm it nor a lover's body, only memories. They were, she supposed, more than many women had.

Still dressed in the black garb of the highwayman, John sat at the massive oaken table in the hall at the Dower House. Two candles in heavy gold holders shed light on the papers spread out before him, but he had not been able to read them for hours. He was simply too weary.

Harry Grove limped in shortly after dawn to stoke up the fires.

"I told ye she'd not be there," the old jockey said as he added logs to the dwindling coals.

"You were wrong."

"So she *was* there. Did it do ye any good?"

John shook his head and pushed the chair back from the table.

"There's got to be an end to it, Harry, and soon." He sighed and ran his fingers through already tousled hair. He could still feel the silkiness of the girl's tresses as he freed them from the confines of her cap. "I want to be myself again, not constantly playing a role."

"The choice was yours."

"Aye, and I don't regret it. But that doesn't mean I can't be weary of the task either."

Leaning back in the chair, he had to stretch to reach the goblet of wine he had poured for himself. It was nearly empty, but the flagon was beyond his grasp. Harry came to his aid, pouring the goblet full with the last drops.

"Are ye ready to deal the final blow?" the old man asked.

"As near to ready as I'll ever be." He picked up several of the papers from the table and scanned them quickly with eyes that glittered with satisfaction.

"Vanderbilt and Townleigh will be bankrupt in a week; they cannot pay the interest they owe Thomas. That's nearly ten thousand pounds out of his treasury and into Kilbury's." One of the papers fluttered to the floor. "Lord Astin's venture, in which Thomas has heavily invested, has already failed. My uncle will learn of the failure tomorrow." Another sheet drifted in the chill air to land on the bare flags. "What I've lifted from Talcott, MacLendon, and Owen has been enough to all but shut down the mines; there's no income for Thomas from that quarter. And we should have enough to see the workers and their families through the winter, at least."

One after another the papers slipped from his hand, each with a tale of riches destroyed and business ventures gone awry.

"Of all those who helped Thomas plunder the Kilbury fortune, the only one I haven't been able to touch is Stanhope. He carries no purse, and his investments are safely out of my reach. Even the elusive Benjamin Miner, whoever he is, has yielded Jack Silver a purse or two." He let the last sheet, covered with numbers, drift downward, then he stretched and yawned and got slowly to his feet. The fluid motion of his body came much more naturally than the clumsiness of the John Colfax he presented to the world. Yet as he bent to retrieve the papers from the floor, he let out a curse of pain.

"Are ye hurt?"

"No, just tormented by hay!" He pulled a long stick of dried fodder from his collar and held it up triumphantly.

Harry folded his arms across his chest and raised an eyebrow.

John hastened to explain.

"She'd been waiting for me outside in the cold until she was nearly frozen. I couldn't have taken her home then. The poor thing would have died."

"So ye warmed her up a bit, eh?"

"That I did, Harry, and nothing more, though it's none of your damned business."

"And what if she was a trap, then what? It'd be me own neck, too, if you was to be caught."

"I thought about that," John replied as he walked to the fire and one by one tossed the sheets of paper onto the now blazing logs. "Whatever else she may be, Betsy Bunch was no trap."

"Just another tavern wench smitten with the legend o' Jack Silver?"

"Perhaps." Yet though she had plenty of opportunity to seduce him, it was clear she wanted no sexual adventure.

Still, her infatuation was as good an explanation as any, and if too many things about her sat uncomfortably on his mind, John forced himself to dismiss her.

Watching the last of his calculations disappear into a curling puff of smoke, he told Harry, "There's no sense worrying about it. I'll not see her again, not as Jack Silver."

CHAPTER
5

Elizabeth did nothing to hide her fury or her shock. They were all she had to cover the nameless dread, the growing horror.

"Father, you can't do this!" she cried.

"I can, I will, and I already have," Edward Stanhope replied with uncharacteristic calm.

She had come to the library in search of a book and, when she found her father inspecting the progress on the wedding portrait, nearly turned around to return to her room empty handed. He stopped her and insisted she stay. Not once had he looked at her, not even when he made the announcement that prompted her outburst.

"There's no reason for it," she insisted, regaining some of her composure though she felt no less outraged. "What difference can a few weeks make, so we can have a proper wedding?"

Edward held his chin in his hand, apparently contemplating the painted likeness of his daughter and the man who would soon be his son-in-law. Elizabeth despised the portrait and could not bring herself to look at it. She wondered if her father's constant fascination had anything to do with a resemblance between her and her mother. There were no portraits of Anne Stanhope in this house, and Elizabeth did not remember the woman who had died before she was two years old. For whatever reasons, Edward had never remarried, and perhaps the wedding portrait brought that fact to mind.

"It can make a great deal of difference," he answered. "I received a message from Thomas a week ago, informing me one of his business ventures has entered a difficult period and he needs additional capital. He suggested that since he is soon to be a member of the family, I might consider advancing him the funds."

"But why should that require an elopement?"

She moved cautiously to a chair by the fire and slowly sank down. Aware that her father had not taken his eyes from the canvas in front of him, she tilted her head back and drew a deep breath meant to calm her. It did not have the desired effect. Her hands, gripping the arms of the chair, still trembled, and a shriek of pure rage threatened to burst from her throat.

"You haven't answered me," she prompted after a prolonged and agonizing silence.

"It's what Thomas wants. And the earl has taken ill."

"No! Not John!"

She regretted the intensity of her exclamation instantly, for the simple reason that it drew her father's attention at last.

Edward gave her an odd look, one she could not decipher as either curious, suspicious, or apprehensive. He did not often stare at her so intently, and the sensation his scrutiny stirred was decidedly unpleasant. She felt like an ox just chosen to be the main course at some barbaric feast.

"Do you still harbor silly fantasies about him?"

She shook her head.

"Of course not," she said, realizing only afterward that it was a lie.

Apparently satisfied with that answer, Edward once again stared at the painting and told her, "Had John been more like Thomas, I'd have married you to him four years ago, when he first came into the title. But he would only have squandered my money, the way his father squandered the Kilbury fortune, and there are doubts he can even sire an heir."

"And have you proof that Thomas can?" she shot back. How else could she defend her clumsy but sensitive friend? Who else would?

Edward never made a secret of his disappointment at not having a son to inherit nor of his desire for a title to match his wealth. Elizabeth, raised without a mother, accepted her responsibility to continue her father's line without question, even when it came to marrying the man he had chosen for her.

"I believe this discussion is at an end. Thomas will obtain the necessary special license and you will wed in two weeks' time. If the earl has succumbed to this latest illness, an ostentatious wedding would be considered in bad taste. And if not, well, the deed will be done all the sooner."

Now she understood. She felt as if a noose were tightening around her neck, and there was no escape.

"He intends to host a ball to announce your formal betrothal, and—"

"And I shall refuse. I am not about to be married in the dead of night by a sleepy country parson. Or, heaven forbid, traipse off to Gretna Green at this time of year."

She had never argued so vehemently before. If Edward was surprised, she herself was stunned—and faintly exhilarated. But Edward maintained his calm. If anything, his reply was quieter and therefore all the more intimidating.

"You will do as I say, Elizabeth, or you will find

yourself in much less pleasant circumstances. Shall I tell you what it is like to be on the streets without a penny?"

"Are you threatening me?"

He glanced at her briefly, long enough to let her know he was not bluffing.

"Yes, my dear, I am."

Icy rain beat a miserable tattoo on the panes of the bedroom window. Elizabeth curled on the window-seat and stared through the streaked glass to the moonless dark beyond. Even had Nell not refused to give her the skirt and cloak and shoes, there would have been no appearance of Betsy Bunch at the Black Oak this night. No one with any sense was on the road in this weather.

"Now you know why his lordship hasn't been around," Nell said with matter-of-fact acceptance of life's disappointments. She slipped two flannel-wrapped bricks between the sheets of Elizabeth's bed. "I must say, the last few times he's been here, he hasn't looked well."

The last time, Elizabeth recalled, was two weeks ago, the morning the portrait had been started. She admitted John seemed pale that day. Still, she refused to believe his illness could be anything other than a mild catarrh, such as nearly everyone caught this time of year. He would throw it off and be visiting again soon, embarrassing her as much as he delighted her with his bumbling, innocent, harmless adoration. An adoration her father had forbidden her to return.

She kept her gaze firmly focused on the rain and asked, "Nell, have you ever been in love?"

"Me? In love? Lord save me, no!" the maid exclaimed.

"But why not?"

"Who is there for me to fall in love with? Fulton, the butler? He's old enough to be my grandfather. One o' the lads from the stables? The Hindu gardener who wears bedsheets wrapped all round his head?" She let out a mirthless chuckle, and her next words were deadly serious. "You've not gone and fallen in love with that highwayman, have you?"

Elizabeth, too, laughed.

Leaning against the chilly stone wall that framed the window, she answered, "No, I've not fallen in love with Jack Silver. One can hardly fall in love with a man she's seen only once in her life and expects never to see again."

An eerie flash of lightning brightened the night for a startling second as though to remind Elizabeth of the lie she told Nell after her nearly disastrous second encounter with the brigand. She had admitted to recognizing him at the Black Oak the night of Thomas's robbery; the rest of the tale she kept safely to herself, even denying she had seen him that following night.

"Or is it his lordship you've a fondness for?"

To that query Elizabeth had no ready answer, especially after her father's similar question that morning, but she suddenly realized she needed one.

"I suppose I once fancied myself his countess, but I think I understood some time ago that he would never see me as anything more than a companion. We are friends, that is all." Two disappointments were as much as she could bear in one evening. Refusing to dwell on the unattainable, either John Colfax, earl of Kilbury, or Jack Silver, highwayman extraordinaire, Elizabeth sighed and rose from her chilly seat. "I just wondered if you knew what it was like to be in love, for I fear if my father and Thomas Colfax have their way, I shall never know for myself."

John stared out the window at the fading winter light while his valet struggled to smooth the fabric of his coat across his shoulders. After two weeks of bogus sneezes and coughs, he was glad to be healthy again. Thomas might be disappointed that his sickly nephew had recovered, but John counted on and therefore encouraged such faith in an early demise. As long as Thomas expected John to succumb to frail health at a young age as his mother had, he was far less likely to resort to active measures to eliminate the single obstacle between himself and the Kilbury title.

"It's the best I can do, my lord," the elderly servant said with a trace of disgust in his imperious voice. "You must have lost weight during your illness."

Slipping easily into feigned enthusiasm, John replied, "Then I shall have a good excuse for indulging heartily in my uncle's feast tonight. Besides, no one will be looking at me; all eyes will be on Thomas's betrothed."

And the sapphires. That was one of several bits of information John had gleaned during his contrived convalescence, which gave him reason to spend most of his time at Kilbury Hall rather that at his usual hermitage in the Dower House. He had hoped to learn much more, not the least of which was how Thomas had obtained the necklace from what John believed to be its final resting place. He wanted desperately to confront his uncle but dared not tip his hand. Not yet.

He did, however, acquire some other knowledge about them and Thomas's plans for them—and for Elizabeth. Not only was Thomas going to announce their formal betrothal and the date of their wedding, but he intended to present Elizabeth Stanhope publicly with the single gift that would seal their relationship as securely as the vows scheduled for June. When he clasped the blue stones around her slender throat, he would proclaim to all present his symbolic ownership of this woman who wore them—and of Kilbury.

Once or twice during those weeks, John caught Thomas with a curious, almost worried look on his face but said nothing about the sapphires. He hoped

Thomas now, a month after bringing them out in the open for Elizabeth's portrait, felt sufficiently secure in his possession of them. As much as John wanted to charge his uncle with the heinous crime that resulted in Thomas's being able to present the Kilbury sapphires to his bride, far more important was the completion of his revenge. The jewels were only a part of that.

The image of them as they had lain against Elizabeth's pale skin filled John's thoughts, and he dismissed the valet almost angrily. He saw the old man shrug, but John had known for years that Albert was one of Thomas's hirelings.

"Thomas may trust you and your like," John muttered when Albert had gone, "but I trust only myself."

He straightened out of his slouch and turned away from the window. His one disappointment tonight was that there would be no cloud cover to provide the shadows Jack Silver preferred. The moon would be bright as day, and almost as dangerous. Still, before the sun rose tomorrow, the last of the Kilbury jewels would once again be in the hands of their rightful owner, and the usurper humiliated beyond repair. John smiled with enormous satisfaction as he took one last look at himself in the mirror. Jack Silver winked back at him.

Thomas served a repast fit for a king, a fact that did not escape Elizabeth's notice. Nor did she fail to note that few of the guests warranted such royal treatment. Even if John, who sat disturbingly near at the long table, had not pointed it out to her, she would have recognized that he alone bore an inherited title.

She ate little and tasted less. All her concentration, all her energy, was directed at keeping a smile on her face and not letting anyone think there were anything wrong with this evening's festivities. Her father had renewed his promise, as he called it, only a few hours ago, and she knew he meant it.

Though Thomas had said nothing about the wedding, she knew he was thinking about it. The occasional glance he threw her way burned her flesh; each touch of his hand sent a chill through her. Now, as they sat together at the head of the long table, he pressed his knee against hers in a way that dared her to avoid the contact.

She gagged on whatever morsel of food she had put in her mouth.

"Are you all right, my dear?" Thomas asked.

The lump of meat went down, but the nausea remained.

"Fine," she answered with a well-practiced smile.

Watching the exchange, John gripped his fork with such loathing that he nearly bent the utensil completely out of shape. He wanted to plunge the sharp tines into her porcelain breast to see if there were indeed blood in her veins or only the cold wine of greed. Instead he stabbed another slice of beef and carried it to his mouth.

As well as he had prepared himself for this night, he still found his emotions almost too near the surface to hide. For nearly three years he had thought of Elizabeth Stanhope as a friend, a companion unrelated to his dreadful need for revenge and retribution. Her agreement to wed Thomas had changed everything. And yet something remained, something John struggled to bury as he had buried all his other hopes and dreams. Only this dream refused to die.

She had greeted him warmly this afternoon upon her arrival at Kilbury Hall, but since then she had hardly a word for him. All her attention was focused on the man who would soon be her husband.

Still, John watched her, a part of him waiting expectantly for her smile, the indulgent touch of her hand on his arm, the soft intimacy of her laughter. But all these things, he was coming to understand, were of the past. He should never have let himself believe she was different. She was, as her attention to Thomas made obvious, her father's daughter.

She also gave considerable attention to the glittering blue collar about her throat. Every few seconds, her slender fingers strayed to caress the sapphires, to lift the enormous center stone in sensuous appreciation of its weight and worth. She wore her hair pinned atop her head in an artless cascade of curls to accentuate the length of her throat and neck, to display the jewels at their very best.

He tried but could not deny that the sapphires had never looked more beautiful. It was as though they belonged around Elizabeth Stanhope's neck, nestled against her skin. He wanted to hate them, as he wanted to hate her, but the feelings refused to obey his commands. The fingers that ought to ache to wrap themselves around that alabaster throat instead longed to caress the satiny skin from the corner of her jaw just beneath her earlobe to that tantalizing shadow above which hung the great blue stone.

He could stand the struggle no longer and dismissed it in order to prepare the final act of his four-year-long drama. Letting his fork clatter noisily to his plate, John slid his chair back with an awkward stagger and got to his feet.

"I fear I am not completely recovered from my illness, Uncle," he mumbled. "You'll excuse me, of course."

The great hall of Kilbury fell into stunned silence that followed John out of the vaulted room and into the corridor. He paused to give his eyes a chance to adjust to the darkness after the brilliance of the dining hall, when Thomas stormed through the doors.

"What is the meaning of this? How dare you disrupt my dinner!"

"I am ill, Uncle. Surely you do not—"

"You've not been ill for days. You had a runny nose and a cough, and you used it as an excuse to indulge your lazy habits. Now you've taken advantage of my generosity again and gotten yourself drunk on my wine."

And you are entertaining your guests in a house that is not yet and indeed may never be yours, John ached to remind his uncle, but he bit the words back.

Thomas muttered an obscenity and ran a nervous hand over his balding pate. For a brief instant, the anger disappeared to reveal the anxiety that lay beneath, but Thomas recovered quickly.

"You don't look very ill to me," he said. "And I don't want Elizabeth worrying over you. Not tonight of all nights."

That comment startled John to a new attentiveness. He had intended to make good his escape and expected no complications, certainly not from Thomas. But he realized he had allowed his emotions to color his perceptions, so much so that he almost missed Thomas's fervent plea. His uncle did not want him to leave, a most unusual circumstance. He had to find out why as well as what was so special about tonight. A mere betrothal announcement seemed an inadequate reason for Thomas's intensity.

"Perhaps it was just the closeness of the room," John posed. He could delay his plans an hour or two in favor of discovering Thomas's. "I do feel better now, and I certainly would not wish to distress Elizabeth on this most happy of occasions."

How absurd that he should let Thomas guide him back into the dining hall, where conversation continued as though nothing had happened. But the facade of John Colfax must be maintained at all costs. The top of Thomas's head barely reached John's shoulder, and though the two men weighed nearly the same, John's weight was muscle and sinew while his uncle was going rapidly to fat. Yet John allowed the impression of childlike innocence to persist and even suffered Thomas to put his hand on the broad shoulder.

It was a gesture Thomas had never made before, and that rang another warning in John's mind. He wondered if Thomas's plans were more nefarious than expected. He had never underestimated his uncle before, but Thomas's desperation may have pushed him beyond his usual limits.

He reentered the dining hall with a sheepish, John-Colfax-the-bumbling-earl expression, and an apology ready on his tongue, but the instincts of Jack Silver took over his thought processes and his powers of observation.

He bowed awkwardly to Elizabeth.

"Too much excitement," he apologized with a grin that passed for a blush.

"Are you certain?" She turned in her seat to look over her shoulder at Thomas. "I don't believe his lordship is feeling well."

"A bit of air was all he needed," her betrothed growled as he pulled out his own chair and sat down heavily.

A footman rushed to hold the earl's chair for him, a gesture which turned Thomas's frown angry. John, well aware that everyone was watching him, resumed his dinner exactly where he had left off.

Except that now he took much more careful note of everything—and everyone—around him, searching for any clues.

The woman who sat at Thomas's left was the wife of Henry Wing-Oliphant, a Sheffield steelmaker who made his fortune manufacturing muskets for the army—and lending money at usurious interest rates. Farther down the table sat Morris St. James, who held three of the Kilbury mortgages, and Andrew MacLendon, who held three more. John knew them all from their business dealings with Thomas, and all of them had been improperly introduced to Jack Silver at one time or another. With one exception.

At the far end of the table sat the one guest whose wealth had not been diminished by an encounter with the highwayman. The Reverend Simon Horne, however, owed his position to Thomas Colfax, who had recommended him when the living came vacant soon after the death of John's father. John, because he held the title if nothing else, made the appointment, but Horne was Thomas's man.

And twice within the few moments John contemplated this unusual guest, Horne removed his watch from its pocket and contemplated the hour. The second time, John followed the man's movements closely.

Horne snapped the watch closed and looked down the length of the laden table. He glanced first at Elizabeth, then the vicar let his gaze wander to Thomas. Had there been an answering glance the first time? John would never know, but he caught the barely perceptible nod his uncle gave to the vicar.

There was no time to analyze that nod, to speculate on why the churchman had been invited and why he was so concerned with the time. Nor was there time to weigh risks, to consider if drawing attention to himself might also trigger recollection or recognition in the parson he had seen at the Black Oak. There was only time to react, to salvage a plan that, after four years of dedication and sacrifice, might be destroyed in an instant.

"I should like to offer a toast," John blurted, getting to his feet with all his usual long-legged clumsiness.

"Not now!" Thomas hissed.

Ignoring the order, John reached for his empty wineglass, then turned too quickly when a footman hurried to refill the goblet. He bumped the servant's arm just enough to slosh the wine in the crystal flagon. A spray of crimson cascaded down the front of John's coat and onto the snowy linen covering the table.

"You clumsy fool!" Thomas thundered.

No mere apologies could salve Thomas's temper, but John mumbled them anyway while he compounded the disaster by trying to help the servants clean up the mess. Half a dozen came running; John made certain he was always in their way.

"I am *so* sorry," he exclaimed as he knocked over a salt cellar. When he reached for a pinch of the white grains to toss over his shoulder, he accidentally leaned on a spoon and sent it into the lap of the woman seated beside him. "Forgive me, madam, please, forgive me."

Over and over he begged the indulgence of Thomas's guests, yet he paid little real attention to them. He cared only about his uncle's anger, which gradually rose to an apoplectic level.

"Get out!" the elder Colfax roared. "Have you not done enough damage?"

"Yes, of course. But I told you I wasn't feeling well."

Slowly, John extricated himself from the cluster of frantic servants who could now be left to tidy up. Still murmuring his apologies, he backed out of the room, with his last glance saved for Elizabeth.

She was near tears. He could see their shimmer behind the sweep of her lowered lashes. A splash of wine had left scarlet droplets on the creamy flesh above the neckline of her gown. She dabbed at them distractedly, the gesture bringing John a strange rush of warmth that had nothing to do with anger. Then, just as he made his exit, he saw her touch the blue stones once again.

They lay like a dozen millstones around her neck. Through the interminable meal, Elizabeth frequently caught her fingers straying to the sapphires as if determined to carry out the wishes she could not consciously effect. Only her concern for John helped her exert the effort needed to keep from flinging the detested jewels the length of Thomas's elegant table. She had noticed John's almost constant attention to the necklace and the obvious affection he had for this last remnant of his inheritance.

She would have followed the earl in his disgraced departure had Thomas not clasped her wrist when she lay her fork beside her plate.

"And where do you think you're going?" he whispered.

"Please, sir, I would like to retire. It has been a strenuous evening."

She did not miss the sudden gleam that came into Thomas's eyes.

"But you cannot think of leaving our guests so soon, my dear. Especially the Reverend Mr. Horne."

The commotion had not yet died. Servants were still clearing away the dishes John had overturned and cleaning up the mess he had made. Yet through their bustling and over the conversation of the assembled guests, Elizabeth was able to make out the vicar's unsubtle motion. He cast a concerned frown at Thomas, then once more took out his watch to check the time.

"And what about your father?" Thomas added, leaning closer to her. "You know how much this evening will mean to him. The consummation of all his fondest wishes."

The double meaning of his words, Elizabeth knew, was completely intentional. Her loathing glance in Edward Stanhope's direction was instinctive.

"I must go," she insisted. "The wine has splashed down the front of my gown and is very uncomfortable."

She had made a poor choice of words, as the weight of Thomas's hand on her knee told her. She could almost feel that hand caressing the flesh beneath her clothes and a ripple of revulsion trembled through her.

Thomas must have mistaken that tremor for one of anticipated pleasure.

"Only another hour, my dear," he purred into her ear.

An hour? Only an hour? Elizabeth dared wait no longer.

Taking advantage of Thomas's preoccupation, she shoved back the heavy chair and evaded his seeking grasp. Her haste set the center stone of the Kilbury necklace to swinging against her skin. Again she felt that overwhelming desire to jerk the thing off and throw it at Thomas's feet.

If the necklace remained around her throat, at least she could hurl her feelings at the man she knew now she could never wed. Whether it was the fact that her father had had to resort to threats to make her keep her promise or a reality she had denied to herself too long, she did not know. But she would deny it no longer.

The words she wanted came to her as she edged away from the table. No one else could hear; no one else needed to hear. She told him quietly, "I would rather spend the rest of my life serving the patrons of a public inn than spend a single night as the bride of Thomas Colfax."

Face red with fury and humiliation, Thomas grabbed for her. Elizabeth, relying on the same skill that had helped Betsy Bunch elude capture at the Black Oak, bolted.

Unfamiliar with the ancient corridors of Kilbury, she hiked the blue satin of her skirts and ran in the direction she knew her room lay.

"Let her go," Thomas muttered to Edward, who had jumped from his own place at the long table to chase his daughter. "She'll not go far. We'll finish our dinner, bid the guests good night, and then deal with her."

"But the wedding? It must be tonight or—"

"It will be, have no fear."

The room was cold, the fire burned down to embers. A single candle guttered on the mantel, casting eerie, uncertain shadows over the unfamiliar room. Elizabeth ducked inside and hurriedly shut the door behind her, then leaned against it to catch her breath. She had taken only one when she spied the reason for the lack of warmth.

Nell Sharpe lay in a comfortable sprawl on the hearth rug. The tip of one of her outstretched fingers was still curled around the handle of a delicate porcelain cup whose contents formed a drying stain on the rug.

With no thought to locking the door, Elizabeth ran to her friend's side and knelt beside her. "Nell, can you hear me? What happened?"

"Don' drink it," Nell mumbled, her voice dreamy, her eyes closed as if in sleep. "I on'y took a swallow, jus' one."

"They drugged you? But why? And who?"

"Don't know. Maybe 'twas because—"

Her voice trailed off completely, though her lips still formed words.

"Nell? Nell! Oh, please, Nell, stay awake just one more minute. Tell me what happened. Everything you can."

She shook the groggy maidservant roughly, then, when Nell began to show signs of once again conquering the temporary poison, Elizabeth ceased her rather harsh ministrations and waited.

"They brought a pot o' warm milk," Nell managed to tell her, waving a limp arm toward the chair and the table beside it. There sat the silver tray and the pot. "Told me it had a bit o' whiskey in it to help you sleep."

Elizabeth imagined the rest. Whoever brought the tainted beverage intended it for her, not suspecting Nell would be powerless to resist it. She had never been to Kilbury and had no idea how to find the kitchen where the other servants supped. Thus she had eaten nothing since leaving Stanhope early that morning. Only Elizabeth knew a spot of warm, whiskey-laced milk would be too tempting for poor Nell's empty stomach. She drank the drug intended for Elizabeth.

"But 'tweren't whiskey. Innkeeper's daughter oughta know."

Those last words were little more than mumbles, and Nell drew her next breath with a gentle snore. The sleeping potion had done its work—on the wrong victim.

And Elizabeth had tarried too long. The soft creak of the door opening behind her brought her heart to her throat. Escape now was impossible; she had been caught like a rat in a trap. Angry and disgusted with herself for how easily she had played into Thomas's scheme, she refused to look up at him.

The voice that addressed her belonged not to Thomas Colfax, however, but to the last person she ever expected to encounter within the ancient walls of Kilbury.

"She'll sleep through the night and be none the worse for it," he told her in that wrenchingly familiar whisper as the door closed with a barely audible click of the latch.

In a single terrified movement, Elizabeth rose to her feet and turned in the direction of that voice.

CHAPTER

6

That lone flickering candle cast his shadow on the wall behind him, making the masked and hooded intruder much more menacing than his gently spoken announcement warranted. Elizabeth's heart stopped. She clasped a trembling hand to her throat as though that gesture would bring back the rhythmic pulse.

A dark brow rose above the strip of cloth tied over his eyes.

"Have no fear, milady," Jack Silver mocked with a low bow. "I have no intention of separating you from your ill-gotten treasure."

A heavy, silent moment passed before she understood him. She lifted the pendant sapphire on her palm as though offering it to him and said, "You think I treasure *this?* I *despise* it. I would give it to you gladly, did it not belong to someone else."

She was clever, more clever than John had given her credit, to take convenient advantage of a fact she had heretofore ignored. She wore the sapphires as if *she* owned them, as if Thomas had a right to bestow them upon her. Yet she obviously did not even suspect that the man whose inheritance she so gallantly defended was the same who threatened to relieve her of it. Still, he did not relax his caution. He could not afford to.

"You misunderstand me, Milady Elizabeth." He waited until the shock of hearing her name had its effect. "I said only that I would not separate the sapphires from you. I intend to have them . . ."

He let the words trail off, knowing she would finish the sentence for him. Her fragile whisper came as no surprise.

"And me, too."

He shrugged. Before she could voice a single word of protest, he advanced toward her with all mockery gone from his manner and a pistol in his hand.

"I have no time to waste and neither do you, milady, if you know what's good for you."

He brushed past Elizabeth and knelt beside the sleeping Nell, who continued to breathe evenly and deeply.

"Was this your doing?" Elizabeth asked.

He straightened and once again trained the pistol on her. Ignoring her question, he said, "You'll need clothes, something other than satin ballgowns. Take what you can carry, for there's no time to pack."

She did not move, not to follow his orders, not to flee, not to fight him. He had expected any one of those reactions, but not her stubborn silence.

"Do you think I would hesitate to use this?" he asked with a nod to the silvery weapon in his hand.

"It would make too much noise."

The highwayman had turned, putting the candle behind him so that his face was all in shadow now. Elizabeth could not see his sardonic smile, but she heard it in his reply.

"So, you are a quick-witted wench. The butt of a pistol on the back of the head is every bit as effective and much more quiet. Or, if you prefer, you could take a few swallows of that milk. I understand the drug works quickly, but not quickly enough to spare you certain, shall we say, indignities."

Damn the woman! Was he to have to resort to knocking her over the head to get her out of Kilbury? He could not help but think of Betsy Bunch, who had risked her very life just to see him. Apparently Elizabeth Stanhope held no such romantic notions.

"I can't leave Nell," she said suddenly. "They'll do terrible things to her."

"To a servant? They'll take no notice of her at all. And I tire of your chatter. Do you get your clothes, or do I take you with nothing but what you stand in?"

Still worried about Nell, Elizabeth knew she had no choice. She was being kidnapped, and she must either cooperate with her abductor or risk needless injury in what would only be a vain attempt to avoid her fate.

Besides, she told herself as she walked to the wardrobe, the alternative was no better. Had she not just run from the most dismal future a woman could face? Had she not challenged Thomas Colfax that she would rather live as a tavern maid than in the wealth her marriage to him would have assured her? She knew Jack Silver, not well but instinctively, and her instincts told her he was cold-blooded enough to steal and threaten, but he would not harm her. Not the way Thomas Colfax would.

"It was Thomas, then, who sent the drugged milk?" she asked as she took a serviceable woolen gown from the wardrobe and draped the garment over her arm. She had not brought much with her from Stanhope. "To what purpose?"

"No good, I assure you. Beyond that, I am not privy to Mr. Colfax's intentions."

She detected a bit of a lie in that statement. Grabbing another gown, she decided to test the highwayman.

"Did you know we were to wed tonight?" She glanced over her shoulder and saw him lift Nell easily and lay her on the bed. He said nothing as he drew the sheet and counterpane over the limp form, but a sharp nod from him sent Elizabeth to pulling more clothes from the wardrobe. "By your silence I assume you are not surprised, yet you say you knew nothing of Mr. Colfax's intentions."

"One has only to examine the facts and the logic behind the gentleman's actions," the highwayman replied. "Now, are you finished?"

He did not allow her time to close the wardrobe door or even time to answer his question. With her arms laden with the clothing she had taken, she could not fight when Jack Silver snapped a length of cloth over her eyes and tied it expertly behind her head. Now even the feeble light of that candle was gone. Blind, she lost her sense of balance, and when she tried to walk, she swayed.

"You'll not stumble, milady," he whispered, his mouth no more than an inch from her ear, his arm curled possessively around her waist. "I'll see to that."

Knowing he risked discovery by snatching Elizabeth while Thomas and his guests lingered over their dinner, John had put his plan into motion several hours early. Though he originally intended to wait until everyone had retired for the night, Vicar Horne's anxiety hinted that Thomas had schemes of his own, and the evidence of the drugged milk was more than enough proof.

He forced her to walk quickly down the corridor to a cold, seldom-used stairway that led directly to the cellars. She stumbled often, trying to hold up her skirt as he dragged her down the stair, but he spared her no pity. He had no time. If they were discovered, he was prepared to use the pistol, though the sound of the shot might bring every soul in Kilbury running to investigate.

But perhaps there was an advantage in acting while

so many of the servants were busy tending to the dinner or resting before the guests retired. He saw no sign of anyone and, once within the cool, dank darkness, allowed himself a sigh of relief.

"Where are we?" Elizabeth asked, her voice a whisper that trembled with terror.

Yet was she really terrified? That question had plagued him since the instant she turned and laid eyes on him. She had been surprised, certainly, to see him in her bedroom, but she neither screamed nor fainted, two techniques with which he was all too well acquainted. Indeed there had been a moment when he thought a look of relief flashed in her eyes, almost as if she were eager to go with Jack Silver.

And there was the matter of the drugged milk. It crossed his mind to wonder why Thomas had to resort to such devices, but it was a puzzle that could be worked out later if necessary.

"We are in a great deal of danger, milady. Now hush, or we'll be in a great deal more."

When he came to the door that led from the cellar to the clear night air, he pushed all such thoughts from his mind. Now was not the time for Jack Silver's romantic fantasies to take over.

At least, he thanked God, Elizabeth had not recognized him. Of that he was more than certain. When he swept her up in his arms, she clung to him almost as if she trusted him.

A little more than an hour since he spirited Elizabeth Stanhope from her room, a disheveled John Colfax opened the door of his chamber and peered out into the corridor.

"Is that you, Thomas?" he wondered aloud, rubbing his eyes with the thumb and forefinger of one hand while he tried to smother a yawn with the other. "And what are you making all this racket for at this hour?"

"At this hour? It's barely nine o'clock. Most of my guests are still eating their dessert."

"Oh." A lame response, but John hoped it sounded typical of the ineffectual fop he had created. "Well, then, why are you not with them?"

Thomas might not be with the crowd of guests he had invited to Kilbury, but he was not alone. Edward Stanhope emerged from the room across the hall and shook his head. A moment later, Vicar Horne stepped out of the room next to it. He, too, expressed a negative response to an unspoken question, punctuating his answer with a shrug of his narrow shoulders.

"It's nothing you need concern yourself over," Thomas replied flatly. "Go back to sleep."

Thomas's lie answered more than a few of John's questions. And the vicar's presence on this futile search confirmed what Elizabeth had said about a wedding tonight.

"I'm sorry I spoiled your dinner," he apologized again, hoping to stall his uncle long enough to learn more about the evening's activities.

But Thomas had no patience and offered no information.

"Go to bed. I have everything under control."

Another lie. Satisfied that Thomas had no idea what had happened to his bride, John did as he was told and closed the door with a silent sigh of relief.

He had barely had time to shed the highwayman's cloak and boots—and persona—and pull a nightshirt over his head when he heard the commotion in the hallway. Now he could afford a few hours' sleep. The first portion of his plan was a complete success.

Though her captor removed the blindfold last night after arrival at their destination, Elizabeth had been unable to see a thing, for the place he brought her to was as dark as pitch—and cold as a tomb. Afraid to venture from the bed where he had deposited her, she huddled beneath the blankets for warmth and managed despite her discomfort and fear to snatch a few hours of dream-riddled sleep. She wakened to a creaking of a door and sat up, abruptly alert, to watch a bent old woman enter the room with a heavily laden tray.

No lamp or candle had been lit, but enough light came in around the closed shutters of the single window to banish the night's utter blindness. Elizabeth discovered herself to be in a room that, though small, was furnished with mismatched but fine old pieces; the bed, chair, table, and wardrobe might have been discards from a manor house half a century or more ago.

"Yer breakfast," the old woman announced as she carried the tray to the table.

Rising to a sitting position, Elizabeth asked, "Is it morning then?"

The crone looked at her but said nothing. She merely gave her charge a quick up and down glance, then shuffled to the rough stone fireplace where she stirred the last embers, invisible under the ashes. As soon as she had a cheery blaze roaring up the chimney, adding warmth as well as light, she left the room. A moment after the door latched, Elizabeth heard the sound of a stout bolt dropping. She was, she knew, securely locked in her prison.

She suspected the woman who brought the breakfast tray was not the person who set the bolt across the door. More than likely Jack Silver had posted a guard, perhaps himself. Elizabeth doubted, however, that anyone would respond to questions.

Considering that at the present she was no worse off than if she had wed Thomas Colfax last night, she stretched and yawned and threw back the covers. No one was going to serve her breakfast in bed, and she was not going to wait until the food was stone cold.

Under the towel covering the tray, she found a

wooden bowl of steaming porridge, two thick slices of bread well buttered, and a pot of tea. Simple fare, but nourishing enough. Jack Silver apparently did not want her to starve.

Nor, it seemed, did he want her to freeze. The table had been pulled comfortably close to the fire, and she noticed a healthy supply of wood stacked near the hearth. In addition, someone had draped a thick quilted robe over the back of the chair. Elizabeth had remembered to bring a warm flannel nightgown but no wrapper. She slipped her arms into this one and tucked her feet under her as she sat down to eat.

And to think.

Nothing made any sense. There had to have been something in last night's strange sequence of events that she had overlooked or ignored that would explain this incomprehensible turn of fate.

But try as she would, Elizabeth could recall nothing she had not already analyzed a dozen times or more during the darkest hours of the night. Perhaps by the light of day, however weak that light may be, she might find some answers.

After the highwayman guided her to the cellar's exit and scooped her into his arms, he walked silently for only a short distance, a hundred paces or so. She had tried to keep count, though the twists and turns he took gave her reason to believe he was deliberately misleading her. And when she shivered in the chill, damp air, he enveloped her in his own cloak as he had Betsy Bunch. Then, without warning, he lifted her onto the saddle of what she assumed was the same gray stallion she had ridden twice before. Still Jack Silver said nothing.

She could not begin to guess how long they rode or in what direction. Again, she suspected the horse's frequent turns were meant to confuse her, and they had. The one clue to her location that Jack Silver could not keep from her was the sound of the wind in the trees. There were, she realized with some dismay, dozens of cottages, lodges, houses, and inns built in the forests within range of Kilbury Hall. For all she knew, she might be held in an upper room of the Black Oak. Or even Kilbury Hall itself.

But she did not think so. This place was too quiet, both last night and this morning, to be a public inn, and she could not believe he would hide her in the same place from which he had stolen her. Having eliminated those possibilities, she had no other clues.

After finishing her breakfast, she poured a second cup of tea and ignored the cold floor to walk barefoot to the single shuttered window. Perhaps the view might give her some hint as to her location, and there was always the chance that the window itself might provide a means of escape.

Both her hopes died when she discovered the shutters nailed tightly shut, with a second set of boards across the outside. Only a single crack let in the light, enough to tell that the day was a brilliant, sunny one but nothing more.

"Why?" she wondered aloud. "Why has he done this? And what does he hope to gain?"

Ransom, she answered herself.

"But if he wants money, why did he not take the sapphires?"

That was the most puzzling question. He had carried her, still securely blindfolded, up several sets of stairs to this room and, after dropping her rather roughly onto the bed, unfastened the long row of buttons down the back of her gown, a task she would have found all but impossible to do herself. He put the nightgown into her hands before he bade her good night. A puff of breath and the sharp odor of burning candlewick told her he had snuffed a candle before he opened and then closed the door.

She had removed the blindfold to darkness as complete as any before until waking this morning.

Before she finished disrobing and then shrugged into the nightgown, she unclasped the heavy strand of stones from her throat and sighed with relief to be unburdened.

The sapphires still lay where she had placed them at the foot of the bed.

"Perhaps he is holding *you* for ransom," she said to the detested necklace, and then she settled in her chair to await the next twist of her suddenly altered fate.

Exhausted but satisfied, John allowed himself an extra hour of sleep the morning after the kidnapping of his uncle's bride. No matter what time he rose, he knew he would learn all the details of the disaster only when Thomas was good and ready to tell him.

As if he needed Thomas to tell him.

He rang for Albert and, after dressing in comfortably outsized clothing, strolled to the morning room for breakfast.

The room was deserted. No meal had been laid on the sideboard, nor was there any sign of Thomas's many guests. John allowed himself a small chuckle.

"So they've left you, Uncle, in your hour of need. Half of them probably spent the night at the Black Oak, afraid Jack Silver would accost them on the roads," he whispered to the empty room.

But he had no time to speculate further on what went through the heads of his uncle's guests. It was much more important that he find Thomas himself and learn his plans.

John found the elder Colfax exactly where he expected, in Kilbury's great hall.

The long table had been cleared sometime during the night, leaving a rather absurd stage for Thomas and Edward Stanhope. Looking exhausted as well as worried, they sat at the head of the table, which was vacant save for the pot of steaming coffee and two empty cups.

In a voice that echoed eerily in the huge, empty room John asked, "Where is everyone? Why was no breakfast laid?"

"You're capable of finding the kitchen, aren't you?" Thomas growled in reply.

"Well, yes, of course I am. But that still doesn't answer my question. Has something dreadful happened?" Eyes innocently wide and curious above the pince-nez, John pulled out a chair beside his uncle and sat down.

"No! Now, leave me alone, you bumbling idiot!"

The explosion came as no surprise, but John concealed his pleasure with a look of shock—and hurt.

"Have *I* done something, Uncle?"

Thomas's face took on the hue of a freshly boiled lobster. Before he could release the rapidly building anger, however, Edward Stanhope laid a hand on the jilted bridegroom's arm.

"We might as well tell him, Thomas."

There was a kind of sad resignation in Stanhope's voice, and it set John on edge. Was it possible the man worried about his daughter? Did he harbor some gentle feelings toward her rather than simply viewing her as a marketable commodity? Perhaps, but he doubted it. He also doubted Edward's feelings would have changed the ultimate outcome of Jack Silver's plan one iota.

When Thomas said nothing, Edward sighed and made the announcement himself.

"Elizabeth is gone."

"Gone? Gone where?"

"We don't know."

"But why would she leave?"

"We don't know that either."

Yes, that was sadness John heard in Edward's quiet admission, but it was also something more. Defeat, perhaps, tinged with a bare whisper of fear.

Edward let out another long, weary breath and

confessed, "She left the dinner a short time after you did, my lord, complaining she was tired. Thinking nothing amiss, we did not go after her to be certain she was all right. An hour or so later, we found her maid, drugged, in Elizabeth's bed. And Elizabeth was gone."

A tremor passed through him. His doughy face was gray as old ashes; his eyes had gone dull. He wore the same evening clothes as last night, but now, wrinkled after a night's exertion, they seemed to hang on him, like the ill-fitting garments John wore as a disguise. He had aged suddenly, as though the events of last night had brought home a terrible reality to him.

Elizabeth's disappearance clearly had a different effect on Thomas. He seethed like a covered pot over a low fire.

"You've searched for her?" John asked.

"Everywhere. All night," Edward answered.

"But why didn't you tell me? That's what you were doing last night when you wakened me, wasn't it?" He turned suddenly angry eyes to his uncle. "Thomas, you should have told me. Elizabeth is my friend. I might have helped."

"Helped? How? By getting in everyone's way? By tripping over every piece of furniture in sight? Bah!" Thomas thundered. He shoved his chair back with a rough scraping sound on the stone floor and began to pace the room, his angry footsteps echoing in the emptiness.

"I sent everyone home with the story of Elizabeth being ill, but who knows how long they'll believe that? How long before the truth gets out that she ran away"—he choked as if his tongue had difficulty forming the words—"on what was to be our wedding night."

"But, Thomas, I thought the wedding was to be in—"

"We were going to elope," Thomas interrupted with

a glare both to John and to Edward clearly meant to silence questions as well as protests.

John, however, ignored his uncle's silent admonition.

"Are you certain she ran away?" he dared, wondering if he risked too much.

"What do you mean?" Edward put in with a new note of fear in his voice.

In a frightened whisper, John suggested, "Could she have been kidnapped? To be held for ransom?"

"Impossible!" Thomas insisted.

He failed to convince anyone, including himself.

"Why is it so impossible?" Edward was sweating, though the room was cool. He rubbed a nervous hand over the gray stubble on his sagging cheeks and then looked at his fingers in disbelief.

Thomas snapped, "I've already interrogated the servants. No one saw anyone either coming or going. If she had been kidnapped, someone would have seen something."

"Not necessarily," John pointed out. "A kidnapper wouldn't allow that, would he?"

He drew a withering look from his uncle, who went on to add, "There was no sign of struggle in the room, and the clothes that were missing were carefully selected, not chosen at random."

Edward, however, refused to be mollified.

"What about her maid? How do you explain that?"

"Simple. She drank the milk, got sleepy, and crawled into the bed, where she fell asleep. Elizabeth found her like that and took advantage of the opportunity to run."

Thomas shrugged, obviously pleased with his explanation. He was startled when Edward failed to accept it.

"Then why was the cup still lying on the rug and her sleeve still wet with the spill?" He got to his feet as though he intended to confront Thomas physically, but then he seemed to change his mind and headed for the door. "I think the boy is right, Thomas. I think someone drugged the milk, perhaps intending to incapacitate Elizabeth rather than the maid. When the maid drank it instead, he lay in wait, knowing that even if Elizabeth did not drink it, she would have no ally against him. She's been kidnapped, and there is nothing we can do but wait until we receive the request for ransom."

"And what are we to ransom her with?" Thomas called after Edward's retreating figure. "She's got the sapphires."

The morning passed slowly, and the afternoon even more so. After eating her breakfast, Elizabeth dressed herself in a simple gown of dark green wool and tried to occupy her time with whatever tasks came to hand. She made the bed, aware as she did so that she was avoiding the pile of glittering jewels at the foot. She could not bring herself to touch the sapphires, not even to put them away. They remained where she had put them the night before.

She tended the fire and hung her clothes in the wardrobe and brushed her hair a thousand strokes with a brush she found in a drawer at the bottom of the wardrobe. It was a man's brush, with a back of fine-grained ebony, but it was all she had available. The counting of the strokes passed a few of the otherwise interminable minutes.

The elderly woman brought a luncheon tray and removed the breakfast dishes, all without saying a word.

"Can't you at least tell me if I am to be ransomed?" Elizabeth begged. "Or what time of day it is?"

But the ancient crone simply stared at her, expressionless, and retreated out the door.

"No, wait!" Elizabeth cried, dashing across the

room to grab the edge of the door with both hands. "Please, could you bring me a book to read or even some kind of work to do?"

The old eyes brightened, but the look they gave Elizabeth was one of pure disdain.

"I'll ask."

As though drawn by the sound of voices, a tall youth appeared at the door. Without a word he took the breakfast tray in one hand and with the other pulled the door shut, nearly catching Elizabeth's fingers between it and the frame. The old woman barely had time to get herself out of the way. One corner of her skirt remained caught, and Elizabeth hoped the boy would open the door again to free the fabric.

But he did not. An unreasonable despair washed over Elizabeth as she watched the folded corner of homespun cloth disappear, pulled slowly free from the other side of the door. For some reason, she felt her own hope disappear along with it.

She turned and made her way to the chair by the fire. She did not even look at the luncheon tray on the table. For the first time since Jack Silver had left her in this room, Elizabeth admitted she was afraid.

That admission opened a floodgate. A hundred horrible possibilities rushed into her mind, overwhelming all her power to deny them. And the most horrible of all pushed its way to the fore until it dominated her thoughts.

"Thomas had nothing to do with this," she insisted aloud. "If he had, why is he not here? Why did he not bring that obsequious vicar and have us wed last night as he planned?"

Logic dismissed one fear, but she remained alone and helpless, lost and frightened. Now the tears came despite her sniffles, despite leaning her head against the back of the chair and closing her eyes.

"Why, Jack?" she whispered as cold, salty rivulets snaked down her temples to her ears. "Why did you have to become real? Why couldn't you have stayed just a dream, *my* dream?"

A painful sob shuddered through her. Giving in to it and to the tears that refused to be denied, Elizabeth curled deeper into the chair.

"Damn you, Jack Silver, damn you to hell."

CHAPTER

7

John did not for a moment entertain the notion that the old woman lied or even made some mistake, but what Peg told him about Elizabeth Stanhope's behavior during her first day of captivity left him more confused than ever.

"She ate all the breakfast but never touched lunch or dinner?" he asked, trying to puzzle it out.

"Not a bite," Peg insisted just as firmly as she had told him the first time.

They faced each other across the ancient table in the hall, John seated, Peg standing out of customary respect for the lord of the manor.

"And when I looked in on her this afternoon, she were sleepin' in the chair. Fire were almost out, so I built it up again, and that were what woke her."

"Did she say anything?"

Peg shook her head.

"Nary a word, 'cept to ask for a book to read."

He had no idea how long the old woman stood there, waiting for his reply while he toyed with the remains of his own supper. A dozen different responses came to his mind, but he rejected them all one by one. Finally, realizing he had been lost in thought for some time, he dismissed Peg with a wave of his hand and a mumbled word of thanks. She bobbed a bit of a curtsey, then shuffled quietly out of the room, leaving him alone with his thoughts.

The day had gone well until now, and he knew success left him complacent and unprepared for Peg's confusing information. But what, he wondered as he laid down his fork and finished the tart wine that accompanied his meal, had he truly expected?

Edward Stanhope had proved no great surprise. Once the possibility of ransom had been broached, he clung to it doggedly and refused to take any action until the kidnapper's demands were made known. He would not even leave Kilbury Hall when Thomas organized a search party.

Thomas, on the other hand, was a veritable fury. He ordered the Hall combed from the servants' quarters in the attics to the deepest, dankest cellars. When not a single clue turned up, he widened the area to include the grounds and outbuildings and led the hunt himself.

They found nothing. No trace of Elizabeth, nor a single witness who had seen anything amiss the night before. A messenger dispatched to Stanhope Manor returned with a shake of his head; Elizabeth had not run home.

John even took them to the Dower House and invited his uncle to search the decrepit building.

Thomas made a cursory tour, poking his nose into rooms empty of everything save cobwebs and dust, climbing stairs that led to garrets with rotted floors and broken windows. He left with a curse for the time his nephew had forced him to waste.

And all the while Elizabeth was sleeping in the tower room, accessible only through one of those empty chambers. Had she screamed or made any break for freedom, Thomas might have been alerted.

But John counted on the loyalty of Peg and the strength of her grandson Ethan to keep the captive safe and silent. They had not disappointed him, though he admitted he owed some of his luck to Elizabeth herself.

Elizabeth. A soft, involuntary groan escaped him. Never all day had she been out of his mind, but while he participated in the search, he had concentrated on keeping the others from learning a single clue that might lead them to her. Now that the day was over, he had only Elizabeth to think about. And what he intended to do with her.

He opened the door silently, not so much out of necessity as out of habit. With caution that had likewise grown instinctive, he blocked her escape at the same time he surveyed the darkened room for traps. Everything was as it should be, as he had expected it to be, except that she slept in the chair rather than the bed.

The glow of the dying fire illuminated her, curled like a child. After closing the door behind him, John took three long strides to the center of the room. He could not take his eyes from her, could not resist the temptation to feast upon his prey while she slept.

The veil of her hair tumbled over one arm to the floor, the silky blue-black strands inviting a man's touch. No smile curved her lips, though that lack did not make her any the less lovely. Feathery lashes brushed her cheeks and fluttered, as if perhaps she dreamed.

Elizabeth Stanhope was, John admitted with no hesitation, a very beautiful, very desirable woman.

Suspecting her sleep was a light one, he scraped his boot on the uncovered floor. The sound brought her instantly awake, instantly wary.

"Oh, it's you," she said.

"You sound a bit disappointed."

Sarcasm, as usual, dripped from his tongue. Elizabeth ought to be accustomed to it, but the memory of the way he had spoken to Betsy Bunch argued against her. Jack Silver could be gentle, he could be tender. But not with Elizabeth Stanhope.

"Were you hoping, perhaps, for Thomas Colfax to come to your rescue?"

"No!"

The word burst from her with such desperation she hardly recognized her own voice. She regretted displaying her feelings so readily before she knew what her abductor wanted of her. Even if it were to her advantage to apprise Jack Silver of some part of the truth, she must do so with caution.

She unfolded her legs from their cramped position and gave in to the urge to yawn and stretch before she arranged herself more modestly on the chair. There was, she noticed with disappointment, no trace of the tray the old woman had left for her supper.

Ignoring her empty stomach and parched throat, Elizabeth turned her attention to the man who stood at the center of a triangle formed by her chair, the bed, and the door to her prison.

"I would be quite content if I never laid eyes on Mr. Thomas Colfax again as long as I live," she stated.

He lifted a dark brow just as he had the night before, only this time he wore no mask. Still, in the poor light provided by the fire, she could barely make out his features.

"Have you another lover?" he asked.

Her laugh was short and soft and almost sad.

You, she longed to tell him, *you, Jack Silver, were my lover. But only in my dreams, and now you've wakened me to a bitter reality.*

She answered with pride and hoped it covered the pain in her declaration. "No, I have no lover."

He took one step nearer, then another, until he was

close enough to extend a hand to her. And though his words had nothing to do with the gesture, Elizabeth found herself unable to resist.

"How strange," he commented, still with that mocking lilt to his voice, as she placed her hand in his. "You are not an unlovely woman, and as heiress to your father's fortune, you would bring more than your face and form to a marriage bed. Yet you say you have no lovers."

Closing the distance between them, he brought her hand to his lips and brushed a lingering kiss across her knuckles.

He never took his eyes from hers. She could not blink away the intensity of his gaze, and though her hand trembled in his grasp, she was powerless to pull free. Not that he held her tightly. His fingers curled around hers with only the slightest pressure. Perhaps that gentleness, that careful restraint, spoke more eloquently of his strength than had he crushed her hand.

"No lovers," she echoed. Her voice, too, was weak, breathy, and little more than a whisper. Had she not been sitting, she was certain her knees would never have held her. Even now a strange dizziness washed over her.

"Not even your betrothed?"

She jerked her hand out of his, nearly bumping his nose in the process. The dizziness passed as well as the weakness, but a tingling sensation remained where his fingers had touched hers and where his lips had grazed her skin. Tingling or no, she would not stand for his insults.

"How dare you!"

"How? Very easily, milady. In fact, I dare nearly anything I wish."

She thought for a moment he might reach for her again. The way he flexed his fingers hinted that he wanted to, perhaps to grab her upper arms and pull her against him, but instead he gave her an unfathomable smile and walked past her to the fireplace.

"I dared to snatch you from the arms of your intended bridegroom, did I not?" he asked as he tossed several pieces of wood onto the embers. "I have dared to relieve Thomas Colfax of a considerable sum of coin, not to mention numerous other travelers who have fallen victim to my powers of persuasion."

Elizabeth had no retort. She heard his every word and yet she heard nothing, her mind filled with that unbidden image of Jack Silver taking her in his arms. He had done nothing of the sort last night, except to wrap his cloak around her so she didn't freeze to death, and she was no more or less at his mercy now than twenty-four hours ago. Then why could she not banish the thought? Because he had kissed Betsy Bunch, who all but threw herself at his feet? Determined not to let old dreams flare to life once more, Elizabeth shook her head clear of them and heard Jack Silver's arrogant boast.

"I dare, my dear Elizabeth, because others have dared even more."

John stood again, facing her with his back to the fire that blazed and lit the room with eerie yellow brilliance and dancing shadows. For a moment he was tempted to laugh off the things he had told her until he realized she was lost in her own thoughts and had probably heard very little. Before he could speculate on what might run in the head of Elizabeth Stanhope, she broke a long silence with words he never expected to hear, not from her, not from anyone else.

"I beg your pardon, Mr. Silver. I'm afraid I wasn't listening."

"'Mr. Silver,'" he repeated with a bit of a chuckle. "Few people call me that."

"I daresay it isn't your given name."

"It's close enough," he said with a shrug as he leaned against the mantel. "And it's of my own choosing."

"As is your line of work?"

She was a bold one to ask such a question of him, but John was beginning to understand that the woman he had taken from Kilbury Hall was not the frightened, selfish creature he had expected.

"It was not my first choice," he told her honestly, "though I doubt you'd believe that."

"And why were you not able to find other employment? You speak as though you have some education, and I have seen no physical infirmities that would keep you from honest work."

Good Lord, she actually expected him to justify his actions to her! Worse, he was on the point of doing exactly that. He stopped himself just in time.

"Let us say that circumstances forced me to a life of crime, which is generally the excuse most felons give on their way to the gallows," he replied. "I, however, have no intention of ending as a rotting corpse in chains on a crossroads gibbet, at least not until I have taken care of certain business matters."

"My ransom, for example?"

He tried but could read nothing in her tone, neither hope nor fear. Studying her face by the light of the fire, he discovered no clue to her thoughts in her expression. Indeed she appeared quite calm.

She had, however, with that simple question given him the opening he needed to broach the subject of her captivity. He wondered, in the seconds before he made the announcement, if she would be so calm afterward.

"You are not to be ransomed. Unless you are discovered, and I do not think that likely, you will be my guest here for the next month, perhaps two. I hope you will find your stay a pleasant one."

The blood drained from her face, and for an instant he thought she would faint. Though he made no overt motion, he was prepared for anything from a sudden swoon to a physical attack on his person. She did nothing, showed no response at all, save to take a deep breath and exhale very, very slowly.

Beneath her gown, her breasts rose and fell with that extended sigh. He remembered how the candlelight had gleamed on the swell of her flesh above the blue satin she had worn the night before. The memory alone was enough to make his own flesh swell in response. Yet he cursed his body's reaction.

Bedding her would not be a distasteful chore if he ignored his conscience. He wondered, however, why he felt such an eagerness to be about the deed.

He glanced to the bed where lay the necklace, the symbol of everything he had lost. Guilt faded as he realized Elizabeth had slept with the gems, not around her throat, lest they scratch her delicate skin, but at her feet.

She clasped her hands in her lap and drew in another slow breath. She no longer looked at him, and he found he missed the defiance, the pride, that glittered in her eyes and masked all her other feelings. She was, he realized, very much like him in that respect. Did she, too, have secrets to hide?

If she did, she continued to keep them hidden as she looked up at him and said without emotion, "So I am to be a hostage. To what purpose? What do you want, Jack Silver?"

He owed her no answers, not even to tell her she was but an instrument of revenge. Her burden of guilt weighed no less than Thomas's, as the stones on the counterpane proved. She claimed to despise the sapphires, yet there they lay, hardly out of her reach and certainly not out of her sight.

If she could lie, then so would he. And in the end,

would her pain not be even greater when she learned of his deception as he had learned of her betrayal?

As before, when he offered her his hand, she placed hers on it without a word. He pulled her to her feet and smiled with satisfaction. For all her brave words, he saw confusion in her eyes, uncertainty, perhaps a sliver of fear.

He twisted her arm behind her, forcing her lower body against him, against the proof of his claim. "What I want, Elizabeth, is *you.*"

Had he not covered her mouth so possessively with his, Elizabeth would have laughed aloud. Did he expect her to believe such nonsense? He had never met her, could not possibly have developed the kind of obsession that would lead him to kidnap her from under Thomas's nose.

And yet he was kissing her, teasing her lips with his until she could no longer resist the invasion of his tongue. He tasted of tart wine and unquenchable desire. He would not be denied and suddenly Elizabeth knew she would not either. The stifled laughter became a sigh and then a moan from deep in her throat.

She would not believe his lie, but she would give in to the desire his lie awakened. She would force from her mind all the truths, all the ugly realities, and savor this moment, however long it lasted. Only the dream mattered now and the man she held so hungrily in her arms.

When John suddenly released her, he left her gasping, her head thrown back like a wanton creature. With each breath, her breasts pressed against him, warm and full, tempting his touch. A frantic pulse beat at the base of her throat; she could deny her passion or tell him it was feigned, but he knew the truth.

"For a woman who has no lovers, you display a

remarkable lack of innocence," he told her, his own breathing not quite steady.

Brought back to the reality she had tried to ignore, Elizabeth blushed and hung her head. Resting her brow against Jack Silver's chest, she could not but notice how rapidly his heart beat. Was it possible, then, that what he said was true? That he had brought her here simply out of desire?

No, no, no, she told herself sternly now that sense had returned, however unwelcome it might be. *He has other motives, I am sure of it.* Still, she took some comfort from his passion; it meant he was not coldly seducing her.

"I am sorry if I offended you," she apologized. "I sought only to please you."

"And just what is *that* supposed to mean?"

"Dear God," she whispered, searching for answers to a thousand questions. His features had taken on a demonic cast that was not altogether frightening but revealed nothing. "What do you want of me? The necklace? Take it. I cannot give it to you, for it belongs to someone else. It is worth a king's ransom, far more than I."

"I told you before, you do not need to give it to me. It is already mine."

"Then what purpose can this torture serve? Shall I confess the truth to you? I had heard that some men prefer their women unwilling, that the sense of conquest arouses them. I thought perhaps you might be that sort and that if I surrendered willingly, you might—lose interest."

Her explanation made some sense, certainly more than anything else she had done, but it was not enough.

And he had not lost interest.

"You think I wish to rape you?"

"Do you not?"

He thought back to Betsy Bunch, half frozen because she wanted to be with him, and he had given her nothing but a few kisses. Elizabeth Stanhope would never believe him capable of that kind of restraint. It was, he decided, his damned fate to be unable to bed the women who most wanted him and forced to bed those who did not.

He laughed again at the irony, then answered his prisoner's question as honestly as he dared.

Circling her face with both hands, he brushed a feathery kiss across her lips and then said, "I wish to seduce you, milady. I wish to initiate you to the thousand joys of the flesh." He kissed her again, still softly but with a hint of passionate pressure, and as quickly broke off. "I wish to enjoy you and make you enjoy me as well."

Her lips were parted, her nostrils flared, her eyes closed. Thick lashes settled against her cheekbones like leaves drifting onto a still pond. If he released her, would she fall senseless into a fragile heap at his feet? He thought perhaps she might.

"This is not what I imagined," he confessed as he drew his thumbs along her jawline. A tremor went through her. "Do you fear me?"

"Yes, I fear you. I would be a fool not to."

Again he stroked her chin, and he threaded his fingers deeper into the thickness of her hair.

He could almost imagine that Elizabeth Stanhope's black tresses, heavy with the scent of lilacs, were Betsy Bunch's golden curls. He remembered the feel of them, the warmth they gave his hands in the cold of the loft. He remembered, too, the wench's fear.

"I think you fear yourself more, Elizabeth."

Dear God, he had thrown her own words back at her! With a wordless cry, Elizabeth wrenched free and ran to the door. She knew it would be locked but grabbed the handle and pulled frantically.

"You cannot leave," the quiet voice reminded her. She spun, her back to the door, her hands flattened against the age-smoothed wood. The man who walked slowly, patiently, confidently, toward her was no more than a shadow, a stealthy silhouette from which she could not escape.

"Neither, for that matter, can I," he added.

CHAPTER

She was a liar, a greedy, scheming liar who would say anything, *do* anything to get what she wanted, John reminded himself with each step he took toward her. With his own eyes he had watched her through that interminable dinner while she caressed the jewels around her throat. And later, when Jack Silver had come into her room at Kilbury, she once again reached to protect the blue stones.

Yet she dared to tell him she cared nothing for them, that she would gladly give them to him, and all the while she slept with them at her feet.

One or the other was a lie as surely as her tale of trying to destroy his desire by giving in to it. At least he knew that was a falsehood. No one, not even Elizabeth Stanhope, could fool him where a woman's desire was concerned.

He was still two or three steps from her when she asked, "Why are you doing this? What have I done to you to deserve this?"

Her words touched that chord of guilt in him and almost halted him, but he came to stand directly in front of her before he answered.

"No, milady, you'll not play upon my sympathies, for I have none. If I did, I would not be an outlaw, would I?"

He touched her again, his left hand holding her chin, the right smoothing back a lock of hair that had fallen over her eye. He planted his booted feet outside hers to trap her between the unyielding oak of the door and the undiminished heat of his desire.

"Do you intend to take me at the point of a gun, the way you rob innocent travelers on the highway?"

She had recovered some of her defiance. He felt it in the way she tried to evade the insistent pressure of his body.

"There are no innocents," he told her as he moved his hand down her throat to the high neckline of her gown. "And I do not believe I shall need the gun. You've provided me with a much more potent weapon."

His mouth came down on hers at the same time he moved his hand to the back of her neck. Struggling to retain a hold on coherent thought, Elizabeth concentrated on his actions. Perhaps if she could keep track of what he was doing, she could control her reaction to him.

But this was Jack Silver kissing her, Jack Silver's hand unfastening the buttons at the back of her dress, Jack Silver's body moving insistently against hers. Dreams mingled with nightmares until Elizabeth twisted her head away from his kiss.

"Stop," she gasped, "please, for the love of God, stop."

"No, Elizabeth, I cannot stop."

She felt his words against her throat while he pulled her away from the door. His fingers quickly freed the rest of the buttons down her back.

"And if I could, I would not."

John pulled the dress from her shoulders and down

her arms, raising gooseflesh on the exposed skin. He kissed her shoulder, his head buried in the cloud of her tousled hair. The scent of lilacs overwhelmed him to remind him of that night in the loft and the girl he had wanted so damned much. Why did Elizabeth have to remind him of her?

And yet it was Elizabeth he wanted, here and now. Elizabeth, who quivered in his arms, whose every breath became a moan of involuntary passion. Elizabeth, who had befriended him four years ago and then agreed to marry his uncle.

His own breath ragged, John backed away from the woman pinned against the door. In the firelight he could see the rapid rise and fall of her breasts under the thin linen of her shift. The woolen gown lay at her feet; she made no move either to retrieve it or to cover herself.

He wanted her. He could remind himself over and over of her sins, her lies, her greed, her willingness to sell herself to Thomas for the hope of a title, but none of it diminished his need for her.

He was losing control of the situation, of himself. He stepped away from her in the hope that distance would return his sanity.

For a breathless moment Elizabeth feared he would retreat. She could not let that happen. Her own attempt to flee Thomas Colfax may have failed, but Jack Silver presented her with another opportunity. If someday in the future she were to be returned to Thomas and forced to consummate the marriage, she would at least have *this* to remember. She would give her virginity willingly, freely, as only she could give it, to the man of her choice. She would not let it be taken from her.

She raised one trembling hand to the narrow strap of her shift and slid it off her shoulder. And prayed she had not gone too far.

Slowly she bared the tantalizing curve of one breast until the fabric of her undergarment hung precariously on the distended bud of her nipple.

He did not retreat. He hooked a long finger under the edge of her shift and determinedly pulled it further down.

She shivered at the breath of cold air on her naked skin. Yet at the same time, a fluid warmth spread through her, kindled where his gaze touched the tightened tips of her breasts. When his hands circled the soft mounds of flesh, she felt as if she would burst into flame.

Then he withdrew his hands but only to unbutton the dark shirt and pull it over his head.

Elizabeth had never seen so perfect a specimen of raw masculinity. Once, when she had gone hiking with the earl in search of wildflowers, they had come upon a group of village youths swimming naked in a meadow pond. Poor John, more embarrassed at the sight than she, had quickly turned her away and sent the boys home with a stern warning against such unseemly behavior. Still, she had seen enough to know what a man looked like without his clothes.

That had not, however, prepared her for the sight of Jack Silver as, shirtless, he tugged off his boots and unbuttoned his black breeches. With each movement, muscles rippled in his shoulders and arms. A dusting of hair softened the sharp planes and angles delineated in the firelight. It beckoned her fingers until she had to clench them into fists at her side to keep from reaching for him.

Her tongue slipped out to moisten her parted lips.

She was aware of his hands now upon her, pushing her shift and her underdrawers over her hips. When she was as naked as he, he scooped her up as if she were a sleeping child and carried her to the bed. The unmistakable scent of him, all warm and masculine, filled her with each breath. And the taste of him, more intoxicating than the finest champagne, engulfed her as once more his lips took possession of hers.

Not for a second did he break the insistent pressure of his kiss, not even when he lay her down on the quilt and stretched out beside her. It was she who shattered the bond, turning her head away to gasp and draw much needed air into her lungs.

"You cannot escape," he told her as he cupped her chin in his hand and turned her to face him once more.

"I know," she whispered. "Not from you, not from myself."

John blamed the firelight for the tricks his eyes played on him. The flames in her eyes were only reflections of the burning logs on the hearth. The fluttery pulse at her throat was nothing more than a shadow of the unsteady light. Even the trembling of her fingers as they feathered down his chest and belly he attributed to the chill the old fireplace could never chase.

But the firelight, the drafty cold of the room, the distorted images of shadows and substance had nothing to do with the eager hands that tightened around his waist and pulled him closer to a fevered body.

A thousand warnings screamed in his head. He tried to think, tried to keep his head clear. The Elizabeth Stanhope he had taken from Kilbury was not the same creature who now sprawled half beneath him. He had expected resistance at least, tears and hysteria more than likely, resignation the best he could hope for, but never this wanton desire.

Forcing himself away from her, he looked down as she opened eyes glazed with passion. Her nostrils still flared with each labored breath; her swollen lips parted as her tongue flicked out to lick away the dryness. He had brought her here for just such a reason, to arouse her and demand her complete surrender, yet now that she was on the brink, he hesitated.

"Have I done something wrong?" she asked, breaking into his wandering thoughts with a breathless whisper. "Do you no longer want me?"

He chuckled and glanced down the length of their almost-joined bodies to the undeniable evidence. "Oh, yes, I want you. 'Tis damned difficult to deny a wanting as obvious as this."

With an exasperated cry, Elizabeth withdrew the arm she had twined around his waist and flung it back onto the bed with a resounding thwack.

"Why should I expect him to behave like a civilized gentleman?" she wondered aloud, staring at the bed canopy though it was lost in shadow. She could not, would not, look at the man beside her. "He is a highwayman, a common thief, who has stolen me from my home and imprisoned me for the stated purpose of satisfying his lustful craving. He will not allow me to be ransomed, nor can I do anything else to avoid my fate. Then he has the unmitigated gall to mock me and—"

His hand clasping her chin cut her off. He turned her roughly to face him, his fingers digging cruelly into her jaw.

"Don't pretend I'm not here, milady," he growled. "Others have made that mistake and lived to pay dearly for it."

"I could never pretend you're not here." She knew her voice trembled, but she met his angry gaze and did not falter. "Nor can I pretend that I do not want you in the same way you want me."

Was she telling him too much? Had she given him another weapon to use against her? No, he already knew, as any man would, that her own desire made her powerless against his seduction.

She had, however, gained some control over her own emotions.

"You told me before that I was not ill-favored." She drew the side of her little finger down the center of his chest to where the dark line of hair narrowed at his navel. He pulled in a single sharp breath, then released it before she continued. "Neither, Jack Silver, are you. Can you not understand how a young woman, promised in marriage to a man nearly as old as her father, might imagine herself with a handsome, romantic adventurer such as yourself? And, when she finds herself actually in that man's company, discovers that she has fallen victim to her own fantasies as well as his seduction?"

His only reply as a snort of bitter, still disbelieving laughter. Before he could put his thoughts to words, Elizabeth went on.

"Yes, I was afraid of you. I still am. But am I not to be allowed to make the best of this, as you certainly are?"

The hand that lay flat on his belly now came up to caress his cheek. Her honesty, her boldness, shocked him and left him with no answer to her question. Was she once again trying to trick him out of his desire, out of his revenge? If she were, she failed miserably, because his need for her grew stronger.

"Last night was to have been my wedding night, and I dreaded it more than I have ever dreaded anything in my life. When I left Thomas's betrothal dinner, I intended to run away. I even told him—"

She bit off the rest of the sentence. To tell Jack Silver what she had told Thomas about preferring the life of a tavern maid to being his bride might trigger the highwayman's memory, and she dared not risk that much. Not yet.

"What you're saying then, if I understand you correctly, is that you prefer being bedded by a common thief to marriage with Thomas Colfax. Hardly the sort of compliment I'm used to."

He was going to make her admit all of it, Elizabeth realized, before he would give her a moment's peace. That was more than she was willing to do, even for him.

She stroked her hand down his cheek once more, feeling the roughness of his beard, the hardness of the muscle that tightened his jaw. Oh, if only she could see him, really see him, but in the darkness of the firelit chamber, he was just shadows, some darker, some lighter. When she touched him, she could imagine the shape of him, but it wasn't the same. And all she could see now were his eyes, blazing silver with passion.

He lay half across her, his chest nearly squashing her sensitized breasts. Her legs, however, were not trapped beneath him. She lifted the left to curl it high over his hip and bring her lower body into intimate contact with his.

His kiss was like fire, devouring her, consuming her, igniting in her a holocaust. The searing touch of his tongue against hers sent waves of heat shimmering through her until she felt as if her entire body were made of molten lava. The conflagration destroyed everything in its path, reason, fear, confusion, and left behind the white hot embers only a storm could quench.

He could not resist her a moment longer. He had waited, wanting her, too long already.

A strangled cry escaped her, escaped even the muffling pressure of his kiss, at the sudden bright pain of his possession. When she tried to break free, he held her thrashing head still.

"It will pass," he murmured as he tangled his fingers in her hair and clasped them around her skull. "Don't move, don't try to fight it."

He had nearly forgotten the suspicion that wormed its way into his thoughts when Elizabeth first responded to his seduction. The discovery of her virginity had allayed that doubt once and for all.

He kissed her cheek as though to apologize for doubting her.

That gentle gesture surprised her as had the way he held himself so still within her, waiting for the pain to subside. In truth, the loss of her maidenhead had not hurt so much physically as it had emotionally. That kiss and the words he whispered after it eased the ache.

"And for what are you sorry?" she asked. "For taking what I gladly gave? Better you than—"

"Hush! Even a rogue and a thief like me knows it isn't polite to discuss one man when you are in bed with another." He moved tentatively, not eager to cause her unnecessary discomfort but unable to hold back his own needs. "I said I was sorry for hurting you the way I did."

"I knew the first time would be painful. A virgin I may have been but not an ignorant one."

He kissed her again, this time brushing his lips across her temple while he whispered into her ear, "A skillful lover knows ways to lessen the pain of a woman's first time, and I regret that it is too late to prove that to you."

But the pain was gone now, and renewed desire demanded fulfillment. She took him deeper and deeper inside her, knowing the haze of mindless passion was about to overtake her again. It mattered not in the least. For the moment the dream was as she wanted it. Jack Silver held her in his arms, loving her, making her forget all the nightmares.

"But it is not too late to bring you pleasure," he told her as the rhythm of his body increased. She was warm and wet and tight around him, as eager to be pleasured as he. And he wanted, almost *needed,* her culmination before he reached his own.

What pleasure could be greater than this? Yet

somehow Elizabeth sensed that there was indeed more. It was a craving of both the body and soul, undeniable as surely as it was unidentifiable.

Fluttering kisses on her face and throat, the highwayman urged her to seek that elusive satisfaction. "Yes, love, yes," he breathed softly. "It's there, it's almost there."

And then the storm burst upon her, frightening her with its intensity. She cried out, not once but a dozen times, as each spasm seared her soul like lightning. She clung breathless to the man whose body still moved within hers, until he stiffened in her arms and, with a cry of his own, expended his passion as completely as she had hers.

The morning room at Kilbury once again boasted a fine assortment of breakfast delights. John made his selections from the sideboard, then walked slowly to the table. Thomas, looking rested but no less angry than two nights ago, sat at the head of the table. A plate piled high with eggs, bacon, and marmalade-smothered toast occupied his almost complete attention. Elizabeth's disappearance had not affected his appetite for long.

"No news?" John asked as he took his place across from the table's other occupant, a morose Edward Stanhope.

"Since last night? No," Thomas answered curtly.

"I went to bed very early, Thomas," John defended himself, enjoying the secret truth in that statement. "I thought perhaps the kidnapper had delivered a ransom demand."

"There is still no evidence to prove she was kidnapped," Thomas snapped. "I wish you would stop assuming that she was."

Edward finally spoke up. In contrast to his host, Stanhope did not look rested. If anything, he appeared more exhausted than the day before. And older.

"The boy can't help what he thinks, and I am inclined to agree with him."

"Then why have we received no demands from this alleged kidnapper?" Thomas wanted to know. "What use is a kidnapping if one does not expect a ransom?" He shoved another bite of toast into his mouth, unmindful of the dollop of marmalade on his chin. "No, the girl has just run off."

As they had so many times before, Thomas and Edward spoke almost as freely as if they were alone. When John finished his meal and excused himself from their company, they looked at him as though they did not remember his ever joining them. His vacant smile assured them he had heard nothing.

And indeed he had heard little that he did not already know, except for one very satisfying bit of information.

Edward had made Thomas a loan in anticipation of the elopement, a loan that he now demanded be repaid immediately in light of Elizabeth's disappearance. Thomas blanched and simply said repayment was impossible.

The untouchable Edward Stanhope had been touched. That knowledge was, in its own way, as satisfying a victory as the taking of Elizabeth's virginity. It did not, however, give rise to the same unsettling emotions the memory of her brought to John as he made his way from the morning room to the library. He did not like the possibility that some of those emotions were spawned by doubt—and inescapable guilt.

CHAPTER
9

John scratched a neat row of numbers onto the ledger page. As usual these late winter nights, wind howled in the chimney and stirred enough drafts to have every candle in the hall flickering dangerously. The old Dower House sadly needed repairs, but they would have to wait.

"A thousand pounds is a small enough start, but a start it is, nonetheless," he remarked as he scanned the column that reached halfway down the page. He set the pen beside the book and rubbed his chilled hands together. "Whatever happens now, at least all of them have repaid part of what they took from Kilbury. Even Edward Stanhope."

"I thought the girl up there was his payment," Harry Grove said with a nod toward the stairs. He sat on a stool by the fire, polishing the black boots Peg had retrieved from the tower room when she took Elizabeth's breakfast.

John muttered a mild oath. Everything, even a pair of boots, brought her to mind, no matter how he tried to dismiss her.

"She's for what Thomas and Edward owe me

personally," he growled. "The rest is the money they stole from my father."

"Can't say as I see much difference."

John closed the ledger and pushed it aside. There were times when he, too, had difficulty distinguishing between the two. At the beginning, all the reasons and explanations had been crystal clear. What had happened, he wondered, to blur the lines?

The fact remained that Thomas, who managed the Kilbury estate while his brother was alive, had mortgaged everything he could, most frequently to his friends and business associates, including Edward Stanhope. Often he lent them the money in the first place, though at much lower rates of interest than what John and his father William before him paid. So Kilbury fell deeper into debt, and Thomas grew wealthy on that debt. He controlled everything save the title itself.

And what price did one put on the honor of a name unsullied for centuries?

"It's the difference between restitution and revenge," John answered as much to benefit his own curiosity as Harry's. "Thomas beggared my inheritance, and for that he and his cohorts owe me. In doing so, however, he displaced families who had been Kilbury tenants for generations, destroyed one of the finest stables ever bred, and left me nothing with which to reclaim what he had lost. He forced me into common thievery and a role that makes me want to vomit at my own actions."

Harry snorted and spat on the gleaming leather.

"Ye never seemed to mind playin' the highwayman once ye got used to it."

"No, it's John Colfax I hate playing. You needn't remind me, Harry, that he's my own creation, a necessary foil to Jack Silver. Necessary, perhaps, but nonetheless an evil I devoutly wish to be rid of." He stood, wanting to head immediately up the stairs to the tower room yet at the same time seeking an excuse to delay facing the woman on whom he had perpetrated another evil. "And now, if you've finished with my boots, I believe I will pay a brief visit to our friends at the Black Oak."

Harry looked up and said, "Ye're askin' fer trouble."

"On the contrary. I took far more risk when I went to watch Thomas's reaction after robbing him. Tonight I go only to listen to the gossip. I doubt Elizabeth's disappearance is much of a secret any more, and Jack Silver's not claimed a victim for a month, so no one will be on the watch for him."

They were perfectly legitimate reasons, yet John knew they were also the flimsiest of excuses. He had to do something to avoid the irresistible pull of the woman upstairs. He could have understood simple lust, but concern over her reaction to what happened between them last night plagued him more than physical desire. And everything, *everything,* reminded him of her. Even the ledger, that long tally of the sums he had taken from Thomas and his business associates.

Had there been no need for the charade of the bumbling John Colfax as the antithesis to Jack Silver, perhaps Elizabeth might have considered another bridegroom.

No, that was a foolish thought. And even if it were not, his scheme had gone too far already.

Harry, as though sensing John's unease, did not leave off his warning. "I don't like it, not at all. But if ye won't be wise, at least be careful. Folk are bound to be nervous."

John pulled on the boots and then took the two primed pistols from the drawer hidden under the edge of the table. When they were secured in his belt, he reached under the table again, this time to retrieve the sword that hung on two hooks behind the drawer.

"Have you ever known me not to be careful?" he asked while buckling on the slender but deadly weapon. "Jack Silver's not been caught yet."

"There's a first time for everything."

"You have my word it won't happen tonight. No one will be on the roads anyway. Thomas is still too frightened after the last time, and Edward won't leave Kilbury until he has word of his daughter." He took the heavy black cloak from its peg by the fire and draped it about his shoulders. "I'm only going to the inn to listen to the gossip. I give you my word. And I must not keep Elizabeth waiting."

Booted and cloaked, he slipped into the clear, windy darkness of the night. A waxing crescent moon rode low in the western sky, affording him ample light to reach the inn. It would, however, have set long before he returned to the woman who waited in the tower room for him.

Kilbury Hall crowned the hill that overlooked the woodland where some medieval Colfax had built the turreted Dower House. In summer, the half-timbered building lay hidden behind the screen of oaks and beeches, but now, on a clear February night, both buildings were exposed to John's scrutiny. As he swung into the saddle, he kept a watchful eye on the road leading down the hill.

He saw no sign of activity. The soft glimmer of lamplight at the windows told him the residents were comfortably settled for the evening.

Still, he remained cautious. Though neither Thomas nor Edward was likely to be out on such a night, John had learned never to ignore improbabilities. He kept the stallion to a quiet walk until they had put sufficient distance between themselves and Kilbury, then he gave the beast its head.

The stallion's hooves beat a rumbling tattoo as he stretched out his ever-lengthening strides. The winter wind whipped the highwayman's cloak behind him and stung his eyes, but he did not pull in the reins. It was as if he, like the stallion, relished this freedom to race, unfettered, after days of forced idleness.

The lights of the Black Oak flickered in the near distance. From the thick plumes of smoke spiraling from the chimneys, the place looked busy, perhaps too busy for a golden-haired serving maid to find time for a solitary traveler. Reminding himself that the companionship of Betsy Bunch was not his primary objective, he guided the gray stallion to the secluded thicket behind the stables, then made his way through the woods to the inn itself. But when he entered the noisy bustle of the common room, he immediately scanned the crowd for some sign of Betsy's presence.

She wasn't there. Though the room was poorly lit and murky with smoke and steam, John's keen eyes saw no one resembling the laughing tavernmaid. The innkeeper's daughter labored beneath an overburdened tray, and even the boy, Robin, had been pressed into service with a huge pitcher from which he refilled tankards of ale. Mary, gaunt and scowling, carried dirty dishes toward the kitchen. As she made her way between the tables, John put himself directly in her path.

With a slight inclination of her head she told him, "There's a place over there by the window." She didn't look up, apparently more concerned about the stack of plates and bowls and mugs than in identifying one more patron when she already had plenty. "I got no one to wait on ye if ye want the private room, so best make do wi' the parson's comp'ny or be on the road again."

Had she not pushed past him, she might have noticed his slight expression of surprise, but before he had the time to regain control of his features, Mary had disappeared.

When he turned to make his way to the vacant place by the window, he recognized the profile of the man who would be his companion: none other than the Reverend Simon Horne.

"Damn!" he swore under his breath.

The risk was incalculable. Horne had seen him that other night, too, and though the vicar had never encountered Jack Silver on the road, who was to say he might not notice some resemblance between the black-clad stranger who frequented the wayside inn and the bumbling, graceless nephew of Thomas Colfax? Yet none of the inn's other patrons this evening offered the chance at information John so desperately needed. Horne was his uncle's servant and a key player in the drama, privy perhaps to secrets even the earl of Kilbury himself knew nothing of.

And the vicar was drunk. Very drunk.

The table by the window was small, with barely room on its surface for a candle inside a sooty chimney, a plate with the remains of Horne's half-eaten dinner, his Bible, and his mug. As John pulled out the chair across from the parson, he noticed the marks of spilled ale and food on the page. Horne had given up reading some time ago.

"May I?"

The churchman looked up, his owlish eyes blinking in a futile attempt to focus on the person addressing him.

"Do you mind if I join you?" John asked again now that he had the vicar's attention. "This is the only place left."

Horne nodded, then shook his head as though not certain whether to answer yes or no. He reached for his tankard only to find it empty. While he stared morosely into the depths, his new companion raised an arm to bring the boy hurrying to the table with his pitcher.

"Another cup for his reverence," John quipped. "And one for myself, too."

He got a penetrating look from Robin Sharpe and

wondered if the boy remembered past visits. Good God, the risks he was taking! Harry was right, but it was too late now.

Then the vicar, still contemplating his empty mug, released an obscene belch. The boy sneered and said, "'Pears to me 'his reverence' has had enough." Even so, he took the mug from Horne's hand and poured it full. "I'll have to fetch another glass for ye, sir."

Was it an excuse to leave and find someone in authority? Someone who would clap cold iron around Jack Silver's wrists? John couldn't resist a nervous glance at his hands. But no, the boy was just looking over his shoulder before he signaled to his sister.

"Hennie'll bring yer cup," Robin said, lifting the nearly empty pitcher, "whilst I get more ale."

John nodded his approval as the boy backed away from the table.

Throughout most of this brief exchange, Horne sat silent, his freshly filled tankard ignored.

"'Tis a quiet place, most nights," he mumbled.

He wrapped both bony hands around the pewter mug but still did not drink. The risks, John knew, were diminishing. There was no hint of recognition in Horne's glassy eyes nor in his self-absorbed manner. Nothing about his companion stirred memories of either a clumsy nobleman at a betrothal feast or a fellow sojourner in an empty tavern. He might even have been on the verge of falling into a drunken stupor, which was not what John wanted.

"Do you come here often?" he asked and was rewarded with a slow nod from the vicar's head.

"Oh, but not so often as *that!*" Horne suddenly exclaimed with a guilty flush. "When I've been out making calls, I do stop now and then on my way home. Not that I'll be going home tonight."

"And why not?"

Horne shuddered visibly and granted John a level if slightly unfocused stare.

"Only a fool would be on the roads alone. Even the coaches have stopped for the night."

Now he drank several desperate gulps and wiped his mouth on an already stained sleeve. When next he spoke, he kept his voice so low John was reduced to reading his lips.

"There's been a kidnapping," he whispered, leaning over the table. His eyes were dull with drink but wide with a kind of fascinated horror. "Mr. Thomas Colfax's bride, Miss Elizabeth Stanhope. And they say that brigand Jack Silver had a hand in it."

"Do they now."

Robin returned with a full pitcher and a clean mug that he set down in front of John with a thunk. Horne, startled, covered his momentary embarrassment by burying his face in his own drink. John smiled but silently cursed the interruption. He was certain Horne teetered on the verge of divulging everything he knew and to bring him back to that same volubility might take more time than John dared to spend at the Black Oak. Still, he had no choice but to try.

"And how did this highwayman accomplish his foul deed? Surely the young lady was not alone on the road."

The vicar tipped up his tankard and swallowed another gulp or two. At this rate he'd have it empty before he said another word.

But when he set the mug down, the words began to flow from him in a flood.

"She wasn't on the road at all," he said with a vigorous shake of his head. "He snatched her right from Kilbury Hall, damned near under Mr. Colfax's nose. I was there when it happened."

"You saw Jack Silver take her?"

Again Horne shook his head, and the action seemed to make him dizzy. He waited just a moment, blinking, before he continued.

"No, no one saw him, but I was at the Hall when it happened. I was to have married them."

He paused and looked up to stare directly into John's eyes. At first John felt a twinge of fear that the ale-fogged memory had finally cleared enough that Horne recognized him. But the expression on the man's face was one of pleading, not accusation.

"I tried to stop him, but he would listen to no one. Even when I told him the Church would not sanction a marriage without consent, he insisted."

An ordinary patron of the Black Oak who came a stranger to Horne's table would certainly have asked to whom he referred. John, however, did not need to ask, and in any case an interruption might halt the steady stream of the vicar's confession. As unobtrusively as possible, he caught the attention of Robin Sharpe who, instantly understanding the need for silence, filled Horne's mug once more.

"He threatened to turn me out of my living if I breathed a word," he whined. "But today one of the villagers was overheard to say he saw Jack Silver that night with Miss Stanhope."

It wasn't possible. No one had seen him and certainly not with Elizabeth; it must be only fanciful village gossip, one fellow claiming to have seen something in order to gain his friends' attention. Yet a little trickle of caution against complacency seeped into the back of John's mind.

"So that's why no one wants to risk being on the road tonight," he said, prodding Horne to further revelations. "They fear the highwayman."

Horne nodded eagerly, as though he were absolving himself of his own guilt.

"Mr. Colfax was furious. He never wanted anyone to know she was gone. He had said she was ill when she left him at the dinner. But servants talk, and the tale soon spread. Run away or kidnapped, I do not know, but it is God's own truth that she is gone."

He lifted his tankard again, but this time the weight of it plus his unsteadiness of hand sent a splash of ale down the front of his coat.

"He did not want me to leave," he said while watching the foamy liquid soak into the fabric, "but I could not stay. Mr. Stanhope said he would leave, too."

"And has he?"

"I don't know. He had a carriage to ready, and Miss Stanhope's servant was still ill, so perhaps he did not. I had my own horse and no reason to wait upon him."

John sipped his ale, only half listening as Horne's whines drifted into incoherence.

It made sense, as the vicar said, for Edward to leave Kilbury and go home to Stanhope once his suspicions of kidnapping were confirmed, if only by village gossip. Edward must know by now that if a ransom request were received, Thomas had no way to pay for it.

And there was but one road between Kilbury Hall and Stanhope Manor.

Horne was all but unconscious when John excused himself from the table. During the hour or so he had spent with the inebriated vicar, the room had grown noisier and smokier. Making his way through the crowd, he exerted no special effort to shield his face beneath the shadow of his hood lest that in itself draw too much attention. He caught snippets of conversations and heard the name of Jack Silver mentioned more than once.

A few weeks ago the irony would have made him smile. Tonight it merely wakened him to a bitter reality.

He was more keenly aware of his surroundings than ever before, the soot-blackened beams of the ceiling, the stones of the fireplace glazed with the sweat of innumerable hands over the centuries. He cast a single fond glance to his favorite inglenook, where now a fat-bellied merchant puffed on a long-stemmed pipe and leaned out of the shadows to engage in a heated debate with his companions.

Though he took his time and even managed to peer into the steamy kitchen as he made his way to the exit, John saw no sign of yellow-haired Betsy Bunch. And he had tarried here long enough.

Outside, away from the warmth and comfort, he let the wind swirling in the courtyard sweep away the last of what he recognized as sentimental fancies. By the time he had slipped unnoticed out of the Black Oak's precincts, his mind was clear and determined once more.

Jack Silver might be able to consort with buxom tavernmaids, but Jack Silver was but a figment of John Colfax's imagination. In a few more months, the highwayman would disappear forever save in the tales and legends of this tiny corner of Somerset. For John Colfax, earl of Kilbury, there could be no laughing, light-skirted Betsy Bunch.

The gray stallion nickered a greeting. The wind had risen, sharper and colder than earlier, and wisps of clouds raced across the moonless, starry sky. Through the branches of naked winter trees, John could still see the warm lights of the inn beckoning to him even as he swung into the saddle.

But he turned away without a backward glance. He knew, with a pang deeper than mere regret, that he could never set foot in the Black Oak again.

CHAPTER
10

Elizabeth sat in the middle of the bed, the blankets tucked around her legs, and began to pull the borrowed brush through her hair. At least if she fell asleep now, she'd do so somewhere warm and comfortable. After spending most of yesterday huddled in the chair, she still felt a lingering stiffness in her shoulders and knees.

Other aches did not bear thinking about.

What was done was done. She was a prisoner of Jack Silver for reasons as yet unknown, and she had given herself most willingly to him, for a reason only too well known.

She should have taken Nell's advice and worked harder to accept Thomas as her future husband. Instead she listened to the stories of Jack Silver and built him into a romantic fantasy. As Betsy Bunch, she sought him out and found him, forgetting as she did so that it was not she, Elizabeth Stanhope, he gallantly rescued from the storm and even more gallantly kissed in the moonlight.

But it was Elizabeth Stanhope who had fallen in love with him—and then given her captor the secret of her desire for him, a secret he could and probably would use to his advantage in negotiating her ransom.

"And what if Thomas no longer wants you now that you've made a gift of your virginity to Jack Silver?" she scolded herself in an attempt to deal with the consequences of her actions. "You could be thrown out on the streets without a penny, as your father warned."

The answer to her question came without thought. She had been prepared to pay that price when she ran from Thomas's betrothal dinner; she was no less prepared now. And if Thomas did ransom her and force her into the interrupted marriage, she would have at least that one heady victory over him—and a memory he could never take from her. Jack Silver had given her a gift of his own.

Despite his claims to the contrary, Elizabeth remained convinced that Jack intended to collect a healthy purse and then let her go. He was probably at this very moment regretting his actions, which might have lowered her value and his profit.

"He can have no other reason for taking me and certainly not for keeping me as long as he said." She had to believe that. If for one single moment she considered that Jack Silver had kidnapped her simply because he desired her, she would go mad. For she would not be able to resist him any more in the future than she had last night, and then she would indeed be ruined forever, beyond redemption. And if a child resulted from this madness, she would be ruined beyond ransom.

No, he did not desire her, she insisted in a reluctant heart.

"Then why did he bring me poetry?" she asked, unable to keep silent as she glanced to the beautifully bound volume of Italian sonnets that had been delivered with her breakfast along with a single candle. "Or is this part of his game, to mock my emotions even when he is gone?"

She stilled the sudden quiver of her hands and smoothed the hair over her left shoulder. She was tired enough to forgo the rest of the ritual, but habit prevailed. She pulled the heavy mass over her other shoulder and began counting strokes again.

You're waiting for him, aren't you? a voice within her taunted. *Not only waiting, but preening.*

A long, regretful sigh, loud in the silence of her tiny room, served as her confession. At least there were no more tears.

Moving out of the shelter of the woods that surrounded the Black Oak, John braced himself against the wind that swept unhindered across the frozen fields. He had the advantage now of clearer sight, without the screening trees, but the wind had gained an eerie substance, a palpable blackness that swallowed what faint glimmer of starlight escaped the increasing cover of clouds. He let the stallion pick his own pace, trusting the animal's instincts over his own.

It was some five miles from the tavern to the hall, a bit less to the Dower House, but in that preternatural darkness, John could make out the gleam of candlelit windows at Kilbury before he had gone half the distance. When the road dipped into the fold between two hills, the lights disappeared, only to wink back into view as soon as he crested the next rise. From this nearer vantage point, however, he noticed other lights, two mere pinpricks, where there should be none: on the road.

A vehicle was descending Kennec Beacon, the highest of the hills between the Black Oak and Kilbury Hall.

The presence of a coach or carriage caused him no particular alarm; he had only to move a few yards off the road and be as invisible as if he hid in the densest summer forest. He was, however, intensely curious and eager to take advantage of the situation. Because, he reasoned, in all likelihood it was Edward Stanhope's carriage that proceeded at a cautious pace down the steep slope. Whatever his other faults, Stanhope possessed enough intelligence to know that he alone had little to fear from an encounter with Jack Silver. Indeed, he would welcome it, for if he believed the highwayman had abducted Elizabeth, only Edward had the funds to ransom her.

John hoped that Stanhope also realized how much Elizabeth's safety depended upon Jack Silver's surviving such a meeting.

Still, he took every available precaution. Waiting at the side of the road, he watched the carriage reach the bottom of the beacon then, after a pause while the driver released the brake, he allowed the vehicle to pass. Only when he was certain it was indeed Stanhope's did he touch his heels to the gray's flanks and follow.

There was no one seated beside the driver nor a groom riding behind. John rode closer, confident the hoofbeats of the two horses in harness would cover his mount's—not that anything could be heard above that wicked wind whistling across the downs. It was then a simple matter to lean out of the saddle and grab hold of the cold ironwork on the back of the carriage. A slip would mean bruises and perhaps broken bones, but more painful by far would be the loss of an invaluable opportunity. John released the gray stallion and swung nimbly up to the roof. Before the vehicle's occupant could alert the driver, he had settled himself onto the seat beside the terrified coachman and placed the icy barrel of a pistol to the man's cheek.

"Give me the reins," he whispered, "and I'll not harm a hair on your head."

The coachman offered no resistance, transferring control of the two horses to him almost before the words were spoken. John kept the pistol in position and ignored the pounding and muffled shouts from within the carriage as he slowed the horses from a comfortable trot.

"Oh, God, ye're goin' to leave us here!" the coachman suddenly wailed. "Like ye did Mr. Thomas!"

"Shut up, you blubbering fool! I want only a few minutes with your employer, no longer than it'll take you to walk to the top of the next hill. I've slowed the horses; you can jump now, and I promise I'll have carriage and contents safely waiting for you a mile down the road."

The drop to the road was not without danger, but the coachman knew he faced greater risks if he didn't jump. A slight nudge from the pistol barrel overcame any protest. Knowing the horses would look out for their own safety, John kept an eye on the coachman as the frightened man leapt to the frozen ground. The impact knocked the breath out of him, but he had sense enough to roll clear of the carriage, and before the horses had gone five paces, the driver was on his feet.

John slapped the reins and the carriage quickly picked up speed again. The thumping from inside stopped; he grinned at the thought of Edward Stanhope slammed back against the squabs.

Elizabeth wakened with a start. The door opened slowly, letting in a wedge of yellow light. Then a grotesque silhouette, hunched under the burden of an enormous box or chest, blocked the light. As soon as he had entered the room, the door swung closed behind him. Darkness, softened only by the glow from the fire, descended once more.

"A gift for milady," a familiar velvety voice intoned.

Before Elizabeth could ask a single question, Jack's strained grunt was followed by a heavy thud. For a moment she wondered if the ancient boards would give way and send the room and all its contents crashing into some even more ancient dungeon. But the floor did not so much as creak under the added weight, so she sat up and tried to make out what her captor had brought her.

As soon as she recognized the trunk she and Nell had packed for the ill-fated visit to Kilbury, she let out a very relieved sigh and only then realized a small part of her brain had imagined Jack Silver presenting her with her own coffin.

"How did you get my trunk?" she asked, trying to cover the unevenness that had crept into her voice. "You didn't—"

"Steal it from Kilbury Hall?" he finished. "No, I'm not so foolhardy as that. I robbed your father's carriage."

"And how is that any less foolhardy? He'd have shot you on sight!"

"Not if he wants you returned to him. But is that concern for my welfare I hear in your voice?"

It was just as well he strode to the bed and sat down, for then she had an excuse not to speak. No lie could have convinced him she was anything but concerned. Terrified, in fact. She glanced to the trunk and shivered to think that it might have been *his* coffin.

He pulled off one cold leather glove and stroked his finger down her cheek.

She jerked away from his touch and said, "Of course I'm concerned," hoping he would attribute her reaction to the effect his cool touch had on her warm skin. "If my father had killed you, what would happen to me?"

"Precisely, my dear." He leaned close enough to brush a kiss on her temple, then removed the other glove. "Which is why I took the risk of approaching him and pointing out that his daughter's, shall we say, holiday would be much more pleasant if she had at least a few of her own possessions."

"'Holiday!'" she snorted. "This is nothing less than imprisonment."

He took her chin firmly in his hand and brought his face so close she could see only his eyes and her own frightened reflection in them.

"You have no idea what imprisonment is, my dear, pampered, cossetted-from-the-day-you-were-born Elizabeth Stanhope." His words were warm on her lips and as bitter as the unsweetened tea that accompanied her meals. "Have you ever seen a cell in Newgate? Or smelled the stench of the Fleet?" he asked. "Have you ever heard the clang of the iron door as it closes out light and freedom and locks in damp and disease, rats and despair?"

Rather than try to hide the depth of his passion from her, he seemed to want her to be completely aware of it. She was, only too well, but she refused to let him get the best of her. She squirmed out of his grasp and scooted to the far side of the bed, beyond his reach—for the moment.

"No, I've not, and—"

"Well, milady, I *have*, and this room is a bloody palace by comparison."

She ignored the frisson of horror that raised gooseflesh on her arms. "If you have, Jack Silver, it was not my doing. I've never accused you or anyone else of a crime nor given testimony that would send you to prison." He had not moved; against the firelight behind him, he resembled a statue carved from the blackest marble.

"Oh, not I, milady, but others. And sent not for crimes but for convenience."

For once she was glad of the dark that hid his face from her. She imagined his lips curled in a vicious sneer, his eyes narrowed, his nostrils flared as the rage simmered. This was not the Jack Silver she knew, not the gentle rogue who had sheltered Betsy Bunch from the cold and kissed her in the stable loft, not even the dashing outlaw who had kidnapped Elizabeth Stanhope on her wedding night and sent her books of poetry to read. Had she let her dreams conjure a romantic fantasy from the gossip spread about the mysterious highwayman when in truth he was nothing but a common felon, destined for a common prison cell—and then the hangman's noose?

"I don't understand. Whose convenience? Thomas Colfax's?"

He didn't respond, though she was certain he had heard her. Instead he rose from the bed and walked to stand in front of the fire while he methodically untied the cord at his throat and shrugged off the heavy cloak. He hung it from his hand for a moment before tossing it onto the chair.

"You've rearranged the furniture."

"I couldn't see," she explained, wondering if he changed the subject to indicate that he had no intention of answering her earlier question. "It was kind of you to send a book for me to read, but I had only one candle, so when it had burned down I moved the chair closer to the fire."

While she was speaking, he walked to the old piece of furniture, lifted it by the carved wooden arms, and returned it to its place on the other side of the table, several feet further from the light and heat of the fire. Elizabeth bit back the rest of what she wanted to tell him about the darkness of the room even at midday and the strain it put not only on her eyes but on her nerves as well. Something, a dreaminess or reverence or *something,* in the way Jack Silver handled that very ordinary old chair warned her she had committed a grievous sin in moving it from its assigned place.

Her apology came without conscious thought.

"I'm sorry."

He sat down and began pulling off his boots. He looked up, the heel of his left foot still notched on his right toe, at her quiet pronouncement. The glow from the fire barely reached his face, distorting the planes and angles into vague shadows, but even at that she saw the frown of confusion slowly form.

"Sorry? For what?"

Sarcasm and challenge filled those three short words.

Elizabeth grasped the challenge and hurled it back at him.

"I don't know, but does that make it any less sincere? You looked so . . . so . . ."

The first boot clunked to the floor. He switched his feet to remove the second but kept his gaze on her. She squirmed mentally under that stare, unable to finish her explanation. How could she tell him she had imagined sadness in his action? Jack Silver, who robbed men at gunpoint and made them walk through blizzards, who kidnapped and seduced a woman he did not know, surely harbored no sentimentality about a collection of wood, horsehair, and faded brocade. Yet that was exactly the impression he had given her.

When he had set the second boot beside its mate and pulled off his stockings as well, he calmly unfastened the buttons on his shirt and drew it over his head. The control in his every movement mesmerized her, because it was so different from the man he had been just a few moments ago. Now he gave no hint of emotion, neither anger nor tenderness.

Had her half-formed comment alerted him to a momentary lapse in that control?

She leaned forward, not forgetting for an instant those eyes that never wavered from her. If, as she suspected, his continued presence and casual disrobing indicated his intention to spend some time in her bed, she had little to lose by repaying his boldness with defiance.

"I said I was sorry because I meant it. Whatever I have done, I apologize for the harm it may have caused, even to the chair. Please believe that I did not set out deliberately to injure it or you or anyone else, but if in my ignorance I did, then I hope you will give me the opportunity to make amends."

Dressed only in his black breeches, he appeared relaxed, but the uneven light and shadow still allowed Elizabeth to note the tensing of his muscles as he gripped the arms of the chair. That she succeeded in arousing such a strong reaction in him satisfied her. It also gave her added confidence and banished a good portion of her fear. She might be Jack Silver's captive, but she had the distinct feeling that if she assumed the role of terrified victim, her captivity would be a good deal less pleasant.

Finally able to tear her gaze from him, she reached for one of the two pillows she had used while she had the bed to herself and moved it to the side nearest the fire.

"I can tell you from experience that that chair is not the most comfortable place to sleep," she said as she pulled the quilt over her shoulder and snuggled into the welcome warmth. Curled on her side, she lay facing him, watching him though he was hardly visible as the last flames winked out and only a dull red glow remained. "But then, I'm certain you don't believe a word I say, so make your bed where you will."

She yawned, then closed her eyes and smiled. "Good night, Mr. Silver."

John counted to ten very slowly, as slowly as Elizabeth Stanhope breathed. She had her arms wrapped around herself under the covers so he couldn't see the rise and fall of her breasts, breasts he longed to curl his chilled hands around for warmth, but he could see the rhythmic movement of her shoulder. Each breath seemed a sigh of contentment, mocking him, beckoning him. And that satisfied smile still curved her lips; he wondered if perhaps she watched him from beneath those lowered eyelids.

But when he stood, her expression did not change. She had either fallen asleep or was confident enough to ignore her adversary.

"I did not come to this room to sleep in a chair," he announced as he grasped the edge of the quilt in one hand and pulled it neatly down to her hips. "Take off that bloody nightgown and warm my bed properly."

She had not been asleep; her barely stifled gasp, however, told him she was near enough to have been taken completely by surprise. And though he stood over her, she kept her now open eyes trained straight ahead, not at him. He read her thoughts in that blank stare. When she briefly lowered her lashes, he almost heard her silent prayer.

Guilt stabbed at him so sharply the words of apology were on the tip of his tongue. To silence them, he had to force into his mind's eye the worst of the memories of Elizabeth as he had come to know her, Elizabeth who would wed Thomas for a title.

Let her believe Jack Silver took her at her word to make amends for unnamed sins. Let her think she bought forgiveness with her body. In a sense it was true, except that there could never be any forgiveness —only revenge.

She lay still, her hands clasped beneath her chin where the buttons of her nightgown began. But for that vacant stare and the rapid pulse at her temple, she might have looked peacefully asleep. Before John had time to repeat his order, however, her fingers began slowly undoing the buttons.

"May I ask a favor?"

She still did not look at him, and her voice, though hardly more than a whisper, lacked its earlier fire.

"I won't hurt you."

He wished he hadn't given her that instinctive response, but it was too late to call the words back. Besides, as he watched her fumble with the buttons, he realized the reassurance was unnecessary.

"I didn't think you would."

"Then what is it you want of me?"

Elizabeth rolled onto her back and looked up at him.

"No, Jack Silver, what is it *you* want of *me?*" She had unfastened all the buttons, baring her throat and the soft upper curves of her breasts. The shadowed valley between them beckoned his touch. "I confess I left the chair too near the fire, but such a crime is easily—"

He lay the tips of his fingers lightly on her lips. He could have silenced her with a kiss, but then he, too, would be incapable of speech.

"I am in no mood to argue or to explain," he said gruffly. "I am cold and weary, and so are you."

If his words hinted that he wished only to sleep, the slow trail he traced with his fingers told of different desires. Down her chin and throat with such silken tenderness that she arched her head back. Under the neckline of her nightgown to where her skin warmed at his touch. On to the soft swell of her breast.

He could have pulled her up and removed the nightgown; she was willing enough, if the quickening beat of her heart beneath his hand and the parting of her lips were any indication. But that very willingness and his own unfathomable need for her flashed a burst of sudden anger through him. He would not let her turn the tables on him. To remind her how completely she was at his mercy, he took hold of the soft linen fabric and tore it, exposing her pale skin all the way to her belly.

"I never want to see you in this rag again."

She flinched at his words but made no move to pull the halves of the torn gown together. "You had only to ask. Instead you ruined it, and it's of no use to anyone."

She half expected him to strike her for her insolence. Braced for a blow she might not see coming in the dark, she still found his soft chuckle no surprise at all.

"Your generosity amazes me, Elizabeth Stanhope. But tell me, what makes you think I am equally generous?"

With the edge of his little finger, he drew a wavering line from the base of her throat to her navel, then slowly lower. She didn't move a muscle except to force one unsteady breath after another into and out of her lungs—and to shudder when he withdrew his hand. He dismissed it as a shiver brought on by the cool air.

He stripped off his breeches and clambered over her to crawl beneath the blankets. Wrapping his arms around her so that she had to twist free of the torn nightgown, he whispered in her ear, "I take what I want, Elizabeth. I give nothing away."

He curved his hand around her breast and found the nipple already hard, another result of exposure to the cold. Yet she felt warm as he pulled her back against his own arousal.

"I'm no bloody Robin Hood if that's what you think."

He turned her to face him, and her reply was lost in a gasp silenced by his kiss. But the words of a frantic question screamed in her brain even as she surrendered to him, a question she had never thought to ask even of herself.

If Jack Silver was not Robin Hood, then who *was* he?

CHAPTER

11

Rain pattered on the roof and walls, and an incessant wind whined in the chimney. Now and then low thunder rumbled as from a distant storm. Elizabeth poked at the fire, added another log from the dwindling stack, and rocked back on her heels. She shivered and hugged her arms more tightly around herself.

After a week of confinement in this room, she had learned to gauge the passage of time with some degree of accuracy—but little else. She had not learned how to make the time pass more quickly nor to keep secret from her gaoler that she measured the hours by how many of them passed between the time he left her and the time he returned. No, that was not quite true, she thought as she rose and stretched muscles grown stiff with cold, because she never really knew when he left her.

Though the sliver of overcast sky visible around the boarded window gave no hint as to the time, Elizabeth estimated she had at least half an hour before the old woman came with her breakfast. She backed away from the fire and allowed herself a grim smile of satisfaction. In half an hour she would have a third candle to add to her stock at the bottom of the wardrobe drawer. She worried occasionally that her captor might find them; he had searched the drawer once before. But then he had good reason. Four days ago he had removed the detested sapphire necklace from the same drawer, where she put it simply to get it out of her sight. Now she felt confident he had no other reason to paw through her belongings.

She walked to the chair and sat down, rubbing her eyes. She suspected she had slept only a few hours. Jack Silver, however, was gone. Long gone.

On the table beside her rested the book he had brought her two nights ago, a battered edition of Henry Fielding's *Tom Jones,* and the pewter candleholder whose base contained a puddle of hardened wax drippings. The old woman brought one candle each day with the breakfast tray. No pleading on Elizabeth's part had so far induced Jack Silver's servant to bring another.

"What I would not give for a lamp," she sighed. "Or a window with the sunlight streaming in."

She dared not wonder if she would ever see sunlight again.

Despair came easily in the morning when Jack's abandonment stripped her of warmth and companionship and when the length of another interminable day stretched before her. For the first few days she found some diversion in the care of the clothes he had brought her and in exploration of the room, but without light, she could see so little and nothing to give her a clue to the location of her prison.

"If I were miraculously transported to Stanhope Manor this instant, I could tell no one a thing that would lead them to your redoubt, Jack Silver," she said to the quiet, empty room. A grim smile of admiration touched her mouth.

"No wonder you've eluded capture so long. No wonder you dare to mock me by giving me a book written by a man responsible for bringing the most notorious highwaymen to the gallows."

Jack had laughed when she pointed out that little irony to him. His gift was not without purpose, that laughter told her.

She granted him the respect he deserved by nodding her head in the direction of the bed where he had lain with her last night and acknowledging "You are clever, Jack Silver. Very, very clever."

By the time the old woman came with breakfast and the day's candle, Elizabeth gathered what determination remained to her. Perhaps the numbness and shock were simply wearing off, but today she felt certain would be different. *She* would be different. She would have three candles—and perhaps the answer to the question that had plagued her for so many days.

"A message from Mr. Stanhope, sir. The man who brought it was told to wait for a reply."

The footman handed Thomas the sealed envelope on a silver tray. Watching from the far end of the breakfast table, John sipped his coffee and exaggerated his squint over the pince-nez.

"Has he received a ransom demand from Jack Silver?" he asked with hopeful eagerness.

Thomas fumbled with the wax seal as though the reminder of the highwayman's involvement made him nervous, but his hand was steady when he withdrew the single folded sheet.

"Edward wants to meet with me as soon as possible." Thomas glanced at the tall windows streaked with rain and growled, "He could not have picked a worse day! I'll probably catch my death of fever, but I suppose there's no way 'round it."

John doubted the complaint was meant for his ears and therefore made no reply. But when Thomas suddenly gave him an interested glance, he was on his guard.

"You're welcome to join me if you wish."

The temptation was strong but not strong enough.

"I think not," he said. "My constitution is not as strong as yours, Uncle. I'd be afraid of falling ill again."

The elder Colfax raised a disdainful eyebrow, but John sensed a simmering disappointment behind Thomas's lack of agreement.

"Send Stanhope's man back with the message that I shall be there at once," Thomas told the footman. "And have the carriage readied. I expect to be gone overnight, no longer. Are you certain you don't wish to come, John?"

He shook his head. He might miss some vital conversation but he was more eager to take advantage of Thomas's absence from Kilbury, the first since the night of the kidnapping.

He recognized impatience as a growing enemy. Spiriting Elizabeth away from Thomas had perhaps been too easy and seducing her definitely so. Overconfidence could lead to recklessness, and he was too near the achievement of his objective to take any unnecessary risks.

So he lingered over his breakfast long after Thomas had departed. Nameless servants cleared the dishes from the table and sideboard, all of Thomas's choosing, even the older ones employed before John's return to Kilbury. As such, they were not to be trusted.

When they were done, he strolled to the library, where two parlormaids were giggling when they should have been dusting. Thomas no doubt would have turned the girls out of the house, but when they saw it was only the earl who discovered their dereliction of duty, they giggled again and resumed their work. With occasional glaces toward them, rewarded often enough with grins and more girlish laughter, he made a show of looking for a book. When he found one that suited his purpose, he left the library and only then headed for his own rooms.

There were neither giggling parlormaids nor spying footmen here. Dropping *Robinson Crusoe* into his pocket, he closed and locked the door behind him, then wandered to the window and pulled back the faded velvet curtain to peer outside.

Rain and a lowering sky shrouded the entire vista in dreariness. Dirty patches of nearly melted snow huddled beneath leafless trees; even the grass had turned a dull muddy color. Winter had not released its grip, but neither had spring yet taken hold.

He looked beyond the lawn to the woods. Through the pale curtain of mist and tattered fog, the dilapidated Dower House was visible as a dark hulk behind a screen of trees. A thin curl of smoke drifted from the main chimney, gray and forlorn as everything else in sight.

Longing tugged at him. The hours he spent in Elizabeth's bed each night were far too short to appease the appetite she aroused in him and, he suspected, in herself. With Thomas gone until morning, he could indulge those appetites and spend the entire night with her rather than abandon her the moment she drifted, warm and replete, into sleep.

"Damn!" he swore quietly, not knowing what or whom he cursed.

He let the curtain fall again, blocking out the view of the place where Elizabeth waited. Blocking the images from his mind was not so easy.

Idleness, he determined, was the cause of his maundering, and he did have plenty of work yet to do.

Slipping into the corridor, he rehearsed half a dozen explanations to give anyone who might question his actions, but he encountered no one on his stroll to the study. This room, unlike most in the Hall, was brightly lit and warmed by a crackling fire, for it was here that Thomas conducted his own financial affairs as well as those of the Kilbury estate.

Despite the warmth, John's blood ran cold. With a glance at the clock on the mantel, he allowed himself an hour, no more, with the ledgers. Though hardly a month had passed since he last examined Thomas's handiwork, he had to be certain he had missed no name on the list of those with debts to pay.

He pulled one enormous book from the shelf and carried it to the desk. With each leaf he turned, years flashed by, years before William Colfax married his beautiful Lenore, years before she bore him a son whose birth nearly killed her. William had taken her away to Italy and Spain and even the jasmine-perfumed islands of the Caribbean. There were the entries, in Thomas's cramped hand, for the funds sent to the earl and his frail countess on their journeys.

John turned the pages more rapidly. He had no time to dwell on his father's error in giving control to Thomas. Had the younger brother executed his duties honestly instead of stealing and lying and cheating, William's wisdom would never have been questioned. But Thomas *had* stolen, and he had lied and he had cheated until there was nothing left of the estate when William died.

Soon, however, the wrong would be righted. John did not smile as he ran his finger quickly down the columns, but he did feel a certain sense of victory, of vindication.

He paid little attention to the bills, though many of the expenses had been exaggerated. It was the receipts that interested him most. Payments for the sale of assets, the mortgaging of properties, the disposal of valuables.

"And you thought you were so clever," he muttered, scanning the familiar names, Edward Stanhope most prominent among them.

The sound of voices beyond the door startled him. He looked first at the clock, afraid that somehow he had tarried too long, but less than half his allotted time had passed. A bare second after that reassurance, however, Thomas pulled the study door open.

"What the hell are *you* doing here?" he demanded.

Undisguised astonishment robbed John of an immediate answer. Speechless, he blinked twice while Thomas marched toward the desk. That momentary numbness proved a blessing, which John's first conscious thought recognized and took prompt advantage of.

"I'm trying to help," he stammered, shifting easily from one role to another. "Is something wrong, Uncle? Dear heaven, you've not been attacked by Jack Silver again, have you?"

Thomas's answering sneer became a red-faced glower as he reached across the desk and snatched the heavy ledger away. John drew his hands back with an exaggerated motion as though afraid to have his fingers smashed.

"No, we were not set upon by robbers," Thomas snapped, returning the ledger to its place on the shelf, "and certainly not by a lone highwayman in broad daylight."

"It happened before."

He should not have reminded the already furious Thomas, but the words were out too quickly. The older man whirled, his face now an apoplectic crimson.

How sweet it would be to see Thomas felled by a stroke, left paralyzed and helpless and at the mercy of the nephew he had tried to reduce to beggary. How fitting for the pompous thief to be condemned to a life of drooling impotence.

"I'd welcome sight of the bastard," Thomas hissed, then waved a hand as if chasing away a pesky fly. "I'm well protected, have no fear. Now, go on about your entertainment and let me handle Jack Silver." He smiled but with no lessening of the disgust in his eyes. And if he said nothing regarding John's interest in the accounts, his actions left no doubt that he neither needed nor wanted any kind of assistance.

Soon, John thought, *soon I'll wipe that goddamned grin from your face forever.* But for a short while longer, though each second pained him, he would continue the charade of ignorance and innocence that allowed Thomas his illusion of power.

He offered no resistance when his uncle turned him in the direction of the door. That door would no doubt be locked from now on.

Careful not to display too much of his own curiosity, John asked, "If not Jack Silver, then what did bring you back so soon? The weather looks to be improving."

"The road is a ruin." Thomas led the way down the corridor to the long gallery. Though John could easily have overtaken him, he hung back as though unable to keep up the pace. "One of the horses stumbled and was injured."

"Not seriously, I hope."

"Not enough to warrant destroying it, but we couldn't continue."

"You'll want Harry Grove to look at it. There's no one better with an injured horse than Harry." Whether or not Thomas wondered why his nephew had taken such an interest in finances, John pursued the changed subject with enthusiasm. "I'll ride down to the Dower House and bring him."

Thomas paused midstride.

"That place ought to be torn down," he said with a scowl. "You can't imagine what a drain it is on Kilbury's limited resources."

More than you know, Uncle mine, more than you know. The litany ran through his head, but he kept his reply subdued, almost apologetic.

"Surely it cannot cost so much for three servants."

"Three! I thought you had only two, Grove and that old woman."

"There's Peg's grandson, Ethan. He lives with her and helps Harry." God, but he hated sounding so defensive. "I am still the earl of Kilbury," he added, hoping he injected the right amount of petulance into his voice, "and I like the Dower House. It's cozier than the Hall."

He clenched his fists at his sides to keep from gesticulating at the barrenness that once was the grand showpiece of Kilbury. How many years had it taken Thomas to strip the long gallery of its magnificence? Where there had once been a dozen, now a single Chinese vase graced the mantel; the others were sold off even before William died. At least the Grinling Gibbons chimneypiece remained; the mellow wood matched the inlaid floor once covered by richly colored Persian carpets, more victims of Thomas's greed.

Yet it was Thomas who shrugged and resumed the conversation.

"As you wish."

"I wish."

His insouciant smile was enough to put Thomas at ease, but there still remained the matter of the injured horse—and an opportunity to make the most of.

When they reached the stairs leading to the entrance hall, John stepped down the first two before he turned to face his uncle again. It suited his purpose to allow Thomas the advantage of height in exchange for the advantage of distance.

"I'll fetch Harry at once. Is there anything I should tell him about the injury?"

For a moment, Thomas's expression went blank, as

though he had forgotten the reason for his return. Or perhaps he was ruminating on another problem.

"No, I've no idea. But aren't you worried about going out in this weather?"

The odd note of triumph in Thomas's question and the slight elevation of one brow set John on his guard. Keeping his own expression innocent, he rested a long-fingered hand on the dark oak of the banister and took another step downward.

"It's only a ten-minute ride, not like the ten miles to Stanhope. And I believe I'll stay the night. The Hall is so damp this time of year."

Without waiting for his uncle's reply, he trotted down the rest of the long staircase. Impatience was the enemy now as much as anything else. He dared not proceed too quickly; if being surprised in the study by Thomas's return had not been a disaster, it had taught him a valuable lesson. No matter how carefully he planned, he could not anticipate every eventuality. Nor could he control all the other players in this drama.

Certainly not Elizabeth Stanhope. And perhaps he would do well to catch her in an unguarded moment.

The fire popped, sending a flurry of sparks toward the open book. Lying on her stomach with her elbows propped on a pillow, Elizabeth brushed away the few bits of ash that fell on the page. She considered again the danger of reading by firelight, then returned to the romance of young Tom Jones and Miss Sophia Western.

The dancing flames, however, made the printed words waver before her eyes. When she blinked, her concentration drifted away from Tom and his beloved but unattainable Sophia—and settled morosely on the detested Blifil.

"I am not Sophia," she said aloud while rubbing her

eyes. Too many hours trying to read by the fickle firelight had put a strain on her vision. Sitting alone in the dark, however, put a strain on her nerves. "And you, Jack Silver, are no Tom Jones."

The logs on the grate settled again, and one tumbled into a bright heap of flame. This time the winking sparks shot out with such force that they landed while still alive. Scrambling to save the book, pillow, quilt, and herself from the dangerous spray, Elizabeth tangled her feet in her skirt and ended up sitting on the wadded-up bedclothes. By then the flickering embers had died, and the fire crackled merrily, like a naughty child behaving itself once again.

She had no choice but to disengage herself from the quilt and rearrange it. Either that or retreat to the safety of the chair and the brighter, steady flame of a candle.

"No, not that," she muttered, extricating the pillow and book from the rest of the heap. "Not yet."

She stood up and began folding the quilt again. With its thickness tripled, it made lying on the floor a bit less uncomfortable. At least the cold didn't seep through.

A wicked clap of thunder startled her. Instinct drew her eyes to the window, where she expected to see sheets of rain against the glass or the trees outside swaying wildly in the wind. Fresh anger knifed through her, but the curse that came to her tongue died there as she felt a draft brush her skirt against the back of her legs.

She spun, the quilt clutched to her breasts like a shield, and faced Jack Silver.

"What are you doing?" he asked, leaning against the door to close it.

"Haven't you the decency to knock?"

He waited, rather than approaching her, but Elizabeth did not lower her guard.

"I never thought I would be interrupting anything."

"Well, you have," she stammered. His presence, so unexpected this time of the day, left her at a loss. She had counted on his usual arrival after dinner.

He mocked her with an exaggerated bow.

"A thousand pardons, my dear," he added with a chuckle. "And here I thought you would be so glad to see me."

CHAPTER 12

And why should I be?"

Jack had surprised her, not only by appearing when she least expected him, but also by the subtle change in his manner. He seemed more casual, even light-hearted, though the underlying intensity remained. Such a contrast left her confused and off balance.

He shrugged, the gesture itself an indication of his altered mood, and moved away from the door before answering, "Because you are lonely and bored, Elizabeth, as you tell me nearly every day. Or should I say every night?"

Another blast of thunder shook the building to its foundations. Elizabeth, who held no fear of storms, clutched the quilt more tightly to her as Jack Silver strolled to the table where the unlit candle stood. He glanced from it to her then unfastened his cloak and tossed it over the chair.

He gave her a hint of a smile as well as a nod in the direction of the pillow and book that lay on the floor.

"Were you planning a picnic?" he asked, one dark brow raised.

"Hardly. I was cold and found it more comfortable to lie close to the fire."

He leaned down and picked up both objects. After tossing the pillow onto the bed, he handed her the copy of *Tom Jones,* then reached into his pocket and withdrew another book. She took them both, meeting his appraising stare without a qualm.

"That's rather dangerous." He put a seductive emphasis on the last word. "A stray spark could have set the whole place ablaze. You might have been trapped."

"Perhaps that was my intention."

"No, Elizabeth, you are not so desperate," he drawled lazily as he walked to the chair and sat down. "Nor, I think, are you cold."

"Do you accuse me of lying?"

"Are you?"

Stretching his legs out before him, he rested his elbows on the arms of the chair and clasped his hands together, a very image of paternal patience. Elizabeth refused to give in to any feelings of guilt, and she would not be treated like a naughty child. Still, if she gave him an answer, perhaps he would probe no further.

"The chair is not comfortable," she confessed, turning slightly away from him, "and the poetry you sent reminded me of a summer afternoon I once spent with a friend. I sought merely to change the scenery, so to speak, and . . ."

Letting the words hang in the air, she hazarded a cautious sidelong peek at the man watching her. The constant gloom had sharpened her eyesight, not enough to make out his carefully shadowed features, but at least she saw the way he leaned forward, his lazy, confident demeanor now tense and expectant.

The silence lengthened until he broke it. "Are you not going to tell me of this summer afternoon and your 'friend'?"

Despite an air of studied nonchalance, his interest, she was certain, could only be attributed to jealousy. It was a small victory, but each victory for Elizabeth Stanhope was a defeat for Jack Silver.

"It was nothing," she replied with a shrug. "I was very young, a naive child. He showed me a kindness, nothing more."

"Nothing?"

Jack Silver regained his composure quickly, for that single word dripped with accusation, with mockery—but not with jealousy. In fact, he sounded more self-satisfied than ever. But the damage had been done. If he did not yet know how much of himself he had revealed, Elizabeth did.

As if Jack Silver had any reason to envy poor John Colfax. Though he must have watched her carefully to have effected her abduction with such ease, her captor obviously knew little about her or he would have known how innocent was her relationship with Lord Kilbury.

To hide her satisfaction, Elizabeth took the three or four steps to the bed and began to spread the quilt out upon it. She laid the books on a corner of the mattress to free her hands. She could not make out the title of the second, but like *Tom Jones,* it was a well-made book and well cared for.

"I assure you, there was only friendship between us," she finally managed to answer the question that had hung in the air so long. "I was barely out of the schoolroom and he much older." She sounded too wistful, too sad, when she intended a casual dismissal of a meaningless memory. "I was also very lonely and perhaps took too eagerly to his friendship. The sonnets reminded me."

She fussed with the bedclothes and plumped the pillows—anything to avoid facing him. The memories were no lies, but she had not expected the recollection of that long-ago afternoon spent with the young earl of Kilbury to trigger such emotion. She did not want Jack Silver to see any evidence of her feelings. If she didn't look at him, she could hold on to an illusion of privacy until she had successfully wrestled with this strangely persistent ghost.

But Jack himself shattered the illusion by snorting a laugh.

"I find it difficult to imagine you lonely, Elizabeth. The only daughter of a wealthy father? You must have been courted by every bachelor from nine to ninety, feted at parties given by their sisters and maiden aunts, waltzed at every ball from Land's End to John O'Groats."

The irony almost made her laugh aloud. But how could Jack Silver know it was crushing, unbearable loneliness that gave birth to Betsy Bunch whom he had held so tenderly? Elizabeth Stanhope was indeed the only child of a wealthy father, but Edward had taken great pains to see that she was not feted and courted at all. She had been almost as much a prisoner in Stanhope Manor as in this tiny room.

"You know so little of me, Jack Silver," she said, resting her forehead against the bedpost. "Imagine what you like; I've told you nothing less than the truth." Her conscience pricked her but she ignored it with no difficulty.

He was clever, so clever. He thought, it seemed to her, of every eventuality, even to lulling her into this effervescent fantasy of her own power, only to dash her hopes and place her more securely at his mercy.

"Damn him," she swore softly.

Perhaps her muttered curse covered the creak of the chair, or perhaps she was too immersed in her murky thoughts, but whatever the reason, she did not react to the sound. By the time she realized what it meant, it was too late. Jack had risen from the chair and come up behind her.

"It appears I have indeed left you lonely too long,"

he whispered in her ear as he enfolded her in a sinuous embrace. "You've begun talking to yourself, a sure indication of incipient madness."

She made only a token effort to escape, knowing any such attempt would be utterly futile. With the warmth and strength of his body molded to her back, he had her trapped.

"I am no fool, Elizabeth," he went on, the words punctuated by breathy kisses to the side of her jaw, beneath her ear, at the shiveringly sensitive top of her spine. "Not even fool enough to underestimate you. Indeed I'd be disappointed if you did *not* attempt to learn my identity. But, my dear, saving your precious candles and expecting me to walk innocently into a well-lit room is not a scheme worthy of you."

She stiffened with the shock and shame of his discovery and held back a sob of defeat that might well have been a cry of surrender. All the while, he nuzzled her neck, the rain-damp coolness of his hair in sensual contrast to the steamy warmth of his breath against her flesh.

"I do not underestimate my enemies, my dear Elizabeth, and certainly not ones as charming as you."

"Not even when you have me at your complete mercy?"

"You are never more dangerous. Or," he added after a telling pause, "more charming."

Elizabeth arched backward to press her head against his shoulder. As Jack kissed her exposed throat, she drank in great gulps of air. The scent of the rain from his hair filled her lungs with a tantalizing taste of forbidden delights and brought all the hopelessness crashing down upon her.

He could come and go as he pleased, could ride through the rain or the snow, under the midnight stars or in broad daylight, could grace her with his companionship or leave her in dark isolation until she went mad. And worst by far was his ability to drive her senseless at his touch.

"I know exactly what you had in mind, my dear," he murmured. "Even if I believed your pretty story of poetry and picnics, I'm not fool enough ignore an unlit candle. When did you plan to light it, Elizabeth? While I slept?"

How could he be so clearheaded, so rational, so *cruel,* when she barely recalled her own name? She drew in another deep breath and another, willing that fragrance of rain and storm and cool open air to break the spell he had woven about her as securely as he had his arms. Bringing all the scattered fragments of her old anger together, she wrenched herself free and stumbled, breathless, away from him until she had put the old chair protectively between them.

"Why do you fight me?" he asked, smiling indulgently and folding his arms across his chest. "You did not fight me last night. Or any of the nights before. What has changed? Not I, certainly."

She made his exaggerated patience her own and said, "I did not truly understand all that had happened, all you had taken from me."

"Taken?" he echoed. His voice remained low, soft, seductive. Even when he barked out a bit of laughter, the velvety midnight quality remained to send ripples of desire down her spine. "Do not blame me, Elizabeth, for taking what you yourself gave so freely."

She trembled with the fury racing through her. Frantic, she looked around the room for anything that might be used as a weapon. Even if it did not gain her her freedom, she wanted to hurt him, lash out at him, make him suffer in some measure as she had. But there was nothing, and even if there were, he could so easily disarm her.

"I did not give you my freedom!" she cried out.

"You kidnapped me, made me your prisoner, gave me no choice! How long do you intend to keep me here, locked in the dark? Until I go blind and can *never* identify you?"

Elizabeth closed her eyes and gripped the back of the chair, her anger now turned inward. Nothing could call back those foolish words. She had revealed too much of her own thoughts and confirmed all his suspicions.

"If you understand me that well, Elizabeth, then you know I mean you no harm. When the time is right—"

"No harm?" The words came out a strangled croak. "What do you think you have already done?"

"Nothing you couldn't explain to a husband besotted with your beauty—or your father's fortune. Unless, of course—but it's too soon to tell about that."

An icy dread pooled just beneath her heart, then spread into her belly and finally further down. If she had not had the heavy cloak to clutch in her numbed fingers and the chair beneath it for support, she might have sunk to the floor.

Her mouth was dry, and her pulse roared in her ears. A dozen exclamations of horror came to her tongue but she had no voice to give them until one slashed its way through her shock.

"You are a monster, Jack Silver."

Driven only by instinct, she drew the black cloak from the back of the chair and held it to her breast as a shield against his still mocking gaze. Yet nothing could alleviate the feeling of nakedness, of powerlessness, that enveloped her. She raised the garment to her chin and fought the urge to bury her face in the smoky roughness of the coarse wool cloth.

"I never claimed to be anything else," he replied, his voice now cold and hard.

He strode to her, his steps deliberate, neither slow nor rushed. Standing behind her, he parted the heavy fall of her hair and draped it over her shoulders to give him easy access to the row of buttons down her back.

She stood still, hardly daring to breathe, as she felt the deft movements of his fingers and the widening expanse of exposed flesh as the dress gaped further and further open.

"I can't believe you would do this."

"Do what? Make love to you in the middle of the afternoon?"

"It is not making love, whatever the time. It's breeding, like cattle or dogs or horses." She nearly gagged on the words, but succeeded in getting them out without choking.

"Is that what you thought last night, Elizabeth?"

He rested his hands on her waist with his thumbs hooked into the open V above the buttons still fastened. At the slightest pressure from his fingers, she leaned back the scant inch necessary to know he had no obvious aversion to bedding her in broad daylight. Even if that broad daylight did not penetrate this room.

"Everything has changed. I did not know then what you intended."

He laughed and popped another button with his thumbs.

"But surely you knew there was a chance you might conceive. And can you deny that you desired me? I do not deny that I desired you. Besides," he murmured against her shoulder as he slid his hands down to her hips, "you said yourself that you preferred me to your betrothed. Do you think Thomas Colfax's motives would be any different? A husband has every right to expect his wife to bear his children."

"But I am not your wife!" she cried.

"You could be if that's what you wish."

Her shrill protest to his impossible suggestion melted into a wail of passion. The highwayman unfastened the remaining buttons quickly and slipped his hands inside the gown at her waist, then brought them up to her breasts. She felt her nipples harden against the rough warmth of his palms. No, she could not deny that she desired him, now or last night or any other time he so much as touched her. Even the frozen dread in her belly warmed, liquefied into an irresistible flame of need surging through her.

Jack Silver's wife? The idea was laughable, more ludicrous than being his mistress, his lover, the mother of his child.

"Dear God in Heaven, why have you done all of this to me? If I carry your child, not even my father's fortune will buy me a suitable husband. I'll be forced—"

Jack interrupted her with a snarled "You considered Thomas Colfax 'suitable'?" and with no gentleness bent her over the chair to face him.

She nearly let go the heavy cloak, but beneath her fingers it was something to squeeze as she tightened the reins on her emotions. He had probed too near the truth, and if she did not maintain some kind of control on herself, she would reveal everything to him, from her masquerade as Betsy Bunch to her hopeless affection for the earl of Kilbury.

She expected him to demand an answer to his sarcastic question, but this man whose demeanor changed almost as frequently as the shifting of the firelight waited in patient silence. He even took a step back, allowing her to stand straight without the ancient oak pressing into her spine. Though he towered over her, his eyes bright and unforgiving, his hands hard upon her bare shoulders where her gown had slipped, Elizabeth found a morsel of calm, enough to think through her reply before speaking.

"My position is not protected by a title or other law of inheritance," she began. She had blurted out so many unconsidered responses before that now these words came with difficulty. The touch of him, the warm nearness of him were potent distractions. "My father could turn me out on the streets if he so desired. If I wish to continue to enjoy the comforts of his wealth and avoid the fate of a woman alone, I must accede to his wishes. His wish is to see his heirs—my children—born into a titled family to safeguard the estate he will give them."

A moment ago, when she phrased the words in her mind, they seemed so logical, so sensible. They were the very justification Edward had used whenever she protested against the marriage to Thomas. Now, as she watched Jack Silver's eyes take on a fitful glitter, she realized the trap he had led her into, a trap of her own making.

She thought she detected a triumphant smile on his lips, but it might only have been a trick played on her by overstrained eyes and overwrought emotions.

But there was no smile, no humor, not even any mockery in his words, only the cruelest of accusations.

"You'd have sold yourself to Colfax like any common whore."

She shook her head vehemently.

"No, you don't understand," she pleaded, refusing to meet those glittering eyes.

"Don't I? Then what do you call marrying for a title if not a form of prostitution? Or can you tell me truthfully that you were marrying Thomas Colfax for love?"

"I—I can't tell you that. You know I can't."

His fingers bit into her flesh with such force that she felt weak with the pain, but she would not cry out. Slowly, however, her hold on the cloak that had become a shield between her body and his slipped. When the cloak fell, so did her gown, down her arms and off her wrists.

"Because the truth is that you agreed to marry him for a title that is not even his until his nephew dies."

"No, goddamn you, Jack Silver," Elizabeth whispered, at last raising her eyes to throw all her anger into one final glaring stare. "The truth is that until I met you, I had no idea what love is."

CHAPTER
13

Silence spun a silken web around them, each invisible strand humming with the tension of their captivity. John found himself staring into the eyes of a woman as transfixed as a lacy-winged insect caught in a spider's trap.

Yet he knew he was no less a victim than she. As her nostrils flared with each ragged breath, he felt the air leave his own lungs in more rapid gasps. When she licked the tip of her tongue across her upper lip and reached a warm hand to stroke a lock of damp hair back from his brow, he could hold back no longer.

He laughed loudly with deep and sincere satisfaction. "Ah, my dear Elizabeth, you are almost convincing."

Her eyes widened in shock, then narrowed in a clear warning. He did not try to stop her nor move to avoid the blow. The sting of her slap was a small price to pay for witnessing her rage.

"You *bastard,*" she hissed, drawing back for another attack.

"Why? Because I failed to believe your pretty lie?" He chuckled again without a trace of mirth and caught her wrist neatly. "Don't waste your energy," he warned, his voice now cold and hard as his grip on her arm. He lifted her hand to place a kiss on her palm. In contrast, the soft flesh was warm, as warm as his cheek. "Save it for—"

"For the bed?" she finished. She tried to snatch her hand away, but he held her fast. "Why should I? You only want to plant your seed in me. Can you not accomplish the same if I merely lie back, spread my legs, and let you—"

"No, damn you," he growled and stole the rest of her bitter words with a hungry kiss.

He wanted to embrace her, to make the cold truth of her accusation the lie he now knew it to be, but she fought him with tight little fists until he held her arms immobile. If she had not tangled her feet in the pile of gown and cloak on the floor, she would have kicked him painfully in the shins—or worse. To prevent her raising a knee to his groin, he tried to pin her against the chair. It wasn't heavy enough and slid out from behind her, almost bringing them both crashing to the floor. Instinctively, to keep her balance, she flung her arms around his neck.

But was it instinct or desire that prompted him to sweep her up and carry her to the bed? Surely his survival did not hinge on the deepening of that kiss he could not find the power to break. Nor could he find any logic to explain why she responded to the touch of his tongue on hers with a desperate moan.

She's lying, she's lying! he told himself with each long stride he took toward the bed.

But the bed was too close, and too much of him remained unconvinced. Even if he accepted her pretty little declaration as a falsehood, how could he deny the evidence of his own loss of control? She was right, it should have made no difference how or even if she responded, so long as the seed he sowed took root and grew within her.

Except that she did respond—and fed a hunger for her he did not dare to explore. She was a writhing warmth in his arms, all naked flesh beneath the twisted linen of her shift. Her fingers clutched frantically, tremblingly, at his hair, holding his mouth to hers as though she needed his own breath to breathe.

Or did he need hers? He could not let her go, not even to free her mouth when he lay her atop the still rumpled quilt on the bed. Sprawled half across her, half beside her, he felt her fumbling now at the buttons of his shirt with such frenzy that one came off. He heard it clatter on the floor, just before he heard the tearing of fabric that meant she had lost patience with the buttons.

Still he moved his lips against hers, took the tip of her seeking tongue between his teeth. He no longer drank the sweetness of her kiss; he swam in it, drowned in it, breathed it, lived it. As her fingers had grasped his shirt and torn it open, so he ripped away the barrier of soft linen that kept him from the silken temptation of her body.

Good God, what had she done to him? He hated her for her lies, hated her for the mockery she made of his memories, but this fury that coursed through him did not feel like hatred. It burned hotter, stabbed deeper, sang wilder in his blood.

Now he was the prisoner, held as much by the slender fingers stroking down his chest to his ribs and behind him to his back as by the magnetic heat of her breasts that he could not resist crushing against him. And when he did try to push himself away, it was she who broke the enchantment of the kiss and forbade him.

"No, Jack Silver," she crooned in a breathy whisper. "You'll not leave me now. You're too close to what you want to give it up."

Damn! He managed to raise himself up on his forearms, but even at that frail distance, he barely saw her, save for the sooty splash of her hair on the pillow and the glitter of her heavy-lidded eyes. He was as blind as he had wanted her to be.

His other senses were intensely alive, however, especially his sense of touch. She was panting, her breath warm on his face, her nipples hot and hard where they came in contact with his own searing skin. And he felt her heart skitter more erratically than his own.

Again he tried to escape; she tightened her embrace around his ribs and whispered a malicious chuckle into his ear. The game had changed, and he had no idea how or when.

Elizabeth squirmed beneath him, not to free herself from the burden of his body, but to settle him securely where she wanted him. He complied readily until he lay above her, though with only one leg between hers. Still, she felt the occasional nudge of his arousal against her thigh and decided her chance of success now rested in caution rather than the recklessness from which the idea of turning the tables on him had sprung.

"You're no better than my father, Jack Silver," she accused in a husky purr intended to sound seductive as well as mocking. "You could have ruined me in a dozen other ways, but I don't think that's what you really want, is it?"

Let him think her hands trembled from barely restrained passion, she prayed silently as she slipped her hand further down his back. Well aware of the danger of taunting him, she could not forget the wildness of his reaction when she threw his intentions back in his face a few moments before. She had seen a hint of something else then, though she had not been prepared and so could not determine its meaning. She desperately wanted another glimpse.

"And what do *you* think I want?" he asked.

The tensing of the muscles beneath her palm told

her more than the unmistakable caution in his tone that her words had hit their mark. She ran her fingers along the top edge of his breeches. She had him on the defensive now. God, if only she could take full advantage before he—

"I said, what do you think I want?"

He ground his hips against hers to underscore the repetition. She had to shake herself free of the effect his blatant display had on her. He was making her forget herself.

"I believe, Jack Silver, that you are jealous of Thomas Colfax, and you'd like nothing so much as to see your child, especially if that child is a son, raised as his heir, perhaps even someday to inherit the Kilbury title."

She smiled, though she doubted even Jack Silver could see in the almost total darkness. The fire was only a shimmering glow, and the storm that continued to rumble around the walls and above the roof dimmed even the fragile line of daylight around the window.

That smile faded as quickly as a flash of lightning when Jack Silver laughed softly and said, "I, jealous of Thomas Colfax? I'd do as well to be jealous of that nearsighted bookworm nephew of his who let Kilbury fall to ruin. Besides, my dear Elizabeth, you assured me Thomas would not marry you if you carried another man's bastard."

His sweetly sarcastic reminder chilled her. Once more, the highwayman was in control. Perhaps he always had been and merely allowed her a teasing moment to think she had gained an advantage. He played with her like a cat with a mouse, letting her escape only so far before he stretched out a paw and batted her back where he wanted her.

And he seemed to have all the cruel patience of a cat. He shifted just enough to extricate first one arm and then the other from the sleeves of the shirt she had ruined, each movement easy and controlled. Was he bluffing? Could she have twisted out from under him and escaped? Or was he so accustomed to disrobing with a naked woman beneath him that she had no chance to catch him off his guard?

She wanted to try, but something held her back. Even when he reached down to unbutton his breeches, she lay still, as passive as she knew how. Dear God, had she become so resigned to her imprisonment that she no longer possessed the will to resist? No, no, she told herself to force back the rising panic, it made no sense to escape from the bed when she remained every bit his prisoner.

But when he settled against her in exactly the same position as before, she could feel the hair on his chest gently brush her nipples. She had to release her breath slowly, trying with all her might to keep it from becoming a moan. If she gave in, all was lost. *She* was lost.

The war waged with desires and denials was not the one she most wanted to win. She would, she swore, surrender on that battlefield if it gained her another far more important victory. He had already taken her innocence and made of her body a willing instrument of his pleasure, and she was in grave danger of losing her heart to him as well, but he had not yet conquered her mind.

"Perhaps," she drawled, stroking the flat of her palms up the corded muscles to his shoulders, "just perhaps, I could convince Thomas the child was his. That's what you're counting on, isn't it, that I'll be so desperate I'll do anything. Of course, if Thomas believes himself to be the father, you would be robbed of your chance to humiliate him. If you wish the child raised as his heir, that would be the price."

"Suppose I want both?"

His reply came too quickly and lacked his usual

arrogance. Elizabeth trailed her fingers ever so slowly down his chest until he drew in a sharp breath and held it. She had planted a tiny seed of doubt in his mind.

"You can't have both, Jack Silver," she scolded, smothering a triumphant smile. "You must choose whether you want to cuckold Thomas Colfax before he's even married or to foist your bastard on him, acknowledged as his own."

He couldn't choose; his long silence told her that much. He wanted more than he could have and didn't like being confronted with that unpleasant truth. Therein lay her hope: that he would recognize the futility of his scheme and release her. Jack Silver did not give the impression of being open to any compromise, but Elizabeth suspected there lurked within him a sense of honor that would respect her besting him at his own game.

He kissed her nose, and she thought she heard a chuckle. Then he brushed his lips across her cheek so softly she was certain she felt the smile of surrender curve them. But when he nuzzled her ear and took the lobe between his teeth, there was no hint of concession in the way he ran his tongue in a lazy circle around her flesh.

"Thomas Colfax will rot in hell before I'll let him have my son," he swore.

She shivered and could not restrain the sigh of capitulation that fought its way out of her. How she wanted to hate him for all the wrongs he had done her and the wrong he yet planned to do. But her body betrayed her, remembering the fantasy that her heart created. In that moment when, without knowing how he had done it, Elizabeth acknowledged the highwayman's complete mastery of her, she could not conjure up any emotion but the pure delight of loving him.

He kissed her throat, cupping her breasts in his strong hands, and her sigh became a moan. The fire of wanting him blazed within her, burning away all other thought, all other need, and when he finally made his possession of her complete, she held him to her, within her heart as well as within her body, and swore she would never let him go.

She slept, though he knew she would waken soon. He slipped silently from the bed and pulled the covers over her as best he could in the dark. Having had enough sense to throw his clothes to the floor, he found them with a minimum of fumbling. Christ, but the room was cold with no fire.

And dark. He had planned it that way, from the boards over the window to the careful rationing of candles, but he realized now, as he stumbled across the room to find his cloak and boots, how desperate Elizabeth must have been for light, and not only in her attempt to discover his identity.

She was clever, he would give her that. He shook his head with a rueful smile. He would have liked to see her reaction when she realized the same "friend" who had shared poetry with her on a long-ago summer afternoon was the brigand who stole her innocence.

He was surprised to find that the thought, after bringing him that momentary pleasure, made him more than a little uncomfortable. What if he had been wrong all these years? Was it possible she told the truth about her betrothal to Thomas being forced upon her? That would explain the drug in the milk and even Vicar Horne's statement regarding a wedding he did not want to perform.

He tossed such doubts aside as both useless and dangerous. He had examined all these details many times in the past four years, including the apparent contradiction between Elizabeth's friendship with

John Colfax and her willingness to wed his uncle. She preferred Thomas and the things she believed he could give her, as her constant attention to the sapphires made quite clear.

And there was the matter of her melodramatic declaration of love for Jack Silver. That alone convinced him she could lie like a paid witness. No, he had made no misjudgments.

His feet were nearly frozen by the time he found his boots but he decided to forgo warmth in favor of silence. Elizabeth might waken if he went clomping around in them, so he picked them up along with the cloak to carry downstairs. He then returned to the bed to make sure she truly slept and did not plan some further mischief.

In the few moments since he left her, she had turned on her side and curled into a tight ball, obviously unable to find enough warmth from the corner of the quilt he had pulled over her. She lay on top of everything else; he would have to wake her to pull the other blankets from beneath her.

There was, however, the cloak hanging over his arm. After setting the boots silently on the floor, he draped the semicircle of heavy wool over the sleeping girl's bare shoulders. Though not enough to cover her from neck to toe, it was better than nothing.

After all that he had done to her, he could not let her freeze.

Bright sunlight shimmered in the cracks between the boards. The storm had passed. But the sun brought no warmth to the room, and the fire shed no light. Trying to figure her way out of the tangled bedclothes, Elizabeth discovered that she had Jack Silver's cloak wrapped tightly around her. He must, she realized, have covered her with it after he left the bed.

She shut her eyes against tears of frustration and futility. Her worst fears had come true, even to the possibility that she might conceive her outlaw lover's child. Yet that alone did not bring the unwanted moisture to her eyes. She had told him everything, *everything,* and he had believed nothing. He dismissed her explanation for her marriage to Thomas, and he ridiculed the confession of love he had wrung from her himself. Yet even that stung less than the arrogant contempt he displayed for the earl.

Why? she wondered.

But she was too cold to ponder such questions now. Without a roaring blaze in the tiny fireplace, the chill and damp crept in to make her very bones ache.

Wrapping the cloak more tightly around her shoulders, she sat up and swung her legs over the side of the bed. Her feet came into contact not with the floor but with a pair of high leather boots.

She had to laugh at the idea of Jack Silver's boots parked under her bed. They'd be wet, though, from his ride in the storm, and if not properly cared for could be ruined. She picked them up and carried them to the hearth.

It wasn't until she set them down on the cold stones that she realized they were not in fact wet at all, nor did they bear a trace of mud or dirt. And the cloak about her shoulders smelled of wood smoke, not of rain.

She knelt and buried her face in the sturdy English wool. Her teeth were chattering, with both cold and an eerie combination of apprehension and excitement. Breathing deeply, she closed her eyes and blocked out all extraneous thoughts to focus on the facts. She must make no hasty conclusions.

The man who wore these things into her room and left them behind had come to her wet and still chilled by a storm that touched neither his cloak nor boots.

He must have worn other clothes, clothes that would mark him no different from anyone else traveling in broad daylight. And then, upon reaching this place where he kept Elizabeth Stanhope prisoner, he donned his disguise.

And what of this place itself? Her room was small, but she remembered climbing stairs that night he brought her. Could this be a servant's chamber, the hearth only sufficient to chase the chill for a few hours at night? Sounds from the rest of the building did not reach her ears even in the silence of the night. At least two servants waited on Jack Silver's bidding, perhaps more, with unquestioned loyalty, for they could not help but know his secret, yet he trusted them when he went out into the world without his disguise.

Elizabeth opened her eyes, afraid of where her thoughts were taking her. She stirred the coals to find the glowing embers buried in the ashes and with some patience brought the fire to life. Still wrapped in the cloak and nothing more, she let the flames warm her.

"Whoever he is, he knows Kilbury Hall too well to be a stranger," she said aloud, remembering how swiftly he had guided her through the underground passages. "And he was there that night with Thomas and John and my father, who would certainly have noticed anyone who did not belong."

Was he one of the Kilbury servants? she wondered. She thought it unlikely, for the youth and the old woman who served here seemed to bear more respect for their master than if he were only another, though higher, servant.

Could Jack Silver have sat at the dinner table with her and she did not notice him? She squeezed her eyes closed in frustration. With the single exception of the nervous vicar, she recalled no one clearly enough to tell whether or not the highwayman had attended. Only when she remembered how John had named each of Thomas's guests did she begin to place faces into her memory.

"Damn!"

John's curse echoed in the solitude.

The old woman looked up from the meal she was laying out on the table.

"Is something wrong, milord?"

He shook his head without moving away from the tall window. Until Peg appeared with food, he had forgotten Harry was at the Hall, tending Thomas's injured horse.

"No, nothing's wrong."

He heard the muted clatter of dishes, the quiet clink of silver, and the aroma of a hot mutton pie stirred his hunger. Still, he stared outside at the late afternoon sun slanting in great golden arrows through the trees, at the droplets from the earlier storm dripping from the branches, at the puddles reflecting an almost cloudless sky. He had blotted out nearly all conscious thought until Peg interrupted his reverie.

"It's her, isn't it. That girl upstairs. I warned ye she'd be nothin' but trouble."

The view from the window lost some of its magic, but he continued to stare at it while admitting, "You did, Peg, and so did Harry. What's done is done, however, and I'll have to live with it."

She snorted her disapproval but said nothing more on the subject. Harry would not have dropped it so easily, which was why John wished the old jockey were here. He needed someone to argue with him, someone who would point out all the obstacles, all the risks, someone who would make him comfortable with his decisions.

"Will there be aught else, milord?" Peg asked.

He was about to dismiss her but instead decided to ask at least some of the questions he would have fired at Harry. Peg had the singular advantage of being female.

"Shall I let her go, Peg? I could take her to Kilbury tonight, while Thomas is gone, and it would all be over."

He took his place at the table and picked up the mismatched silver before he dared look at the servant. Her expression told him she had not been completely surprised by his question. Nor was she about to give him any but a carefully considered reply.

"No, milord, it'd not be over," she said, shaking her head slowly from side to side but keeping her eyes on him, "and ye know it well as I. She was a virgin when ye took her that night. Ye know she carried no man's babe then, but if ye send her back now, ye'll never know if yer own heir grows in her womb."

He shrugged, then focused his attention on the steaming pie in front of him. Peg's remark was nothing he did not already know; he had told himself as much a dozen times before he ever touched Elizabeth Stanhope and a thousand times since.

"Ah, ye think it matters so little now, and perhaps, after all ye've done, nothing does matter. But ye've asked me, and I'll tell ye true, whether ye be Jack Silver or John Colfax, earl of Kilbury."

Her voice, low and hoarse with age, belonged in the darkened tower room, not here in the hall where sunlight still painted shadows outside the tall windows.

"I don't think ye *can* take her back. I don't think ye ever will."

CHAPTER
14

The exercise of her mental faculties buoyed Elizabeth's spirits and infused her with energy through the afternoon. One by one, as though John were beside her whispering their names, she recalled the other guests at that horrible betrothal dinner. So certain was she that one of them must prove to be Jack Silver that she dressed and brushed her hair and tidied up the room in preparation for her release.

But Mr. Henry Wing-Oliphant, the Sheffield steelmaker, was far too short to be Jack Silver, and Mr. Lawrence Salem, who had sat directly across from John, was too old. No disguise, however clever, could have transformed any of the gentlemen Thomas had invited to Kilbury that night into the man who later kidnapped her. And seduced her. And told her he wished to father a child on her.

A sudden chill, like cold water overflowing a pool, rushed through her. It washed away all her hopes and left behind only the clear reality she had tried so hard to deny.

"You've been a very cooperative victim, Elizabeth Stanhope." She berated herself with unrestrained disgust. "You've done everything that scoundrel asked of you and more, even falling in love with him. All because you were stupid enough to believe in a romantic fairy tale."

She stood by the bed and looked down at the torn shift spread out on the quilt. The damage was not irreparable, and she had intended to ask for needle and thread to repair it.

"Why should *I* mend it?" she asked, turning away from the bed and seeking physical activity to fight the tears of defeat and humiliation stinging her eyes. "*You* tore it, Jack Silver. *You* mend it!"

Though the room was too small for respectable pacing, Elizabeth managed four full strides from the bed to the wall, all the while railing against the nightmare reality she could no longer deny.

"You *are* a monster, Jack Silver," she cried as she looked for something to kick, to throw, to destroy. The small, leather-bound edition of *Robinson Crusoe* lying on the table came to hand first and an instant later crashed with a dull thump against the door. "You are a despicable, cruel bastard who deserves to be drawn and quartered and I shall laugh at your execution."

But she was not laughing now. She was sobbing uncontrollably as she snatched the hapless Tom Jones and his long-suffering Sophia from the chair and hurled them after Mr. Crusoe with a double thud as the heavier volume hit door and then floor. Hot, bitter tears streamed from her eyes, blinding her to her surroundings but not to the horror and pain inside.

An animallike howl of despair escaped her as she grabbed the torn shift from the bed. It was a mute reminder of all her foolish romantic notions as well as the harsh reality. The gallant outlaw she so proudly claimed had taught her what love is was nothing but a common, brutal felon.

With a violent oath, Elizabeth ripped the shift as

neatly down the middle as Jack Silver had torn her nightgown. Bits and pieces of linen fabric flew wildly to the strangled accompaniment of curses Betsy Bunch once had blushed to hear in the Black Oak Inn.

"Damn you, damn you, damn you!" she shrieked and flung the tattered scraps into the fire. Over her own screams she heard the pounding of running feet outside her prison cell. When the door opened, she ran to it, but strong arms stopped her and dragged her back into the room. Darkness, inside and out, descended once more.

At Harry's entrance, John looked up from the ledger page. The candles had burned low; one guttered out in the draft. By a conservative estimate, the hour must be close to midnight.

Limping more noticeably than usual, the old man hobbled to the welcome warmth of the fire and said, "I expected you to be abed long before this, milord."

An innocent enough statement, spoken without either sarcasm or censure and requiring no response. John knew, however, by the way Harry lingered to stretch his gnarled hands toward the flames that he would not leave without an explanation.

"Miss Stanhope indulged in a temper tantrum," he replied as he returned his attention to the ledger. The numbers that blurred a few minutes ago now stood out clear and precise once more. "And I had work to do."

Peg would fill Harry in on the details John had no desire to discuss. It was she who had burst into the quiet of his dining hall with a barely coherent report of strange noises coming from the tower room and demanded he investigate at once. He had opened the door and been assaulted by a sobbing bundle of hysteria, all wild fists and tumbled hair and tears. He could not even be sure she knew who held her and wrestled her back into the room. The dropping of the bolt as Peg locked them both in brought a wail of such despair that John shivered and wondered if Elizabeth had indeed gone mad.

For the next hour he listened to her curse him through a thousand hells even while she clung to him like an orphaned child. He held her, saying nothing, until she fell asleep utterly exhausted in his arms.

That, however, was hours ago.

"I told ye it'd be different now ye've told her why she's here."

"That changes nothing," John insisted. "And I did not tell her. She figured it out for herself."

"So ye said, so ye said. Ye give the girl fair credit for some brains. But that don't explain why ye're warmin' yer backside at the fire instead o' warmin' yer—"

John swiveled sharply in the old wooden chair.

"For someone who was against this enterprise from the first, you're suddenly very eager to push me into Elizabeth Stanhope's bed." Harry gave him a look that could have been grin or grimace, then turned away. John's temper cooled to be replaced by concern. "What happened at Kilbury? I expected you hours ago."

He braced himself for the worst possible news. As one of the few servants left from the days when John's father controlled the estate, Harry was held in a certain amount of distrust by Thomas's staff. In the stables, however, some of the old grooms and stableboys remained who respected the crippled jockey as well as his unwavering loyalty to his—and their—true employer.

Had Harry learned disturbing information? Could Thomas somehow have discovered the nature of the activities at the Dower House? Did John's explanation for his presence in Thomas's study this morning arouse more suspicions that it allayed?

No, Harry would not have withheld information. Whatever kept the old man at Kilbury Hall so late was something else, but it was enough to stretch John's nerves tighter.

The old voice was laden with weariness that went beyond disgust. "He ruined the mare. The coachman told him she wasn't fit to drive, that she should have been unharnessed and led back slowly. I did what I could."

John barked a vile oath, then slumped in his chair. "But that would have left Thomas stranded," he sneered. "Better to destroy a fine animal than Thomas Colfax should sit in his carriage and be bored for an hour."

He took one last glance at the account book. The numbers seemed meaningless now. Money, even the thousands of pounds Jack Silver had removed from the pockets and bank accounts of Thomas Colfax and his cronies, could not begin to compensate for the lives, human and animal alike, sacrificed in one way or another to a single man's greed.

He closed the book, letting the pages slide against one another with a susurration almost like a human sigh.

"Did you put the mare down?" His voice was no louder.

"No, not without his authority."

"Will she suffer?"

"There's a boy with her to keep her quiet, Dwyer's son, not one of them new slips. With rest and care, she'll be fine."

John heard the words, almost the same as were uttered all those years ago when another horse had been injured—and a man nearly killed. He knew what had *not* been said; those words were far more important.

The mare would survive, but she'd be useless for her intended purpose. Sold for a guinea or two to a farmer or carter who could afford no better, she was doomed to live out a few more years in misery—if Thomas didn't order her destroyed at once.

Reminding himself that the present must be dealt with before the future, John pushed the chair back and got to his feet. Harry rose, too, and rubbed his thigh, the unconscious gesture of an elderly man seeking to ease the pain of an old injury. He had ridden John's mount to Kilbury earlier, but there was no horse to bring him to the Dower House at this late hour. He had walked the half mile and more in the cold damp evening air.

He was a little man, no taller than Elizabeth Stanhope and now bent with his more than sixty years. Yet he had lost none of the wiry strength that kept him on the magnificent horses bred at Kilbury. John felt that strength in the hand Harry rested on his arm.

"It's not like Conquest, lad." The ancient voice was stronger, too, though still a whisper. "Thomas meant no harm this time, not really. No one was hurt, and I'll do what I can for the mare."

A wry smile turned up John's mouth.

"We've been together too long, you and I, Harry," he said, clasping his own long fingers around the old man's. "We think too much alike. Sometimes I just think more slowly than you."

Grizzled brows knit above worried eyes.

"You were right, and I was wrong, Harry." The admission came more easily than he expected; the past hours alone had given him time to think it all through. "It's time to end it now, before anyone else suffers." Leaving the old man by the fire, John strode toward the stairs, but halfway across the darkened hall, he paused, then slowly turned. "Revenge is a kind of greed, too, isn't it?"

John slipped silently through the door, listening as well as looking. Nothing moved save the vague, distorted shadows of bedposts twisting like tormented dancers on the wall opposite the fire. Darkness clung to the rest of the room, especially the corners, and the only sounds were the gentle crackle from the hearth and the sighing of a spring wind outside the window. The pile of tumbled bedclothes might conceal Elizabeth, asleep where he had left her, but in the uncertain light John refused to accept the obvious.

He leaned back against the door until it latched. Did the click cover the sound of a woman's sudden intake of breath? He couldn't be sure, and then Ethan slid the outer bolt into place, masking any other noises. Until the boy's footsteps faded, John heard nothing else.

He walked to the bed. Amongst the shadows he made out the darker mass of her tangled hair on the pillow. He touched her shoulder hesitantly, then withdrew the instant he felt her involuntary wince.

She pushed the blankets away. Beneath them she lay naked and acquiescent.

"You are very late, Jack Silver," she whispered.

"Get up," he growled without moving a single step toward her. "And put your clothes on. I am taking you home."

CHAPTER
15

She made no effort to cover her nakedness but stammered, "I—I don't understand. What about the child?"

"The child?" He drew the sheet over her but could still see the curve of her breasts under the linen, the nipples tight and hard against the rough fabric; one slender leg remained exposed. He had to drag his gaze away from her or he dared not trust himself to approach her. Shocked as he was by her behavior and disgusted with his own, he remained vulnerable to his body's instinctive reactions. If he had any hope of carrying through on his intention to return her to Kilbury, he could not come closer to her until he had some control over those instincts. "I've changed my mind."

"You've changed your mind?"

Her question echoed in the stillness as he strolled to the hearth where she had left her dressing gown. He found the garment warm, as if she had just stepped out of it. The image burned in his mind. To counteract the power of that vision and to keep his fingers from caressing the fabric as though it were her skin, he tossed the robe toward her. She caught it with surprising deftness.

"Put it on."

As if she had heard nothing else, she repeated in a distant, disbelieving whisper, "You've changed your mind?"

"Yes, damn you, I've changed my mind!"

Shrinking from his anger, Elizabeth let both sheet and dressing gown slip in her hurry to put some distance between herself and the man whose scowl was positively diabolic in the fragile light.

"You can't!" she blurted out, then bit her tongue before she said anything else. Once again he had caught her off her guard.

"Are you saying I can't change my mind or I can't take you home?" he asked.

His voice was low and smooth, not calm but tightly controlled, with the ever present hint of sarcasm. In sharp contrast to the gentleness he had shown earlier, she sensed a reckless danger about him now that left her not frightened but very wary.

"You can't take me home," she answered. "I would be locked out. After what you did at Kilbury, abducting me from right under Thomas's and my father's noses, every door will be secured. You would have to wake someone, and surely they would catch you then."

"I could leave you somewhere close and let you find your own way. And servants have been known to leave doors unlocked."

"They have, but are you willing to take such a risk? Or that someone may not be watching for just such an eventuality?"

"I've taken greater risks before. And why are you so eager to stay? You should be glad of the chance to escape my brutal captivity."

Did he wince as he repeated one of the lesser

accusations she had hurled at him earlier that evening?

She could not hate him. She had tried, conjuring up every crime he had committed against her and more. But while she consigned him to eternal damnation for kidnapping her, for ruining her, for admitting he intended to get a bastard child on her, he said not a word in his own defense. He took the blows from her fists without a sound, without a retaliation. She blushed now, remembering her wild shrieks of despair that turned to wretched sobs as he held and comforted her.

Only later, when she wakened from the fitful sleep that followed her tears, did she recognize his silence as an admission of guilt.

"You can marry Thomas and perhaps he'll never notice your lack of, shall we say, innocence."

She bit back yet another desperate attempt to convince him she would not wed Thomas Colfax. Far more important was her need to keep Jack from returning her before she had the answer to that most desperate of questions. If he did not believe any of her other entreaties, she would not waste time reiterating them now. She would instead play upon his curiosity —and the compassion she sensed beneath his sarcasm.

"And what of you, Jack Silver? You'll never know either." With the dressing gown securely tied around her waist, she knelt on the far side of the bed and waited for his answer. When none came, she dared go further. "It will be at least a week before I can expect to learn I do not carry your child. But if the answer is otherwise, you'll have to wait a bit longer. You said Thomas Colfax would burn in hell before you'd let him raise your son, but if you send me home tonight, you'll never know."

Still he said nothing. Elizabeth inched across the tangled bedclothes toward the pillow.

"It is late," she whispered, "and we are both very tired."

His hand already on the buttons of his shirt, John took one step toward her. She had not answered his question. He did not care.

Elizabeth lay on her back, her head turned to the right, facing the window. The light had brightened steadily until she knew the sun was well above the horizon.

Beside her, Jack Silver slept on, his left arm flung above his head. Beneath the covers, the fingers of his right hand were curled lightly around her wrist. She had wakened when the light around the window was but a pale shimmer and tried to find a more comfortable position. Her wrigglings must have disturbed him, for he mumbled something and grabbed her arm possessively. Then, as the minutes passed, he relaxed his grip and his breathing steadied into the peaceful rhythm of deep, contented sleep once more. But she did not move, not even to pull away from his grasp.

Not even to look at him.

Not even when he whispered her name.

"I'm awake," she said.

He yawned and stretched with raw abandon, but he never let go her wrist. He was as naked as she, and she felt the muscles of his thigh knot and then relax against hers, followed by a sensuous stroking of his foot up the outside of her ankle to her calf. He nudged his toe under her knee until she was forced to raise it. As she did so, he slid his leg under hers so that she could not avoid awareness of his arousal.

"Did you sleep well?" he asked as casually as if they were polite guests greeting each other over breakfast.

"No, I did not."

He placed her hand on his belly, then stretched both arms over his head to yawn again. It was, she thought, most impolite of him, since it implied that he had slept marvelously well. But then, he was not faced with a most uncertain future.

"And why not? Did I snore? Did I steal all the covers and leave you shivering?"

Before she could pull her hand away from the intimate place he had put it, he rolled onto his side and gathered her neatly in his arms so her bottom nestled even more intimately against him.

"No, you did not snore or leave me shivering." Indeed, he had kept her snugly warm, but she would not admit that. "You simply left me wondering what you intend to do with me."

He nuzzled the nape of her neck and muttered, "You're a damn prickly wench in the morning. And here I'd wondered what it would be like to waken in your bed."

"Now you know."

"So I do. In truth, it's not entirely unpleasant."

Had he completely forgotten last night? He certainly acted as if he had, jesting with her and cupping her breasts in warm hands until her nipples ached for the touch of his fingers. She sighed with exasperation.

"Is this not what you wanted, my seductive Elizabeth?" he asked. "Did you not coax me here last night when I would have taken you home?"

She twisted out of his embrace and scooted beyond his reach. The red dressing gown lay at the foot of the bed, though she had no idea how it had failed to be knocked to the floor during the night. She blushed at the thought of that almost desperate lovemaking, then quickly shoved the thought aside as she grabbed for the robe. Ignoring the way she exposed herself in the process, she pulled it on and tied the sash around her, just under her breasts.

Not until she had finished did she realize Jack Silver had lain calmly on his side of the bed and watched her without making a move to stop her.

"Would you like to go home now?" he asked.

"In broad daylight?"

He shrugged and lay back, lacing his fingers behind his head.

"I can arrange it."

For all his nonchalance, she sensed a wariness in his tone.

"Someone would recognize you."

"I did not say I would take you."

She turned away from him, her heart pounding. He had all but confirmed her suspicions that he concealed a familiar identity, if not familiar to her then at least to others who knew her and to whom she could describe him. She hugged the knowledge tightly.

"Shall we call a truce, Elizabeth? Or at least consider this match a draw? You were right last night. I was exhausted and not thinking clearly."

"And now that you've had some sleep you are once again bent upon using me for your revenge?" she snapped. "I don't know which version of Jack Silver I—"

"Watch your tongue, Elizabeth, or I shall indeed send you back to Stanhope, pregnant or not."

That silenced her and gave John a chance to run his fingers through his hair and sweep away a few clinging cobwebs from the corners of his mind. He had indeed slept well, but not long enough. Even now he was fighting an urge to close his eyes and shut out all the problems facing him until at least noon. They would, however, still be waiting for him then.

He had told her only part of the truth and also part of what he told her was a lie. He did not mind admitting that exhaustion caused last night's debacle. If he had had a handful of wits about him, he would never have considered letting her go and for the very reason she mentioned. Whether or not Elizabeth Stanhope bore responsibility for the acts of her father and her betrothed, any child she might carry was certainly innocent. He had meant what he said: He would never allow Thomas to raise that child. If it meant murder and the risk of hanging, well, he had already faced that risk more times than he could count. But there were ways of seeing to the child's welfare. A letter to his solicitor should be enough.

She intruded upon his thoughts with an impatient "Well? What are the terms of this truce?"

"Terms?" he echoed. God, he had very nearly fallen asleep again. "Ah, yes, the terms. For my part, I shall keep you here until it is determined whether or not you have conceived. Now, what will you offer me in exchange?"

"O—Offer you? I am to offer *you* something in exchange for the privilege of remaining your prisoner?"

"Exactly. You, my dear, are the one who wishes to stay."

He was infuriating. Worse, he was right. Elizabeth slumped down on the edge of the bed, her back to him. As usual, the room was cold, there was no fire, and her body was making other needs known as well. How was she to think under those conditions? Yet think, she must.

"I agree not to throw tantrums and frighten your servants. And if you'll bring me needle and thread, I'll mend the shirt I tore."

In her mind's eye she saw him, relaxed, self-assured, with a hint of a wicked smile playing about his lips while he considered her offer. She would recognize that smile anywhere if ever she saw him beyond these four walls. And if she did, she had only to kiss him once to know for certain.

"I think that will do for today, but what about tomorrow? And the day after? Surely a week or two of my hospitality is worth more than a mended shirt."

"I have nothing else to give you." She stopped only

long enough to take a deep breath, then when he did not interrupt her, she continued a bit more calmly. "I do not know what you want, Jack Silver. You said you wished to bed me, and so I gave you my virginity as willingly as I could. Should I not have? Would you have preferred to rape me? Are you angry with me for cheating you of that perverted pleasure?"

"No, I am not angry," John said simply. That she considered him capable of such barbarity bothered him much less than his own uncertainty as to what he would have done had she resisted him. Could he have taken her against her will? And did her willingness negate the fact that he had kidnapped her?

"You have availed yourself of me at your leisure, as though I were some music box to be wound up when you wished to be entertained and then left on a shelf, still and silent and content. You made fun of me when I complained of being bored or when I just wanted someone to talk to. Has it never occurred to you that I am a human being, that I crave companionship? Dear God, I thought my father was inhuman because he would not let me go to London, but even within the confines of that mausoleum he named after himself, I had servants to talk to, things to do. If I could not visit London or Bath, I was free to ride into one of the villages or—"

Once again Elizabeth paused, this time to flick away droplets of despicable moisture that insisted on trickling from her eyes and to bite back a dangerous confession. If the arrogant highwayman learned of her girlish affection for the earl of Kilbury, he might use it as against her. He already had a sufficient arsenal.

And though the gentle, studious, often clumsy John Colfax might be no match for Jack Silver, Elizabeth recognized he also held a fragile ray of hope for her, perhaps her only hope.

She refused to wipe away any more tears, lest

acknowledging them open the floodgates of despair. Instead, she straightened her shoulders and said, "That is my offer. If you find the terms unacceptable, set your own or return me to Stanhope."

The silence stretched longer and longer, until Elizabeth wondered if perhaps her captor had fallen asleep. She listened and found his breathing just slightly uneven, as though he were testing her patience. She refused to turn around. Her pride was suddenly a great deal stronger than her curiosity.

And when he did finally reply, his voice startled her so that she almost lost that control.

"I'll accept your offer but only for today." John flipped back the covers and stifled an exclamation at the cold that raised gooseflesh. He swung his feet to the floor, though he was somewhat prepared for that shock, then rose to fetch his clothes. As he pulled on his breeches he told her, "By tonight, when I return, I expect you to have—"

"No, wait!" she cried out. "I'll answer your questions. Any questions. About Thomas, about my father. As many as you like. As many as I can."

He finished buttoning his pants and with a grunt at the shiver brought on by exposure to the chill picked up his shirt.

"You're overly generous, my dear." The idea must have come to her suddenly, barely formed, with no time for her to determine its best use. Or perhaps she thought to substitute quantity for quality. She had no way to know his sole interest lay in her father's finances, a subject about which a spoiled daughter was likely to be painfully ignorant. "And how do I know you have answers to the questions I might ask? Or even that you would tell me the truth?"

"You don't. But neither do I know how many questions you may ask or what means you have to prove me a liar. My offer stands, Jack Silver, provided you agree that whether you run out of questions tonight or in a week, you will not take me back to Stanhope until . . . until we are certain."

In one sense, she drove a hard bargain. In another, she took an enormous risk. Her information bet against a highwayman's honor.

She was almost kneeling on the bed, facing him now with the crimson robe gaping open. Yes, it was a gamble, but he had played for higher stakes at much higher odds.

"I'll accept your terms," he said, "on the condition that if I catch you in a falsehood, you'll be taken home at once. Agreed?"

"Agreed."

Harry was nowhere in sight when John came down from the tower room. Peg brought him a message with his breakfast that Harry had already gone to tend Thomas's injured horse. The old woman said little else and offered no opinion when John told her to take a lamp and sewing supplies to Elizabeth's room. He downed a cup of scalding coffee and left most of the rest of his breakfast on the plate, then went to his own room to discard the black breeches and shirt and don the wrinkled clothes he had worn yesterday. With his John Colfax persona securely in place, he set out for the Hall.

Though the sun was well up, the March morning remained brisk, with a sparkling frost still crunchy on the grass underfoot and a skim of ice on the puddles. No other trace of the storm lingered. The sky stretched in unblemished blue, save for a raucous flock of crows wheeling overhead. Their noise made the gelding nervous; John touched his heels to the horse's flanks and let him spend his energy in a run up the hill.

It was not a long run, not nearly long enough to

supply the mental cleansing of hard physical exertion. Perhaps tonight Jack Silver would ride. John allowed the possibility to bring a smile to his face. But it was only a possibility.

He rode directly to the stable range, where a lack of activity confirmed his suspicion that Thomas had not yet returned from Stanhope. Hoping, though not expecting, that he might gain access to the Kilbury ledgers again, John left the gelding in Harry Grove's capable hands, then headed down the graveled walkway that led to the garden entrance.

An unfamiliar urgency lengthened his strides. Though any one of the gardeners or other servants was certain to remark on his impatience, a sharp contrast to his usual pace, he did not slow. A few days ago, even yesterday perhaps, he would have heeded his own warning and slipped into the carefree role he had perfected over these four long years. But now the play was nearing its end. He was eager to cast off the jester's motley.

As expected, the door to Thomas's study was securely locked. A passing footman gave him a slightly disapproving glance, which John returned with a cold stare. He suddenly had no patience with Thomas's toadies; he was tired of pandering to them, of being always so apologetic as if he had no right to his place in Kilbury Hall.

"Where is the key to this room?" he demanded, taking a great deal of satisfaction in the amazement on the servant's startled face.

"I—I don't know, milord. That's Mr. Thomas's study, and he won't like it if—"

"Find it. And bring it to me in the library."

The man drew himself up in his Kilbury livery as if to continue his protest, but John confounded him by simply turning and walking away.

He had to. Arguing with the man would have served

no purpose save to reveal far more than John dared. Such carelessness prompted him to curse himself as he strode toward the library.

This time he listened to the warning. Perhaps it was that look of amazement on the footman's face that alerted him to the danger. One servant might report that the earl asserted his authority, but as long as no one else corroborated such an outlandish tale, no damage would be done.

Still, it was not easy to slip into the old habit. The very difficulty alarmed him. It took conscious effort to slow his steps to a leisurely stroll when every muscle of his legs wanted to stretch out with some kind of strange exhilaration. He had to concentrate on each joint to relax it to that loose-limbed, stoop-shouldered gangliness that hid the truth.

Why? he wondered, entering the peacefulness of the library. Why was it suddenly so difficult to don a disguise that was, in essence, himself?

Lit by sunlight and warmed by a cheery fire, the room was quiet. Almost too quiet, he thought but blamed the sensation on the difference between the silent solidity of Kilbury that shut out all outside noise and the tumbledown ruin of the old Dower House that let in all the sounds of nature. And today there were no maidservants to giggle at his presence. Even so, he redoubled his effort to maintain the facade.

Looking for books to take to Elizabeth, he walked slowly about the room. No more sonnets; they belonged to the carefully cultivated John Colfax. He dismissed any curiosity about the motive that had driven him to make such a choice in the first place. She must expect—and receive—something quite different from Jack Silver.

He reached for a well-worn edition of *Moll Flanders*. A smile spread across his face as he opened the cover and read the inscription scrawled across the end papers. "To Jack, who has memoirs of many women of pleasure. Merry Christmas."

The last line was unrecognizable to anyone who did not know Ainsley Arlington.

They had enjoyed that last holiday at Oxford, Ainsley the wastrel fourth son of a wealthy marquess and John, the studious heir to Kilbury. Neither of them gave a thought to the future, expecting life to go on as it always did. It was Ainsley's idea that night, after a quiet dinner in the rooms they shared, to visit a pleasant little tavern. There was a girl Ainsley had his eye on.

John slammed the book shut and shoved it hastily back into its slot. He wished he could put his memories on the shelf as easily as a book. Just as the thought of Ainsley's sultry Oxford beauty brought Betsy to mind, so did Betsy remind him of Elizabeth. Or perhaps it was the other way around.

A fine, leather-bound edition of More's *Utopia* caught his eye. After ascertaining it contained no identifying marks, he tucked it under his arm and looked for at least one more. He had just leaned down to pull Walpole's *Castle of Otranto* from a lower shelf when shouts in the corridor stopped him.

He straightened, book in hand, and turned instinctively toward the door. Thomas's voice carried only a sense a panic, though his words were not yet distinguishable.

He burst through the library door almost exactly as he had burst into the Black Oak the night Jack Silver lifted his purse, but the feeling of smug satisfaction John felt that night was replaced with a sense of dread anticipation.

"So! There you are!" Thomas cried.

The expression on his face was an unreadable mixture of triumph and fear, as if he would be smiling if he were not so out of breath. But it was the feverish gleam in his eyes that sent a current of alarm along John's every nerve.

He refrained from the flippant answer on his tongue and said, "Of course, Uncle. Whatever is the matter?"

From inside his coat, Thomas retrieved a handful of papers. They were as neat as his person was disheveled, from his wrinkled clothes to his unshaven cheeks and uncombed hair. Slapping the documents on the desk by the fireplace, he opened a drawer and withdrew a quill and bottle of ink.

"Sign these," he ordered.

"What are they?"

John knew what they were without asking. He had seen their like too often before. There was little enough property still belonging to Kilbury that had not already been mortgaged, but Thomas obviously had found a few scraps. John wondered only what excuse his uncle had concocted this time.

He approached the desk slowly. Thomas, still breathing heavily, held out the pen and slid the papers toward John for his signature. The smile and the triumph behind it became more pronounced.

"I finally received Jack Silver's ransom request."

CHAPTER
16

And mortgages on Kilbury are the price of Elizabeth's release?"

He wanted the words back, but they were gone too quickly. Thomas, however, appeared not to have noticed the sarcasm. John struggled to bring his temper under control; it had never been so difficult before.

"No, you idiot, but how else am I to raise two thousand pounds?"

"Two thousand!"

For once he did not have to feign his shock. He had not taken the pen yet, and Thomas finally lowered the instrument to the desk.

"Yes, two thousand pounds, and I haven't got it," he said. "And before you ask why Stanhope himself doesn't put it up, it's because the stubborn fool thinks I had something to do with the kidnapping. He wants security."

There was more to the story, John knew, if only an explanation for Thomas's lies. But how much? And how long did John Colfax, earl of Kilbury, have to learn it all?

He swore softly, stalling for some of that time. Thomas's blatant request for the ransom at least assured John his uncle did not suspect him of involvement; Jack Silver's secret thus far remained safe. Edward Stanhope, however, was another matter, and there was always the possibility that someone else had seized upon the opportunity of Jack Silver's silence to fleece both Thomas and Elizabeth's father.

He must not act in haste. Making the wrong decision could seal his fate as certainly as signing Jack Silver's death warrant. He could, however, begin with a question or two.

"Have you the note?" he asked, blindly skimming the first of the documents.

"What note?"

"The ransom note from Jack Silver. I should like to see it." He lifted only his eyes to peer at Thomas over the lenses of his spectacles.

Thomas fumbled for the pen, an obvious ruse to cover his confusion. Nothing, however, could cover the steady reddening of his face. "I don't have it." He glanced away for only the briefest of moments, but it was enough. "I left it with Stanhope."

"But I thought you said you received it. Did Jack Silver not send it to you here at Kilbury?"

"What does it matter to you?" Thomas finally thundered, thrusting the quill at John. "Edward has the note and the two thousand pounds. And it is not as if she were *your* bride."

With the mask back in place, John met that furious stare and replied, "But it is *my* estate, Uncle."

Thomas showed no surprise as, calm returning, he leaned forward across the desk. "No, John, it is *my* estate to do with as I please. It has been for years, ever since your father put it into my keeping. You have no other heir, nor is it likely you will ever have one."

He ended his remarks with a scathing leer, clearly meant to cast doubt on his nephew's manhood. At that John took satisfaction. Whatever his earlier slips, he had not destroyed the carefully constructed image of John Colfax in Thomas's eyes. There was also the memory of Elizabeth, Thomas's bride-to-be, giving herself and her virginity so eagerly to Jack Silver. Even now that unlikely heir could be growing in her womb.

His confidence as well as his persona once more in place, he knew he had no choice but to sign the documents. Refusal, even hesitation, was out of the question.

"You wound me, Uncle," he said as he reached for the quill.

He would mortgage the last of Kilbury and perhaps the last of his pride, but if in doing so he bought himself a bit of precious time, perhaps all was not yet lost. And Thomas would pay. He would pay very dearly.

John dipped the nib in the bottle of ink Thomas slid forward and then neatly scratched his name and title on the bottom of each page.

The tub was small and cramped, but the water steamed with delicious heat. Though Elizabeth longed to stretch out and sink until the water reached her chin, she contented herself with a good scrubbing and the luxury of washing her hair with her favorite lilac-scented soap. When she emerged from the cooling bath, her skin was wrinkled and she had to flex her knees several times to relieve the stiffness, but she felt almost reborn.

She dried with the single towel, then walked to the table and turned up the wick on the lamp. For a moment, the light hurt her eyes, but she became accustomed to it more quickly than when the old woman first lit it.

And pain or not, the light was so welcome Elizabeth stared at the wavering flame in delighted fascination while she ran her fingers through her hair and wrapped the damp towel around it.

Light made the room less cell-like, and Elizabeth felt less trapped.

"Perhaps it is just another part of his scheme," she said aloud. "First he deprives me of all human comforts, then expects me to be grateful for each little kindness." She shook her head, which loosened the towel. "I cannot help but be grateful anyway."

She strolled to the bed, where the old woman had laid out clean underclothes alongside another pile of garments. These, too, had been freshly laundered, but Elizabeth had never worn shirts of dark, coarsely woven linen. They were Jack Silver's shirts, brought to her for mending. In the lamplight, she could not mistake the ragged tear down the front of the first.

She blushed and snatched a chemise over her head so hastily it tangled with the towel on her hair.

"In another week I shall be free of you, Jack Silver," she whispered as she dropped the towel to the floor. "I shall see sunlight again and come and go as I please." She smoothed the chemise over her hips, noting that the fabric had not been pressed. "My clothes will be properly cared for, too," she said slowly, unable to keep her fingers from straying to her belly or her mind from thinking the unthinkable.

What if she did not start her monthly course in a week's time? What if, despite all her denials and her refusal even to consider the possibility, she did indeed carry Jack Silver's bastard child?

Three words shivered from her lips. "It is possible," she whispered as she clasped the already wrinkled linen in her fists.

She finished dressing in silence, frightened silence. Thomas would never accept such a child, never, not at any price. His dreams utterly destroyed, Edward Stanhope would almost assuredly banish her, perhaps to the streets where he said he had made his own fortune.

But before Thomas could reject her or her father disown her, Jack Silver had first to release her. Would he if he knew she had conceived? Or would he condemn her to bear his babe as it had been conceived, in darkness and in solitude?

She sank down on the chair, her hands limp on her lap. Numbness, worse than any chill, seeped through her, for no matter what happened, only the most bleak future awaited her.

"If there is no child, and Jack keeps his bargain to return me to Stanhope, Father will have me wed to Thomas Colfax. I know it." Putting the thoughts into words made them even more horrible, more sickening. Yet she gained strength from the admission. "Is that why I begged to stay here, Jack?" she asked her absent captor. "Because I would rather never see the sunlight again than be forced to—"

She could not finish. The image of lying with Thomas Colfax as she had lain with Jack Silver brought the taste of bile to her throat.

Glancing around her at the tiny room that had become her entire world, she realized the four walls were less of a prison than the emotional dungeon that awaited her outside. She did indeed long to see sunlight again, but she had never truly been free to do as she wished. Her masquerades as Betsy Bunch were proof of that. For so many years she had felt trapped within the confines of Stanhope Manor, her life circumscribed by the limitations her father set for her. No suitors, no friends.

Only Thomas Colfax for one and Lord Kilbury for the other.

It was John, she recalled with sudden clarity, who had inadvertently planted the desire in her to escape that life, a desire that resulted in her begging Nell to help her create Betsy. Though she had known the heir to Kilbury almost since her birth, she did not become truly acquainted with him until after his father's death and John's return to the estate from Oxford. It had been a year or more since she had seen him last, and that first glimpse, at the funeral on a bitter, windy day in January, shocked her.

She remembered him as a handsome young scholar, tall and thin, with laughing eyes and a ready smile, though of course she was much too young to attract his attention. But that day, when he buried his father, there was something she at only seventeen noticed. Perhaps it was shock or the knowledge that he must change his own life forever. He looked hollow, empty, almost frightened. And when she saw him next, only a few months later, she hardly recognized him.

They established an odd friendship, though she had known even then that there was far more romance on her side of the relationship than was safe. John, perhaps because he was so much older than she, never seemed to notice her adoration. He talked of Oxford and London, of Paris and Rome, as if they were imaginary worlds instead of places he had been. He made her want to visit them, even while he painted frightening, intriguing portraits of the world beyond this rural tranquility and extolled the virtues of rusticating, of staying right here in Somerset for the rest of his life.

Elizabeth blinked and shook her head, sending strands of wet hair to stick to her cheeks. Why had she become so lost in those memories? And why was there a strange pang in her heart? John was happy, as happy as he could expect to be, she supposed. The responsibility of his title did not sit comfortably on his scholar's shoulders, and she admitted that of late he acted more and more preoccupied. But she could do nothing for him.

Nor did she dare sit and ruminate further. What

would be would be, and she was better off not encouraging madness by dwelling upon it.

She walked to the bed and picked up the highwayman's shirt to examine the long tear down the front. Mending was an infinitely practical activity, yet even that brought her predicament to mind. Was the wistful girl who had lain in the summer grass and read poetry with the earl of Kilbury also the wanton who tore the clothes from a seductive outlaw, who reveled in his sensuous mastery of her body, who clung to him in the breathless throes of passion and confessed that she loved him?

A shudder rippled through her. The fire had burned low while she bathed, and though the shimmering halo around the window remained midday bright, Elizabeth remembered it was still a wintry early March out of doors.

"It is as if the whole world has disappeared," she murmured, tossing the shirt onto the chair before she tended the fire. "I can hardly remember it."

One log followed another until the fire blazed, and she backed away from the heat, realizing she had piled too much wood on the coals.

"You could have set the whole place on fire," she scolded, using another piece to poke and rearrange the logs. "Best pay attention to what you're doing."

There was, however, no reason to waste the advantage of the delicious heat. Ignoring the shirt she was supposed to be mending, Elizabeth took her brush from the drawer in the wardrobe and settled herself in front of the fire to dry her hair.

The tangles were terrible. One by one she combed them out, pausing frequently to give her arms a rest. It was such a simple task when Nell did it, but then Nell did not have to reach up behind herself and tug at knots she could not see.

She set the brush in her lap and stared blindly into the flames. "Poor Nell, what has happened to you?"

Surely by now Nell had recovered from the effects of the drug intended for her mistress, but Elizabeth worried about other consequences. Edward might have dismissed the maid or worse. At least Nell had family to rely on. She might be disgraced, but she could always return to the Black Oak.

Elizabeth froze. If Nell had been dismissed and gone back to her family, would she reveal Elizabeth's secret? Would she tell Hennie and Mary and Robin that the laughing Betsy Bunch was in truth Elizabeth Stanhope, the spoiled heiress of whom they made such sport? There was always the possibility, too, that Nell might use her knowledge to blackmail Edward Stanhope. Appearances and reputation meant everything to him; he would do nearly anything to maintain them.

And what of the highwayman who frequented the tavern? Elizabeth recalled that first night when she had fallen on his lap in the cozy corner by the fire. She had recognized Jack Silver instantly, and she was certain he knew it. Had others? Was he, in fact, a regular customer of the inn, known and protected by its proprietors?

She shook her head and picked up the brush once more. Stroking the bristles through her hair slowly to still the trembling of her hand, she whispered, "They don't know him, else he'd not have hidden from Ned and Mary that night in the stable."

But doubts remained. Doubts and fears. For even if the rest of the Sharpe family did not know the silver-eyed traveler who warmed himself in the inglenook, Nell did, through Elizabeth's description, and Nell also knew the secret of Betsy Bunch.

John waited until Thomas was well gone, then swore long and softly with all the enthusiasm and inventiveness of a scholar. Mere words, however, could not effect a thorough ventilation of his anger and frustration. Rather than risk displaying his fury to any of Thomas's servants, he retreated to the confines of his room. On the way, he filched a decanter of Thomas's favorite brandy from the drawing room and made certain at least one footman saw him do so.

Thomas had given him no chance to read the half dozen or so sheets of foolscap, only time to sign his name at the bottom of each. And then the lying bastard had gathered them up and departed, shouting orders to have a fresh horse saddled for his ride back to Stanhope. Not even Jack Silver could catch him before he reached his destination.

"If you're counting on me to follow, Uncle, you'll be sadly disappointed," John said as he closed and locked the door.

He pulled the stopper from the decanter and poured a long swallow down his throat. The fine liquor burned first, then warmed. He waited until the warmth pooled, then swore again.

With long strides he crossed the room to the window and stared out at the clear bright morning that mocked his anger. He was exhausted. He had slept too little in the past week, and what sleep he got was often shallow and disturbed. But this latest disaster left him in a state of vibrant frenzy. He needed to *do* something to release it—and he could do nothing.

If he had had access to Thomas's study and the ledgers, this might not have happened. He would have known exactly how desperate his uncle's financial situation had become. But could he ever have imagined Thomas would resort to fabricating a ransom demand?

No, he admitted, he could not. He also admitted with no lessening of that burgeoning energy that he had been lucky in the past. At any point in the past four years, Thomas could have committed a similar folly. Only the confidence John's own image encouraged kept Thomas within his cold, calculating habits.

He would not allow four years of careful planning to be destroyed by a single moment of heedless anger, his own or anyone else's. With another swig of brandy to douse his fury, he began to bring his temper under control.

Though he wished he had been given the time to read the documents and determine precisely which properties he had signed away, it really did not matter. The deed was done and he could not, short of revealing his own secrets, have refused to sign. Whatever they might be, the few properties of the Kilbury estate that remained unmortgaged would not bring a thousand pounds on the open market, much less two. John knew it, and he had no doubts that Edward Stanhope, who was far more clever than he was honest, knew it as well. Thomas had to be supremely desperate.

Desperate men often made desperate mistakes. John toasted that possibility with another swig and turned away from the window, leaving the decanter on the sill. He had no intention of getting drunk. There was far more satisfaction to be found in pouring Thomas's expensive—and probably smuggled—brandy into a chamber pot.

Still, he felt the effect of three healthy swallows of potent liquor. He found he could flex his fingers without wanting to wrap them immediately around Thomas's throat. A few turns around the room worked some of the tension from him, so that when he returned to the chair by the window, he could stretch his legs out in front of him and lean back rather than perch on the edge, tense and ready for an imminent attack. He even managed to reach into his pocket and retrieve one of the books he had selected for Elizabeth's entertainment.

If the brandy helped him to gain control of his temper, it also released certain inhibitions. Running the fingers of his right hand along the spine of the

Walpole novel, he could not chase Elizabeth's image from his mind or erase the effect of that image on his body.

Elizabeth, dressed only in firelight. Elizabeth, naked against the pillows. Elizabeth, damning him in one breath and declaring she loved him in the next.

He wanted her. Now, here, in his house, in his room, in his bed. There was no reason why he could not have her. If not here, then he had only to return to the Dower House and the room in the tower, where she waited.

Drawing in a deep breath that came perilously close to a groan, he forced himself not to rise from the chair. No woman had ever tempted him the way Elizabeth Stanhope did, but he would not give in to that temptation. Not now. Not yet. There would be time later.

He smiled at the thought and reached for the decanter and one last swallow of brandy. No matter what capital Thomas raised from the mortgaging of those few pitiful scraps of Kilbury's once glorious estate, he would still be broken financially. Between Jack Silver's raids on Thomas's business associates and John's discreet investment of the proceeds of those raids, the man who had pillaged his brother's and then his nephew's inheritance would be lucky to escape debtor's prison. And though Edward Stanhope's wealth might buy Thomas's way out of gaol, it could not buy what only John was able to give freely: Elizabeth and a titled heir to the Stanhope fortune.

And how was Thomas to explain the failure of Jack Silver to return his victim after the payment of the ransom?

CHAPTER
17

The scrape of the door roused Elizabeth from a light doze. She glanced up from the book that lay open on her lap and tried half-heartedly to stifle a yawn while she wondered just how long she had been asleep and how she would explain such laziness to Jack Silver.

But instead of the highwayman, the old woman shuffled in as she had twice before since morning. This time she carried a large tray, like those used at the Black Oak for serving patrons. One by one, she set a number of dishes from it on the table, including a platter covered with a tarnished silver dome. Before Elizabeth had a chance to ask what special occasion merited such a feast, the silent servant leaned forward and snuffed the flame of the lamp.

The room plunged into darkness.

"What are you doing!" Elizabeth exclaimed in sudden panic.

She would have jumped from the chair and physically stopped the old woman from taking the lamp had not a voice from the doorway said, "My dear Elizabeth, you did not think I would let you have the light while I am here, did you?"

Once again, she was left blind, except that the frustration was greater now that she had had a day of respite. A wordless growl curled from her throat as he held the door open for the woman to depart with the lamp and empty serving tray in hand. Even the light from the corridor was dim in contrast to what Elizabeth had enjoyed, so that Jack Silver's silhouette appeared vague and more shadowy than ever. She blinked and rubbed her eyes in an attempt to bring her tiny world into focus again.

The door did not close immediately, and Elizabeth's attention was drawn to the sound of other footsteps entering her prison. The youth who had brought her bath now dragged a second chair into the room. Jack Silver followed, directing him to place the chair on the other side of the table from Elizabeth. For the space of a heartbeat or two, she wondered if she had a chance to escape with both men otherwise occupied and no one between her and the door.

The lassitude that had her nodding all afternoon left her no energy for a sprint out of the room and to whatever lay beyond. She discarded the idea almost as quickly as it came to her. And by then, the youth had backed his way to the door and her escape was cut off.

To break the silence that followed the closing of the door, she said, "I mended your shirts."

The highwayman stood in front of the fire that was once again the only source of light. Resting one forearm on the high, carved back of the chair, he leaned forward to pick up the single unlit candle from the table.

"I expected no less of you," he replied as he turned to touch the wick to a fiery coal on the hearth. "You have proven to be a singularly honorable captive."

Was he mocking her or complimenting her? Something, perhaps the very softness of his voice, told her he meant exactly what he said.

"I have tried to be. It seemed the wisest course."

He set the candle in its holder on the table and then strolled to the bed, where one of the shirts lay. He picked it up as though to examine her handiwork, though how he could see anything in the pitiful light escaped her. Still, she felt on trial and hoped he would find her work satisfactory.

Running a finger down the neat seam she had stitched, he nodded with what appeared to be approval. After spreading the shirt once more on the counterpane, he tossed another log on the fire and came back to the table. Now he sat down across from her, his long-limbed body seeming to flow into the ancient chair as if he were some barbarian potentate settling onto a throne. She watched him, waited for his verdict with her breath growing tight in her lungs and her fingers closing around the second shirt still draped over her lap.

He had, with his usual skill, placed the candle perfectly. It shed enough light to illuminate the meal, but the shadows it cast on Jack Silver's face turned his features to an eerie mask, frightening and yet hauntingly familiar.

"We feast tonight," he said, gesturing to the assortment of dishes. "Partridge for milady's evening repast."

"You're joining me?"

"Do not sound so horrified, my dear Elizabeth. Surely if you've no scruples against sharing my bed, you'll not mind sitting at the same table."

"No, I don't mind at all. I'm just surprised."

And wary. For all his bonhomie, she still sensed an edge in his voice. Jack Silver did not play the role of genial host well. He was almost as clumsy at it as the earl of Kilbury, though in an entirely different way. Perhaps that was why he chose to ignore her remark— or at least forbore to respond to it.

"You are quite skilled with a needle," he commented as he served her a portion of the crisply roasted fowl. "Perhaps I should keep you after all."

Something fluttered in Elizabeth's belly that had less to do with her ravenous hunger than with her own thoughts on her future.

"This morning you were only too eager to be rid of me. Surely our bargain alone has not changed your attitude." She gave him a puzzled glance, though she was not sure he could see her any better than she him. "Has something else happened?"

She was certain that something unexpected had caused his delay. The last hint of daylight had faded around the window long before she piled the fire high against the evening chill. It was blazing merrily when she nodded off after sewing the last button onto Jack's shirt. Now that blaze was an incandescent heap of coals, ready to be refueled. Her dinner—*their* dinner —was at least two hours later than usual.

"There is no danger to you, Elizabeth, and no more to me than I am accustomed to."

"But if you are in danger, then I am, too," she said, taking the plate he offered. Instead of the usual pewter, this was fine porcelain, nicked in two places on the edge but so thin and delicate even the firelight shimmered through. There was wine, too, poured from a dusty bottle that Elizabeth suspected came from the Kilbury cellars, pilfered perhaps the night Jack led her through them. He filled a glass for her, then another for himself. "What would happen to me if you were captured? Or . . . ?"

"Or killed?" He spoke the word too easily, like a man who either has given the possibility no thought at all—or too much. "I've left instructions, should that unlikely event occur. You must not worry about it, my dear. Now, a toast to tonight, to this moment."

He raised his goblet and she touched hers to it without thinking. The soft ring of crystal dispelled the momentary gloom, though Elizabeth noted that the glasses were of different patterns and that the base of Jack's was, like the china, badly chipped. She wondered where he had found—or stolen—them. Like the furniture, they must have come from a noble estate.

But she had no more time to speculate on the provenance of Jack Silver's table setting. The wine was crisp and cold, teasing her tongue as seductively as the glitter in his eyes teased her heart.

She set the glass down and picked up her fork. The first bite of rice, heavily laced with curry and herbs, melted in her mouth. It was all she could do not to gobble everything at once. With the beginning of an embarrassed flush warming her cheeks, she glanced up to see if Jack had noticed her gluttony.

She found him staring at her, a strip of partridge dangling from his fork.

"Have I done something wrong?" she asked.

"Not at all. I am glad to see your appetite so much improved. Or is it simply that you prefer this to plainer fare?" He popped the morsel into his mouth. "Alas, I cannot hope to compete with the likes of Thomas Colfax when it comes to setting milady's table."

Elizabeth nearly gagged. Thomas had served partridge at that dreadful banquet a week ago. She could not recall if she ate any of it then, but the serving in front of her lost a good measure of its appeal. The bite in her mouth tasted rank, too, but she managed to swallow it before saying, "I have told you before I would not care if Thomas Colfax choked to death on his own pigeon pie." To emphasize her words, she plunged her fork once more into the fowl and pulled off another strip. "I suppose this is poached from Kilbury land?"

"What little of it is left."

The edge to his voice was bitter, almost angry.

Again that odd sensation fluttered in Elizabeth's midsection. She recognized it now as a combination of expectation and triumph. Jack Silver never intended her to see his emotions so clearly. How much more might he reveal if she goaded him?

"Perhaps," she said as she brought the tidbit to her mouth, "if you did not poach so freely, the game would have time to replenish itself."

Waiting for his reply, she fastened her gaze on that glitter in his eyes and pulled the bit of partridge from the fork with her teeth.

"Ah, but it's not the game that's dwindling. It's—"

Elizabeth struggled to swallow, but her throat closed up. She snatched her napkin to her mouth and spat into it. Then she reached for the wine and took a most improper gulp in an attempt to wash away the lingering foulness.

She didn't realize until she set the nearly empty goblet down that she had broken into a cold sweat and that Jack Silver was staring at her with a very puzzled frown.

"Forgive me," she apologized, "but it—it tasted spoiled. Perhaps it had been hung too long."

He shoved his chair back, dangerously close to the fire.

"I snared that bird myself only yesterday. It was not hung too long."

The taint lingered on her tongue, and she tried not to think of the other piece she had swallowed. The curry and other flavorings to the rice had masked the taste of spoiled meat then.

"Then I think someone has tried to poison me."

John studied her, taking in the gleam of sweat on her brow, the trembling of her hand as she reached once more for the wine. Though he was certain the partridge had not been poisoned, he was equally certain Elizabeth was not lying. Nor, he realized with an odd sense of relief, had she accused him.

He walked around the table to stand behind her. It would have been just as easy to lean across the table to sample the meat he had given her, but he was afraid of revealing too much and not only because of the candlelight. He had never had so much difficulty disguising his feelings as tonight. He even realized, too late, that he had left the carving knife within her easy reach.

Resting his left hand on her shoulder, he reached over her right to spear the slice of partridge from her plate. One bite told him there was nothing spoiled about the bird at all.

She tilted her head back, and if he had not come to his senses quickly, she might very well have got a clear look at him.

Striding to his own chair, he said gruffly, "It's neither spoiled nor poisoned. If you don't like it, don't eat it."

Let her put it down to a highwayman's less than noble palate if she so desired, he thought as he poured her glass full once more.

She voiced no complaints about the wine, a fine old burgundy he found in the dungeonlike cellar beneath the Dower House. Twice she drained the goblet. Her appetite, however, faded. She toyed with the other food on her plate, eating only sparingly of the rice and artichokes. She did not touch the partridge again.

Nor did she speak or look up from the meal. Finished well before her, John poured his own glass full with the last of the wine and watched her.

Unlike him, she had no reason to avoid the candle's light. It fell full on her, accentuating the high curve of a cheekbone, the arch of a brow, the swirl of a tendril of hair that came loose from the simple coil atop her head. Envious of the way it caressed her jaw and curled down her throat, he wanted to smooth that strand back where it belonged. The thought sparked a glow in his loins until she hazarded a furtive glance in his direction and he caught the look of resigned terror in her eyes.

From the beginning, he had expected her hatred, so much so that he still found her passionate declaration of love impossible to accept. The Elizabeth Stanhope he carried in his mind would never have fallen in love with him. But she insisted she had, and the notion somehow pleased him that she might not be the creature he had so long imagined. Seeing her passion turned to fear, he felt the wine in his belly change to vitriol, burning with unbearable agony.

She had lowered her eyes again when he said as gently as he could, "I will not harm you, Elizabeth. You have my word."

"The word of an outlaw? A highwayman and a poacher? A kidnapper?"

"Have I ever lied to you?"

"You *are* a lie, Jack Silver!" Now she looked up, her eyes ablaze, her nostrils flared with fury. "Tell me who you are and why you hold me here against my will, and then perhaps I'll believe you when you say you mean me no harm."

She reached for her glass, but it was already empty. John poured the last dregs from the dusty bottle into it and watched as she downed it in a single gulp.

"Not against your will, Elizabeth. I will return you to Kilbury or your father's house tonight if you wish." He spoke slowly, soothingly, with little intonation. Whatever made her think the meal was poisoned, the fear had combined with the potent wine to make her irrational, the last thing he expected from her. Indeed, he had hoped the wine would relax her.

"You twist my own words against me," she railed at him. "You think that if I do not want one thing, then I must want another. It never occurs to you that *I* might want something entirely different, something you never considered."

She picked up the empty wine glass and would have

hurled it into the fire had John not caught her wrist. Holding her firmly, he took the crystal goblet from her and set it carefully on the table.

"You can be a damned destructive wench."

The fight went out of her, changed to a frightened quiver as he brushed his lips across her fingers.

"Can you not at least tell me why you've done this to me?"

The answer should have been so simple. The words were there, ready to mock her and everything she represented. But when he forced them out, they came with a rasp of desperation no less intense than hers.

"No, Elizabeth, I cannot."

"Then let me go. Dear God, let me go."

He need only loosen his hand around her wrist; he held her in no other way. Yet he felt the fever-heat of her. He wanted to crush that warmth and softness to him without layers of clothing between them. He wanted her naked and willing in his arms, not fighting him, not cringing from his touch.

"Let me go," she pleaded once more.

She tossed her head, sending that wild mass of hair down her back. He longed to tangle his fingers in it, to hold her still while he plundered her mouth with savage kisses. He wanted to feel those silken strands drift over his skin as he pulled her on top of him and plunged into the satin-smooth depths of her.

"No," he told her in a voice harsh with the effort to control a need he had never experienced before. He was aware of her hands resting on his shoulders, but he did not remember letting go of her wrist or even of walking around the table to take her in his arms and pull her tightly against him.

"Please, Jack, please," she whispered.

He watched her lips form the words, felt the softness of her breath against his own mouth.

"No, Elizabeth, I will not let you go."

The words became kisses he burned along her jaw

and chin. She tilted her head back even further with a frenzied moan that might have been his name. He pressed his mouth to the hollow at the base of her throat and let his tongue feel the wild beat of her pulse. Again she begged him, repeating that frantic plea over and over.

"Please, Jack, please let me go." Her hands tightened on the muscles of his shoulders, then slowly stroked up his neck. "For the love of God." He wondered if she knew she had threaded her fingers into his hair even while she implored, "Let me go, now, please!"

Her last was the cry of a woman as far gone in passion as he. He raised his head to give her the only answer he could.

Her eyes smoldered with unquenchable fire. She was free; he had wrapped his arms around her waist but it was she who held herself to him so tightly he could almost feel the sweet moistness of her. Yet still her lips moved with the silent denial.

At least he was able to give voice to his own, though that voice was hoarse and uneven. "No, Elizabeth, I will not let you go. I *cannot* let you go," he murmured as he let her pull his head down once more. "Never, never, never."

CHAPTER
18

From the instant Jack Silver gathered her into his arms, Elizabeth surrendered heart and mind, body and soul to the exquisite need he awakened in her. She had fought it as long as she could until his own confession of desire defeated her resistance.

He showered a dozen kisses on her eager lips while he carried her to the bed. With each kiss came another declaration, another promise.

"You are mine, Elizabeth." Another kiss. "All mine. Forever."

"Forever?"

"Forever. No one else shall ever have you."

He laid her facedown on the bed and quickly began to unfasten the buttons of her gown. There was neither nervousness nor hesitation in his sure fingers. Where she should have felt the cool air on her naked skin, he warmed her with heated words and more fiery kisses.

"I want you, Elizabeth." Kneeling beside her, he pushed the gown from one shoulder and ran the tip of his tongue from the nape of her neck nearly to her elbow. "Do you understand me? I want you, not because of Thomas Colfax or your father or—"

"Don't speak of it." She pulled her arm free of the confining sleeve and rolled to the center of the bed. She reached up her fingers to his lips to silence confessions better left unsaid. "I understand much more than you know."

He grasped her wrist and pressed a kiss to her palm with an intensity that both frightened and aroused her. Did he mutter a curse against her flesh? She felt the movement of his lips, the heat of his breath, but above the pounding of her heart she heard nothing.

She pulled away and wriggled out of the rest of her clothing while Jack removed his shirt. Stretched languorously naked on the bed and mesmerized by the gracefulness of his body silhouetted against the firelight, Elizabeth watched him.

"Hurry," she whispered.

He glanced over his shoulder at her. She detected a ghost of a smile in the shadows that were the planes and angles of his face.

"Impatient, are you?"

"Yes," she murmured, trailing her fingers down his spine. As he bent to pull off his boots, she flattened her palms on his shoulder blades to feel the play of the muscles, then stroked lower before she wrapped her arms around his waist and fumbled at the buttons on his breeches. Beneath the tight fabric he was hard and throbbing, and the thought that she could bring him to such need increased her own. Curling herself around him, she kissed the warm, slightly sweaty skin along his ribs. She tasted him with the tip of her tongue, even nipped his skin between her teeth.

He fell backward with a sudden gasp, breaking her embrace and pinning her to the bed with his shoulders across her belly. Before she could catch the breath he had knocked out of her, he lay atop her, his knees nudging hers apart until she cradled his length comfortably between her thighs.

"Now you are mine, Elizabeth," he declared in a passion-roughened whisper as she opened herself and took that sweet, satiny shaft deep into her soul.

She lost count of the number of times during the night she wakened to insistent caresses, to kisses at the back of her neck or a warm hand curled around her breast. Each time he apologized for disturbing her, but with his apologies came whispered words of seduction beyond her power to resist. And when, exhausted, she drifted into the dreamy euphoria that passed for sleep, his arms still held her within a warm, replete cocoon.

But she was not surprised to find herself alone when she opened her eyes to a room bright with lamplight. Nearly all trace of his presence had been erased; his clothes, including the two shirts she had mended, and the remains of last night's dinner were gone. Only the tangled bedclothes and the second chair by the table testified that it had not all been a dream.

Elizabeth blushed to think the nameless old woman had come into the room while she and Jack Silver slept twined naked in that tumbled bed.

She might have lain abed the rest of the day, sleeping away the exhaustion, had she not spied a breakfast tray on the table by the returned lamp. Though everything on it was probably stone cold, her stomach loudly informed her she had eaten little the night before.

Not bothering to look for her dressing gown, Elizabeth wrapped herself in one of the sheets and looped the trailing end of it over her shoulder. It smelled of sweat and sex, of Jack Silver and the shameless creature who yielded everything to him, of darkness and passion and unimagined delights, and she hugged it tightly to her breasts as she crossed to the table.

The tea was barely tepid. After pouring her cup half full, Elizabeth took the kettle to the fire to warm the rest. Whoever brought the breakfast tray had also cleaned the old ashes from the hearth and built up the fire as well as replenished the store of wood. Yet still Elizabeth shivered at the sight. She disliked the idea that Jack Silver was making her more comfortable here, that perhaps he meant exactly what he said last night.

"No, he was merely caught up in the moment," she scolded, staring into the dancing flames. "He cannot intend to keep me forever."

Putting the denial into words broke the spell. She drained the last of the now-cold tea in her cup, then strode to the washstand to perform a simple but thorough toilette. She let the sheet fall to the floor, unmindful of the chill. The water in the pitcher was cold, too, and rather than take the time to heat it, Elizabeth scrubbed her body unmercifully with an icy rag that would not lather. The afterglow of sexual satiety had faded to be replaced by grim reality.

Yesterday she had believed Jack Silver would release her when, as she fully expected to do, she presented proof that she did not carry his child. Now, curling herself up on the highwayman's massive chair to chew on a piece of stale bread and examine the two volumes added to her meager library, she was far less secure.

She tried to reassure herself with a stern "He gave his word. Do not thieves have a certain honor?" But deep inside her, doubt clung stubbornly.

To silence the doubt, she took *Utopia* from the table and opened it. At least it and the Walpole novel Jack had brought her last night were books she had not read before, and she could hope to be entertained.

But after a single page of More's imaginary ambassadorship to the Flemish court, she closed the book. "I would rather have more mending," she muttered, "than be reminded how small my prison is."

She had no idea what time of day it was, not even whether still morning or already past noon, though she suspected it was earlier rather than later. She did not feel as rested as she should have had she slept past the middle of the day. Perhaps, when the old woman came again, she could be prevailed upon to divulge at least the hour, though Elizabeth would not have wagered her hope of freedom on the possibility.

The kettle began to hiss. She filled her cup, this time glad the tea was hot. She considered taking up her own chair again, but Jack's was nearer the fire, and she preferred to have the lamp over her left shoulder rather than her right.

"Excuses," she told herself truthfully. "You want to sit in his chair because you won't give up stupid, useless romantic notions."

But she sat there anyway, almost as if daring her common sense to make her do otherwise.

"The man has ruined you," she went on mercilessly. "Even if he meant what he said last night—all that nonsense about 'forever'—whatever would you do for the rest of your life with an outlaw?"

She took another slice of bread from the tray and bit off a large chunk. For a moment that stopped her ramblings, but only for a moment. Yet almost instantly, other thoughts crept in, fears she had submerged beneath more obvious and immediate ones. Was a forever with Jack Silver any worse than a lifetime with Thomas Colfax? The instant she washed the stale, dry stuff down with a swallow of tea, the words began to tumble once more.

"He'll hang someday. Oh, he's clever enough not to have been caught so far, but they're all caught eventually, and they all hang." A nervous shudder rippled through her. In her mind's eye she saw the ghastly silhouette of a felon's body dangling from a crossroads gibbet. When the corpse swung toward her, she reached desperately for the other book. It would, she swore, keep her imagination occupied.

But haste and the hideous vision that refused to fade made her clumsy. The slim volume slipped from her fingers and fell noisily to the floor. It landed facedown and open with several pages badly creased. Mindful of how Jack had scolded her for her destructive tendencies, Elizabeth immediately picked up the book to smooth the damaged leaves.

Beneath it, knocked loose by the fall, lay a small rectangle of paper, its two ragged edges indicating it had been torn from the corner of a larger sheet. Not daring to hope it might reveal the identity of her captor, she raised the small vellum rectangle to the light.

"Kaspar Kennicott, Esquire," she read aloud. "A solicitor?"

The second line of printing gave a London address.

She did not believe Kaspar Kennicott, London solicitor, was masquerading as a highwayman in Somerset; the book, however, might have been stolen from him. Or, she admitted, lent or sold to the person who called himself Jack Silver.

Whatever the case may be, Mr. Kaspar Kennicott's informal calling card was the first clue Elizabeth had to unraveling the secret. It wasn't much, hardly anything at all really, but more than the nothing she had begun with. She was not, however, sure exactly what use she could make of the information.

"I cannot write Mr. Kaspar Kennicott and ask him if he is the notorious highwayman Jack Silver," she told herself with bitter frustration. "And certainly not until I am free."

Still, whatever the value of the solicitor's address, she had no intention of letting it fall into her captor's hands. After reading the address again and again and committing it to memory, she tossed the scrap into the fire. Flames curled around the paper for a second, as if it were immune to them, then suddenly it shriveled and flared into a bright tongue of incandescence. Only when it had been utterly consumed did she open the book again and begin to read.

Thomas did not return to Kilbury that night, nor did he send any message. John, not willing to arouse any suspicions among the staff, dared not leave when everyone would expect him to be awaiting his uncle's return. He contented himself with uneasy pacing in the library. From the tall windows he looked toward the distant wood and the ancient building sheltered there, but as darkness descended, the Dower House disappeared into shadows.

He continued to stare long after night had blotted out everything save his own reflection in the diamond-paned glass.

It was almost as if he could see her in that tiny room, waiting for him. Wrapped in the red dressing gown, with her hair loose about her shoulders, she was sitting in the chair, *his* chair, by the fire. Did she wonder why he had not come to her? Did she worry that he had been captured and dragged off in chains to be tried and convicted and executed for crimes he never denied committing?

He shook his head and rubbed tired eyes. His imagination was getting the better of him. He needed sleep, real sleep, and more than the few hours he had snatched after leaving her bed this morning. Damn the woman! He should be thinking of the questions he would ask her, the questions she had promised to answer in exchange for another week in captivity, not mooning like some lovesick schoolboy. What had she done to his carefully laid plans? What had she done to *him?*

"Are you quite all right, milord?"

John turned at the softly spoken question. Patton, the footman who had brought him the key to Thomas's study, stood just inside the library doors.

"I'm fine. Why do you ask?"

Even to his own ears, the words did not sound right. They did not belong to that other John Colfax, the one he had created so carefully over the past four years, a pliable, trusting soul who would never be so suspicious. He felt like a man fumbling in the dark for a flint to strike a candle and coming up empty-handed. That other self remained out of reach.

"I merely came to see if there was anything you needed. It's past midnight and the rest of the staff are abed."

"And you should join them. Heavens, I had no idea it was so late!" He nearly gagged on the words, but that sufficed to tell him he had once again captured the essence of that other John Colfax.

Forcing his body to assume an attitude of defenseless vulnerability, he turned from the window and walked toward the door. Patton backed away with a subservient bow, but when John opened the door, the footman hesitated.

"Are you not going to bed?"

"As soon as I draw the curtains, milord. Unless you need me to light your way?"

"No, I'll manage. Thank you, though."

He thought to slip down to the Dower House, justifying the action with worry that perhaps Thomas had unraveled the scheme and located his missing bride. Patton's attention, however, dissuaded him. Whether acting on Thomas's orders or on some devious purpose of his own, the footman was clearly a spy of some kind. Relieved only because he heard no footsteps following him, John climbed the stairs to his room. He did not mind the dark.

* * *

The day passed quickly, perhaps, Elizabeth surmised, because she had slept late. The night, however, was a different matter. Jack Silver had neither come to her nor sent a message explaining his absence, and she could not shake the uneasy feeling that crept into bed with her when she could no longer hold her eyes open. He was free to do as he chose, regardless of his bargain. He could hardly blame her for not keeping her part if he did not ask her the questions she had promised to answer.

Still, her dreams were unpleasant, though she could not remember them clearly upon wakening, and she faced the next morning with a deep-seated apprehension.

"I have no reason to worry," she told herself sternly as she dressed. Such one-sided conversation no longer felt uncomfortable. It was no worse than talking to the old woman who never replied with more than a single-word answer and often not even that. "Jack Silver has avoided capture for years, far more successfully than some of his more notorious brethren. If anything had happened, surely his servants would know."

Throughout the day, neither the old woman nor the youth showed any sign of a change in their circumstances or that of their employer. Elizabeth's meals arrived on schedule, water was brought for her washing and wood for her fire, even the lamp was kept trimmed and filled.

The monotony should have reassured her; it did quite the opposite. By nightfall, she did not know whether to scream in frustration or weep with fear. Unable to concentrate on a book or sit still for more than a few minutes at a time, she paced the tiny room. The whine of a rising wind in the chimney and the rumble of distant thunder that presaged yet another storm added to her agitation.

"He said I would be taken care of in the event

anything happened to him," she recalled. "And, damn his thieving soul to hell, why should I worry about him? He is an outlaw, a common felon who convicts himself with his own words."

But *how* would she be taken care of? By being returned to Thomas Colfax? As if to escape that eventuality, she stretched her strides out longer and longer; her already cramped quarters closed in on her. She came to the wall beside the door and pounded her fist angrily on the smooth old oak paneling until her hand hurt and her shoulder ached from the repeated shock.

"I am either a fool or a madwoman," she whispered, breathless from the exertion. She forced one measured breath at a time into and out of her lungs, but that did not slow the reckless pounding of her heart.

Yet even above that wild pulse roaring in her ears, she heard the approach of voices. She hardly dared to breathe in an effort to distinguish the speakers and what they said, to no avail. The wall and door were too stout, the oak too solid for words to penetrate.

Still she listened as they came closer and closer until finally she was able to determine that at least two people stood somewhere on the other side of her door. One of them was almost certainly the old woman, but no matter how hard she tried, Elizabeth could not identify the other. It might have been Jack, it might have been the silent youth, it might have been Thomas.

They stopped some distance from the door. For a minute or more, the conversation continued, the voices steady with no trace of anger or argument.

Two days and nights had passed since she last saw Jack Silver. Though nothing indicated he had fallen victim to any mishap, a flicker of Elizabeth's old rebellion flared. She would not sit idle, waiting to be transfered from one captivity to another.

She ran to extinguish the lamp and cast the room in murky shadows once more, then returned to flatten herself against the wall by the door. If she had become accustomed to the comings and goings of the old woman and the boy, perhaps they had become just as accustomed to her own acquiescence. Her escape could catch them by surprise and give her another few seconds' advantage.

More thunder rumbled, low and powerful. Elizabeth wriggled her toes inside her slippers. The flimsy footwear would do her little good if she succeeded in her escape, but they were all she had. Nor had she any cloak to protect her from the cold rain and wind. Even as she prepared to bolt, she accused herself of foolishness. The plain iron candlestand would have made a respectable weapon, but it was out of reach now and she dared not risk the few seconds needed to secure it. And to wield it she would have had to let go the heavy skirts she clutched out of the way so she could run as unencumbered as possible.

The scrape of the bar being lifted from the door went through her like a streak of lightning, energizing her. Foolish or not, she poised ready to sprint for freedom.

She waited only long enough for the ancient servant to enter the room. Before the other, unseen person could close the space between them or shut the door, Elizabeth butted her shoulder into the old woman's back. With a grunt, she stumbled; Elizabeth darted behind her, out the door and into the corridor.

A beam from a hooded lantern blinded her, but she did not stop. Squeezing her eyes closed against the brightness, she dodged the invisible bearer of the light. The passageway was so narrow she brushed against the wall. The collision slowed her flight by no more than a heartbeat, yet she knew the loss of a single precious moment meant the end of her freedom.

"Damn you, Elizabeth, what do you think you're doing?"

His voice was a whisper, hot with anger and something else. His hand was a vise on her arm, clasping her with such force that her own momentum spun her toward him.

He swung the lantern out of her reach and called to someone to take it from him before she knocked it to the floor and set the whole place ablaze.

She wanted to run away from him, into the dark and the night and the storm, and yet when he dragged her into a harsh embrace, she clung to him fiercely.

"I thought you'd been taken," she whispered, staring up into that shadowed, unreadable face. "I feared Lord Kilbury had hanged you."

CHAPTER
19

He wanted to laugh, but not at the absurdity of her fear. Instead he experienced a strange and unexpected delight so deep and dominating that for the moment it erased all those angers and hatreds that had followed him for so long. Harry worried about him and Peg, too, though neither of them would admit it, but that Elizabeth Stanhope feared for his safety brought a decided smile to his lips.

He quelled the laughter, but try as he might, he could not suppress the joy. He told himself there was a logical reason for her reaction.

Cradling her head on his shoulder, he stroked her hair comfortingly. The urge to kiss her and reassure her almost overwhelmed him. He resorted to sarcasm to dismiss that urge and asked, "Am I to take this unconventional greeting as a sign that you worried about me?"

For a long moment she said nothing, but he did not miss the slight stiffening of her body. Whether it was a warning that she intended to make another break for freedom or a reaction to his sarcasm, he took no chances. He nodded to a grumbling Peg, who muttered about being too old for such foolishness while she held the heavy door open. Though he could easily have lifted Elizabeth into his arms and carried her once more within the confines of her prison, he merely guided her, keeping one arm securely around her waist. She did not resist, yet he allowed himself no delusions as to her willingness.

Neither did he permit that sweet exhilaration to persist. It distorted his thinking, and more that than ever before, he needed his mind clear and sharp.

"You were foolish to try to escape, Elizabeth," he told her. "You have no idea the dangers waiting beyond this room."

The door closed, the latch clicked home. He relaxed his hold on her but remained cautious as she spun away from him and crossed the room to stand before the fire. If she was trying to lure him into the light, she failed.

"And just what are those dangers?" she demanded. "Can they be any worse than what I face right now?"

"I believe the understanding was that I would ask the questions."

She shook her head.

"You tricked me into making that bargain. You never had any intention to take me home."

"Are you so certain?"

"Why did you stop me just now? If you truly wanted to be rid of me, you'd have let me go."

"Perhaps I'm eager to hear the answers you'll give to my questions."

Again she shook her head. The long gossamer streamers of her hair danced in the light from the fire behind her and beckoned his touch. Only her acid retort kept him at his distance, but his fingers still rubbed together in anticipation. Damn it, why could he not stop wanting her?

She held her chin high and said, "If you were so eager, you would have been here last night."

"But you said you feared I had been, shall we say, detained. Do you no longer give me the benefit of the doubt?"

Unmoving, he waited. She did not alter her proud, defiant stance, but her silence told him the truth she could not disguise. She *had* been afraid and perhaps regretted exposing the depth of her vulnerability. She then used anger to try to cover her fear. Discovered, but not defeated, she drew in a sharp breath, then exhaled slowly. A mere nod of her head was her only admission.

"I'm genuinely touched at your display of concern, my dear Elizabeth," he said as he turned his back on her and reached to open the door, "but I suspect you were more worried about your own safety should I fail to return."

"No, that's not true!"

He heard her take a step, perhaps two, toward him, then she retreated. Her response was too spontaneous and too intense to have been anything but the truth, not at all what he expected. And certainly not what he wanted. The knowledge that he had succeeded in making Elizabeth Stanhope fall in love with Jack Silver should have given him a sense of smug satisfaction. Instead he tasted a triumph too bitter to savor, too sweet to trust.

The door handle grew slippery with the sweat of his hand upon it. A voice deep inside warned of risks and dangers more deadly than any he had encountered before. And for what reason? Did it matter whether she stayed with him of her own free will or not? That kind of surrender had never been part of his objective.

Besides, he reminded himself now that he no longer had that enticing image of her in front of him, he had accomplished exactly what he set out to do. Now that Thomas was ruined financially, Jack Silver could fade into legend. The real John Colfax, not the simpering oaf the twelfth earl of Kilbury had been for the past four years, would preside over a prosperous domain returned to its former glory.

John wondered why that future, which he had dreamed of for so long, suddenly loomed empty and hollow.

Then behind him Elizabeth began to laugh. He heard the first quiet chuckle clearly, only to have another booming roll of thunder drown it out. By the time the echoes faded, however, she was laughing uproariously.

He turned to find her doubled over, her hands on her knees. Uncontrollable giggles racked her, making the tousled curtain of her hair shimmer. She staggered to the nearest chair and dropped onto it with her face buried in her hands. For a moment he wondered if she were crying rather than laughing or if she had simply broken and gone mad.

But surely neither weeping nor madness could create such a delightful sound. This was the music of unbridled merriment, as bright as larksong after a storm. He had never heard her laugh before. A polite chuckle, perhaps, as on the day they had come upon those village boys in the pond. She had snickered a bit then, though probably at him for his overly pompous defense of her innocence.

An innocence he stripped from her. Her laughter mocked him and made him feel uncomfortably guilty.

"Have you taken leave of your senses?" Good God, he sounded as pompous as that popinjay nobleman!

She wiped away tears, leaving moist streaks that gleamed in the firelight. A broad grin lit her face as she struggled to contain even more mirth.

"Not I, Jack Silver," she managed to declare before an irrepressible giggle escaped her.

And she was laughing at him. He knew it by the way she flipped her hair back from her face and glanced sideways, her eyes sparkling with secret amusement. Her devilish smile both taunted him and beguiled him.

Again she curbed the laughter, though with obvious effort. She closed her eyes and leaned her head against the chair—*his* chair—to take slow, deep, calming breaths.

Her lips still curved in a mystery-laden smile, she told him, "You don't even realize it now, do you?"

"Realize what?"

"No, of course you wouldn't. It was the last thing you ever expected to happen." She sighed and turned her head just enough to give him one of those bewitching sidelong glances. "Now it *has* happened, and you simply do not know what to do about it."

This had gone far enough. The woman had lost her mind. He should have recognized the signs days ago. First she threw a childish tantrum and tore her clothes to shreds, then accused him of poisoning her with one of the finest partridges ever taken from Kilbury's woods. Now, with no provocation, she was laughing hysterically and talking in nonsensical riddles. Much as he hated to do it, John admitted his only choice was to instruct Peg to bring the bottle of laudanum-laced wine. In the morning, his captive would waken in her own bed at Stanhope Manor. It was not the ending he had envisioned to this part of his scheme, but neither did he want a madwoman on his hands.

He pulled the door open only to have her tell him, in a low, throaty whisper, "You can't run away from it, Jack."

He slammed the door with a force equalled only by the window-rattling thunder. "What the devil are you talking about?" he roared above the storm and watched as Elizabeth rose from the chair and took a single step toward him.

"You've fallen in love with me, Jack Silver. No, don't try to deny it," she admonished. "I've already recognized your symptoms, for they are the same as my own."

For several electrified seconds, neither of them spoke, and Elizabeth hardly dared to breathe. She had taken an enormous gamble not only in revealing her suspicion but in taunting him with it. It was a chance she had to take if she hoped to uncover the truth. Though she was not yet certain she had won the wager, her heart, pounding as if it would burst, finally resumed a more normal pace when she realized he had chosen not to leave.

She never expected him to capitulate easily. No man as fiercely independent as a highwayman who had eluded capture for almost four years would readily admit to having been emotionally seduced by his own victim. So his derisive bark came as no surprise. He had similarly dismissed her own confession.

"You confuse lust with love, my sweet."

She arched one brow and walked closer. "Do I? Then why are you so torn between letting me go and keeping me here?"

One more step and she would be close enough to insinuate herself into his embrace. The bar on the outside of the door had not been shot home. She did not for one second believe this was due to any lapse on his part. He may have succumbed to the purely human frailty of love, but she doubted he would ever let something so unimportant rob him of the caution that had served him so well over the years.

She had no real hope of being able to escape, but if she managed to open the door and gain a quick glimpse at what lay beyond, she might be able to add some scrap to her minuscule repertoire of knowledge about the place where she was being held.

The difficult part would be tearing herself away from him long enough to drag the door open. Nearness to him had a way of making her forget nearly everything else.

"It is not a matter of being torn, but rather of weighing the alternatives and their consequences," he said, answering a question she had almost forgotten asking. "For instance, now that Thomas has raised a ransom, I have to consider whether or not to take it. And if I do, shall I let him have you or double-cross him?"

Another blast of thunder shook the very floor beneath her feet. It was nothing compared to the shock that reverberated through her with the echo of his words. Her knees went so weak she was afraid she would fall, but she could not bring herself to lean on him for support. Neither, however, could she back away.

"But you said you asked no ransom. Is this yet another of your lies?"

"No, Elizabeth, not a lie at all. I asked no ransom, nor has Thomas offered one. I only said he has raised the money on that pretext."

"But why would he do such a thing? Surely when I am not returned—"

It made no sense at all, not even enough for her to complete a speculation. She waited for him to give her an explanation; she got only a stony stare from eyes turned to gold by the reflection of the fire. He had given her all he intended, which was enough to raise questions and increase her already monumental confusion.

She pivoted slowly away from him, aware she might never have such a perfect chance to get a glimpse outside that usually barred door. Had he guessed her intention and made up the ransom story to keep her from the attempt? In one respect, she had to admit, he was right; she had no idea what danger lurked beyond her prison. Then again, perhaps he was merely manipulating her. Frustrated, Elizabeth let out an explosive "Damn!"

The highwayman said Thomas had not offered the ransom. Then how did Jack know of it? His intimate knowledge of Kilbury Hall implied he had spent some time within its walls, and again Elizabeth considered the possibility that he was a servant, but again she dismissed the notion.

She glanced over her shoulder at him. He remained every inch a puzzle. He was no lackey, nor was he one of the local villagers or farmers. Whether as Elizabeth Stanhope or Betsy Bunch, she knew the inhabitants of her limited world too well, and none of them bore the slightest resemblance to the man standing between her and the door.

Then she remembered the card that had fallen from the book. Perhaps Jack Silver *was* Kaspar Kennicott after all.

She envisioned this man a bewigged barrister, defending innocent clients or prosecuting the guilty with impassioned eloquence; no stretch of her imagination could picture a stodgy solicitor in some musty, dusty office. Curiosity, ever a force to be reckoned with, urged her to confront him with her scrap of secret knowledge. She bit her tongue and said nothing.

At last it was he who broke the silence. "Shall we get on with it, Elizabeth? You did agree to answer my questions, and I do not have all night."

The sarcastic words demanding to know what he planned to do on a cold and stormy night nearly choked her in their race to leave her throat, but before she could form the question, she had her answer. He had said he needed to consider whether or not to take the money Thomas had raised.

"Good heavens, you're planning to steal my ransom money, aren't you?"

He had the nerve to shrug, fold his arms across his chest, and say, "The idea crossed my mind, yes. But whether I do or not is really no concern of yours,

Elizabeth. It will not affect my plans for you. That said, shall we get on with *our* business?"

Whether he acted upon the idea or not that night or any other, Elizabeth was unable to learn. Over the next several days, whenever she broached the subject of the ransom, Jack either ignored her or caustically reminded her it was none of her business. She began to wonder if the tale were true or if he had made it up only to torment her. At least he came every day, sparing her the worst agonies of worrying.

He followed no schedule. He appeared one night just as Elizabeth sat down to her dinner, the next day in the middle of the afternoon, while she was reading. One morning she wakened to find him sitting in his accustomed chair, calmly pouring himself a cup of tea, as if he had been waiting for her all night. Some days he even visited her twice, with the result that she never knew from one minute to the next when to expect him. She became ever alert for his footsteps outside her door, and concentration on anything while he was gone became virtually impossible.

While he was there, he asked questions, dozens of them, but they, like so much about him, made no sense. Most concerned her father's business associates, about whom Elizabeth knew very little beyond their names. He displayed no surprise at her answers, as though he knew them almost before she did. She suspected she in fact told him little he did not already know.

By the same token, he imparted virtually no information to her. Day after day, she racked her memory for any detail she had overlooked, the one clue that would unravel the entire mystery. She knew it was there somewhere, eluding her as craftily as Jack Silver himself had eluded the keepers of the law.

Of one fact she was certain, however, and it gave her both a sly satisfaction and a secret hope. Whoever hid behind Jack Silver's masquerade, that man had indeed fallen in love with her.

If she had not confronted him with her suspicion, and if he had not sidestepped his retort, she might have held some doubt. But as the days passed and he took such blatantly obvious care to avoid her touch, yet at the same time studied her with naked desire in his eyes, that satisfaction grew. Sometimes she tested him, drawing out her answers with silences so long she was sure he would forget the question. And invariably he had.

She was, however, running out of time. Though the individual days passed with unbearable slowness, before she knew it the week was gone. On the one hand, she faced that last day with some relief, but much less than she had anticipated. On the other hand, she discovered an inexplicable fear of leaving this tiny, dark chamber and reentering the real world.

"You're a fool," she muttered over the usual breakfast of bread and tea. Around the window the soft light of an overcast day gleamed. "You should be ecstatic at the prospect of finally seeing the sky again, rainy day or no."

But it was not the weather alone that affected her mood. She had recognized the familiar signs two or three days ago, the tenderness in her breasts, the ache across her lower back. She had told him that within another day, two at the most, she would have the proof positive that she carried no child. That, too, should have given her relief, but she discovered herself on the verge of tears at the very thought.

She scolded herself sternly. "Not only a fool, but a stupid one. At least without a child to give testimony to what has happened here, you may be able to put the pieces your life together."

A shudder passed through her, and an insidious dread curled like nausea in her stomach. To exorcise it, she rose and tossed the dregs of her tea onto the fire.

Steam and sparks exploded up the chimney, taking with them on their flight Elizabeth's own dregs of worry and doubt.

When Jack first allowed her the lamp, she had promised herself to explore the room as she had not been able to do with only a candle. With perhaps only hours left to do so, she resolutely turned up the wick and began a minute examination, from the dark corner beyond the hearth to the wall behind the wardrobe.

She checked every stone of the fireplace but found none loose. She stroked her hands over every inch of the ancient oak paneling in search of a spring mechanism or other device, but no sections of the walls shifted to reveal secret passages or hidden doors.

Balancing on a chair, she lifted the light high to check the shutters over the window. They could not be pried loose, nor could she see a single thing through the tiny cracks, no matter how she squinted or angled her head. She even let the fire die almost to nothing so she could look up the chimney. It, too, provided no means of escape or clue to the location of the building that served as her prison.

She gave up her investigation only moments before the old woman brought the midday meal. There was no difference in the servant's behavior, but Elizabeth felt the woman's dark eyes on her every second of that brief visit. Did guilt visibly alter her features? She refused to let it affect her; she waited patiently, an open book on her lap as if she had spent the morning reading, and did not let that audible sigh of relief escape until the elderly woman had closed the door behind her.

Then she immediately resumed her exploration, beginning with the furniture. All the pieces were old and heavy, but if a single clue was there to be found, she would find it.

With more determination than strength, Elizabeth

pulled the massive wardrobe away from the wall to examine both the back of the wardrobe and the wall itself. She found nothing. A search of the drawers and doors and shelves likewise proved fruitless. There were no secret compartments, no false bottoms, no clues.

After crawling out from under the bed, where she had gone in search of hiding places beneath the floor as well as beneath the mattress, she sat down and rested her head against the ancient footboard. "Even if I discover nothing now," she consoled herself with a disappointed sigh, "I shall know every detail of this room. I shall be able to provide such a description that surely anyone who has seen it will recognize it instantly."

It was small consolation but better than nothing. And though she ached with exhaustion and looked over her shoulder at the bed with a distinct desire to sleep, she knew she had only hours, perhaps only minutes, before Jack Silver returned.

She cursed her failure to make this search earlier, but there was nothing to do for it now. She got to her feet and wiped her dusty hands on her skirt. Jack's heavy, thronelike chair was the most recent addition to the furnishings and offered the most possibilities. Elizabeth strode purposefully toward it and with no hesitation tipped it over to examine the underside. She set the lamp on the floor and turned up the wick.

Like the rest of the furniture, this chair was intricately carved, even under the seat. Elizabeth became so intrigued by the myriad swirls and curves cut into the dark wood that she did not hear the footsteps approaching in the corridor until too late. Before she could scramble to her feet or right the chair, the door opened.

"What are you doing?" the old woman asked.

Struggling to untangle her skirts, Elizabeth stammered half a dozen incomprehensible bits of gibberish no one would take as answers. Not that Jack Silver's servant cared; as though she relished the prisoner's discomfiture, she marched into the room and picked up the lamp. Elizabeth had not even a second to protest before the old woman snuffed the light. Blinded, she looked up as another shadow moved in the darkness. She made out the silhouette in the doorway.

"Our final night," he said.

CHAPTER
20

He never spoke of the time of their parting. Although Elizabeth counted the days in her heart, she found that hearing the words from Jack himself made the reality undeniable.

And unbearable.

Three strides brought him to her. With one hand he lifted the overturned chair and set it on its legs again. For a moment he stared at her, making her feel an odd combination of fear and arousal. Warmth pooled deep in her belly and then even lower, and her nipples hardened as though he had already stripped her naked. She wanted to back away from that unreadable glitter in his depthless eyes, yet she found herself drawn even closer by the same mesmerizing power.

"Destroying my possessions again?" he asked as he sat down.

Shaking off the effects of that momentary insanity, Elizabeth tilted her chin defiantly and replied, "No. I was looking for something."

If seated he was forced to look up at her and the intimidating strength of his stare lessened, she now squirmed with guilt she had no reason to feel. Damn the man! He played such havoc with her emotions she could scarcely think.

"And what did you expect to find on the bottom of an old chair?"

Why must he mock her at every opportunity? Was it not enough that he could strip away her emotional resistance with a single word and seduce her with a glance?

"I honestly do not know, but if anything would give me the slightest clue to your identity, Jack Silver, I'd be sure to spot it."

He raised a dark eyebrow and stretched his feet toward her until the toes of his boots touched the hem of her gown, then asked, "Did you find such a clue?"

The words of denial almost escaped, but Elizabeth contained them. If she did not control her wayward tongue, she would soon have no secrets left.

"I'd be foolish to tell you if I had, wouldn't I?"

Though his smile did not alter, he nodded in acknowledgment of her cleverness.

"Shall I fear for my life tomorrow when you are returned to your father and Thomas Colfax?"

That second reminder of their impending separation and what awaited her sent a shiver through her, but she would not let him have an easy victory. Two could play this cat-and-mouse game, and Jack Silver had been an excellent teacher. Turning from the highwayman's steady gaze, Elizabeth held out her hands to the warmth of the fire before she said, "Perhaps you should."

His silence told her that arrow hit its mark. She nocked another and let it fly.

"Perhaps you take too much for granted."

"Perhaps I do."

The chair creaked a warning as he stood but too late to help her. She spun around, hands raised in tightly clenched fists to ward him off, only to have her wrists immediately clamped in his inescapable grip and then trapped behind her as he brought her body roughly against his.

Holding her, no longer able to deny the effect she had on him, John fought to retain the last shreds of a control he had thought never to lose. This desire for her was like a disease for which there was no cure; at times during the past week he actually made himself believe he had recovered until he saw her again, heard her voice, smelled that gentle essence of lilacs and woman, watched the subtle and seductive movements of her body. Each day, each night, the effort to resist the temptation drove him to the brink of madness. Now, as he leaned over the precipice, he knew surrender would not save him.

"Do you accuse me of taking *you* for granted, Elizabeth?"

"Yes!" she spat.

"A few days ago you accused me of having fallen in love with you."

"I was wrong."

No, you were right, he wanted to tell her, but she gave him no chance. Words tumbled from her lips just inches from his own. He could have kissed her to silence, but he did not.

"And I was a fool to think I had fallen in love with you. The man I fell in love with existed only in the dreams of a silly girl who believed marriage ought to have something to do with romance. She did not love or even like the man she agreed to wed, and so she sought another."

Something was wrong with her confession. Like too many other things about this woman, it was unlike anything he expected. She herself was unlike anything he had expected, from her wanton passion to this savage self-deprecation. Each time he tried to force the real Elizabeth into that image of the selfish, greedy, heartless bitch, a part of her refused to fit, until what he saw now bore no resemblance to the woman he had stolen from Kilbury Hall a mere two weeks ago.

"I never thought I'd come face-to-face with you, Jack Silver. At times I suppose I considered you a figment of my own imagination."

Was she, in turn, a figment of his imagination? No, not unless the sweet ache of arousal was a dream as well. Oh, dear God, why could he not stop her words and bend her body to his will? Because, he knew with frightening clarity, he did love her, and the satisfaction of lust alone would never be enough.

And she could never love him. He could not let her.

"Reality rarely lives up to our dreams," he told her, surprised at the steadiness of his voice. "If it did, we'd have no need for dreams."

She laughed but without that joyous music he remembered. And her eyes that had twinkled with merry tears reflected only bitterness. She did not blink as she said, "Ah, you ape the romantic, Jack, despite what we both know to be truth."

"Do we *ever* know the truth? Or do we simply choose what we want to believe and all the rest is lies?" Letting go her wrists, he slid his hands downward from her waist to bring her more intimately against him. She uttered a little gasp, nothing more, but made no attempt to escape. "I want you, Elizabeth, and that is truth. Why I want you, I do not know. Love? Lust?"

He shrugged, a simple flexion of the muscles of his arms and shoulders that in other circumstances would have done nothing more than indicate his lack of an answer to his own questions. But with Elizabeth nestled between his thighs and his hands still curved around her buttocks, that innocent gesture increased the intimacy.

"At least," he whispered, daring to lower his head so that his mouth was no more than an inch from hers,

"I do not deny wanting you. Will you deny that you want me when I can feel the heat of you?"

"Damn you." Even her curse was breathless with arousal, but she stared at him with eyes wide and clear. "I swear, if ever you do release me, I will hunt you down and make you pay for everything you have done to me, Jack Silver. Everything."

This was no idle threat. He read the implacable determination, colder and harder and more deadly than mere hatred, in her eyes. Because she did not hate him. The love he saw beneath the determination served to twist the pain inside him into agony almost beyond bearing.

"Then perhaps I shall never release you."

He permitted her no reply but captured her open mouth with his. She stiffened in his arms, and even her lips tightened with resistance. But the passion of her would not be denied. He felt it in the way she moved against that throbbing hardness he pressed to her belly, in the way her hands clenched into fists at his back and then slowly relaxed.

Just as slowly and just as surely as her resistance melted, so the idea of making her his wife, once voiced in jest, began to insinuate itself into his thoughts.

At first he dismissed it as insane, so much so that he withdrew from the addictive honey of Elizabeth's kiss to stare down at her.

No, he had not lost his mind. Lips moist and parted and swollen, eyes dreamily half closed, nostrils flared with each gasping breath, she was more beautiful than he ever imagined. The woman he had watched while she sat beside Thomas Colfax at her betrothal dinner just two weeks ago had been beautiful, too, but *that* Elizabeth Stanhope had not aroused in him the kind of insatiable desire he felt now.

He had lost his heart, and at a time when he could

not afford to do so. Damn! Why did he not simply tell her the truth? Surely she would understand.

Once he had seen a stallion nearly kill himself trying to jump a fence that separated him from a mare in season. If he thought this Elizabeth, the one who looked at him now with passion-glazed eyes and whose hands were tugging his shirt free, would understand—and forgive—his actions tonight, she would also understand them tomorrow or the day after when this four-year-long nightmare came to an end. And if not, if she were in truth the schemer, the liar, the heartless creature who had sat like a marble goddess for her wedding portrait with Thomas, then the secret of Jack Silver would remain safe.

For tonight, however, she was his.

He lowered his mouth again to hers and began unfastening those damned buttons.

"When?"

The single word, though whispered as softly as Elizabeth knew how, echoed in the darkness. She had tried to find the right words to ask the question, but every phrase seemed wrong until finally only the one word mattered.

The man lying naked beside her, his arm around her shoulders to cradle her head on his chest, murmured the answer she dreaded.

"Soon."

She sighed and curled more tightly against him. She felt him stroke her hair, tangled now beyond redemption, and then softly kiss the top of her head.

A strangled sob knotted her throat, but she gathered what little remained of her pride and forced it down. Neither taunting nor threats had moved Jack Silver, and she was certain he believed nothing she said. Why should he? She had contradicted herself so many times even she was not sure of the truth. Any tears she shed would only be those of self-pity. She had been, from the very start, the outlaw's willing victim, and he had taken complete advantage of her. He would release her minus not only her virginity and her heart but her self-respect.

"Then perhaps we should go now," she said, "before . . ."

"Before you tempt me to make love to you again?" He laughed, this time the gentle laugh of a lover. "You already tempt me, Elizabeth. You make me wish I could indeed keep you forever."

At least there was that much truth between them.

"Is there no way, after—after tomorrow, that we could be together?" she dared to ask and immediately wished the words back.

She thought his heart, so strong and steady beneath her ear, missed a beat, but it might have been an echo of her own. The rhythm resumed, no faster, no slower.

"Tell me of a way to enter Stanhope Manor without being caught," he replied with a chuckle that sounded more nervous than amused.

Now it was indeed her heart that skipped and started. Damn him! Would he use even her final, desperate grasp at a moment of romance to further his thievery? Besides, he knew of Betsy Bunch's comings and goings through the garden gate. It was a wonder she hadn't heard servants' gossip about some trades-man seeking the maid.

She could not hide the bitterness in her voice. "There is none any more. I discovered one of my maids sneaking out to meet with some rascal late at night and cut off her means of escape."

"Did you turn the worthless slut out into the cold without a character?"

He spoke so easily, with so little emotion, that she almost believed he had completely forgotten poor Betsy. Except for that mention of turning her out into the cold. He remembered, and Elizabeth grasped at that memory.

"I considered it."

"But you didn't?"

"No, I didn't."

If she had not had her head on his chest and her hand on his belly, she would not have known he sighed.

"And what of the rascal she trysted with? Was he discovered, too?"

Elizabeth almost laughed.

"No," she said with an exaggerated sigh. "She claimed he was just a traveler she'd never meet again, though I doubted her story, for she painted such a wildly romantic picture of him." She added a disdainful sniff for emphasis. "As if he were a knight in shining armor on a silver steed instead of an itinerant peddlar, if he was even that."

"I do believe you are jealous of the poor wench because your own romantic bubble has been burst, Elizabeth."

John yawned and stretched with exaggerated arrogance, then rolled away from her to sit on the edge of the bed, ignoring the little yelp that squeaked from her at his rude departure from her embrace. The way his fingers trembled as he raked them through his hair alarmed him, but a few deep breaths brought him back to normal. The fire had died an hour or more ago, and nighttime chill set in; he welcomed it to cool his blood and clear his head.

He had not meant to waste so much time in her bed. And it would be so easy, so delightful, to spend the rest of the night with her. Even now, after making love to her twice with more passion and abandon and pleasure-prolonging restraint than he had thought a human being could endure without going mad, he felt the familiar tightening in his loins again. No, the time had not been wasted; he had no regrets. As he began the fumbling search for his clothes, he knew he could never have denied himself—or her—these final hours. Neither, however, could he deny that time had run out.

"What are you doing?" she asked, a silken voice in the darkness behind him.

"Getting dressed. I'll give you some privacy to do the same while I fetch us a late supper. And then it'll be time." He wished he had been less blunt, but the words needed to be said if he were to convince himself of the reality.

It was all much easier once he left the room. In the narrow corridor lit only by a guttering candle in a pewter dish, he breathed deeply of air that did not smell like Elizabeth. Then he dropped the bolt securely across the door and headed down the stairs.

Harry was waiting for him, asleep in one of the great chairs that nearly swallowed the wizened old frame, but waiting nonetheless.

"I wondered what happened to ye," he asked, wakened in the middle of a snore by the sound of John's boots on the flagged floor. "Ye've not changed yer mind, have ye?"

"Have no fear, Harry. She goes home tonight. Is everything ready?"

Harry nodded and slipped out of the chair to limp to the fire where a pie warmed on the grate. "Aye, it's ready. The horse is saddled and, from the looks of him, impatient. Ethan's been to the Black Oak, says it's quiet. Only Ned's nags and two others in the stable."

He lifted the pie gingerly to the tray on the table where dishes and silverware as well as a dusty bottle of wine were already laid out.

"Excellent," John said. "Enough to bring someone to the stable in the morning, but not too crowded." He leaned over the steaming pastry to inhale the savory aroma. It stirred an almost forgotten appetite. "More of Thomas's pigeons?" he asked with a sly grin.

"Ye told Peg to help herself, milord. An' she did 'em

proud, too." The old man smiled, then frowned with a upward nod of his head. "That one upstairs best not be complainin' about this dinner. There be nothing wrong wi' Peg's pigeon pie."

Indeed there was not if the rumblings from John's stomach were any indication.

"I'm quite certain there isn't. Now, what about the wine?"

"The powder's in the goblet, just like ye said."

By the light of the candles on the table, John could barely see the tiny pile of white dust in the bottom of one of the two tarnished silver goblets. In the darkness of the tower room, Elizabeth would never see the drug. And as long as he kept it diluted by adding to her wine, she would drift gradually into sleep, allowing him ample time to ask the last—and most important —of his questions.

He felt an odd reluctance to take this final action, though he knew of no alternative. Harry must have sensed that hesitation, for he said, "It's all but over now, milord. And I must say, it's gone far better that I would ever have guessed when ye started this wild scheme. 'Tis fair to say I might even miss ol' Jack Silver."

"Not I, Harry, not I." He stared into the goblet and longed for the respite of dreamless sleep. He could not remember when he had last enjoyed that luxury. "I'm tired of the lies, of one damned masquerade in the dark, another in the daylight. Sometimes I can't remember who I really am or which role I'm playing."

"Ye never had that trouble before."

Harry's accusation could not have been more clear.

"Taking her was a mistake, I admit," John said calmly. Hefting the tray himself, for Peg had long since gone to her own quarters, he thought again of Betsy Bunch at the Black Oak, with her ready laugh and frightened kisses. "I should have settled for the sapphires. But what's done is done."

He wondered, climbing the stairs and wending his way through the mazelike corridors of the upper floors, if he ought to have told Harry about the idea that came to him in those last moments before he left Elizabeth's bed, the idea of asking her to marry him. No, there was nothing the old man could do, and he would only ask a hundred questions for which John had no answers.

At least Betsy had not been turned out of her position at Stanhope. There was nothing he could have done to save her from that all-too-common fate. Elizabeth's future, however, he did have some control over, if not as Jack Silver then as John Colfax, Lord Kilbury. And perhaps more than just "some."

Elizabeth closed the lid on the trunk and fastened the brass latches with a series of sharp clicks. She had neatly folded and packed all her clothes, even though Jack had said nothing about her taking them. If she had to leave everything behind, it would not matter, but packing gave her something to do while waiting for his return.

With a sigh, she sat down on the trunk and gazed about the room. Her captivity had, if nothing else, given her a new appreciation for small pleasures.

"I shall climb stairs again," she said with a wistful laugh. When her stomach growled, she added, "And I shall order what I like for dinner."

She glanced toward the table where she had shared so many meals with her captor and lover. Two candles flickered there now, beside the stack of books he had brought her. The dark, lonely hours pressed in on her even as they were about to end. Why then, she wondered, did she dread stepping beyond that barred door? Freedom awaited her.

"I shall walk in the sunlight until my nose is covered with freckles, and I shall dance in the rain at midnight," she told herself firmly to dispel all those gloomy thoughts. "I shall go to London and visit the king."

No, not the king, a small voice inside her whispered. *I shall go to London and find Kaspar Kennicott.*

"You've hardly touched your food. Are you not feeling well?"

Elizabeth glanced up sharply at the highwayman's question. Had she only imagined the hint of expectation in his voice? She read nothing in his features, for he had placed the candles in the center of the table. When Elizabeth looked in his direction, she saw only the flickering flames and the glitter of his eyes in the distant shadows.

"I'm nervous, that's all."

She poked her fork into another morsel and brought it to her mouth. Thank God, it wasn't a piece of pigeon. She had nearly gagged on the first bite, which tasted every bit as spoiled as if it had been slaughtered the same time as last week's partridge. Yet Jack ate with relish and his serving came from the same dish as hers. She did not fear poison, but something had certainly set her off her taste for food.

At least she knew it was not a symptom of pregnancy; the signs to the contrary were only stronger now. Besides, this was no morning nausea nor a strange craving, just an inexpicable offness to the taste of something she normally enjoyed.

She chewed thoughtfully and swallowed, then rather than risk any more of the pie, she blurted, "I'm frightened if you must know."

He poured more wine into the goblet in front of her and asked, "Of what? Of your father? Thomas Colfax?"

She shuddered and reached for the wine. It, at least, did not taste rotten and washed away the lingering corruption in her mouth.

"Of everything. I do not know what the world will

be like or even what I will be like. I told you before that my father threatened to throw me out on the street if I did not do as he wished."

John watched each time she brought the goblet to her lips. The opium powder's effect came on gradually, and he had already seen the signs that she was falling under its influence. Her speech slurred, though only slightly, and her movements took on a dreamlike aspect.

"If he does, then I shall—"

A single sharp tap at the door stopped him short. For an instant he dared to think he had imagined the sound, until, a second later, it came again.

He barked a low, gruff "Come in!"

The massive panel swung inward. The broad-shouldered youth, his shaggy hair disheveled with sleep, stood in the hall with a fresh taper in his hand.

"A visitor," he mumbled.

CHAPTER
21

Tying the belt of a worn blue dressing gown about his waist, John peered over the pince-nez as he entered the Dower House's small, dark drawing room. The lenses sat crookedly on his nose, distorting an already unpleasant sight.

"Good God, Uncle, it is half past one in the morning! What are you doing here?"

Thomas looked up from a drunken sprawl on a delicate French chair much too small for his bulk.

"I need money. Why else do you think I'd set foot in this mouldering old relic? Why can't you stay at the Hall, where I can find you when I want you?"

When you want to steal *from me, don't you mean?* John almost spat, but he dare not risk an argument with Thomas now. Besides, there was nothing left for Thomas to steal. "I haven't a penny. You know my finances far better than I."

Thomas must be very drunk and in very desperate straits if he did not bother to cover his demands with excuses. At any other time John would have done his best to take advantage of Thomas's desperation, but tonight there was no time. Even now the drug in

Elizabeth's wine was taking her nearer and nearer to oblivion. John had counted on her last few moments of lucidity for the final questions, the ones that had haunted his sleep and his heart all week. If, thanks to Thomas's untimely visit, she slipped into the abyss before John had those answers—

"There's always more," Thomas stated.

John shook his head. The room was icy, with no fire laid, yet beads of sweat glistened on the other man's brow.

"There must be!"

The outburst must have frightened Thomas, as though he suddenly discovered he no longer commanded the situation as he always had in the past. He struggled to his feet but after a few unsteady seconds sank once again onto the chair. He looked as if he might stay there forever.

John clenched his hands into fists inside the pockets of his dressing gown. The facade took more and more of his energy to maintain, but when he spoke his voice was calm and unworried. "You're overwrought, Thomas. Allow me to offer you some brandy, and then Ethan can escort you to the Hall. A good night's sleep will make—"

"Oh, stop it, you idiot! I haven't had a good night's sleep since that bastard Jack Silver stole the sapphires!" He slumped again; the effort of trying to control his temper and the disappointment of failing sapped his strength. "But I'll take your brandy or whatever swill you give that name to. Send your half-witted lackey for a bottle, and we'll drink together. Maybe it'll make a man of you!"

Thomas burst into eerie, cackling laughter that lasted only a moment and then died as suddenly as it had begun, leaving behind otherworldly echoes. The flames of the two candles Ethan had lit on the mantel danced crazily; grotesque shadows cavorted about the room. Aware that Thomas watched those phantom shapes with frightened eyes, John signaled to an unmoving shade by the door. The boy mimed the act of sprinkling something into a cup, but John gave him a short negative shake of his head. Ethan slipped out into the darkness beyond without a sound.

The candles stilled, and John felt as if a refreshing breeze also had died. He smelled the reek of liquor on Thomas's panting breath and the stink of fear that oozed from his pores. His own anger mounted, like a fire that consumed without heat and left only cold ashes behind.

The temptation to tell Thomas everything was greater than John expected, perhaps because this intrusion had caught him unawares. He told himself the triumph would be all the sweeter when the humiliation was made in public rather than here in the silent ruins of the Dower House. So he waited, saying nothing, hiding his loathing and fury as he had done for so long while Thomas regathered his courage and pride.

"In vino veritas," the older man chuckled. "You think you are the only one with some Latin, but the truth is that I am not the ignorant lout your father treated me as. Shall I tell you, now that I am nearly as drunk as the lord I shall soon be, the truth about your father, my late and most unlamented brother, and that scheming bitch who bore you?"

The mask slipped. Grabbing Thomas by the lapels of his crumpled coat, John hauled the limp, terrified drunkard to his feet.

"You bastard!"

Thomas's eyes widened. His breath, foul with liquor and fear, made John gag.

"So, the whelp has a temper after all."

"I do, Uncle, and you'd be wise to remember it." Lowering Thomas slowly to the chair was not an act of kindness but a display of strength, a silent threat. "Ethan will bring the brandy. You are welcome to drink it all if you like. When you are ready to return to the Hall, Ethan will escort you to the door. Or you may spend the night here. But I warn you, Thomas. Do not attempt to leave this room alone."

The older man's mouth opened and closed wordlessly. The only thing that worried John about the possibility that Thomas might die of an apoplexy was that such a death would cheat him of the triumph so close within his grasp. Such a worry, however, paled in comparison to the worry that sped him out of the drawing room and to the narrow stairs leading to the tower. He heard the curses Thomas hurled after him, but now they carried no sting.

"You put the drug in the wine, didn't you?"

Elizabeth tried to raise her arms and wrap them around Jack's neck as he scooped her off the floor, but her limbs refused to respond.

"Yes, love, I put the drug in the wine," he agreed. "That's the fourth time you've asked me. Now, answer my question, please? How did Betsy Bunch enter Stanhope without being seen?"

She wavered, not sure if she should be angry with him for thinking of one woman while he still held the other in his arms or pleased that her disguise had worked so well he could not tell the two were one and the same. The dilemma as well as the success of her charade made her laugh.

"She was clever, wasn't she? All those nights she crept out of her nice warm bed and sneaked out to meet her lover and no one was ever the wiser."

"Yes, very clever. How did she do it, Elizabeth?"

John glanced up at Harry, who held Elizabeth's cloak draped over his arm. The old man shook his head.

"She's too far gone," Harry whispered.

When Elizabeth failed to respond to the sound of another voice, John reluctantly agreed with Harry's appraisal. He stood up, cradling her against his chest as he had so many times before. Now, however, he did not carry her to the bed in anticipation of making love to her, though the desire to do just that almost turned him back from the door.

Harry held the door open.

"Ye should have given that stuff to yer unc—yer other visitor as well," he grumbled. "Would've made things a damn sight easier."

John caught the almost slip and paused to give Harry a warning glance.

"It isn't over yet, my friend. There are still plenty of risks. Having that one out of the way would make little difference. Besides," he added, tamping down the hatred against another sudden flare, "I want him conscious in the morning. I don't care if his head feels the size of St. Paul's dome; I want that bastard conscious."

He followed Harry by sound and instinct through the dark rooms and corridors of the Dower House. Here and there moonlight streamed through uncurtained windows, casting its usual ghostly shadows on floors and walls and shrouded furniture. Though he trusted Elizabeth was far enough under the influence of the drug to risk not blindfolding her eyes, he did not chance carrying a light. There was always Thomas's coachman to worry about. Peg had been enlisted to watch the driver, but there was no way to know if Thomas had brought other spies with him.

Nor was John sure exactly how much of the drugged wine Elizabeth had consumed. After leaving Thomas to his brandy, he hastened back to the tower room only to find Elizabeth slumped in her chair, the empty goblet dangling from her fingers. Some of the spilled wine still pooled on the floor, but most formed a sticky dark stain at the hem of her gown.

He could only hope she drank enough that what

happened from now on remained at best a hazy dream.

At the kitchen door, Harry hobbled ahead to turn the key and lift the latch, then swing the panel inward on well-oiled hinges. Cold air rushed in, and John felt the woman in his arms shiver.

He helped Harry wrap her in her cloak, a task made more difficult by her regaining some consciousness. She struggled weakly with uncoordinated limbs and in a slurred, frightened whisper asked, "Where am I?"

"On your way home."

"But I don't want to go home!"

Though feeble, her protest rang with terror in the midnight stillness.

"Hush, hush, love, it's all right." Under his breath he muttered another curse on Thomas.

She quieted, but he felt the lingering tension in her body as he approached the gray stallion tethered beneath the trees that shaded the old carriage house. A stranger passing by would never see the dappled specter, especially on a night like this. The trees rustled in the wind and an owl fluttered across the moon on silent wings. Not a cloud marred the sky, leaving the moonlight to bathe the world in silver shadows.

John slipped the reins free and mounted easily despite his burden. Once settled in front of him on the saddle, Elizabeth shuddered with a sleepy sigh. Again, the memory of another woman riding thus intruded upon his thoughts, but the memory was subtly altered, as if he had taken some of the drugged wine himself. Instead of the awkward shyness of Betsy Bunch wrapped within his highwayman's cloak, Elizabeth Stanhope shared his warmth that bitter night, just as she did now.

Dismissing these errant flights of fancy, he nudged the stallion with his heels. The beast, too long confined, sidestepped just once. It was enough to disturb her drugged slumber.

Her first words were mumbled and incoherent. But there was no mistaking her next statement.

"Don't make me marry him, Father," she begged with a chilling tinge of a threat in her still slurred and drowsy voice. "I despise Thomas Colfax."

The hood of her cloak fell away as she shook her head in dream-trapped denial. Tears glistened on feathery lashes that slowly fluttered open. Eyes bright and dark with the effects of the drug and the moonlight searched for reassurance.

He did not know if she saw Jack Silver or her father's face from her dream.

"Didn't I swear Thomas would never have you?"

"Then why must you do this?" she asked. "I never gave away your secret, never!"

She knew nothing, he was sure of it. He nudged the stallion away from the carriage house and into the woods, where night sounds and distance would keep anyone else from hearing Elizabeth's voice.

If she had drunk even half the wine left in her goblet when Thomas's arrival interrupted their dinner, she should have been unconscious now. Instead she drifted surrealistically between dreams and reality, between past and present. Sometimes she spoke to him, and then her voice was clear, but other curses and threats seemed directed at someone else, her father or Thomas perhaps.

"I'd sooner spend my life as a tavernmaid like Betsy or kill myself and be damned to hell than spend one moment as Thomas Colfax's countess."

Something curdled in his belly like milk in vinegar. Only John's death could give Thomas the title, a daunting enough prospect, but not the one that caused his gorge to rise. The image of Elizabeth in Thomas's bed, her glorious hair spilled on his pillow, her joyful body pinned beneath his sweating, grunting obscenity turned John's stomach because a mere two weeks ago, he had been willing, even eager, to use her as the instrument of his revenge.

He leaned closely over her, protecting her from the scrape and slap of low branches until the stallion broke out of the brush and onto a narrow, moonlit path. How instinctive that sense of preservation came now, without thought, without effort. Again he cursed, for there was little else he could do for her. And he had already done far too much to her.

It was still several miles to the Black Oak by these woodland ways, and keeping the gray to a steady walk ought to afford time for Elizabeth finally to fall asleep. If she dozed only for an hour, it would be enough. Enough to leave her without the agony of a farewell.

The night's silence magnified the slightest sound. More deliberately cautious than ever, John listened for any hint of pursuit. No hoofbeats followed on the path, no branches crackled in the wood. Only Elizabeth's occasional whimpers broke the stillness until, finally, she drifted into sleep in his arms.

The stable loft at the Black Oak shimmered in silver light streaming through the tiny window as John carried Elizabeth up the creaking ladder. She had not stirred once; the opium, the wine, and her own exhaustion had finally done the trick.

It was what he wanted, he told himself as he lay her on a thin pile of hay. No last-minute pleas, no tears, no recriminations.

Working quickly, he gathered more of the sweet-smelling fodder into a heap, then spread his own cloak atop it. A few seconds later, he had Elizabeth snugly wrapped in a double layer of heavy wool and buried beneath the added cover of the hay. To ensure that someone found her as soon as the inn wakened, he pulled a strip of black silk from his pocket to tie around one of the ladder rungs. It would serve as a signal of Jack Silver's presence and spark a search.

Only a few hours remained until then. John needed every moment of those hours to set the last act of this comedy turned tragedy in motion. Yet he could not make himself leave the loft or even rise from beside the sleeping Elizabeth, though the danger grew with every second he tarried.

"Damn you, Thomas," he swore for the thousandth time.

If he had not, he might not have remembered that Thomas posed an even greater danger. He had to be returned, conscious or not, to Kilbury as soon as possible before he wakened and took it into his head to begin rambling about the Dower House in search of some overlooked treasure he could convert to his own use.

John stood and brushed dust from his knees. A piece of the dry, prickly stuff landed on Elizabeth's cheek. He should have left it, but the temptation to touch her one more time overwhelmed him. He pulled off the glove and stroked his finger down her cheek.

"Farewell, love."

Her lashes fluttered and a sleepy frown creased her brow, but she did not open her eyes.

Go, a warning screamed in his head. *If she wakens, you'll never leave her. Go!*

He knelt again and leaned down to kiss her.

"Good-bye, Elizabeth."

She sighed and burrowed deeper into her cocoon.

Time is running out! Leave her now!

"Where are you going?"

Her voice was soft and sleepy. If he said nothing in reply, she would slip back into that dreamworld with no memory of waking.

"I can't stay, love."

He smoothed the hair at her temple until the lines of worry on her forehead eased. Her breathing deepened, and he thought she had fallen asleep again.

"You could have stopped it, you know," she murmured with an eerie clarity. "All Father ever wanted was the title."

There was one thing to be said for the anger. It got him to his feet and gave him the fortitude to walk toward the ladder. It also aroused his curiosity. Who was she speaking to? Not Edward this time, nor Thomas. And the Jack Silver she knew had nothing to do with the earl of Kilbury or his title.

Let it go, the warning voice urged. *It makes no difference now.*

Ignoring it, he turned and strode back to her, knelt beside her once again.

"Then he should have married you to the earl himself instead of playing for that fat toad who might never inherit."

She flinched as though his fury penetrated her dream. More disgusted now than angry, John rocked back on his heels and rested his head on his knees.

The question had lurked in the back of his mind for days, perhaps even since that first night, but he never dared explore it. It had nothing to do with his plans and would make no difference in the outcome. But tonight, when Jack Silver's performance was nearly finished, he had intended to ask her. Indeed, if he had any hope of playing another role, he needed the answer.

"Why would he chance your spending the next fifty years as nothing more than Mrs. Thomas Colfax or even the bastard's widow when you could already be countess of Kilbury?"

Her sigh was loud and long, almost impatient or

exasperated, as though only an imbecile would not know the answer to so simple a question. As he glanced at her, her face sharply illuminated in the moonlight, she gave him a brief, indulgent smile just before she closed her eyes.

"Because you never asked me."

CHAPTER
22

The nightmare did not end with Elizabeth's return to Stanhope Manor. Day and night, awake or asleep, she found no escape from the relentless demons. The memory of waking in the loft of the Black Oak's stable with her father and Thomas bellowing orders until she had to shriek for silence invaded her dreams. She remembered blinking at the sunlight streaming through the dusty air. Too many days in the darkness of the highwayman's lair had left her all but blind. The searing light, more than anything else, told her Jack Silver was gone.

Thomas, however, refused to leave. After accompanying her and her father home, he installed himself as a guest who gave every indication of staying.

During the three weeks since that morning, Elizabeth hardly dared to leave the sanctuary of her room. At first she pled the painful sensitivity of her eyes to the light and the headache that lingered long after the sleeping drug wore off. Even those complaints did not deter Thomas. Twice he dared to knock on her door and demand admittance. Her unfeigned shrieks of terror and Thomas's beastlike bellows drew the attention of servants less loyal to him than his own, and under Edward's direction the assault ended.

And another began. If Edward's siege was quieter, less violent, it was every bit as persistent. His first questions were the obvious and expected ones, posed almost as soon as she regained consciousness. Had she recognized her kidnapper? Did she know where he had taken her? Had he harmed her in any way? She could not even answer those simple queries save to beg to be left alone, and her father had complied with her wishes but just until she could no longer plead the effects of her captivity.

By then, she knew only one question—and one answer—mattered to him. He did not ask it for he did not need to. He need only wait, as both she and Jack Silver had done, to learn if she had come away from her ordeal bearing the irrefutable proof of the highwayman's most unforgivable theft.

The thwarted bridegroom had not tried to claim his bride for over a week, yet Elizabeth tested the lock on the door almost hourly. And she did not sleep a night without at least one dream from which she wakened in an icy sweat of terror.

She had simply exchanged one prison cell for another, and if this one offered more amenities, it also reminded her of how much she had lost.

Standing at the window that overlooked the garden, she gazed down upon a now familiar and thoroughly loathsome sight. Though the spring morning was brisk, with a steady wind blowing in from the sea, her father and Thomas Colfax strolled among the greening beds of flowers. Edward shook his head emphatically while Thomas gesticulated, even coming to stand directly in front of the older man and block his path.

A series of rhythmic taps on the door distracted her just as Thomas and Edward walked out of her line of sight. She turned from the window and crossed to unlock the door and admit Nell. While the servant carried the breakfast tray to the table by the window, Elizabeth relocked the door and checked to be certain it was secure.

"I wish I could hear them," she said. "If I knew what they were planning, it would make my own task easier. Did you learn anything this morning?"

Nell shook her head.

"It's why they go outside to talk," the maid said, "so's no one can hear 'em. Best eat yer breakfast before it's cold. Shall I burn today's letter from Mr. Thomas?"

Elizabeth approached warily, as if Thomas's presence were a tangible thing through the letter he had placed, as he did every morning, on her breakfast tray. At first she had returned them to him unopened, but he merely sent them back with another added.

"Yes, burn it." Her voice rasped, she had become so terrified of him and of what he would do to her when he learned the truth. "Why do you even ask? Why indeed do you continue to bring them to me?"

Nell shrugged and tossed the sealed vellum envelope into the flames.

"It's not my place to guess whether you'll want to read one someday nor to refuse it when he gives it to me."

"May he burn in hell forever," Elizabeth swore with cold passion, wondering if she meant to curse Thomas Colfax or the man who had abandoned her to him. Three weeks and not a word, not a sign, from the highwayman. Not that he ever said he would contact her, she reminded herself bitterly, but he *had* sworn that Thomas would never have her. Elizabeth retained little hope of avoiding the marriage Jack Silver had apparently only postponed. "And you may burn his letters in front of his very nose if you wish."

"What of the one from his lordship?"

Another piece of the nightmare. This was the third

note from John and no doubt contained the same polite, solicitous phrases as the first. Or perhaps, she thought as she picked up the folded sheet of cheap, flimsy paper with her name neatly written on the outside, he offered an explanation for the cryptic message he had sent exactly one week ago.

"I'll read it later," she answered, tucking it under her plate as she sat down to a heartier breakfast than normal.

Nell had already busied herself with the usual tasks of making the bed and laying out clothes for her mistress. On the surface, nothing had changed. The routine was as it had always been. Except that when Elizabeth stole cautious glances at the maid, she often found Nell staring right back.

She put it down to curiosity. She had, after all, said little about those two weeks spent with the outlaw, not even to forestall the inevitable gossip and speculation. Now, with Thomas increasing the pressure to conclude the agreement arranged before Jack Silver's intervention, she wondered if perhaps she should have told Nell everything.

Then again, she had little doubt Nell already held her own suspicions. A woman might keep a secret from a man, even from her lover, but not from her maid.

"Good God, how did a man stand to wear one of these things every day?"

John tugged the moth-eaten wig more securely on his head, but nothing could make it comfortable. Still, the angry countenance staring back at him from the mirror was one even he would not have recognized. The dull reddish hair made him look sallow, almost sickly, in the late afternoon glow that lit his room at the Dower House. In the smoky lamplight of the Black Oak, *he* might be mistaken for a corpse.

Satisfied that he had altered his appearance sufficiently for at least one night's visit to the inn, he stood and let Harry help him into the carefully padded contrivance that would bind his left arm to his chest as well as add a paunch to his belly.

"I still think ye're worryin' too much about nothin', milord," Harry suggested. "Maybe she never got the letters. An' if, as ye think, 'twere truth she spoke that night in the stable, maybe she just forgot. If she really thought the earl of Kilbury was Jack Silver himself, do ye think she'd not have said something by now?"

They had had this conversation a dozen times in the past week, since the delivery of John's third letter to Elizabeth—and no response from her. Harry always managed to convince him that her final words in the stable loft were nothing more than an expression of her confused state of mind. She had earlier that night imagined herself talking to her father, why not also to John Colfax?

"I don't know, Harry, I just don't know. But something isn't right." He slid his arm into the sling and watched over his shoulder as Harry tied the string. "If she agreed to marry Thomas for the sake of a title, why hasn't the wedding taken place? It can't be because Thomas is afraid she's bred a bastard; he's been lodged at Stanhope pressing for an elopement since the day Edward fetched her back from the inn. It has to be because Elizabeth herself is balking. She's answered none of Thomas's letters either."

A quick tug on the string released the whole apparatus, and though Harry groaned at having to do it all up again, John smiled with satisfaction. He tested the mechanism once more, then pulled on an oversized shirt. The cover of a coat and light cloak completed the illusion of the missing arm. It was perhaps too elaborate for the single instance he intended to use it, but if caught in his disguise, he did not wish to be disadvantaged by it. And what he planned for tonight was, in its own way, more daring than any of his previous escapades.

"And how do ye know she's not answered him?"

"She hadn't as of yesterday," he admitted. "If anything had changed today, Thomas would surely have returned to Kilbury. If she rejected him, he'd have no reason to stay; and if she accepted, he'd have her wedded and bedded within the hour."

He was able to hide the anger such a thought still raised, though it had taken him nearly all of the last month to achieve that kind of control. He had had far less patience these past four weeks than in the four years that preceded them. Perhaps, he thought as he took the loaded pistols from the hidden drawer where the sapphires lay in innocent splendor, his eagerness to see it all done had much to do with the fact that he expected the deed to be accomplished much sooner. Instead, this entire month had crawled by with nothing resolved. Thomas still sat comfortably albeit nervously in the role of master of Kilbury, Edward still paraded about Stanhope, and Elizabeth—

Elizabeth still haunted his dreams.

He hadn't let Harry know how the full extent of the effect Elizabeth's final comment had on him. For days he had battled against a torrent of self-recrimination. "Had I but known" echoed in his head over and over until logic silenced it. He *hadn't* known she was willing to marry him, nor was there any guarantee that Edward, who never broached the idea, would have agreed to an alliance between his daughter and the earl of Kilbury two or three years ago. By the time Elizabeth's betrothal to Thomas was proposed, the damage had already been done. John Colfax was a laughingstock, and he had no one to blame but himself.

Nor, however, could he expect anyone else to repair the damage. That, too, he must do himself, which was why he had coerced Harry into contriving this elaborate disguise.

"And what will ye do if ye don't get the answers ye want tonight?"

Inaction contributed to his impatience as well. Striding about the room to adapt his gait to the change in balance created by the pinioning of his arm, John felt the almost soothing rush of excitement flow into him. He had waited, perhaps too long, and now he was once again taking action.

"I do not expect answers tonight," he said. He stopped at the window to gauge the waning daylight. In an hour another full moon would rise, as clear as the night he had last seen Elizabeth. He need not even close his eyes to picture the way the light had silvered her features, framed by loose wisps of midnight hair. "I intend only to leave a message."

"And not wait for a reply?"

"If one comes, it won't be for days. I could hardly wait at the Black Oak that long."

Behind him, Harry began lighting the candles as the twilight deepened. John drew the curtains and turned away from the window, though it was unlikely anyone would see him.

Perhaps he was wasting his time trying to contact Betsy Bunch, but the girl might be persuaded to tell Jack Silver the means of entering Stanhope Manor unseen. If she did not, he was no worse off than now. If she did, he could confront Elizabeth himself.

"I don't like the way ye say that," the old man muttered. "Ye've kept yer secrets before, but not like this."

"No, Harry, not secrets. I've told you everything."

Harry looked up and swore. "Like hell ye have. Since ye left the girl at the inn, ye've told me naught of yer plans."

With a laugh and a swagger that almost turned into a stumble, John answered, "Because I've never *had* any plans. And it's Thomas who kept all the secrets. I've gone through every drawer and every cabinet, read every ledger and letter in his study, and there is nothing, *nothing,* to tell me where to find the rest of the mortgages. Until I know who and where this Benjamin Miner is, the money I've taken from Thomas and his friends is worthless."

He tried the swagger again and this time kept his balance.

"Then what good's the message at the Black Oak? What's it got to do with mortgages?"

"Nothing at all, Harry. For that, I must do what I should have done weeks ago." And would have done, he said only to himself, but for five words murmured in a moonlit loft. "Have everything ready for me to leave for London day after tomorrow. It's time I pay a call on old Kaspar."

Elizabeth checked the locks on the door one more time before she walked to the secretary and sat down. She had snuffed all the lights save one on the desk; the scent of burnt candlewick stung her nose. If anyone interrupted her, she could plunge the room into absolute darkness and give herself the moment she needed.

But it was unlikely anyone would disturb her at this hour. Even the persistent Thomas abandoned his pursuit in favor of the charms of a liquid mistress after midnight. Nell, before retiring to her own bed, had reported him well into his cups more than an hour ago, woozily ensconced in the library where Brinslow Copperstith's wedding portrait hung over the mantel.

Taking a deep breath, Elizabeth pulled the top drawer as far out as it would go. Rather than reach inside, she slid her hand along the bottom and loosened the three sheets of paper held there by four silver pins wedged into the wood.

The seals on two were long since broken; not even bits of wax clung to the paper any more. Elizabeth unfolded them one by one and smoothed them on the desktop, then repositioned the lone candle to shed more even light. The third letter, its blob of red wax intact though the edges of the paper showed signs of wear, she set off to the right with her hand resting atop it.

The first, if two brief paragraphs could be considered a letter, arrived the very day of her return to Stanhope, but she had not read it immediately. She had wakened that evening too groggy and feeling that her head had been split open by a very dull sword. Thinking Nell would be tending her, she voiced a thick-tongued plea for water, but instead of the familiar maid, a sour-faced woman rose from the chair beside the bed and muttered, "I'll fetch the doctor." That worthy proceeded to prescribe a sleeping draught, which Elizabeth had no strength to refuse. The vile-tasting liquid, so unlike the sweet wine Jack had drugged her with, was poured down her throat.

Perhaps it was the darkness that brought the memory into such sharp focus. Perhaps, she hoped, other mysteries would come clearer as well.

She reread John's letter. There was no mystery in the few sentences. He expressed his delight at her safe return, his sympathy on any injuries she may have suffered, and his offer of whatever kindness she might demand of him. It was exactly what she would expect of him: concerned, gentle, generous, and signed with a scholar's ornate script.

The second note bore no signature and only four words across the middle of the page. But there was no doubt in her mind that the same hand had penned both missives.

"'Consider the question asked,'" she whispered, forming each word slowly and distinctly. "What question? How am I to consider it if I do not know what it is?" Exasperation edged her voice. Slowly, she forced calm to return.

She slid the third letter closer. In the week since Nell brought it on her breakfast tray, Elizabeth had contemplated opening it too often to count the times. Yet there it lay, still sealed, unread, beneath her hand.

Had she finally learned a lesson about giving in to curiosity? She shook her head. The temptation was greater each time she pulled the letter from its hiding place.

"I should have burned it along with each one Thomas sent," she whispered, trailing trembling fingers across the waxen seal. "I felt no curiosity about them, none at all."

No, it was guilt that stayed her hand, guilt that made her hide the letter. A guilt mixed with hope and fear, dread and joy, anger and shame.

"Is it so wrong to want what I want?" she asked and angrily broke the seal.

The words blurred before her eyes, and only then did she realize she had been crying. With the back of her hand she wiped the tears from her cheeks and blinked to clear her eyes. But even as she did so, she paused and turned her attention away from the letter to listen, undistracted and without the crinkly rattle of the paper in her unsteady hand to mask the sound.

The voice, not loud and still distant, could only be Thomas's. No one else would be awake at this hour. For several seconds, Elizabeth listened in horrified disbelief as he came closer to her door. The babbling incoherence of his speech testified to the extent of his drunkenness. But behind those unintelligible mumbles she discerned another voice, one she knew even better than Thomas's.

Her father's.

"You've no right, Colfax!"

A thud followed Edward's whispered outburst, as of something heavy being shoved against the wall, then silence. Had Edward pushed Thomas, or had Thomas merely stumbled? Elizabeth held her breath, listening.

"Ev'ry right, Stanhope," Thomas insisted, spitting the name with an emphatic sneer so clear Elizabeth in the safety of her room winced. "I ransomed the bitch, din't I?"

The crack of flesh on flesh jolted her. After a moment of what she could only imagine was shocked silence, Thomas growled a string of obscenities.

Edward cut him short.

"You ransomed her, all right. With my money and your nephew's estate."

Elizabeth glanced at the pages on the desk and at the third now crumpled in her hand. Was it in fact John who had secured her release from Jack Silver? She could easily believe it of him, and yet he made no mention of it. Hastily smoothing the crushed letter, she wondered if the outlaw knew or cared where the money had come from.

She read no further than John's customary greeting before the argument resumed outside her door. Thomas must have shoved his way past Edward, for his voice came nearer with each word.

"There's nothing left to him but the entail—and the title. I've taken the rest."

"I don't care about the rest! Damn you, Colfax, I want that earldom for my grandson! I'll see her wed to John if that's what it takes."

Now she felt as well as heard the impact of a body against a wall. The flame of her candle wavered, making the words on the page before her dance. Once again she tried to press out the crinkles, but once again Thomas Colfax's voice intruded.

"You'll get no earldom that way, you fool," he hissed. "That whey-faced twit get a child on her? Pah! Never!"

He spat like a common lout on the street, and this time it was Edward who swore. But he kept his voice low, and when Thomas burst into drunken laughter, Elizabeth could not distinguish her father's words. She had no difficulty understanding what Thomas said next.

"Raise an outlaw's bastard as earl of Kilbury? I'd kill him first and the child, too, before—"

Then he was pounding at her door, demanding entrance, shouting curses and unintelligible obscenities. The outrage lasted only a few seconds, but it was long enough to stir the other inhabitants of Stanhope. Doors opened and closed as servants wakened and rushed to discover what had disturbed their rest. Among them, no doubt, was Nell, but Elizabeth dared not look for assistance from her maid.

The assault on her door abruptly ceased, with Thomas's continued curses indicating he was being dragged away by some of her father's servants. When the curses degenerated into sobs and finally faded altogether, Elizabeth had to strain her ears to hear Edward dismiss the rest of the curious staff who had gathered in the corridor. Quiet, if not silence, returned, though the fearful echoes of the tumult still rang in Elizabeth's ears along with the terrified rush of her pulse. She did not remember rising from her chair but discovered now that she gripped the back of it as though she meant to use it as a weapon.

Could she? she wondered. Or were there others, more effective?

"Elizabeth!"

Edward's low-voiced order froze her.

"Unlock the door! I can break it down, you know. Or set a guard. Is it not better that this be kept from the servants? Thomas was drunk, nothing more."

She needed time and knew there was but one way to buy it. Opening the door to her father involved a risk, but it was a chance she had to take. Allowing him to place someone outside her door would cut off her only hope. She shoved John's letters roughly into the drawer and blew out the candle. A soft shimmer of moonlight illuminated the window, keeping the room from pitch blackness. Elizabeth hoped her eyes, once so accustomed to the dark, were sharper than her father's. Then, heedless of the still hot wax that dripped onto her hand and the seat of the chair, she grasped the candlestick and hefted the chair and padded toward the door, still without a word.

In a more conciliatory tone, Edward began again, "It must be done, Elizabeth. Nothing has changed."

She judged the distance by the thin line of light visible at the bottom of the door and set the chair down. It was heavier than she expected, but she gave herself not even a moment to rest. Each second was too precious to waste. Planting her feet firmly, she reached over to turn the key in the lock.

"It's open," she said with no further invitation.

She feared the irrepressible defiance in her voice would hasten his entry, but it seemed to have the opposite effect. She used that momentary pause to tighten her grip on the chair. Listening for the twist of the latch, she held her breath.

As though anticipating an attack and hoping to catch her unawares, Edward shoved the door inward. Unimpeded, it slammed back on its hinges. The force of the push brought him one stumbling step into the room, and that was all Elizabeth needed.

She swung the chair low, no more than a foot above the floor. The back legs caught his knees, the front his belly, not a crippling blow but enough to pitch him face first toward the floor. If he had fallen to the floor, he might have been able to push himself up quickly enough to avoid the next blow, but Elizabeth released the chair the moment it hit him. In the dark and unable to reclaim his footing, Edward presented a perfect target.

She brought the bottom of the heavy candlestick down on his head. He grunted and fell again but continued to struggle. Once more Elizabeth hit him, feeling the sharp pain that told her her hand rather than the candlestick made contact with his skull. This time, finally, he lay still.

On her hands and knees, Elizabeth drew great deep breaths and waited for her heart to stop pounding. She still clutched the candlestick, minus its taper, and could not bring herself to fling it away, though her action suddenly filled her with horror and disgust.

"Think what he would have done," she told herself in justification. "Think what he would have let that monster do."

Slowly, becoming aware that she had sustained a few bumps and bruises in addition to the strain of her battle, she got to her feet. Though she had only minutes in which to effect her escape, she could not make herself move any faster.

She closed the door first, then, passing Edward's prone form, nudged her father with her toe. He groaned, and she raised the candlestick again, but when he made no other motion, she sidled to the desk, never turning her back to him. There she found her weapon's mate and took it to the fire to light it.

Her first task was to find the key and refit it into the lock to prevent anyone else from entering. Only when that was done did she take the candle to examine her father.

His breathing was even, with a distinct snore. There was no smell of liquor about him. Gingerly, Elizabeth reached out her hand to touch the back of his head. She found the beginning of a lump but no obvious wounds.

And then there was no more hesitation. Into a black reticule she dropped her jewelry and the few coins she had in her possession. She had not worn mourning since John's father died more than four years ago, and the clothes would be out of style, but she assumed fashion would hardly be the concern of a young widow too poor to afford a servant to accompany her. She had just pulled the black gown from the back of her wardrobe when a quiet tap on the door froze her.

"It's me, Nell. Are you all right, miss?"

Elizabeth raced to the door and unlocked it with hands that shook so badly she dropped the key. Poor Nell had barely time to utter a squeal of surprise before Elizabeth grabbed the girl's arm and dragged her into the room, then shoved the door closed again. Nell stood in shocked silence, staring down at Edward's unconscious form sprawled in the middle of the floor.

"Don't gawk," Elizabeth said. "I've no time to waste. I'll explain as much as I can while we work."

She took Nell's hand in her own and slapped the empty candlestick into it.

"If he moves, dispatch him," she ordered, untying the sash around her waist. "And where is the small valise?"

In a chilling monotone Nell replied, "On the top shelf. Is he dead?"

"No, he's not dead, just unconscious."

"You did this to your own father?"

"I had to do something. Thomas threatened to kill both John and the baby if I didn't go through with the marriage."

She found the valise and pulled it from the shelf, then threw only the most necessary items into it.

"So it's true," Nell whispered. "I thought so. You've been finicky about your food, not likin' your old favorites, sayin' things didn't taste right. Mam were like that with cabbage when she were with Robin; couldn't abide the smell of it. Do *they* know?"

Elizabeth skimmed out of her nightdress and tossed

it into the valise. While she pulled on a pair of drawers and tugged a chemise over her head, she answered Nell's questions.

"If you mean have I told them I'm carrying Jack Silver's child, no. But Father suspects. I believe he was willing to go to the earl and propose a marriage between us and used the possibility of the child as a threat to Thomas. Thomas said he'd never allow such a marriage nor allow John to raise a bastard as his heir."

She shivered and reached for the dusty black gown. She could not put into words her other thoughts. Her forlorn hope of pleading with John to wed her was dashed when she recognized her symptoms as evidence that Jack Silver had succeeded in his scheme. She might have swallowed enough pride to ask John to accept her, but she would not impose another man's bastard as heir to Kilbury. Had there been any word from the outlaw, she would have waited. Thomas's threats and her own desperation forced her to act instead of wait.

Some of the shock had worn off Nell, who now came to offer welcome assistance, though it meant she had to set the candlestick down on the desk. Elizabeth stood still long enough for Nell to do up the buttons.

"So you're running away?"

"What would you have me do? Wait for Thomas to kill my child? Even if I married him, do you think he'd let it live once he knew who fathered it—and how I felt about him?"

"But where will you go? And how will you travel?"

"I can't tell you where I'm going." The gown fit snugly across the bosom and through the waist, which Elizabeth put down to the fact that she was no longer a seventeen-year-old girl, but it was comfortable enough. She lifted the reticule and tapped it. "I've my jewelry and some money. Later, I'll send you a letter through Hennie."

"Send me a letter! But surely you won't be traveling alone. What will people think?"

"Whatever they wish." When Nell opened her mouth to protest more, Elizabeth placed her hands on the maid's shoulders and stared her into silence. "Don't come after me, Nell. I'm doing what I have to do for myself and for my child."

The girl sniffed, and a huge tear suddenly rolled down her cheek.

"'Tis all my fault. I should never've let you play at being Betsy Bunch. You'd never've met that rascal Jack Silver."

Elizabeth shook her head.

"Betsy had nothing to do with it," she insisted while scooping essential items from her dressing table into the valise. She pulled her brush hastily through the tangles of her hair and twisted the whole long mass into a tight but rather untidy knot at the back of her head. With a few pins to hold it in place, she quickly tied a black, crepe-trimmed bonnet over the whole. "If anything, what you taught me about Betsy and her kind will help me when I need it most. Besides, I'll need someone I can trust here at Stanhope, and there's no one I trust more than you."

Nell lifted tearful eyes to her, making Elizabeth experience again that pang of guilt. This might not be the right decision to make, but she could think of nothing else to do. Nor did she dare wait. Not even one extra moment.

She walked around her father's snoring form to the door and turned the key. Nell approached hesitantly.

"Will you come back?"

"Yes, eventually."

Elizabeth kept the maid in front of her as she opened the door. Then, just as Nell turned to ask "When?" Elizabeth brought the silver candlestick down on the back of the girl's head. Nell crumpled without a sound at her feet.

With cold determination, Elizabeth dragged her back into the room and pulled a quilt from the bed to cover her.

"I'm sorry, Nell, but I do not want you coming after me," she whispered as she paused to catch her breath. "And perhaps they'll not suspect you of aiding me." Then, as she closed the door and turned the key again, she said, "I shall return as soon as I find Jack Silver."

CHAPTER
23

Long days of travel and nights of little sleep left Elizabeth exhausted by the time she reached London. She peered out the coach window at a cold, drizzly day. After the green of Somerset, she found the murky grays and browns of the city stark and unfriendly.

"Not a very cheery place," she remarked to her companions, a faded-looking woman of some fifty years and her spinster daughter. They sat across from her in the damp, musty-smelling coach that had brought them the last leg of the journey. "Is London always so dreary, Mrs. Vail?"

"Soomtimes it's nowt so bad," the Yorkshire widow replied.

Elizabeth had listened to the woman's tale during the long hours on the road and learned much that helped her solidify her own portrayal of a young woman cast into the world alone.

"And ye'll get accustomed to it after a while."

One part of her role Elizabeth did not have to learn; many of her qualms at making her way in this strange new world were very real. Never had she imagined so many streets, so many buildings piled one atop another, so many people and vehicles. Not for the first time since her flight from Stanhope she wished she had indeed let Nell accompany her. And she wondered what madness had possessed her to run in the first place.

She had only to think of the child growing inside her and the man who swore to kill it to remember and to firm her resolve. A shiver rippled through her as if icy rain had sluiced down her back.

Dorothea Vail patted one of Elizabeth's hands.

"It'll get easier, dear, trust me. Ye're younger'n I were when I lost my Tom, and I had no babe on the way, but there aren't nothin' ye can do. Now, dry yer eyes. We're almost to the inn. My sister, Mrs. Dunton, will see ye have a hot supper and a good night's sleep before ye go lookin' for yer cousin."

Elizabeth dabbed at her eyes with a black handkerchief. Tears came too easily, often when she least wanted or expected them. They had led the quiet but inquisitive Dorothea Vail to ferret out the fact that Elizabeth, posing as the widow of a Gloucestershire vicar, was carrying her late husband's child. If Mrs. Vail had been unwilling to help a shy, withdrawn young woman, she immediately took charge of the situation when she discovered there was a child on the way.

And for that assistance Elizabeth was more than grateful.

The inn, identified by the sign swinging wildly in the storm as the Blind Pilgrim, was a more welcome sight than any other she had seen. The coach pulled into the yard and within moments a young boy who reminded Elizabeth of Robin Sharpe opened the door and offered her a hand down.

She had reached London. Alive. Undiscovered.

* * *

The glow from half a dozen lamps and a cheery fire on the grate failed to dispel the gloom of a rainy morning. Ushered into the Stanhope library at an uncivilly early hour, John blamed the weather for delaying his departure for London. Yet now, pacing the length of the room while he waited for a servant to fetch Edward, he knew he had used the rain and the muddy roads as a convenient excuse. His business in London could wait, as indeed it had for four years or more, but Elizabeth was here, in this house. So was Thomas.

The library reeked of spilled brandy and old vomit. There was other evidence, too, that led John to believe his uncle had spent many a night in this room dominated by Elizabeth's portrait. The marks of scrubbing on the hearth could only mean the filthy swine had pissed into the fire.

But it was the stench of Edward Stanhope's lies that permeated the atmosphere like some choking miasma. The way he smiled too graciously upon greeting his guest and glanced too nervously at his daughter's portrait warned John to believe nothing the man said.

"What do you mean, Elizabeth cannot see me? Why not?"

Edward gave him another smile, less gracious this time, before he answered, "She wished to go away for a while. Somewhere quiet." Another glance at the portrait and now the smile faded altogether, replaced by an expression of abject weariness. "This has been quite an ordeal for her, you understand."

The pretense that had been slipping all morning disappeared entirely. "And what of Thomas? Has he gone with her?" John demanded.

Edward retreated toward the open library doors, his eyes wide, his face pale and pasty. A week ago John would have apologized immediately for snapping such a question, but there was no longer any reason to hide. Let Elizabeth's father see the real John Colfax, deal with the real earl of Kilbury.

"I believe your uncle is still asleep, my lord," Edward replied. "He was not feeling well last night."

"Drunk as a lord, was he?"

Edward's wince confirmed John's suspicion.

Nothing at Stanhope was as he expected. Frustrated, he paced to the window, not caring what Edward thought of the protracted silence.

Beyond the rain-streaked glass, the gardens where he had walked with Elizabeth were emerging from winter's drabness. No matter how he concentrated on the business at hand, the past kept intruding. He heard her voice, her soft laughter, smelled the lilacs she gathered and that now were an integral part of the woman he could not exorcise from his dreams—or his soul.

Damn the woman! Where was she? Why had she waited a month to decide she needed a holiday? And why had she replied to not a single one of his letters?

Edward's nervous cough broke into his thoughts. The old John Colfax would have taken such a cough as a hint. Though Edward Stanhope would never order a peer of the realm to quit his house, he was not above intimating that he would be much happier without this unwanted presence. That other John Colfax would have offered awkward apologies and made his exit.

John discovered to both his dismay and his amusement that he no longer had the power to conjure that other self into existence. He tried, but he might as well have tried to strike a fire in wet wool. Oddly, the failure neither disturbed nor alarmed him. He felt almost relieved.

He shifted his focus from the storm to the faint reflection of Elizabeth's father in the glass.

"Is something wrong, Stanhope?"

"Not at all." A lie. Too much eagerness tinged Edward's denial. "I would ask the same of you, my lord. You seem a bit distracted this morning."

Distracted! Good God, he was on the edge of raving lunacy! He had kidnapped and seduced a woman who was not at all what she appeared to be. Then he fell in love with her because she was *everything* she appeared to be. And now she had *disappeared,* leaving him in doubt of everything else he had believed about her. He had, he thought, every right to be distracted.

Such distraction was not, however, a luxury he could afford.

"As a matter of fact," he answered, studying that faint reflection with all the concentration of a wolf stalking prey, "I feel better than I have in some time, although I must confess to a touch of disappointment."

The figure in the glass stiffened. Behind it, almost invisible but for the darkening sky outside and the angle at which John stood, another vague, ghostlike form moved into the eerie roomscape. But Thomas Colfax did not enter the room; he hovered, like an impatient vulture.

"Disappointment, my lord?"

Edward, obviously aware of Thomas's presence, reacted much as a rabbit might with a snare before him and a fox behind.

"I thought, since there had been no wedding immediately upon Elizabeth's restoration, that she might have changed her mind."

The reflection was too faint for John to tell if any more color drained from the terrified man's already ashen complexion.

"No, of course she hasn't."

There was far less eagerness in this denial, and Edward failed to disguise an incipient desperation. With unexpected answers forming in his mind, John turned from the window slowly enough to give his uncle a chance to slink out of sight, though he did not doubt Thomas lurked within hearing range of every word spoken.

Nodding a curt dismissal to Elizabeth's father, John strolled toward the door and said casually, "I had thought to ask for her hand myself, but I see that is unnecessary. Good day, Stanhope."

The desperation shifted to a look of horror. Edward's mouth dropped open and his slack jaw quivered with voiceless words. But he did not need to say anything; John already had the answer to the first part of the riddle. Elizabeth was gone but not on some recuperative holiday. She had not been able to escape Jack Silver, but perhaps her experience as his captive had helped her break out of the pampered prison her father built around her.

It was not the answer John wanted, nor was he reassured by it. Too many other questions rose at once, but with them came a welcoming surge of hope and energy.

Striding through the sterile elegance of Stanhope, he demanded his coat and ordered his horse brought around. If the servants, who had never seen the earl of Kilbury so authoritative before, gave him quizzical looks, they also jumped to do his bidding. Edward, hurrying in his wake, urged caution.

"Please, my lord, the weather is worsening," he pointed out.

Snatching his coat and cloak from a cowering maidservant, John told his frantic host, "Then I've not a moment to spare, have I?"

The man was no less terrified than the girl who had run, skirts raised, from the entrance hall. Though nearly as tall as John, he seemed shrunken to no more than Harry Grove's height, with his shoulders hunched forward as he twisted his hands one around the other.

He was still standing there when John signaled to the butler to open the door.

Through the steady rain, John rode the long miles to London. Forced to leave the gray stallion behind, he cursed each of the unremarkable horses beneath him as thoroughly as he cursed Edward and Thomas and even himself for his stupidity. He spent the first miserable, sleepless night at an inn that reminded him painfully of the Black Oak—except that no laughing, bright-eyed Betsy Bunch graced the smoky common room with her smile. So he drank his ale and ate whatever food was placed before him, then crawled into a bed empty except for dreams.

Overruling Harry's protests, he traveled light, with haste more important than comfort. There was no way to tell how long ago Elizabeth had fled Stanhope or even if she had come to London, though John could not imagine her running anywhere else. To his knowledge she had no relatives at all to take her in. Her only other connections were through her father's business enterprises, most of which were in London. Yet even if she had no more than a day's lead on him, there were a million places a young woman could hide in the teeming city. And a million dangers waiting for the innocent.

A blinding storm and a balky mount brought him barely ten miles closer to London the second day, but by nightfall on the third, he reached his destination. Darkness and a shroud of fog blanketed him as he walked from the inn where he left the last of his mounts and gulped down a plate of something hot, his first meal since dawn. There would be neither fire nor supper to welcome him at the Kilbury house on Waverley Square.

He had no idea of the time as he mounted the familiar steps and reached into his soggy pocket for the key. Other houses on the square showed lights in upper windows, but number eleven was utterly dark. John turned the key and nudged the door open.

Secured from the damp and chill outside, the vestibule wrapped him in something akin to warmth. He slammed the door shut behind him, not bothering to lock it, and stripped off the cloak and coat. They landed with a squishy thud in a wet heap on the marble floor. The key slipped from his fingers; he heard it slide across the tiles but made no effort to find it. It would be there in the morning.

Leaving the vestibule for the hallway, he gave in to a loud, exhausted, yet satisfied yawn. The air of long disuse still clung, like the smoke from William Colfax's cigars. John remembered the pungent sting that always lingered long after one of his father's London parties. It was as if the earl and his delicate countess had just bid their guests good night, so real was the memory.

He did not enter the rooms that opened off the hallway—the drawing room, the music room, the dining hall—but headed for the stairs and hoped he had the strength to climb them.

He had his hand on the banister and his foot poised above the first stair when a whisper of sound froze him. A second later, he identified the noise as the faint padding of bare feet on the floor behind him.

"Well, well, well, what have we here," were the last words he heard.

"Is it to your liking?"

Elizabeth pivoted slowly. Even through the obscuring veil, she found the parlor bright and cheerful, a most pleasant contrast to the other accommodations she had investigated over the past week. Perhaps the fact that the sun finally shone over London buoyed her spirits and made this house more attractive than the others. It was small enough to be called a cottage, more easily managed by the limited staff she intended to engage, but not so small as to make the next part of her scheme unworkable.

"It is," she sighed, unable to keep her relief from her voice. "I shall take it for two years, if that is acceptable, Mr. Kennicott."

With a polite nod of his head, the white-haired solicitor replied, "I believe it can be arranged. With payment in advance, I'm sure his grace won't quibble."

"And you understand the need for discretion?"

Again Kennicott nodded, but this time with a hint of solemnity. A man of middle height and trim, energetic build despite his age, he conveyed an air of patience and affection, emphasized by the gentle pat he gave Elizabeth's hand as he linked it through his arm.

She had waited several days after her arrival at the Blind Pilgrim to go in search of the man whose name she found in Jack Silver's book. Exhausted by her journey as well as the inescapable fact of her pregnancy, she rested under the care of Mrs. Vail and her sister, Olive Dunton, wife of the Blind Pilgrim's proprietor. There were times when she thought she might be content to remain at the inn forever, to bear her child and raise it as the offspring of a mythical vicar while she served ale in the taproom.

But on the few occasions she ventured out of her shabby room, she found herself studying the faces of each and every person who passed through the Blind Pilgrim. Always she looked for a man who might be Jack Silver, though she carried no clear picture of him in her mind's eye. There would be no peace for her until she found him, and she dared not wait any longer to continue her search.

Having established herself with Mrs. Vail and Mrs. Dunton as Eliza White, known familiarly as Lizzie, Elizabeth maintained that identity when she set out to find Kaspar Kennicott. He proved to be remarkably easy to locate, a well-respected solicitor who occupied impressive offices. In fact, the ease with which she found him gave rise to new suspicions and fears that she had walked into an elaborate trap.

She dismissed her worries as ridiculous. What need had Jack Silver for convoluted and risky schemes in London when he already had her in his clutches? And if the highwayman were but an instrument of Thomas Colfax, there was even less reason to involve someone in London.

Whether Kaspar Kennicott believed her story of a secret marriage that ended in tragedy, he treated her as what she claimed to be, the daughter of a rusticating aristocrat whose position allowed for no scandal. He plied her with no questions, not even when she deliberately gave him no address at which to contact her. He simply did what she requested and accepted the money she paid him.

"Mrs. White, you must put your mind at ease," he said, leading her to the door. "I have given you my word that your business with me will be conducted with the utmost confidentiality. You are not the first young woman to find herself in this unfortunate situation."

Elizabeth allowed him to guide her outside, then she waited patiently while he closed and locked the door behind him.

"You forget, Mr. Kennicott," she said when he took her hand again, "that I do not consider my situation unfortunate. Inconvenient in some ways, but not without its advantages."

He chuckled and settled his fashionable hat on his head.

"A certain freedom, you called it, though I fail to see how a woman, living alone, will be able to exercise that freedom to any extent."

Elizabeth took a deep breath as Kennicott helped her into the discreet black carriage. She had seen much of London from within this vehicle while Kennicott escorted her to various properties, from elegant and ostentatious townhouses to the quiet cottage she had just decided to occupy. She waited until he joined her and the driver had the single bay trotting smartly down the street before she broached the next subject.

"That is exactly where I will ask for your further assistance, Mr. Kennicott," she said. "I do not intend to live alone."

The laughter he tried to conceal with a sputtering cough brought a flush of anger to her cheeks until she realized her foolish mistake. Then she was grateful for the thick veil that hid the evidence of her monumental embarrassment. Twice she tried to explain herself, and twice shut her mouth in humiliation.

It was Kennicott himself who saved her.

"My dear Mrs. White, I beg your forgiveness. I am an old man who spends too little of his time in the company of lovely young women. I allowed myself the flattery of imagination." He held up a hand to forestall her response. "No, my dear, do not argue that I have not seen your face. Whatever secret you hide behind that widow's veil remains inviolate. The particular beauty with which my mind's eye has endowed you may not allow me to recognize you, but I do not doubt you are a most becoming creature. That said, and my foolishness behind us, let us proceed to business. I presume you wish me to engage a suitable companion for you."

Elizabeth very nearly ripped the hat with its shrouding veil from her head. She wanted suddenly to throw her arms around Kaspar Kennicott and pour out the ghastly truth, every detail of it. There was such trust in his voice, such honest acceptance without reservation, that she felt ashamed of her deception. If he were anyone else, she might have released that last bit of caution. But he was a man who practiced law, who upheld it and held it in reverence, and the man she sought was a criminal.

The deception, the masquerade, must continue.

"Not a companion in the usual sense," she replied. If any tension or uncertainty remained in her voice, she hoped the veil muffled it. "I want no impoverished gentlewoman, although it will be important that this companion be financially dependent upon me. You will compose the necessary legal documents ensuring this relationship. I will make a generous settlement when the companion's services are no longer required."

Though the veil severely limited her vision, Elizabeth noticed Kennicott's sharp, intelligent features twist into a wary frown. She waited for his interruption, then went on when he said nothing. The words came easily now, or perhaps she simply could not bear to hold the thought inside any longer.

"Age is of no consideration, nor physical appearance, provided the person possess sufficient good health. I must, however, insist upon intelligence and education as well as some familiarity with the niceties of polite society. I do not wish to be saddled, even temporarily, with a crude, illiterate lout."

Kennicott rubbed his chin thoughtfully.

"And how long have I to find this paragon? While there are many women with the qualities you require available for such a position, not all of them will be eager to risk—"

With a soft laugh of satisfaction at her own cleverness, Elizabeth broke into his warning. "Oh, no, Mr. Kennicott, you misunderstand me. I do not want a female companion. I want you to find me a husband."

CHAPTER

Newgate was never silent. Prisoners shouted or cursed or fought; chains and shackles rattled; even the noise of traffic from beyond the prison's walls filtered in to disturb the despair that passed for peace. John managed to block out most of the sounds, but enough pierced even his most fervent concentration that he never forgot for a single instant where he was and where he had been since regaining consciousness nearly a week ago on the floor of a filthy, wretched cell somewhere within the bowels of hell.

If he ever saw Elizabeth Stanhope again this side of the grave, he would be able to tell her from his own personal experience that the tower room where she spent two weeks was a virtual paradise compared to this.

He had regained consciousness five days ago in this solitary cell, clear evidence that whoever engineered his arrest wanted him kept as ignorant and defenseless as possible. His first act was to send word to the one man in London he trusted, and though Kaspar Kennicott had so far been unable to gain John's release from this festering hellhole, the lawyer visited him faithfully every day and slowly filled in the missing pieces of the puzzle.

The sound of the turnkey unlocking the door penetrated his thoughts. A raspy voice mumbled something incoherent, but John was familiar enough with the gaoler's speech to recognize the announcement of a visitor. He swung his legs over the side of the cot and slowly eased into a sitting position as the door opened with a creak of ancient hinges.

John squinted against the light. Kennicott entered with a whispered word to the turnkey, then pulled up a crude stool and sat down.

"You're looking better," the lawyer greeted. "Not well, but better."

In no mood for idle chatter, John growled, "I look like hell and I feel worse. Don't humor me. Do they intend to try me or let me rot?"

The door clanged shut, and he winced as the echo reverberated mercilessly within his brain. The worst of the pain in his head had subsided to a dull and intermittent throb days ago, but dizziness and blurred vision still troubled him. Sharp turns, even a quick sideways glance, could bring him almost to his knees, but at least he had hope that that, too, would pass in time.

He had come to despise hope.

"Rot, if I were to guess." Kennicott's matter-of-fact sarcasm and steadfast refusal to permit his client's indulgence in self-pity held John's attention but only for a moment. "I believe, however, I've discovered the means to cheat Thomas of his desire."

"I'll not pay him."

"I did not ask you to. Thomas would never be satisfied with mere money anyway."

"He wants me dead without my blood on his hands."

Kaspar shrugged in agreement.

"From the looks of you, you are well on your way to complying. Have you not eaten?"

"I've had no taste for food."

Until the headaches eased, he'd not been able to keep anything in his stomach. Sometimes just the sour smell of the slop they brought was enough to make him retch. Starvation might be a slow death, but it was preferable to living in this hell.

There were other injuries, further evidence that whoever attacked him was not content with merely rendering him unconscious. He suspected the tender spot on his left side was the result of a well-aimed kick. The bruise had left him too stiff to examine it, but a deep breath still brought twinges of pain. Blood matted his hair where the first blow had been struck an inch or two above his left ear, though that was the only place his attackers drew blood, except for the scabbed-over burns on his wrists from the ropes he had been bound with.

Such injuries would not ordinarily be life-threatening, but in Newgate a man could die from a stubbed toe. Too many hours riding in the cold rain with too few meals left him in even greater danger of illness. He had no idea if the annoying hoarseness in his voice came from screams brought on by nightmares or from the damp that never left this place.

He became aware that Kennicott was studying him and that the solicitor had taken a neatly folded piece of paper from a pocket inside his coat.

"What is that?"

Kennicott spoke slowly, smoothing the paper on his knee. "A marriage license."

John laughed until the rawness of his throat turned laughter to a choking cough.

"Prison marriages have been outlawed for years," he croaked. "And unless you've not told me the truth, I'm not about to hang and leave a debt-free widow."

He snatched the license from Kennicott and held it

up to catch the faint light coming through the barred window in the door. Even squinting, he could not make out the name. His eyes refused to cooperate, and the effort made him dizzy again.

"She's already a widow," Kennicott explained, taking the license back, "or so she claims. She wants a husband, not a corpse, and she's willing to pay."

"To give her bastard a name, no doubt." Disgusted, John flopped back on the cot and laced his fingers behind his head. If he couldn't read the damned license, he might as well stare at the ceiling. But even then, something twisted in his belly, stronger than the nausea and more painful than the hunger. Above the prison stench, he smelled lilacs. "Do you think I'd let some bitch foist her brat off as the next earl of Kilbury?"

"To keep yourself from rotting in Newgate, yes, I believe you would do damn near anything." Kennicott lowered his voice to a whisper. "What makes you think I've told her who you are? Swallow some of that damned Colfax pride—before it kills you. You *could* hang, you arrogant whelp, if your uncle discovers what you've been doing the past four years. All he needs is one tiny bit of evidence against you. While you sit here, coming down with a good case of gaol fever, who knows what he might find? And when he finds it, he will have you exactly where he wants you."

Refusing to look at the lawyer, John reluctantly admitted everything he said made sense—horrible sense.

Thomas had tricked him into signing the deed to the one piece of property not part of the Kilbury estate that could be sold rather than mortgaged. Simple logic would have Thomas selling the Waverley Square house or using it to pay off some of his many debts. But Thomas saw a more practical use for the house John inherited from his mother.

"I fell into his trap, didn't I."

"You could not have known."

John shook his head and coughed again.

"He installed his thugs in the house, knowing I'd go there eventually. I obliged him by going sooner rather than later. The instant I crossed the threshold, his men attacked me and called the watch to have me arrested for trespass and thrown into Newgate to await trial, whenever that might be. If I'd been killed instead of merely injured in the struggle, well, who could be blamed?"

The pain mounted as he gave free rein to his temper. Another spasm of coughing racked him, forcing him onto his side. When it passed, he found he had once again clasped his hands around his head, as though that would keep his skull from exploding.

Talking made it worse, for his throat as well as his head, but he dared not stop the words. They were his only link to sanity and rational thought.

"I'm thrown into gaol, unconscious, like a common felon. And conveniently unidentified. Should I regain my senses and give the magistrate my own version of what happened, including proof that I am indeed the earl of Kilbury, he might let me off. To ensure I remain safely in custody, Thomas files other charges against me involving the debts he has run up in my name."

"You signed the notes, John."

"Don't remind me!"

"You underestimated him. He is not—"

"No! I did not underestimate him at all." There were now two Kaspar Kennicotts sitting beside the cot; John addressed first one, then the other. "He underestimated me."

Putting his thoughts into spoken words helped, but it also took a severe toll. The cell spun madly, first one way, then the other, until he felt as if he were lying on the ceiling and looking down. His throat was on fire but the rest of him felt cool, as though he stood in a cold spring rain.

He struggled to sit. He had to sway to keep up with the rhythm of the revolving room.

"Thomas expected me to defend myself with or without proof. Having none, I chose to remain unidentified, though it's meant a week in—*this*. Give me the license, Kaspar. We'll backdate it a few weeks. My wife won't mind, will she?" There were a quill and a bottle of ink on the cell's tiny table. Reaching for them, he nearly collapsed. "Go to the magistrate tomorrow. Tell him I'm very sorry for what I did. Pay my fine. Plead my desperate and very pregnant wife. I was drunk that night and forgot where I lived. Used to rent that house on Waverley Square from his lordship, the earl of Kilbury, till he sold it. It's taken you this long to get a statement from his lordship."

"But, John, *you're* the—"

John shook his head violently, ignoring the pain.

"I'm Jonathan Largent, occupation gentleman," he replied. "Thomas expects me to admit who I am. I don't think I'll oblige him."

The letters on the license remained a blur; Kennicott pointed out the place to sign. With what he intended to be a flourish, John signed the other name, then let the quill drop from his fingers.

"Remember, bring her tomorrow as soon as possible," he said as he lay down.

Again the coughing seized him so hard that he felt little pieces of his skull crack loose. Kennicott said something about afternoon, if it wasn't too late. John only nodded, not sure why afternoon was to be considered late.

Elizabeth held a scented handkerchief to her nose, but it did little good. The overpowering stench of Newgate made her gag.

"It won't take long, my dear," Kaspar Kennicott

told her as they followed the turnkey through the dank passages.

She tightened her grip on his arm. Since bringing her the news no more than an hour ago, nothing he told her prepared her for this. All that came to her mind were the bitter accusations Jack Silver laid at her feet all those weeks ago, of the men and women he claimed she had condemned to this fate.

In her worst nightmares, she never imagined such a hell existed. The odors were tangible, almost visible, in the clinging damp of the air. They seemed to absorb the feeble light of lanterns and torches. Even when she risked lifting a corner of her veil, only darkness greeted her.

Within the cell, however, all sensations intensified, entering her being, as though by becoming part of her, they could leave the prison when she did.

Her flesh crawled with the filth. It seeped through her clothes like vile worms burrowing through carrion. And the sounds, muffled now by the enclosing walls of the cell, echoed inside her head. She wanted to scream and drown them out but feared the spirit of some desperate soul would turn her cries to forlorn moans.

At Kennicott's gentle urging, Elizabeth stepped forward, approaching the cot where the prisoner— now her husband—lay with his face to the wall. A pathetic stub of candle on the table provided the only light, and she had no choice but to lift the veil.

"Jonathan?" she whispered. "'Tis I, Lizzie, come to take you home."

She heard the turnkey, guarding the door, snicker, then sniff and wipe his nose on his sleeve. Behind her shoulder, Kennicott cleared his throat. But the man on the cot lay motionless. Dear God, what if he were dead?

She did not realize she had backed away from him until she bumped into the sturdy presence of the solicitor. He steadied her with a pat on her shoulder, then tried to push past her to the cot. She stopped him.

"He is my husband," she said. "It is my duty."

She placed a hand on her belly to calm the nausea as well as to remind herself why this horrible deceit was necessary. She would, she swore again, find her child's father, no matter what it cost. When Kennicott came to her with the news that he had a likely candidate for her spouse, he described a man who fit Elizabeth's needs perfectly. He did not tell her until she accepted this Jonathan Largent as her husband that he lay in Newgate.

She forced herself to think of all Jack Silver's bitter words. Was Jonathan Largent one of those innocent unfortunates who found themselves the victims of someone else's greed? Had Jack Silver imposed so much guilt on her that she came to this stranger's aid to expiate a vicarious sin?

No wife, however deep her mourning, would approach her husband veiled. Secure in the dismal gloom, Elizabeth lifted the swathing fabric over her head and reached out a gloved hand to the shoulder of Jonathan Largent.

Through the thin leather of her glove and the filthy linen of his shirt, she felt the steaming heat of him. With a tiny cry, she drew the hand away as he shuddered and mumbled what might have been her name. Then he rolled over and faced her.

She screamed once. Burying her face in her hands, she spun away from the sight of a man on the brink of death. The hollow, bearded cheeks, the fever-haunted eyes, the parched lips forming insensible words. Beads of grimy sweat on his brow matted his hair to his skin. These would never leave her, for they were the living image of the horrors Jack Silver had planted in her mind.

Kaspar Kennicott caught her and would have hastened her out of the cell, but Elizabeth stopped him. Shaking from head to foot, she pushed away from him. With no one to lean upon, she found her own strength.

"You did not tell me my husband was ill," she said, willing her voice steady. "We must take him home immediately."

The fever lasted three days. It never reached the point of delirium, for which John was marginally grateful. Though weak and listless and plagued still by the headaches and blurred vision that tormented him in Newgate, he remained capable of attending to his personal functions but little else. He slept almost constantly, waking often for brief periods of aching misery.

There were moments when he would devoutly have welcomed oblivion. When the woman looked at him for the first time in that hideous cell and turned away in horror at what she saw, his pride took a blow he never expected. For the next hour, while he submitted to Kaspar Kennicott's fussy help getting out of Newgate and into the carriage that would take him heaven only knew where, he wanted to ease her mind, tell her he did not always have the appearance of a monster. But he could not do it, because he had not the strength nor even the conviction that it would have been the truth.

The jolting and swaying of the carriage brought another onset of dizziness and nausea. Kaspar must have ordered the driver to race through London's streets. John curled into a corner of the carriage, closed his eyes, and counted every bloody second of the interminable ride.

He remembered little of their arrival at the house except that again he had to accept Kaspar's assistance or he would never have reached the upstairs bedroom. The solicitor did not leave when it came to the task of stripping off every stitch of prison-befouled clothing.

John protested but with little real vigor. He could not even get his fingers to stop trembling long enough to unfasten a single button.

He had got down to his small clothes, filthier than all the rest, when the woman—good God, this pale-faced, black-garbed creature was his *wife!*—brought hot water for him to wash. She left hastily, and he forced himself to concentrate on cleaning himself as best he could. Aching, shivering, still tasting the gall of Newgate in his mouth, he collapsed on what he knew was her bed and slept.

When he wakened, Kennicott was there again, putting clothes in the wardrobe, making John wonder if the household had no servants. But he had no energy to ask questions, and by the next day—or what he thought was the next day—both a brisk, business-like woman with the air of a housekeeper rather than a ladies' maid and a stocky, one-eyed manservant had made their presence known.

Once, and only once, his wife herself entered his room. He had ordered the curtains kept drawn, for his eyes remained sensitive to the light and his head still throbbed, but the fabric was old and on a sunny day could only dim the room, not fully darken it.

The sound of her entrance, whether a door opening or closing, a footstep on the bare floor, the rustle of her skirts, brought him out of a fitful doze. The fever had broken, leaving him clearheaded at last though weaker than ever. He rubbed his eyes in a vain effort to bring them into focus; she remained only a softly defined silhouette of a slightly built woman in a loose gown that gave a tantalizing hint of high, full breats. Her belly was not yet sufficiently rounded with child to show, but he needed nothing to remind him of her condition.

"Get out!" he croaked.

She turned slowly, unperturbed, and whispered, "Jonathan?"

He wanted to fling off the covers, grab her by the arms, and bodily remove her from his sight, but he hadn't the power to lift the sheet. Even his voice refused to produce a suitable roar; he scraped out a raspy "Leave me alone," before turning on his side with his back to her.

She left without another word and did not return.

He dreamt of lilacs.

Elizabeth resented every moment of Kaspar Kennicott's interference. She also admitted in the late night darkness of the little room she had intended to be her husband's that without the solicitor's assistance, she would never have survived.

He all but carried the man called Jonathan Largent up the stairs that first night, then reminded her of the risks of contagion that effectively relegated her to the kitchen and heating water for the man's bath. He would not listen to her protests that he had put Jonathan in *her* bed.

When he returned the next morning, he pointed out with unassailable logic that she was in no condition to care for the house as well as a sick husband without at least two servants. With her reluctant authority, he procured James Park, a capable if somewhat taciturn manservant who had lost an eye at Waterloo, as well as Mrs. Emma Davis, a widowed Scotswoman whose efficiency surrounded her like a halo.

And that, Elizabeth hoped, would finally free her of the day-to-day responsibilities so she could begin her search for the identity of Jack Silver.

It did not.

Once again the highwayman's accusations haunted her. She was indeed pampered and cosseted with no idea how to run the simplest household. Even her nights at the Black Oak, though they gave her some hint as to how the rest of the world lived beyond the sheltered confines of Stanhope Manor, never prepared her for the ordinary business of linens and laundry, of crockery and cream, of bread and budgets.

In addition to all that, she had to remember not to behave like Elizabeth Stanhope. Betsy Bunch was only a temporary and occasional role; Eliza White, the vicar's widow, must be a constant manifestation if Elizabeth was to become comfortable in the role. She could never raise her voice and only rarely her eyes. Even the way she moved had to change; she became more gentle and submissive.

She dared not resort to false hair as she had in playing Betsy, but the image reflected in her mirror was not a face she recognized. Weeks of worry and fear and no appetite hollowed her cheeks and put deep shadows under her eyes; frequent bouts with tears added a red puffiness to her nose. Her skin was pale as milk, exaggerated by the unrelieved black of mourning.

Slowly, Eliza became a part of Elizabeth's life. Only occasionally, as when she spoke with Kaspar Kennicott, did she allow a portion of her real self to emerge.

They sat in the shade of a blossoming apple tree that crowded the tiny garden at the rear of the cottage. The solicitor had come to visit her husband, but Jonathan had not yet returned. Almost since the day he had first staggered from his bed some three weeks ago, looking gray and gaunt as a drowned corpse, he left the cottage long before she rose and went about whatever business he pursued. He gave her no opportunity to ask questions and returned late, often after she had gone to bed for the night. Today, with both Mrs. Davis and James Park out of the house on errands, she felt lonely and abandoned and invited the solicitor to stay and have tea with her.

"I very nearly had to chase Mrs. Davis out of the house. I'm sure she considers me incapable of looking after myself for an afternoon."

He gave her a very forthright look over the rim of his cup and said, "No doubt she thinks you are a young woman of rather high station who has, for a very obvious reason, married beneath her."

Tilting her head down so the short veil of her bonnet afforded concealment of her furious blush, Elizabeth fervently wished she had sent Kaspar Kennicott on his way. "I suppose that is what you told her?"

With a small smile, he shook his head. "My dear Mrs. Largent, I did what I had to do. I told both Mrs. Davis and James Park that the positions offered to them required the utmost discretion. If they performed their duties to their employer's satisfaction and did not gossip, they would be well paid and sent on their way at the end of their service with an excellent character." He set his empty cup on the table and shrugged expressively as a Frenchman. "If one does not tell servants the truth, one cannot stop them from speculating."

"Are you suggesting I tell them the truth?"

He laughed but leaned over to pat her knee with a familiarity she found much more reassuring than annoying.

"Tell them whatever you like. Perhaps, owing to your lack of experience, you hadn't noticed that they defer to you rather than to your husband. That was another subtle instruction I gave them. If they took it to mean that their mistress controlled the purse strings because the money was hers and not her husband's, is that not what you wanted?"

"And what does my husband have to say about this?"

"You will have to ask him, my dear."

"I am asking you, Mr. Kennicott. You appear very well acquainted with this Jonathan Largent." The question had been nagging at her almost since the moment he ushered her into that cell in Newgate.

Kennicott, his smile never changing, nodded and said, "I have known the gentleman for some years, yes."

She wanted to snap at him and accuse him of using her to free his thieving friend from gaol, of taking advantage of her generosity, but something stopped her. Perhaps it was the cold logic that emanated from Kaspar Kennicott's wise eyes. She, too, had taken advantage. She had come to him for help and he had done she requested, providing her with a husband who so far met every one of her demands.

Now it was Elizabeth's turn to laugh, a rueful little chuckle. Once again, she had received exactly what she asked for, and it was proving to be more than she expected. "You must forgive me, Mr. Kennicott," she apologized. "Blame it on a woman's—"

The garden gate crashed open and Jonathan Largent, his face a mask of fury above the dark beard, destroyed the quiet peace.

"I've found him," he said, his teeth clenched as though that would contain his rage. "The man who bought the house is none other than Benjamin Miner."

CHAPTER

25

John stood at the window that overlooked the cottage garden. His wife, no doubt still stunned by the rudeness of his arrival, sat in her chair beneath the apple tree. He was glad now that she had ousted him from her larger, more comfortable room at the front of the house. From here he could watch and be certain she did not listen at the door.

"You're certain it's Miner?" Kennicott asked. "The name is not that uncommon."

"But the circumstances are. I talked to the servants and the tradesmen. They've not been paid, though they don't seem worried—yet. They said they'd been instructed to send the bills to the tenant, one George St. James, who filed the housebreaking charge against me. He hasn't been near the place for three weeks until today. He's a clerk in a counting house who can't afford the rent and knows he's being used to shield someone else. He said the landlord is Benjamin Miner."

The name left a taste as foul as Newgate on his tongue.

"Not a trace of him for almost twenty years, and suddenly he shows up as the new owner of my mother's house. Damn!" He slammed his fist down upon the windowsill. The woman below looked up at the sound. The short veil fell back, but the branches of the apple tree provided an effective screen that not even his improved eyesight could penetrate. "Who is he, Kaspar? How can a man lend my uncle thousands of pounds and collect interest on those mortgages all these years and still remain a mystery?"

"You did it well enough."

"That was different. I operated outside the law."

"And did your operations ever affect Mr. Miner?"

"Frequently. He holds more of the mortgages than anyone else except Edward Stanhope. I intercepted several payments intended for Miner. None of Thomas's creditors escaped."

"Perhaps you should have followed the courier instead of relieving him of his currency."

John shook his head.

"I tried, Kaspar. He spent the night at a local inn and boarded the London mail coach the following morning."

The woman in the garden rose from her chair and turned to reenter the house. She moved with an oddly seductive grace, considering how she pressed one hand to her back in a way that emphasized her pregnancy. John watched her until she disappeared inside.

"Tell me about her," he said, staring now at the chair where she had sat. "I want to know about this woman who, for the time being at least, is my lawfully wedded wife."

Elizabeth picked at her food, her eyes downcast but focused on nothing. A dozen thoughts swirled through her head, most of them questions about the name Jonathan Largent had spat when he burst into her quiet conversation with Kaspar Kennicott. She was certain she had never heard of anyone named Benjamin Miner, but the name echoed in her head with eerie familiarity. When she tried to excuse it as one of those queer incidents of hearing something for the first time and yet thinking it has come from memory, she failed.

Jonathan rarely returned from his day's activities in time for the evening meal, and when he did, Elizabeth discreetly took hers in her room. Tonight, however, after leaving with Kennicott for several hours, Jonathan arrived just as she was taking her solitary place at the table. To her extreme discomfiture, he joined her.

The bottle of wine he set unceremoniously beside his plate was not the only indication that he had been drinking. He offered her none, just kept his own glass full while eating and making small talk about the weather, the fish Mrs. Davis had prepared for their dinner, the announcement in the newspaper that a highwayman by the name of Charlie Haddow had been convicted and would hang the following Monday.

She gasped at the last and dropped her fork with a clatter to the plate.

"Oh, sorry," he apologized in an offhand manner. "Not the thing to discuss with a lady in your condition, is it."

"No, it isn't," she replied, keeping her head down and hoping he did not notice the way her fingers trembled as she picked up the fork and tried to eat again. "And certainly not when one has so recently escaped the unfortunate Mr. Haddow's fate himself."

"Ah, *touché*, Lizzie, my dear."

The teasing laughter in his low, still-raspy voice sent a tremor through her. Why had she baited him? She should simply have accepted his apology and ignored him, as she usually did. But his presence was unsettling; she found her thoughts ranging in too many directions, out of control. From Benjamin Miner to Jack Silver to Jonathan Largent—and back again.

"You are a clever wench, Lizzie, but then you are well aware of that, aren't you?"

"I don't know what you mean, Mr. Largent."

"Why so formal, my dear? After all, we are man and wife. And you know exactly what I mean."

So now he was baiting her. There was a sure way to avoid being hooked and netted.

Elizabeth pushed her chair back and rose in a single motion. The fish had gone cold, and she no longer had an appetite for any meal shared with this arrogant man.

Across the table, she glared at him and at the bottle of wine.

"Good night, *husband*," she said in a voice as devoid of emotion as she could make it. There was no reason for anger nor for any other strong feelings toward a man who was nothing more than a convenience at best and an annoyance at worst. Yet she felt a fountain of them bubbling inside her as she walked away from him.

He caught her before she reached the stairs. She had not thought to run, but then she had not thought he would come after her either until the instant he clamped his hand around her arm and held her.

She did not turn, and he did not force her. For a long heartbeat they stood thus. She heard the rasp of his breathing, the effect of the fever and cough that had not completely left him. The stairway was dark, for she had not taken a light when she left the table. Against the black upper reaches, she saw again the face of the man in Newgate, the beard, the untrimmed hair, the wild eyes and wondered why she felt so little fear.

"You are drunk, Mr. Largent," she said. He neither loosened his hold nor made any effort to pull her back.

"I've been drinking, yes, but I'm far from drunk,

Lizzie. It takes a great deal more to put me under the table."

Elizabeth licked her lips at the memory of the wine she had shared with Jack Silver. Something light and sweet fluttered through her midsection, then drifted lower to settle in that secret core of her being. The hand on her arm eased its grip, then stroked down to her elbow, her wrist, her hand.

With a sudden cry, she jerked free and raced up the stairs. Blinded by tears as well as darkness, hampered by skirts that tangled around her ankles, she stumbled more than once. And Jonathan climbed the stairs right behind her. She heard his steady footfalls and, above the pounding of her own heart, his urgent plea.

"Slow down, Lizzie. You'll fall if you aren't careful."

She paid no heed. The touch of his fingers on hers still burned like a brand. She made the top of the stair and ran for the safety of her room. Though the door had no lock, she slammed it shut. Even a second or two delay would be enough for her to reach the fireplace poker. When Jonathan Largent burst through her door, she would face him with at least one effective weapon.

But he did not burst through the door. He opened it slowly and stood on the threshold.

John did not have to see her wide eyes, her trembling lips, to know she was terrified. He could smell her terror, even taste it in the air through which she had passed.

Dressed in the widow's black that had turned her face to little more than a stark, pale mask, she was all but invisible in the darkness of the room. But he had heard the clatter of the poker and guessed, from the direction of her voice, that she crouched with the weapon in hand, waiting for his attack.

Without taking another step forward, he asked, "Are you all right?"

"I'm fine. Now get out."

His eyes slowly adjusted. The blurriness that had plagued him since Thomas's thug cracked his skull was less severe but still enough to be a nuisance, especially in the darkness.

He kept his voice low and steady as he might croon to a fractious horse. "You needn't put down the poker, Lizzie, if it makes you feel safe, but I shan't come closer. I only wish to apologize and make certain you weren't hurt running up the stairs."

What was the matter with him? Why didn't he just say he was sorry and leave the wench alone? Let her take her black-garbed body to her solitary bed while he comforted himself with the wine.

"I wasn't hurt. Now please, Mr. Largent, leave me alone."

For all her brave front, for all her cleverness, she was still a woman alone, a woman who, whatever her own sins might be, carried a child as innocent as the one he had tried to give Elizabeth Stanhope.

And that was why he could not turn away from her, why he had gone after her and taken hold of her arm and then touched her hand. He could blame the wine all night long, but the wine had little to do with his action beyond the fact that it was almost as fine and old as the bottles he had shared with Elizabeth.

This Eliza White, whether widowed or merely abandoned, reminded him too strongly of the woman he, too, had abandoned. She was as slight as Elizabeth despite the pregnancy that had just begun to round her figure and perhaps made more frail by the mourning clothes and the loss that required them. She lacked Elizabeth's sparkle, her defiance, the way she always met his eyes without fear. Yet he saw in her a trace of Elizabeth's determination. Alone against the world, she had not surrendered.

He pulled the door closed and let the sound of its

latching cover the words as he whispered, "Good night, Elizabeth."

Elizabeth listened, her fingers aching from her death grip on the poker, while his footsteps marked his passage to the stairs and then down. Drained of all strength, she collapsed onto the bed. The poker slipped from her hands to fall with a thud on the floor.

She made no move to retrieve it. It might have protected her from an assault by Jonathan Largent, but it could do nothing to save her from a far more dangerous enemy.

Herself.

She did not like Jonathan Largent. Pity and her own desperation had combined to make her take advantage of the opportunity offered by the man in Newgate, but he had done nothing since then to improve her opinion of him. Conveniently, he seemed to share the same attitude toward her: indifference tempered by a grudging gratitude.

But that brief touch of his hand on hers had brought to life a flame she thought cold and dead as ashes, the searing, scorching flame of desire Jack Silver had ignited months ago.

She did not, *could* not, feel such desire for a man like Jonathan Largent. He was, most likely, a common thief. And the only difference between her husband and Jack Silver was that the highwayman readily admitted his crimes. Hardly a distinction.

She wiped her hand on the counterpane over and over again. As the subtle tingle began to fade, reason returned.

Rising tentatively from the bed, Elizabeth placed the blame squarely on exhaustion and her own failure to carry out the mission she had set herself. She had spent too much time organizing her household, a task that should have been left to Mrs. Davis. She had spent too much time proving—perhaps only to herself—that she was not the pampered bitch Jack Silver had named her.

"Not that he'll ever know it," she muttered to the darkness as she began undressing.

She had spent no time at all on her search for the man himself.

She pulled off the cap that concealed her hair and shook the tousled locks free. Though her arms ached from those furious moments of wielding the poker, she made her way to the tiny, neat dressing table and fumbled for her brush. If she did not take the time to braid her hair, it would be tangled beyond hope by morning as she remembered too well from her weeks as Jack Silver's captive.

She sank down on the stool and buried her face in her hands. Dear God, must *everything* remind her of that man? From the wine her husband drank to the simple act of brushing her hair, she could not escape Jack Silver. And even if she could, there was always the child, quickening to life within her.

"I *will* find you," she vowed.

Her search would begin tomorrow.

Kaspar Kennicott set the perfectly matched rubies back into their velvet-lined box.

"Mrs. Largent, I am a solicitor, not a banker."

Elizabeth kept her hands folded on her lap rather than taking back the box when Kennicott closed it and pushed it toward her in perfect alignment with three others.

"You handled the other transactions for me, Mr. Kennicott. I trust you are knowledgeable enough to convert these as well." She met his stare without blinking. If her plan was to succeed, she must secure Kennicott's assistance. "And, considering my unusual circumstances, I trust you to maintain the discretion I have hitherto relied so heavily upon and for which I am eternally grateful."

She moved her hands over the soft curve of her belly. Though she could have worn any of her dresses still, she chose to leave off the constricting stays in order to emphasize what most women would have taken extreme pains to conceal.

"I told you, Mr. Kennicott, when I first embarked upon this venture, that my goal was to provide for a child who, through no fault of his own, might find himself in a position of disadvantage."

The speech, rehearsed in the wee hours of a sleepless night, came more easily than she expected.

Kennicott nodded and replied, "A goal I cannot but find admirable, Mrs. Largent. But you propose to enter a world you know nothing about. Men of business will not readily take to a woman's interference."

"Which is why I needed a husband. A protector, if you will, even if in name only," she reminded him. With a deep sigh, she allowed her shoulders to slump for a moment and turned her gaze away. "I fear I have been less than completely truthful with you, Mr. Kennicott. You have been kind enough to accept my tale of misfortune without question."

"You paid me well enough to do so."

Ignoring the hint of humor in his remark, Elizabeth went on.

"My late husband took his own life, Mr. Kennicott. No, please, I do not ask your sympathy. He was a weak man, driven to his death by certain men who had taken advantage of him."

"And you wish revenge upon them?"

"Not at all. I wish only to ascertain their identities and clear my husband's name by repaying his debts while at the same time making investments for my future and that of my child. That is why I do not wish to engage the services of a banker, Mr. Kennicott. Only of a solicitor who will provide me with the proper introductions and handle the necessary legal niceties. And," she added with the barest hint of a smile, "remain discreet."

Only conscious effort kept her breathing normal, and nothing could slow the desperate race of her pulse.

She had acted instinctively when she fled Stanhope Manor over a month ago, but she trusted her instincts. Last night, as she plotted her course of action in the dark silence of her room, she knew she had made the right choice. Jack Silver had eluded discovery, she was certain, because although the highwayman haunted the roads of rural Somerset, his unmasked counterpart, the man she sought, must not live there. Surely after four years someone would have recognized him.

There was also his choice of victims. Virtually every one was connected in some way or other to Thomas Colfax or, though less often, to her father. Clearly, as her own kidnapping and the treatment she received at the outlaw's hands proved, Jack Silver carried a personal malice toward those two men. She knew little of Thomas's business dealings, but her father's connections all lay in London. If he had made any enemies, they were likely to be there rather than in the countryside where he was treated with respect. The same with Thomas Colfax, who had done so much to maintain the Kilbury estate for his brother and nephew. She wished to learn who those enemies were, for she was certain therein lay the secret to Jack Silver's identity.

The presence of Kaspar Kennicott's name and direction in the highwayman's possession added further confirmation to her logic.

If the calm, unpretentious solicitor did not accept her tale, Elizabeth knew the scheme was doomed. In the tiny hours of the morning, just before she finally fell into a brief and fitful doze, she realized that Kaspar Kennicott, for all her suspicions, remained her last and best hope. He had undoubtedly used her to secure the release of his friend. But if Jonathan Largent was a thief, so was Jack Silver, and the connection could provide Elizabeth with the information she required if, as she fervently prayed, Kennicott agreed to help her.

"You ask a great deal of an old man who is set in his ways. Will you grant me a day to think upon your proposition?"

A cry of defeat rose in Elizabeth's throat. A day! When she had already lost a month of precious time? But she realized, even as she swallowed the cry and fought to keep her features composed, that Kennicott had not rejected her offer. In fact, he was reaching for the box that held the rubies.

The argument was nearly an hour old, having begun the instant John entered Kennicott's offices on the heels of his early-arriving clerk. Unable to face Lizzie even in passing, John had left the cottage almost at dawn as he had the day before. He had not, in fact, laid eyes on her since he closed her bedroom door two nights ago, another woman's name on his lips.

He shook his head vigorously, barely giving Kennicott a chance to finish his statement.

"No, Kaspar, not yet."

"And why not? Why wait?" The old man leaned forward, his forearms on the edge of his desk. "Because you want to strike a killing blow, am I not right? There's a far greater risk buying them all at once, you know. More satisfaction perhaps but more risk. She wants introductions to men of business. What better introduction than to send her out to buy back the mortgages as investments?"

"And what of the risks to her?"

"Do you care?"

"Hell, yes, I care!" John thundered, getting to his feet to resume his pacing. "Good God, Kaspar, what kind of bastard do you take me for?"

"I'm not sure. What kind do you take yourself for?"

"Not the kind who puts innocent women and children, especially unborn ones, into that kind of danger. Besides, what can she know of business? She says she doesn't know enough to pawn the jewels and get a fair price for them, but she intends to invest the proceeds? She's lying to you, Kaspar. You've fallen her victim."

"You're a good one to talk about lies, John Colfax, earl of Kilbury," Kennicott snorted. "And if you'd been listening to me instead of concocting your own excuses, you'd know she has no intention of making investments. She wants to pay off her late husband's debts as soon as she can find the creditors. One of them, she says, is Abraham Melford. The others I've never heard of, but that name caught my attention. Melford holds one of the older notes."

"And he's bankrupt. Or nearly so." John stroked the growth of beard on his chin thoughtfully and pivoted neatly to make another pass of the room. "He could sell the note."

"He could indeed."

"To the widow of Jonathan Largent?"

The ingenious picture was taking shape.

"Precisely," Kennicott intoned. "I believe you begin to see the advantages of such a strategy? To yourself as well as to your wife."

John groaned and grabbed the back of the chair. As he leaned heavily upon it, he hung his head, recalling that desperate instant when he came so close to wanting to make the woman his wife in deed as well as name. He looked up slowly and asked, "Was she upset yesterday?"

"No, not particularly. Why? Did something happen between you?"

With a sardonic smile, John replied, "Come now, Kaspar, you sound almost as if you wish something had."

The old man scowled. "You could do worse."

"Widow or not, she carries another man's child. And given the fantastical stories she's led you to believe, the woman is no doubt a crook of some kind. A thief, more than likely," he said with a wave of his hand toward the row of small ebony boxes lined up along the front edge of the desk.

But the memory of the stark terror in her eyes told him she was no thief, no criminal. If anything, she had been the victim of one. Innocence shone through her fear, the kind of innocence that could not be feigned.

"I don't think she's a thief. The sapphire is paste."

John picked up and opened the first of the boxes. Nestled on its bed of black velvet, a blue oval stone winked back at him. The size of his small fingernail, it probably graced a ring, but it reminded him of those other blue stones, which he could not think of without seeing them around Elizabeth's neck, against the satin of her skin, in the seductive, enticing shadow between her breasts.

He snapped the box shut on the false jewel. "Do whatever she wants," he said. "Buy back my father's notes, one at a time if need be. And, Kaspar, watch out for her. I came here to find another woman, and I intend to do so."

CHAPTER
26

Nothing, Elizabeth reflected as she took a moment to adjust her bonnet against the light October drizzle, had gone as planned. Nothing.

She wondered, on days like this, where she found the strength to continue. Each failure intensified her sense of futility, and after months of far more failures than successes, she told herself she ought to have sense enough to give it all up. Jack Silver had left no trace in London, neither in the subdued elegance of Fleet Street banks nor in the noisome bustle of the docks. At least none that she could uncover.

Doing her best to maintain an air of grace despite her ungainly shape, she slipped her gloved hand into James Park's and allowed him to help her down from the phaeton. The stench of the docks had unsettled her stomach, but she swallowed the nausea with grim determination. Time was running out; she had none to spare for queasiness.

"Shall I wait outside, madam?"

James's question broke into her thoughts. There was just the slightest hint of disapproval in his voice these days. Whether it was for the places she ordered him to take her or for her insistence upon going to them when she ought to be sitting at home awaiting the birth of this child, she did not know. She accepted his censure as a form of affection. She came very near to thinking of him as a friend, save that James kept his distance.

Two ragged boys ran up, scrapping between them for the honor—and coin—of holding the sedate chestnut who pulled the vehicle.

"No, James, I think it would be best if you accompany me. Give the boys a ha'penny each, with another if they do not bloody each other's noses before we return."

She walked up the steps and glanced at the bronze plate, symbol perhaps of more prosperous times and brighter hopes, set into the wall beside the dingy door. According to the proud letters, the firm of Wilke and Race, Shipping, had been founded in 1785. Wilke was one of those names she had given to Jack Silver as part of her infernal bargain. Her father had done business with Wilke, of what nature or how many years ago, she could not remember. Race, the other partner, held one of the mortgage notes Kaspar Kennicott had sent her to buy. She might well have declined this particular mission had Kaspar not told her of the partnership. That odd coincidence had happened only once before, though with disappointing results. The man, Jacob Townleigh, had died several months earlier. His son accepted payment and turned over the note—and knew nothing of Edward Stanhope, Jack Silver, or Benjamin Miner.

She could only hope today proved more fruitful.

James, carrying a heavy satchel in the crook of one arm, opened the door. She entered a tiny, musty room lit by the miserable gloom that passed for sunlight coming through a high window and a fat candle on an ancient stand towering above the mounds of dusty papers on an equally ancient desk.

A gnome with a bulbous nose that sported a large, hairy wart looked up. If Kaspar had not warned her in advance, she would have gaped at Hamilton Wilke as if he were an ape in a menagerie.

"You must be Largent's widow," the gnome said as he walked around the desk.

Elizabeth nodded. "I am Mrs. Largent, yes," she replied, neither correcting nor affirming Wilke's assumption.

He eyed her the way a farmer might eye a cow or horse at a gypsy fair—with open skepticism. Elizabeth waited, not patient but weary, while he made his inspection. The child within her protruding belly kicked with enough vigor to cause pain, but she barely winced. It was an almost constant thing now, this kicking and twisting. And soon to be over.

"Come to buy up old Race's note, so the lawyer says." The singsong rhythm to his words fit his gnomelike appearance.

"Yes. I've brought the payment."

There was no fire in the grate. Wilke's gaze from pale watery eyes added to the chill. He circled her, passing between her and the patient James.

"Five hundred pounds plus the missing interest?"

"I beg your pardon?" She snapped around to face the voice that came from just behind her right shoulder. "I know nothing of any missing interest. I was told the note was for five hundred pounds."

Wilke grinned, displaying fine white teeth, and slicked his hands over his bald pate.

The hair at the back of Elizabeth's neck prickled as if lightning were about to strike. Though the day was gray and gloomy, no storm threatened; alarmed, she glanced over her other shoulder to make certain no one stood between her and the door. James had placed his hand on the handle.

"It's an odd thing about that note," Wilke muttered, strolling back to his stool. "Ye're a bit far along with that child to be out 'n' about, Mistress Largent, are ye not?"

She had faced that question more and more of late. Her answer remained the same.

"The sooner we conclude our business, Mr. Wilke, the sooner I and my child will be safely home." Withdrawing from her reticule the papers Kaspar Kennicott had drawn up, she approached the dust-encrusted desk. "You may read them over before you sign, Mr. Wilke. Mr. Park, will you bring Mr. Wilke his money? I expect he will wish to count it. And then you may leave us."

Wilke stretched out a hand and took the roll of documents. Elizabeth released them quickly, before he had a chance to touch her hand. He gave her a sly sneer that sent a shiver of loathing down her back. When he had broken the seal and unrolled the first page, she nodded to James. He stepped forward and placed the leather satchel on a corner of the desk. He made it quite clear that he did not like leaving her alone with men like Hamilton Wilke, especially with large sums of money, but always before he had followed her orders. This time he hesitated until she turned her head in his direction.

There was no mistaking his glower, but he departed. She suspected he would not be more than inches from the door.

Hamilton Wilke, now apparently absorbed in the legal documents before him, reached into an open drawer and pulled out a pair of round spectacles. When he had the wires wrapped securely around his ears, he moved the iron candlestand so two of its legs held Kennicott's papers flat.

"As you can see, Mr. Wilke, I am buying the note as an investment," Elizabeth began, the long-memorized phrases coming easily to her tongue. On days like this, when she was almost too tired to stand, she worried that she might forget something in the middle and have to start all over. "My husband endured some misfortunes in his own financial dealings, and I wish to avoid such a future for my child. Are you aware of other men of business, such as yourself, who might be willing to entertain a similar transaction? Who have notes they would be willing to sell for cash?"

Hamilton Wilke ran one finger under each line of Kennicott's writing. "Sell their capital? Not likely. None that I know of leastways."

"I was told a gentleman by the name of Andrew MacLendon is looking for investors, but I have not been able to locate him."

Wilke glanced up, peering over the lenses of his glasses, but immediately resumed reading.

"Never heard of MacLendon," he muttered.

Elizabeth had been careful at each of these meetings to mention no more than two or three of the names she recalled. Though she understood this caution could cost her valuable information, she also believed someone, somewhere, would recognize at least one. No one ever did. Today, however, she knew she had to risk everything.

"I am also looking for Benjamin Miner."

Wilke raised his large head slowly. His eyes, peering at Elizabeth first over his glasses and then through them, narrowed to bleary slashes. "Ye're not alone, Mistress Largent. There are many of us been lookin' for Ben Miner these last twenty years."

Elizabeth had never experienced such cold, living hatred in her life. It oozed from Hamilton Wilke like liquid frost, pooling around him and then spreading to encompass the entire chamber. He never moved his finger from the page, but Elizabeth sensed the threat in that very stillness. If Benjamin Miner had walked in at that moment, Hamilton Wilke would have strangled him with his bare hands.

She swayed under the force of that malignant

hostility but did not move toward escape. She had inquired after the mysterious Benjamin Miner several times before, but those who recalled the name at all gave only the vaguest of responses. The man was dead, some said, or they recalled the name but nothing connected with it. Most had never heard of him.

But Hamilton Wilke remembered him well. Frightened yet desperate for the information, Elizabeth waited in silence. Again the child kicked, and the dull ache in her back grew worse.

When Wilke spoke, his voice dropped to a sinister, threatening whisper. "Ben Miner disappeared twenty years ago, maybe more, with every penny I had to my name. Said he was going to invest it in some scheme wi' a friend of his, the son of a duke no less. Talked a good tale, Ben did, and we all trusted him. Till he took our money and never showed his face again."

"Where did he go?"

"Anyone who knows never said a word. Ben Miner vanished into thin air, with my three hundred guineas. For all I know, the bastard married the duke's daughter and lived at Kensington Palace while his old mates starved and rotted and died in prison for the debts they couldn't pay."

Remembering the man in the Newgate cell, Elizabeth felt again that rush of guilt, as though she owed Hamilton Wilke an apology for what Benjamin Miner had done so many years ago, perhaps even before she was born. But her apology would make no difference, so she bit the words back except for one quiet question. "Did you go to prison, Mr. Wilke?"

Wilke's every word dripped with venom as fresh as his memories were old. "No, not I. Race did, though, him with a wife and family. Two months he were in that place and never were right after. It killed his wife. Died bearin' a stillborn son the day after Race come home from the Fleet, she did."

Elizabeth did not realize how far she had backed away from Wilke and his palpable hatred until she came in contact with the door.

"If it weren't for his daughter, Race would've done himself in, and it wouldn't've taken much. Coughed all the time, and he took to drink. There bein' no one else to look after the poor girl, I set the money aside for the rent each week, for coal and milk and whatever else she needed. Saw to it she were taken care of, I did."

"I'm sure she was very grateful, Mr. Wilke."

"Grateful? She never knew. I never told her. Like I never told her about this note. Just sent her the interest and told her it was from her father's part of the business." He snorted, an animal-like sound that echoed in the still, dusty room. "It were, I suppose. I gave him the money when I bought him out."

"You bought him out? He's not your partner?"

Wilke shook his head and removed the spectacles from his nose.

"I've no partner, Mistress Largent." When she looked over her shoulder to where the brass plate was on the other side of the wall, he chuckled. "Sentimental of me, ye might say, to leave his name there, but truth is, I've had no partners since the day I gave Race that five hundred guineas for his half of the firm."

That wasn't right, and she knew it.

"But Edward Stanhope invested in your business, didn't he?"

Reaching for the moth-eaten quill and dusty bottle of ink that had been nearly hidden between two piles of papers, Wilke shook his head again and said, "Not him, whoever he is, not anyone."

Her father's name had roused no response in the man who dipped the quill in the ink and scratched his name laboriously across the bottom of the page. Hamilton Wilke remembered Ben Miner as if the rogue had not but left the office, but not Edward

Stanhope, with whom he had done business surely within the past year.

"Are you certain, Mr. Wilke? I was told Mr. Stanhope—"

"You were told wrong, Mistress Largent. I've never heard of Stanhope, and I've taken in no partners." He blew on the ink to dry it before rolling the old note into a tight tube. "Race were drunk one night and come in here beggin' me for the money. Said there were a man sellin' property in the country. Race wanted to take his little Sarah out o' London and I thought maybe he'd do it, so I gave him the money. Made him sign his half of the business over to me just in case. Next day, he brought me this."

She had watched often enough before as men dribbled sealing wax along the edge of the rolled documents and never before felt her curiosity awaken. This interview with Hamilton Wilke, however, had gone nothing like the others, one and all brief meetings, with a few questions asked, the papers signed and sealed quickly, the money transferred. If what Elizabeth learned fell far short of her expectations, at least she never came away knowing less than she started with.

Now she had even more questions—and so much less time in which to find answers. She stepped forward, ready to stretch out her hand to take the mortgage note from Wilke, but he did not offer it to her. Instead, he lay the neat cylinder close to his elbow, as if daring her to come within his own reach to take it.

Elizabeth very nearly took up the challenge.

"I said before it was an odd thing about this note," he repeated, lifting the candlestand from the new documents that provided for the transfer of the debt to E. Largent, widow. "Poor Race thought he were buying the property, but next morning when the gin left him, he found out 'twas only a mortgage. He'd been swore to secrecy about it, warned never to tell no one. He knew he'd given away all he had left, that he'd go back to gaol when he couldn't pay his debts, and there was nothing for Sarah, not a farthing. Made me swear, he did, not to tell her what he'd done."

He scratched his signature onto the documents, then slid them toward Elizabeth for hers. When he handed her the quill, she hesitated, afraid he would take the opportunity to try to touch her again but instead he lay it down within her easy reach.

"And did you tell her, Mr. Wilke?" she asked, giving her hand a moment to stop its trembling.

"No, Mistress Largent. I never told her. Race put a pistol to his head that night, and there weren't no reason to give the poor girl any more grief. I shut the note away, thinking it were worthless. But the payments came, without fail, every quarter save two. When that scoundrel Jack Silver robbed me of the interest twice, I still never told her. Made it good out of my own pocket."

She met his rheumy stare because she felt it demanding her attention. The pale eyes glittered expectantly, triumphantly. Whatever secret he held, he would not divulge it until she had signed her name. She dipped the quill, still warm from Wilke's own hand, and carefully scribed her name while he told her what she had already begun to suspect.

"Ye see, Mistress Largent, there weren't nobody else knew of this note save Race and the man who made it. Race is dead these many years, so it won't take me long to find out who you are and what you're up to."

Beyond the tiny yard, the afternoon mist was becoming a murky evening fog that distorted sounds of traffic into eerie, muffled echoes. As he had done a dozen or more times in the past hour, John snapped his watch closed and tucked it back into his pocket without taking note of the time. "She's late," he muttered, making one last survey of the road. "Too late."

Three strides brought him to the door he had left standing open. The warmth and cheer of the cozy sitting room welcomed him as he reentered the house and reluctantly closed the door. A fire crackled on the hearth and lamps glowed with mellow light. The place wanted only a tabby cat curled on the rug—and a woman in the chair beside the knitting basket.

"How could you send her all the way to the docks, Kaspar?"

The lawyer crouched by the fire and with a pair of tongs plucked out a coal to light his pipe. He drew steadily on it for a moment, then said, "I did not send her anywhere. She demanded to take Race's note in no uncertain terms."

"Then you should have stopped her. It's too far and too dangerous for any woman, let alone one in her condition."

Kaspar puffed a ring of fragrant smoke around his head.

"Is that a note of husbandly concern I hear in your voice? You seem rather solicitous of late. Shall I send to Bow Street for a runner?"

"I fail to see the humor in that remark."

"It was not meant to be humorous."

"And by that you mean what?"

If a fight with Kaspar would relieve him of this unbearable tension, he'd gladly beat the old man to a bloody pulp. When the lawyer attempted to place a hand on his arm, John shook it off until Kennicott's chuckle told him he had acted like a petulant child.

But it was so damn hard not to be angry, not to want to lash out and expend the energy that built inside him. He should have learned patience from the four years spent engineering his revenge on Thomas. The past six months, however, seemed far, far longer. Lizzie had the honor of buying back the Kilbury mortgages Thomas had pressured John and his father before him into signing. Each time John went through the legal formality of transferring the debt to himself, he felt cheated of the victory. Nor did he have the consolation of being one whit closer to learning where either Benjamin Miner or Elizabeth Stanhope had disappeared to.

He had already fallen into a black reverie when Kaspar tapped him on the shoulder and said, "Come, let us walk outside for a while. Perhaps we shall meet her at the end of the lane and allay your fears all the sooner."

The insistent tone in Kennicott's voice coupled with a discreet gesture with the pipe reminded John that Mrs. Davis was well within hearing distance in the kitchen.

Another near slip. It wasn't that he didn't trust the housekeeper; he no longer trusted himself.

Kaspar led him out of the house and onto the brick walk that led to the gate. A neighbor passing on his way home called a greeting. When John returned the pleasantry, he realized he did not know the man's name. Six months in this house and he did not know his next-door neighbor's name.

There were others in the lane, some walking with eagerness to reach the homes they had left hours before, others trudging with weariness.

"I envy them," he said, watching the man he had spoken with enter his home and the welcoming embrace of his wife. "I never wanted this intrigue and danger. A quiet, settled life for me, a docile wife, a cozy fire, horses to race at Epsom and give me all the excitement a man could want. Nothing more. Certainly not *this*."

He would have slammed his hand on the iron gate, but Kaspar lifted the latch and opened it, sparing him a possible injury.

"And I assure you, Kaspar, I have no husbandly

feelings toward Lizzie. If I did, her actions today would have destroyed them. Whyever would the woman insist on going to the docks to see Julian Race?"

"Oh, she couldn't have been going to see Race. He died years ago."

John was about to ask who she *was* going to see when the rapid tattoo of hoofbeats swirled through the mist. Looking toward the sound, he saw the phaeton he had insisted Lizzie purchase enter the circle of gaslight at the end of the lane. Park, an excellent driver despite his handicap, was driving too recklessly for safety at this hour of the night in a fog growing increasingly murky.

"Something's happened," John breathed, and before the second word had left his lips, he was sprinting the few yards back to the cottage.

CHAPTER
27

Elizabeth lay her head against the damp cushions, too weary to open her eyes even when she felt the vehicle shift as James stepped in to help her down. The simple act of raising her hand required more strength than she could command at that moment.

It didn't matter. Strong arms slipped beneath her knees and around her shoulders and lifted her bodily from the phaeton. She made a futile grab for the bonnet and veil that tumbled from her head, but they fell to the floor beyond her reach.

"I'll get the door, sir!" she heard someone shout as though from a long distance until she realized it was James, running ahead, and that his voice was muffled because Jonathan held her tightly against him.

"Why must all the women in my life be fools?" he growled.

She very nearly asked him who the other women in his life were and why he thought them fools, but by then he was snapping orders to all and sundry while he carried her up the stairs.

"Kaspar, fetch us some brandy. Mrs. Davis, is the

fire laid in Mrs. Largent's room? I'll want some hot bricks for her bed, and, James, see to that horse at once."

While he fumbled opening her door, she managed to tell him, "For a man who is frequently gone for weeks at a time and can hardly be bothered to come home at night, you're certainly quite comfortable telling my servants what to do."

He made no reply, just stepped into the room and then out of the way to let Mrs. Davis past him. The housekeeper turned down the bed and piled the pillows high, while Elizabeth watched with a growing unease. She was unprepared for the intimacy of being in a man's arms, of waiting for him to carry her to her bed and lay her down upon it. A woman eight months gone with child ought not to feel such a flush of anticipation, especially when the man who held her was one she did not love.

Whether she loved him or not, it felt so right after the days and weeks and months of disappointments and loneliness to curl into his embrace. If she closed her eyes, she could almost imagine her husband was Jack Silver, sweeping her off her feet to ravish her in the seductive seclusion of that dark little room.

But instead of Jack, it was Jonathan Largent settling her against the pillows, then offering her the brandy Kaspar Kennicott poured into a tumbler.

"Drink it," he said in that slightly hoarse, prison-roughened voice so similar to Jack's velvety whisper.

She downed the fiery liquid in a single gulp that left her gasping and choking and momentarily blind and no less wrapped in memories of the man she could not find. The child moved within her, the ever-present reminder of her failure, the ever-present reminder of her love. When Jonathan pressed the glass into her hands again, she did not hesitate to pour the brandy down her throat.

"Easy, easy," he said, his hands closing around hers to pull the glass from her lips. "Too much and you'll get sick. Especially on an empty stomach."

She opened her eyes to find the room dark save for the light from the fire. A click from the latch told her Kaspar and Mrs. Davis had left; she was alone with this virtual stranger who was her legal husband. A painful sob rose from her heart at the memory of another firelit chamber, of being alone with a man she did not know and dared not trust. She swallowed the ache and covered the cry with a question.

"How do you know my stomach's empty?"

He took the glass and rose from the bed. She felt strangely abandoned, but he went no further than the end of the bed, where he began to remove her shoes.

"I heard it grumbling when I pulled you out of the phaeton."

She tried to pull her feet up and out of his reach, but the mound of her very full belly got in the way. Besides, he was too quick and had one of her ankles firmly in his grasp. Embarrassed, she let the other foot slide down beside it.

He dropped the first shoe to the floor and went to work on the laces of the second. "I should think you'd have more concern for that baby than to go around starving the poor mite before it's even born."

"Are you implying I'd starve it afterward?" He rubbed her ankles as if he knew how tired they were, and Elizabeth could not hold in a sigh of pleasure at the soft, massaging strokes of his fingers. "And what do you care about it? It's not your child."

He rolled down the first stocking so skillfully his fingers never touched her skin. When he began the second, she flexed her ankle to force the contact. The shock that exploded up her leg was ten times more intense than the explosion of the brandy. She remembered that horrible night when he had touched her hand and she chased him away with the poker. Even that did not compare to what she felt when Jonathan's fingers barely brushed her calf—and this time she did not pull away.

He did, as if nothing had happened, then left her wriggling her bare, tired toes as he walked back to the side of the bed.

"It's a child, Lizzie, who asked for none of this," he said. "It had no say in either its existence or its circumstances. Now, let's see if you can stand up and get out of those clothes. You smell like a fishmonger."

He took her hands and gently pulled her up so she could swing her legs over the edge of the bed. He even gave her a moment to rest before the effort of getting herself to her feet. In that moment she looked down at her grotesque shape and started to laugh—or cry.

"Call Mrs. Davis," she said, conquering the tears. Now was not the time to give in to them, not in front of him. "You don't need to help me."

Jonathan was right; she was a fool. A fool to think he or any man would find this misshapen, ungainly body in any way attractive.

But he didn't call for the housekeeper. Instead, he reached for the topmost button, right under Elizabeth's chin, and began working down the entire row.

"I want to help you, Lizzie. I want to show you that you needn't do everything alone. You needn't take foolish risks."

She wanted to turn away from him, from his kindness and gentleness and the fiery touch of his fingers through the layers of her clothing, but she couldn't. His voice soothed her into acquiescence. It contained none of Jack's teasing sarcasm or unbridled passion, yet in her mind it was Jack Silver who warned her of the dangers to be found on the London docks and in the London streets.

And it was Jack who picked up her hand and held it while he freed the buttons at her wrists so he could slide the sleeves down her arms. It was Jack, not Jonathan, who tugged her to her feet so the gown fell to the floor around her naked ankles. And when she flinched because the child kicked and tumbled within her, it was Jack Silver whose hand brushed against her belly and felt the movement.

She wept for an hour or more, first in his arms until the most violent sobs eased, then curled on her side with one of the pillows clutched to her breast. She said nothing, no matter how he encouraged her to talk, so John let her spend her tears until at last she fell asleep, utterly exhausted.

Whatever had prompted her fear that other night, so many months ago, no longer held her in its terrible grip. Instead of cringing from his touch, she seemed to welcome it, and when the tears came, she clung to him with frightened, but not terrified, desperation.

He stroked a few dark wisps of hair at her temple. A childlike shudder quivered through her, but she slept on. He hadn't tried to loosen the tight coronet of braids atop her head and suspected she'd have a headache from sleeping with it. Better to let her sleep, however, than waken her by trying to undo the intricate coiffure.

He thought of Betsy Bunch and her yellow curls, how they had tumbled into his hands when he snatched off her cap. And Elizabeth's shroud of ebony silk that fell down her back beyond her waist. By the neatness of her braids, he guessed Lizzie's hair was shorter and not nearly so luxurious as Elizabeth's, but caressing those wisps away from her cheek he felt again the satiny texture. Her bonnet had kept out the stink of the docks, and if he dug deep into the recesses of his memory, he could still recall the scent of lilacs, the scent of Elizabeth.

There had been times in those first few weeks of his inconvenient marriage when he marked an eerie resemblance between the two women. He blamed the lingering effects of his beating and the wretched days in Newgate. Blurred vision and fever dreams had transformed the pale, thin Lizzie, with her timid voice and stoic manner, into someone quite different, someone who vanished on his waking.

Dear God, he wondered, as he wondered a hundred times a day, where had Elizabeth gone? On his first brief visit to Kilbury after barely a month in London, he collected the reply to the message he had left for Betsy at the Black Oak. Written in Nell Sharpe's unpracticed hand, the note told him exactly what he expected, that Betsy had left Stanhope Manor weeks before. The implication was clear: Elizabeth had taken the girl with her.

At least she was not alone and not burdened with a child the way poor Lizzie was.

He pulled the sheet and comforter over her. The child whose movements had brought on her weeping slept now as soundly as its mother, even when John tucked the comforter around the bulge of her belly.

The house was quiet now. Mrs. Davis had poked her head in the door once with a look that suggested she was prepared to take his place, but John silently sent her on. He should, he thought, now that Lizzie was sleeping peacefully, seek his own bed, but he was reluctant to leave her.

Against his better judgment, he got up and pulled off his boots. Then, fully dressed, he lay down behind the woman bundled in the bedclothes and curled his body protectively around hers.

From an elegant silver pot, Kaspar Kennicott poured steaming coffee into two cups. "You come pounding on my door at eight o'clock in the morning to tell me *this?* Why not just let me read about your death in the newspaper?"

John, rubbing a chin shaved for the first time in nearly a month, sipped the bitter brew, then shook his head.

"I've no intention of getting killed. But unless I do something, we're very likely to go on as we have for the past several months, and I'm tired of it."

"So you intend to beard the lion in his den."

"If I must." That said casually, he then leaned forward, his elbows on the table and explained with passionate earnestness, "Kaspar, there's no other way. Thomas is too frightened to do anything to me now. If I wait any longer, he will be beyond fear."

"Lesser men than you have been undone by over-confidence."

"The warning is taken, my friend. But Thomas cannot take the risk." Extending one finger at a time, he enumerated the points that had brought him to this decision. "Using a nonexistent ransom demand as an excuse to raise cash, he tricked me into signing the bill of sale, then he sold the house to Benjamin Miner, with whom he conspired to trap me. I walked into the trap and ended up in Newgate. His cronies reported the events to him, and he prepared the secondary charges of indebtedness, should I fail to die. Being the perverse fellow that I am, I refused to oblige him."

"With some assistance," Kennicott pointed out.

John acknowledged that and went on, "When our little widow appeared on the scene, she did more than rescue a dying man from prison. She allowed him the opportunity to assume a new identity—and gave Thomas more questions to puzzle over. It would have been one thing for his prisoner to disappear, even under another name, but when presented with the fact of the man's marriage, poor Thomas had to wonder if he hadn't sent the wrong man to gaol."

"A confusion you compounded when you returned, hale and hearty, to Kilbury two months later."

John laughed and reached inside his coat to pull a thick envelope from his pocket. "You warned me against that visit, too, Kaspar, and the others since. I promise you, this will be the last until I'm ready for the final blow."

He laid the envelope, sealed with a thick blob of red wax, on the table between himself and the lawyer. Kennicott fingered the familiar Kilbury seal impressed in the wax.

"What is this, your last will and testament?"

"Among other things."

Kennicott looked up sharply, but John met the bright old eyes with a smile.

"I'm a practical man, Kaspar. I'd not rest easy in my grave if the world did not know what Thomas did. There may be no way to keep him from inheriting Kilbury if I should fail to return, but I've done my best. And I wanted to make certain Lizzie and her babe are taken care of."

When he had wakened at dawn, Lizzie slept on as if she had hardly moved since falling asleep. If he had waited another hour, he would have time for one last look at her. He realized then that in the half year he had lived with her, he had never seen her face. It seemed impossible, and yet it was true. There were shadowed glimpses over silent suppers and occasional encounters on a dark stairway, but he left the house often before she had risen and he rarely returned before dark.

Perhaps she wished it that way. Perhaps, had he not been more concerned with other matters, he might have investigated the widow Lizzie White and found that she, too, had secrets to hide just as he did.

He ran the back of his hand under his chin and gave Kennicott the last of the instructions. "I want you to sell the sapphires, Kaspar, and invest the money for her. If I don't come back, that is."

"The Kilbury sapphires? For God's sake, John, they're all that's left. After what Thomas did—"

"I know. That's why I want to get rid of them, and what better way? Even if I should find Elizabeth, I'm certain now she meant what she said about hating them. I buried them with my mother because she loved them, but she would never have wanted them to go to such waste." He was able to smile in remembrance now, but the grief at her loss had left its mark on an impressionable boy.

"That's where you're going, isn't it. To fetch the sapphires and confront your uncle."

"I am only going to ask him about Benjamin Miner, nothing else. I have no intention of baiting the man. You forget, Kaspar, he has nothing left to lose; I have everything."

Elizabeth gave her temper free rein.

"What do you mean, I'm not to leave this house? By whose orders?"

She had slept well past noon and wakened both rested and hungry—and eager to pay another call on Kaspar Kennicott. In better spirits than at any time in the past several weeks, she dressed and combed out the tight braids that circled her head. The baby was exceptionally active, but for once his antics brought her smiles instead of grimaces. Within the month, he would be squirming in her arms instead of her belly. Before then, however, she had to finish what she had started.

Mrs. Davis, her arms crossed over her chest, apparently had no intention of letting her. "Mr. Largent," she said, her rolling burr making the name sound more impressive.

"And since when does Mr. Largent tell me what to do?"

"Since ye damned near kilt yerself, that's since when," the housekeeper scolded. "Now, ye sit yerself doon right here and have yer breakfast, and then ye go right back up ta yer room and rest. If ye've nae thought fer yerself, at least have a care fer yer bairn."

As if he had heard, the baby somersaulted with such vigor Elizabeth clutched both hands to her belly.

Mrs. Davis walked to the table and held out a chair. "Aye, lass, he's dropped. Willna be long now."

"How long?"

"A week, perhaps two. Wi' yer first, it may be a wee bit longer, but soon. Now, sit and eat."

If the housekeeper was surprised at Elizabeth's sudden acquiescence, she gave no sign. And once seated, with a bowl of steaming porridge before her, Elizabeth rediscovered the appetite that had her stomach grumbling the afternoon before.

She had gobbled nearly half the porridge before she saw the folded note lying across the table at the place where she usually sat. She had hardly given a thought to the fact that Mrs. Davis put her at Jonathan's customary place, but now something squeezed inside her at the sight of that note. And it was too far away for her to reach.

She had to ask the housekeeper for it.

"He's gone again, isn't he?" she said as she unfolded the stiff piece of paper.

"Aye, early this morning."

Elizabeth read the few lines slowly, thinking his handwriting was terribly difficult to read until she realized her own tears blurred it. It was the unexpected kindness in his words, she told herself, that made her cry when she did not think she had any tears left.

She wiped them away quickly and set the note down beside her bowl. "He expects to be gone only a week this time," she told the housekeeper, then resumed eating though with far less appetite.

Jonathan had never written her a note before. Always he simply told her the night before he left, never giving her an explanation or telling her where he was going. It had never bothered her—or had it? Or was she always so caught up in her own business that she had no time left to be curious about his?

Well, she was curious now and, she admitted with some surprise, worried.

The tenderness and concern Jonathan Largent demonstrated last night had overwhelmed her, so unexpected were they. Once during the night she had wakened and found him sleeping beside her, just his hand resting on her shoulder, an affectionate rather than passionate possessiveness. She tried to snuggle against him but found he lay atop the blankets, not under them with her.

Yet she also remembered the way he had stiffened when his hand brushed her swollen belly and the child moved against it.

"Men!" she sniffed in exasperation and to cover another welling of tears. "I swear, there isn't a one of them on the face of the earth who knows what he wants."

But for all her exasperation, she tucked her husband's note into her pocket.

By the time she finished her much-delayed breakfast, it was too late to have James drive her to Kaspar Kennicott's office, even if the man were willing to do so. Elizabeth forced herself to be content spending the rest of the day more or less as Mrs. Davis directed, except that she refused to go to bed. Still, there was something pleasurable in the ordinary activities of an expectant mother, stitching the warm quilts and gowns for the child's first cold months, knitting tiny mitts and boots.

She went to bed that night with a promise to herself to rise early and overrule any orders keeping her from paying a call on Kaspar Kennicott. One day spent on domesticity was fine, but she had so few left, she dare not waste another.

The next morning, however, broke stormy and cold with a nip of winter in the air. At breakfast, Mrs. Davis gave her a look that said more clearly than any words that Jonathan's orders were not to be defied today.

James offered no hope either. Carrying a large, canvas-wrapped bundle, he came in from the garden and said, "It's a blessing for the horse to stay at home in this weather. Think of all the poor beasts that must go out in it, catching their deaths just as any human would or sliding on the ice and breaking their legs because some fine lady must go calling."

But there was a twinkle in his eye as he spoke.

Elizabeth felt a flush of guilt creep up her throat, a flush that advanced to the roots of her hair when James set his burden on the floor and removed the canvas cover to reveal a handsome oak cradle.

"Oh, James, it's beautiful!" she breathed. Ignoring the rest of her breakfast, Elizabeth knelt beside the cradle and gave it a gentle nudge to set it rocking. The wood was smooth and glossy with patiently polished wax, the hood decorated with a wide band of carved leaves and rosettes. "You did this for me?"

He blushed, she was sure of it, but took pride in what he had done.

"You and Mr. Largent have been good to me," he said. "Weren't many would give a man with only one eye a chance."

She thought of Harry Grove, kept on at Kilbury because the earl would not turn him out despite the injury that cost him a leg. The world was not without it kindnesses.

She ran her finger over the delicate work, marveling at the intricacy of the design and the quality of its execution.

"I were apprenticed to a cabinetmaker before I

thought the army more exciting," James explained. "I asked Mr. Largent if 'twould be all right. He gave me leave to buy the wood and have the bill sent to him."

Elizabeth looked up. "Jonathan did that?"

"Aye, he did, and yesterday, before he left, he asked to see it. Real pleased he was. Gave me a gold sovereign and said I should never worry about employment again."

Elizabeth rarely strayed far from the cradle all that day. She directed James to move it into the parlor, beside her chair, so that as she finished each quilt, she could place it inside. Now and then she reached down to set it rocking.

She could not, however, forget the nagging worry raised by Hamilton Wilke's threat. Perhaps it was the reality of the impending birth that kept the questions roiling in her mind the following morning. After a day of rain, the sky fairly glistened blue, and Elizabeth found herself filled with restless energy.

"I shall compromise," she said to Mrs. Davis, who had brought in a basket of cold, crisp apples from the tree in the garden. "I give you my word I will not go to Mr. Kennicott, but you must allow me to write to him. And then James must take him the letter and wait for a reply."

"And then what?"

Elizabeth smiled at the Scotswoman's suspicion, because Mrs. Davis evidently had come to know her very well.

"And then I should like you to accompany me to the bookseller's on the next street. It is a fine day, and I shall wear my cloak so no one sees how monstrous huge I've grown."

"Now why would you be wantin' to buy a book? There's plenty here."

On either side of the fireplace, shelves lined the walls like a small library. For a man who spent so little time in his home, Jonathan had filled nearly half the shelves with books.

Elizabeth shook off a momentary puzzlement and answered, "I want to buy a Bible in which to record the baby's birth. And I wish to pick it out myself if you don't mind."

She waited, apprehensive, until Mrs. Davis gave her very grudging assent.

"I suppose 'twould be all right. But no further, ye ken? The bookseller's and then home."

The air was clear and brisk with that special smoke and spice pungency of autumn. Wrapped in her cloak, Elizabeth breathed deeply in appreciation of her brief freedom. Though the bookseller's shop was ordinarily no more than a ten-minute walk from the cottage, she knew it would take at least twice that long today.

Perhaps, she thought, it was the earlier exertion of writing a long letter to Kaspar Kennicott that left her so drained. She had done nothing but sit at her desk, but the mental effort proved as exhausting as any physical labor. She had to concentrate on telling the lawyer only those facts she felt he needed to know concerning her identity and the provisions she had made for the child. If somehow Hamilton Wilke's tale reached her father or Thomas Colfax, she did not want Jack Silver's child to be at their mercy. It would have been so much easier to pour out the whole tale, as she had come so close to doing the night before Jonathan left, but in the end, she threw a dozen sheets of paper into the fire and gave only one to James.

She did not expect him back for several hours, plenty of time to stroll leisurely with Mrs. Davis to the bookseller's.

The tiny shop smelled of leather and paper, of ink and dust. The wizened proprietor never looked up at her entrance nor offered to help her, and she found that strangely comforting. She had suffered from a surfeit of attention lately.

She passed over the small, personal testaments and psalms. There was one exquisite Bible, with gold edges and page after page of illuminated text, a masterpiece of the engraver's art, but she could not justify the exorbitant price. On a lower shelf, however, she found exactly what she was looking for.

The bookseller finally acknowledged her presence when she dropped the heavy book on his counter.

"Will that be all?" he asked in a voice as dry and dusty as the rest of the shop.

"Yes. And could you send it round to the house? I'm afraid I'm not able to carry it home."

He squinted at her as though he'd forgotten the spectacles perched atop his head. Or perhaps they were permanently tangled in the uncombed thatch of white hair. Then he reached for a small card and the quill already stuck in the ink bottle.

"The name?"

"Mrs. Jonathan Largent. I live in the—"

"Oh, I know where you live. Your husband comes in here often enough." The wrinkled little face lit up. "Did you find the writing paper to your liking?"

"He bought it here?" It had been a small gift, one she hardly gave any thought to. "Yes, it was very nice. I write a great many letters, you see, and he said he wanted me to have it."

"A fine young man." The quill scratched again. "Quite a scholar, too. You don't find many outside the nobility who know how their names have been corrupted over the years, but he knew his. Laughed out loud when I mentioned it. Said he ought to have learned *something* at Oxford."

Something prickled along the back of Elizabeth's neck and curled in her stomach like a snake preparing to strike. She barely heard the bookseller's words, for

354

she had already looked at the card with her husband's name in the original French.

"L'Argent, Jonathan L'Argent," she whispered, as she reached out a trembling hand to turn the card right side up. "An Oxford scholar, an impoverished nobleman." She scanned the old man's neat script over and over until the paper rectangle fluttered from her hand and drifted to the floor. "Jonathan Silver."

CHAPTER

28

John slammed the ledger closed with a violent curse. All around him, books and papers lay scattered in total disarray. He had left not one corner of Thomas's study untouched, not one account book unread. And he knew no more about Benjamin Miner than when he left London three days ago.

Nor about Elizabeth Stanhope.

His elbows on the desk, he buried his face in his hands and yawned. He needed sleep. Desperately. The weather held clear, and he had covered the distance to Kilbury in less than two days, but with only one brief rest. He arrived yesterday to learn Thomas was at Stanhope Manor, and though the temptation to confront both his uncle and Elizabeth's father together was strong, John resisted and spent the evening, the night, and now most of the morning in Thomas's study, poring over twenty or more years' worth of Kilbury accounts.

In vain. Benjamin Miner remained but a name scrawled across a sheet of parchment or entered neatly in the ledger. By John's estimate, the unknown Miner held close to one-fourth the mortgages against Kilbury lands. Edward Stanhope held another fourth, while the balance, through the efforts of Kaspar Kennicott and the blind cooperation of Lizzie Largent, had been redeemed.

And to what purpose? Kilbury Hall was a ruin, a cold, damp mausoleum stripped of its treasures, a desecration for which he had no one to blame but himself. For the sweet and fleeting taste of revenge, he had allowed all this to happen.

Whether the ruin could be restored, he did not know, nor could he even begin to imagine the cost. Kennicott had invested Jack Silver's booty wisely, so there was enough to redeem the mortgages from Stanhope and Miner, but there would be little enough left. In time, perhaps, John hoped Kilbury would provide for itself, but he never expected the damage to be so great.

The creak of the study door startled him out of a light doze. He raised his head just as Thomas marched into the middle of the chaos.

"What do you think you're doing here?" he bellowed in the same voice he had proclaimed his robbery by Jack Silver to the patrons of the Black Oak.

John wiped the memory from his mind and replied with weary impatience, "I'm looking for something."

"This is my study! You have no right to be here!"

John pushed his chair away from the desk and got to his feet. He barely kept his eyes open as he advanced with measured strides toward his uncle. Thomas stumbled backward, knocking over a pile of account books, until he encountered the door. By then John was nearly upon him and able to reach over the shorter man's shoulder to shove the door closed. The impact reverberated through the very stones of the silent house.

"Kilbury is mine, Thomas," he informed his uncle.

"You may have stolen bits and pieces of it over the years, but this house, this study, these ledgers, all are mine. Not yours."

Thomas opened his mouth as if to contradict that claim, but John simply pushed him away from the door and walked out.

"I am going to the Dower House to sleep," he announced as he proceeded down the hall, not caring whether Thomas heard or not. "I shall see you in the library at two o'clock. I suggest you be there."

Thomas Colfax slumped like a huge sack of suet in the cracked leather chair by the fire. John, still wearing his coat after the long walk from the Dower House, stretched his hands out to warm them and wondered if his uncle would melt into a puddle of grease on the hearth should someone push him closer to the flames.

"Of course, the place has gone to ruin," Thomas whined. "If you'd been here this past year instead of leading a gentleman's life of leisure in London, you'd not be so surprised."

"If tramping all over London in search of Elizabeth Stanhope is leisure, then yes, I suppose that is what I've been doing."

Thomas puffed himself up and declared, "I hired Bow Street Runners to find her. How did you expect to succeed where professional detectives failed?"

John watched his uncle in detached fascination the way he might observe a grotesque but interesting scientific specimen. Did the man actually believe his own lies? Apparently he did, for he looked up with wide, innocent eyes.

"Damn you, you hired *no one!*" John thundered, and Thomas's innocence shattered.

He cringed, sinking deeper into the chair. Feeling no pity, John attacked relentlessly. All the rage, all the frustration, all the pain, poured from him.

"I covered the city from Barking to Richmond, every inn and hotel, every cheap boarding house and,

358

yes, even the brothels." He had to stop and swallow the bile that rose in his throat at the memory of those hideous nights, of the women and children, boys as well as girls, who sold themselves for others' pleasure. But there were other visions burned into his brain worse still, and they would never leave him.

"Have you ever gone to a morgue, Thomas, and looked at a body pulled from the Thames? After the fish and eels have nibbled at the swollen, bloodless flesh for two or three days? I have, too many times to count. And not once did I encounter any Bow Street Runner looking for Elizabeth Stanhope. Only I, Thomas, only I went looking for her. And she was to have been *your* wife."

He turned away in disgust as Thomas began to blubber. "I thought she'd come back," he whimpered. "And I had no money."

For a brief moment John believed his uncle was telling the truth until he remembered the two thousand pounds raised as Elizabeth's ransom. But only Jack Silver could know that ransom had never been paid; John said nothing about it, though he wanted desperately to throw the lies in Thomas's face.

He raked his fingers through his hair, trying to sweep Elizabeth from his mind as cleanly as he had last night when he spent all those hours with the account books.

Ignoring Thomas's unintelligible mumblings, he asked, "Who is Benjamin Miner?" And when Thomas continued to babble, he asked the same question again more sharply.

The once-innocent eyes blinked and fat tears rolled in greasy streaks from them.

Between hiccoughs, Thomas stuttered, "H-he h-holds some of y-your father's m-mortgages."

"I know that. I want to know who he is and where I can find him."

Thomas shook his head violently from side to side until spittle flecked his lips and flew from his mouth.

"I don't know!" he shrieked. "I don't know, I don't know! Oh, why can't you leave me alone? Can't you see I know nothing? Not about Elizabeth and not about Benjamin Miner!"

He drew his knees up and wrapped his arms around them, then tucked his head down into the crook of his arm, against the back of the chair.

"You pay the man five thousand pounds interest from my estate every year, and you expect me to believe you don't know who he is?"

"I don't, I don't!" The screams came muffled from the quivering figure. "Ask Stanhope! He set it up; he knows Miner! Ask him!"

Then he would say no more, just mumbled or shrieked insensibly and waved a flailing, dismissive arm. John would have stayed and waited for Thomas to come to his senses, but a knock on the door demanded his attention.

Leaving Thomas to his wails and hiccoughs, John strode to the door and pulled it open. Patton, the footman, stood in the corridor, a sealed letter in his hand.

"For Mr. Colfax, my lord," he said.

John almost snatched it from Patton's hand but instead gestured the man into the room. There was nothing left to be learned from Thomas Colfax.

"You may take it to him, Patton."

John slept hardly at all that night, despite the exhaustion that had him nodding over his supper. In the drafty comfort of the Dower House, he scratched out page after page of instructions at the table where he had once plotted his revenge against Thomas. Broken windows and cracked roof tiles were to be replaced, chimneys cleaned, a hundred minor repairs made that he suspected had gone unattended for years.

He chuckled as he penned the orders to whatever housekeeping staff Thomas still retained. Mrs. Davis would have Kilbury Hall spotless in half a day. Perhaps he could persuade her to leave Lizzie's employ when this little charade was over.

But he didn't want to do that. Nor did he want to offer James Park a position at Kilbury, though he knew the one-eyed carpenter would jump at the chance. Lizzie would need them both, especially after the baby was born.

He lay down the pen and rubbed his eyes. He had to stop thinking about the woman, about the house he had shared with her all these months. After the cold desolation of Kilbury Hall, the cottage seemed even more warm and homey. He remembered that vision of the parlor the night Lizzie came home from Race's: the fire, the books he had bought for the shelves on the wall, the basket of knitting on one side of Lizzie's chair. She would have to move the basket, he thought with a smile, when James gave her the cradle.

He flexed his fingers not only to remove the cramps from an evening of writing but also to chase away the faint memory of feeling an unborn child move in its mother's womb. God, how it had startled him! He never expected it to be so quick and energetic. And then that night, lying beside her while she slept, he had cupped his palm around her belly and let the tiny being kick against him until it, too, tired perhaps from its play, fell asleep.

"It's another man's child," he reminded himself as he picked up the quill again and pulled another piece of paper from the stack in front of him. "And Lizzie will be perfectly fine. She's clever and capable of managing on her own."

But at dawn when, after only a brief nap in his

chair, he set out for Stanhope Manor, he could not keep from thinking about Lizzie, about the child she was soon to bear. If he had got a child on Elizabeth, it, too, would have been born soon.

The blessing was that he had not, after all, saddled her with a bastard. For all the other injuries he had done her, he could be grateful she had escaped that ignominious fate. And he had been foolish enough to think that she loved him.

"You arrogant ass!" he chided himself, turning from the main road onto the drive that led up to the elegance of Stanhope Manor. "She was clever enough to claim she loved Jack Silver and manipulated him until he released her—before he did further damage. No woman with the brains to do that would consider marrying a fool like John Colfax. She's probably made her way to London and married a sensible, decent man."

He very nearly said "a sensible, decent man like Jonathan Largent," until he realized there was nothing sensible or decent about the man who married Lizzie White. Only that he wanted to be, or perhaps could have been.

Stanhope Manor glistened in the early morning light as if the sun had not yet burned off the glaze of frost that etched the fields and woods surrounding it. But as John entered the mansion and followed a stone-faced footman, he sensed a distinct unease within the house.

If Kilbury Hall felt cold as a grave, Stanhope Manor was as silent. The elegant furnishings showed no signs of wear, the chandeliers sparkled in the morning sunlight, the rooms were all comfortably warmed by glowing fires. None of the servants he passed spoke, not even in the usual whispers of gossip. They hardly looked up. And the footman who at last ushered John into the drawing room walked on tiptoe rather than make a sound.

In the middle of this silence, surrounded by the familiar trappings of wealth and comfort, sat Edward Stanhope.

He might have been a waxwork figure, carefully posed in his chair, but his chest rose and fell with regular breaths, betraying a spark of life. The hand that lifted the tumbler of brandy to his lips quivered uncontrollably. Had there been more liquor in the glass, it would have spilled onto his trousers.

He swallowed half the brandy in a single crude gulp, then got unsteadily to his feet. "Good morning, my lord."

First Thomas, now this.

"You're drunk."

"Oh, no, my lord," the articulated corpse said. "A gentleman is never drunk at this hour of the morning."

"Then you are no gentleman, Stanhope, for you are most assuredly drunk."

The man winced as if he'd been struck and tossed down the rest of the brandy.

"I don't care if you're a gentleman or a chimney sweep, Edward. I only want information."

With the slow, overcautious movements of a man attempting to conceal his inebriation, Edward crossed to the console where the decanters of brandy sat. Still holding his glass, he chose one of the decanters but then acted confused, as though he could not figure out how to remove the stopper with both hands already occupied.

"Elizabeth isn't here, you know," he said, glancing from the crystal bottle to the glass and back again. "And she hasn't changed her mind about marrying Thomas. Not at all."

Edward's comments startled John, but they did not confuse him. He remembered that last conversation all too clearly. And though it was seven months or more in the past, the intervening time apparently did not exist for Edward Stanhope.

He strode to the console and took the decanter from Edward's hand. As he pulled out the stopper and poised the crystal bottle over the empty tumbler, he said, "I came to talk about Benjamin Miner, Edward, not Elizabeth. What can you tell me about him?"

He tipped the decanter but not far enough for the amber liquid to flow out. Edward's hand began to tremble in desperate anticipation.

"Miner's dead. Are you going to pour?"

A thin trickle splashed into the glass, but John stopped it before more than one or two swallows filled the bottom. Edward gulped them down and immediately thrust the glass under the decanter's mouth again.

"You're lying, Stanhope. You bought a piece of my property from Thomas. The money was to go for Elizabeth's ransom. Do you remember that?"

The head bobbed up and down, and glass clinked against crystal.

"Thomas wouldn't show me the ransom letter, you see, so I demanded security."

"But when Elizabeth was returned, did you give the mortgages back?"

A frown creased Edward's brow. He looked up, his eyes meeting John's for the first time. The vacant glaze remained. "He never asked for them."

"And you sold the house on Waverly Square to Benjamin Miner."

The empty tumbler slipped from Edward's hand and crashed among the other glassware on the table. He reached frantically for it, cutting his fingers on the sharp fragments.

"Miner's dead, dead, I tell you."

John grabbed one wrist and pulled the bleeding hand up to Edward's face.

"He's not dead, and you know it. I want to know where he is." With his other hand he dribbled several drops of brandy onto the cuts.

Though the older man clawed at the fingers around his wrist, John held fast. The brandy stung the scratches as sharply as it had Edward's cuts, but he did not loosen his grip.

"Where is Benjamin Miner?"

More brandy until Edward howled with the pain. In the struggle to escape, he lost his balance and fell to his knees. Servants, alerted by his screams, broke into the drawing room; John held them at a distance with a furious glare. One woman buried her face in her apron and began to weep, but she came no closer.

He held the decanter to Edward's mouth and let a thin stream flow down the man's throat. Some of it trickled down his chin; he reached out his tongue but couldn't reach it.

His face level with Edward's, John asked once more in a low, almost gentle voice, "Who is Benjamin Miner?"

"He was a very bad man, my lord. Not a gentleman at all. He stole a great deal of money from his friends."

"He stole my *house,* Stanhope. Where is he?"

"He disappeared. Vanished. No one ever saw him again."

"How convenient! He disappeared just like Elizabeth and poor Betsy Bunch."

"Oh, no, Elizabeth hasn't disappeared. She's resting. Before the wedding."

Disgusted, John flung away the sticky, bloody wrist he had gripped through this whole futile conversation and slowly straightened. Edward sat down hard, his legs splayed out in front of him, and clutched one bleeding hand in the other.

"There will be no wedding, Stanhope. Elizabeth is

gone, as gone as Betsy Bunch, as gone as Benjamin Miner."

He would have hauled Edward to his feet had not two of the servants rushed to their employer's aid—or to his own. He shook them off, but one stepped between him and the man on the floor.

"If it please your lordship," the footman whispered, offering him a handkerchief to wipe the blood and brandy from his hand, "there is nothing you can do."

John looked at Edward being helped to his feet by other servants. Already the silence, broken by John's shouts and Edward's cries, had crept back in. Voices were hushed, movements slow and controlled.

"My God, his daughter disappears and could be dead for all he knows, and all he can think to do is drink brandy at nine o'clock in the morning."

To his surprise, the footman shook his head. "Miss Stanhope isn't dead, my lord."

John grabbed the man by the shoulders but then immediately released him. "Have you proof? Do you know where she is?"

One of his fellows, who had directed the teary-eyed maid to the broken glass on the console, chastised him with a vehement "Shush," but the footman went on. "She sent notes to her maid, Nell Sharpe. Nell burned them, said she didn't know where Miss Stanhope was, only that she was safe."

John wanted to dance with the footman and kiss the maid who was picking up the broken glass. If he was no closer to finding her, at least he knew she was alive.

"Then I must speak to Nell immediately. Send someone for her. And what of Betsy Bunch? She, too, disappeared."

The reply was a slow shake of the footman's head. "Nell's gone. Mr. Stanhope dismissed her months ago. Of this Betsy, I know nothing, my lord."

Even when John described her, the footman repeated the gesture.

John strode to the girl at the console, who dropped pieces of broken glass into her apron and wiped tears on the back of her hand. "Did you know a girl, a parlormaid perhaps, named Betsy Bunch? I had a note from Nell Sharpe that Betsy left the same time Miss Elizabeth did."

The girl sniffed and tried to bob a curtsey. "I never knew no Betsy, milord. I been here since I were ten; ain't never been no Betsy Bunch at Stanhope."

It wasn't possible. He had seen her twice enter the gate. And Elizabeth herself confirmed it, said she had caught Betsy sneaking out at night. He had donned the elaborate disguise as the one-armed man to leave word with Hennie Sharpe that he was looking for his sister, Betsy Bunch. On his first visit back to Kilbury, he had gone to the Black Oak and received the message, in Nell's rough hand, that Betsy was gone.

Had they lied? Or was this frightened girl, no more than fifteen or sixteen years old, lying along with the footman and Edward Stanhope? And if so, why?

One person would know: Nell, who no doubt had gone home to her father's inn after losing her position at Stanhope.

He ordered the footman to have his horse brought around, then took a final look at Edward Stanhope, who sat in his chair once again with a fresh glass of brandy while his valet bound the cut fingers in bandages.

"He's not always like this."

John turned to find the little parlormaid at his elbow. She sniffed again and looked up at him with no apology in her red-rimmed eyes.

"It's because of the baby."

John could hardly put the question into two simple words. Something fierce and hot and dreadful was coiling and twisting and slithering through him. He feared the answer, feared the knowing but feared the not knowing more.

"What baby?" he managed in little more than a hoarse croak.

The other servants had gone on about their business, leaving him alone with the girl, except for Edward and the valet, who were too absorbed in their own business to hear what he had to say to a weepy parlormaid.

And then she said to him the words that he knew would bring him the greatest joy and the greatest terror he had ever known.

"Miss Elizabeth's baby." She blinked once, and more tears rolled down her cheeks. "Jack Silver's baby."

He dug his heels into the big hunter's flanks, but the animal had no more speed to give him. After five miles at this, the strongest horse would begin to flag. But there was still another mile to go. John kicked the horse again.

He leapt off the winded beast before it came to a complete halt in the Black Oak's courtyard. A boy ran up to take the reins, but John didn't wait for him. The horse was too exhausted to do anything but stand stock still, head down, sides heaving.

The common room was all but empty. John recognized Hennie and Robin Sharpe as the only occupants, and they were engaged in a heated game of knots and crosses on an old slate.

"I want to see your sister, Nell," he shouted.

"What for?" Hennie asked. "Oh, begging yer pardon, my lord."

She slid off the bench and bobbed a nervous curtsey, but Robin was less quick to acknowledge his rank. Neither of them walked any closer; Hennie, perhaps, backed away.

John strode further into the room and, his voice lower now, said, "I wish to speak to her about Elizabeth Stanhope and Betsy Bunch."

The girl glanced quickly at the staircase, then turned away but too late. John had heard the light tread descending from the upper floor. If it slowed because the person recognized him, he didn't care. Hennie had already given her sister away.

Robin, however, was a different matter. The sly grin he took no pains to hide hinted at more than a lack of respect. It spoke of secrets.

"There be no Betsy Bunch," he said, the smile unwavering.

Hennie spun on him and snapped, "Hush, you!"

John looked from one to the other, the boy defiant as a young cock, the girl frightened but clearly possessing the same knowledge.

Whatever the boy said, John had seen Betsy for himself, and yet something kept him from blurting out that truth. It had nothing to do with the fact that John Colfax, earl of Kilbury, had never been to the Black Oak when Betsy served, that only Jack Silver had seen her, had caught her on his lap when she stumbled away from an enraged Thomas Colfax, had kissed her and stolen a poor old woman's supper for her, and suffered an intense and gentle desire for her such as he had never suffered for anyone else.

Except Elizabeth Stanhope.

Elizabeth, whose hair smelled of lilacs and springtime and laughter, just like Betsy Bunch. Elizabeth, who said she would rather work as a tavernmaid than marry Thomas Colfax. Elizabeth, who wanted to see the world though her father would not let her go to London. Elizabeth, who willingly yielded him her body in an outlaw's bed, unafraid, as if she had known all along he would not harm her.

He whirled at the sound of Nell's footstep on the last stair. For a long moment she stood, her eyes lowered, her face turned away from him, but he sensed neither mockery nor fear in her stance. When she looked up, he saw only guilt and sadness.

"I searched for them, you know," he said, his voice and body tight with anger. "For months, asking if anyone had seen two women traveling together. I went so far as to imagine they might have switched places, Betsy in Elizabeth's clothes and Elizabeth dressed as her maid. Once, just once, I thought I had found them, but the woman was traveling without a maid, and she was not Elizabeth."

No, she was a young parson's widow named Lizzie White, and she had left the Blind Pilgrim months before he questioned the woman who had ridden in the coach with her. But there was no sense telling Nell that story.

"Damn it, I asked Elizabeth to marry me!"

Nell let out a shriek and covered her mouth with her hands. Thinking she was about to flee back up the stairs, he ran and grabbed her arm to drag her to the table where the slate still showed a half-finished game. He pushed her down onto the bench, beside Hennie who immediately put her arm around her sister's shoulders.

But Nell seemed to need no comforting. Or perhaps that look on her face said that no amount of comfort could erase the pain.

And perhaps she was right.

At least the boy no longer grinned like a hound with a week-dead rabbit.

They sat like statues, three silhouettes against the mullioned window until Robin sidled between the tables and chairs toward the taproom.

"I'll get ye some brandy, milord," the boy said.

John merely nodded and pulled out a chair at the nearest table. He took a good look around the familiar room. Nothing had changed since that stormy January night when Betsy tumbled onto his lap. The Black

Oak was a pleasant inn, with its smoke-blackened beams and yawning stone fireplace, the plank tables and the inglenook where he had warmed himself after lifting Thomas's own purse.

The quiet thump of the bottle and glass being set in front of him finally broke into his thoughts. A more subdued Robin Sharpe moved back to the table with his sisters and sat down.

"So Elizabeth was Betsy," John said, pouring the glass full. He understood now why Robin mocked him for his ignorance. Had the boy known from the first? No, probably not, and if not for the woman in London who waited for her husband's return, John himself would have found the whole situation hilariously funny. Instead it was bitterly ironic.

The first swallow of brandy burned and brought back a moment of that dreadful dizziness he had experienced in Newgate. He shook it off and let the second gulp slide in a smooth, molten path down his throat.

When he looked back at his trio of hosts, he realized they were staring at a stranger. Hennie and Robin had served a few mugs of ale to a cloaked wayfarer, and Nell had taken messages from a very different John Colfax from the one who sat here now.

"Why did she not answer my letters?" he asked, though he knew the answer.

Nell faced him squarely and with no apology said, "She carried Jack Silver's child."

He heard no accusation in her simple statement, but the guilt twisted in him all the same. It made no difference that he now knew Elizabeth had lied, telling him there was no child. She had cleverly negotiated a way out of the situation and took it. Whether she told the truth about loving him, she was still a woman about to be abandoned with a bastard child in her belly.

"Did she go to London to get rid of it?"

He did not blame her. He himself had given little thought to any child he might father on her, only to the pain it could inflict on others. Perhaps she meant to spare it some of that pain.

"No, my lord, but if you think to find her and marry her now, it's too late."

The silhouette that was Nell Sharpe shifted on the bench as she reached into her pocket.

He refused to believe Elizabeth was dead, and if she was alive, it was not too late. His marriage to Lizzie was a sham; it could be annulled. Yet that thought, too, brought immeasurable pain and guilt. He poured himself another swallow of brandy and tossed it down quickly, while Nell smoothed the crinkled piece of paper on her knee.

"She's already wed, my lord," she said, "months ago."

It was not possible.

He set the glass down with exaggerated calm and rose just as slowly. He lifted the chair and set it back down with hardly a sound rather than scrape it across the flagged floor. Hennie seemed torn between backing away from his approach and staying close to Nell, but Robin stepped forward, ready to defend his sisters.

Nell did not retreat. She held the letter out to him. He took it but did not read it. He simply caressed the heavy paper with his thumb.

"When?" he asked.

"In the spring."

It was not possible. Not possible at all. Yet the feel of the paper told him it was true. He crushed it, letting the hard edges and corners bite deeply into his flesh. He wished it were glass to cut and wound him in penance for his stupidity, his blindness, his cruelty.

"Do you not wish to know his name, my lord?"

He opened his hand and stared down at the wad of

stiff writing paper purchased months ago in a London bookseller's shop.

A raw wind swirled dead leaves in the courtyard as Robin Sharpe brought a fresh mount from the stable. "The bay is sound but he'll not go another six miles, my lord."

John looked over the dark gelding the boy had chosen and pronounced him fit. He swung into the saddle and was about to head the horse out of the yard when Robin took hold of the bridle.

"Beggin' yer pardon, my lord," he began with all that mockery back and no attempt made to hide it, "but just who is this Jonathan Largent Miss Stanhope wed? And how did ye know it was he?"

"He's a thrice-lucky fool, Robin, and that's all a clever lad needs to know."

The boy nodded, but even when John tried to turn the gelding away, Robin held on. He brought his other hand to his chin and scratched it with obvious exaggeration before he looked up again with a wide grin. "Well, again beggin' yer pardon, my lord, that bein' the case, I think ye ought to trade this nag for a fine gray stallion if ye wish the fastest ride to London."

Then he let go the bridle and slapped the gelding on the rump.

CHAPTER

29

Elizabeth gathered enough strength to ask if she were dying.

"Hush, now, child, it won't be much longer now," Mrs. Davis said, drawing a cool, wet cloth across Elizabeth's forehead. "'Tis almost over."

Though Mrs. Davis seemed to speak with undue enthusiasm, Elizabeth took comfort in knowing that the end was near. She no longer feared death; she cursed it for drawing its task out so long.

She tried to lick her lips, but even her tongue lacked moisture. An arm reached behind her, lifted her, and a glass of cool water was pressed gently to her mouth. She wanted to gulp it down, to put out the fiery agony that suffused her body, but she heard that stern voice tell her to sip slowly.

"Take the glass from her if she insists on drinking like that."

It was the doctor, the nameless physician Kaspar Kennicott had sent for hours ago—or was it days ago? Elizabeth had not wanted him, but Mrs. Davis said something about the baby not being turned, and so Kaspar had sent James to fetch this master of cruelty.

The blessed water was taken away, leaving Elizabeth to gape like a tiny bird until she fell back on the pillows.

"I am dying," she croaked, "and you deny me some little comfort?"

She did not hear his answer; her own scream drowned it as a river of twisting torment rushed over her, crushing her, squeezing her, battering her with the relentless pressure of death—and life. She fought it as she had fought all the others, but it was stronger. It drew its strength from her, gaining what she lost. When at last it retreated to leave her breathless and conscious only enough to know that it would attack again, she sensed no mercy in the respite.

Yet she accepted it as she accepted another stroke of the cloth on her brow.

A violent crash, like a gigantic thunderclap, shook the house, even the bed on which Elizabeth lay. Storms held no terror for her, but when she opened her eyes, she saw sunlight streaming in through the window. There was no storm, yet the thunder continued, rhythmic in its violence, until one of the shadows moving across the band of sunlight shouted for it to stop.

Elizabeth laughed, a sound she recognized as a hoarse, maniacal cackle, but she could no more hold it back than she could deny her body's effort to wrench this child out of her.

And then the thunder crashed so close she felt the reverberation of it. Again the shadows shouted, and again she laughed, but then the pain gripped her and all sounds vanished beneath the echo of her own screams.

This time it lasted forever until she could scream no more. She surrendered to the pain. She would no longer fight it, no longer resist the impossible demands it made on her. She would let it do to her as it will.

Then it released her, not into the stillness and a damp cloth to refresh her, but into the storm that continued to rage around her. When she tried to rise from the bed, no hand held her back. She blinked weary eyes against the lightning that flashed across the window and saw that it was not lightning, but only those indistinct shadows crossing the sunlight.

Where before there had been only two shadows, now there were three. They writhed in some macabre dance, like angels wrestling for her soul, until the thunder that surrounded them separated itself into voices.

"She is my *wife,* damn you! I have *every* right!"

"Mr. Largent, she is about to deliver a baby!"

"Do you think me blind? I can *see* what she is about to do, and I intend to *be* here when she does it!"

"But, Mr. Largent, husbands do *not* attend their wives in childbirth!"

She wanted to shout at them to stop, but already she felt the onset of another pain. Gasping, she could only whisper his name over and over and over until the whisper became a moan and the moan became a wail.

A hand suddenly grasped hers and a voice told her to squeeze it, to break every bone in it. She squeezed. But the pain did not go away.

He told her to scream and to curse—and to fight and to live. She screamed and she fought. But the pain grew worse.

She felt his lips brush her cheek as she arched her head back and lifted her shoulders from the sweat-damp sheet. But there was no escaping the pain, not even to draw enough air into her lungs to scream.

"Now, Elizabeth, now," he begged.

She heard the bones in his hand crack and splinter even as she felt her own body tear into bloody shreds.

He was a tiny mite with a round little face and a cap of dark hair. Asleep now in the crook of his mother's arm, he seemed quite unconcerned about the tumult his arrival had caused.

"Do you want another pillow?"

Elizabeth looked up from her son's sleeping face. In the chair by the window, his unreadable features clearly lit by the afternoon sunlight, sat the man she had thought never to see again. Her lover, her friend —her husband. Her seducer. Her savior.

"No, thank you. I'm quite comfortable."

She did not even know what to call him.

She had clung to him in those final moments of bringing her child into the world. After Dr. Belmont laid the bloody, squalling infant on her belly and cut the cord that tied him to her, she could not pry her fingers from the hand that gave her her strength.

Nor had he seemed willing to leave. Both Dr. Belmont and Mrs. Davis argued that he ought not to be there, but only when Elizabeth asked him for some privacy did he get to his feet and walk slowly to the door. She had no idea until then that he had knelt on the floor beside her bed nor did she know for how long. Even when he left, he waited just outside her room. She heard him arguing with Kaspar and James until Mrs. Davis threatened to pour boiling water on all of them, and they retreated down the stairs.

So she had her privacy to tend to the intimate needs following childbirth, to have the sweat and blood washed from her body, to have her tangled hair combed and plaited, to feel the cool sweetness of fresh sheets beneath her and a clean nightdress against her skin. But Mrs. Davis barely had time to lay the tiny baby boy in Elizabeth's arms before an impatient knock came at the door. And he strode in without waiting for permission.

He said nothing, just sat in the chair by the window until Mrs. Davis left. He nodded at her admonition that the new mother needed to sleep. And after ten minutes of silence, he asked Elizabeth if she wanted another pillow.

What, she wondered, did *he* want? She could read no expression in his features, nor had the few words he spoke to her given any clue to his thoughts. She supposed he had a certain right to be angry with her, but—

"How long have you known?" he asked, his voice calm, betraying no emotion. Yet the intensity was there beneath that quiet surface.

"Only a few days. After you left, I went to the book shop and the proprietor told me about your name. I mean, about Largent and L'Argent. You're really quite clever, you know."

His sigh was as sudden as a shout and the realization took her by surprise.

"Did you think I knew sooner? If I had, I would never have chased you off with the poker." She blushed at that frank admission, but the memory aroused her curiosity. "And what of you, my lord? How long have you known?"

He smiled and gave her nod of acknowledgment. "Only two days ago. I went to see Nell Sharpe and recognized the writing paper I had bought for you."

A thousand other questions must wait for answers. Whatever had kept her awake this long was fading. She yawned, and the tiny bundle in her arms was suddenly very, very heavy.

"It's time you get some sleep. I'll fetch Mrs. Davis and have James bring the cradle."

As if anticipating those requests, Mrs. Davis opened the door. John, obviously resenting the intrusion as much as Elizabeth, cast the housekeeper a livid glare, which she answered with an outraged sniff.

"Bring it over here by the fire," she ordered, striding right past him. "He's a wee one, comin' early as he did, and it won't do to have him take a chill."

It was no wonder James hesitated to enter such a

tableau. Or perhaps he understood someone else should have the honor. Elizabeth watched, her eyes filling with tears, as John rose to take the cradle from the servant's hands.

He was nearly as exhausted as she. His every movement showed stiffness and pain, and weariness tinged his features. Yet when he hefted the weight, his shoulders straightened, and he carried the cradle with visible pride to place it beside the bed, where the warmth of the fire was steady and Elizabeth could easily reach to rock her son to sleep.

This was the first time, since the ordeal of the birth, John had come so close to her. He had only to put out his hand to touch her, but she looked too fragile to withstand a feather's brush. Purple shadows beneath her eyes testified to the long hours of her travail; the pulse in her throat beat beneath translucent skin. Still, she managed a smile, and he knew too well the strength concealed behind that delicate exterior. He expected his hand to bear bruises for a week.

Mrs. Davis pushed past him to take the baby from Elizabeth and put him in his cradle, but John stopped her. Flexing his abused fingers, he asked, "How soon might I be allowed to—"

"Not for a month, at least!" the woman snapped, horror rounding her eyes. "The puir lass hasna breathed twice since birthing this one and ye're all ready to gie her another. Ye ought to be ashamed o'—"

"No, Mrs. Davis," he replied, laughing, "though 'tis good to know I must not wait till this one's weaned to enjoy other pleasures. All I want to know is how soon I can hold my son."

Clearly humiliated, the housekeeper had the good grace to say nothing as she backed away from the bed. But John detected a hint of a smile on that stern face.

And then Elizabeth was offering the infant to him without a word, without a caution. He had never seen such absolute trust, and it filled him with awe. Was this her way of asking for the same in return?

"The Marquess of Rand once told me," he said, sliding his fingers under the tiny head no bigger than his palm, "that a man ought never to see his children until they were old enough to speak and pay proper respect. Damned fool, if you ask me."

"Mr. Largent, such language!" Mrs. Davis admonished.

He looked up from his contemplation of the impossibly small human creature in his hands and glanced at Elizabeth. "She doesn't know?" he asked in a hushed whisper.

Elizabeth shook her head. "I told no one."

"Not even Kaspar?"

"No one."

He laughed out loud with undisguised joy and delight until the baby began to howl. At once, Mrs. Davis was there to take the child from him, but he would not let her. He wasn't sure his threatening scowl was enough to intimidate her at this point, but she backed up enough for him to kneel and place his son in the cradle.

Hands on her hips, Mrs. Davis scowled down at him.

"Now, ye've seen yer boy and held him in yer two hands. 'Tis time for the lass to sleep before the bairn wakes with an empty belly. Ye can't be helpin' her wi' that, so ye might as well take yerself doon the stairs and hae a drink wi' yer friends."

His knees protested, and he winced when he leaned on his bruised hand, but he got to his feet and reversed the advantage of height.

"My friends can wait," he said.

The baby seemed determined to make up for his lack of size as soon as possible by nursing every two hours, which left Elizabeth virtually unable to regain her strength. Yet whenever she wakened, John was there, dozing in his chair by the window or already up and lifting the squalling infant from his cradle. On more than one occasion, she stole an extra hour's sleep while her husband paced the floor.

But during those frequent feedings, while the baby suckled and slept at her breast, she found the time to ask and answer questions, if only one or two at a time. By the end of the first week, she had assembled an incredible jigsaw of chance and mischance, of luck and logic.

It all made perfect sense, once the pieces lay joined to form the whole picture, from Jack Silver's intimate knowledge of Kilbury Hall to Kaspar Kennicott's address in a book John had borrowed from him years ago. And if she was amazed at the pains he had taken to conceal his identity for so many years, he was no less impressed with her ability to gauge people's expectations.

"We see what we expect to see," she explained one night while fumbling to untie the lacings of her gown. "And conversely, the unexpected becomes invisible. I did not *expect* to see *you* in that Newgate cell and therefore I did not." To silence the baby's screams, she had given him a knuckle to suck on, but she knew he would discover the ruse quickly. "Just as Betsy Bunch *belonged* in the Black Oak. Oh, drat, there's a knot and I can't undo it with one hand. Can you bring the light closer?"

"If I do, it's likely to drip. Here, let me try." He set the candle on the table beside the bed and leaned over to untangle the ribbons that fastened the front of her gown. "Not only what we expect to see, but what we *want* to see as well. To ease the pain of losing you to Thomas, I wanted you to be as greedy and grasping as he. And I became blind to the truth."

Though she had lost a good deal of her modesty over the past few days to the point where she no longer felt shy exposing her breasts to let the child suckle, this was the first time John had touched her, and she felt a vague apprehension. She did not think he would draw away as he had that night before he left for Kilbury, but neither was she certain he would be anything more than unemotionally helpful.

And she wanted him to be so much more.

She watched his fingers, so long and yet so deft with the narrow ribbons. He could not help but touch her. Did he feel the race of her heart, the singing of the blood in her veins? She thought she detected a slight tremor in his hands as he pulled one ribbon through another, but she put it down to haste. No doubt he merely wanted to finish the job so his son could eat. But when the knot was freed and she raised her hand to open the gown so the tiny mouth could fasten on the nipple that already leaked a drop of rich milk, he pushed her hand aside.

"Let me," he whispered.

He lifted the fabric away from her skin to bare her left breast. Instinctively, the baby found his source of sustenance and began to suck greedily. But as Elizabeth watched, hypnotized, those long highwayman's fingers drew back the other side of her bodice.

"I cannot blame you for lying and telling me there was no child," he said. "I gave you little reason to trust Jack Silver."

"But I didn't lie!" she protested, then stammered a sheepish "I was mistaken. I didn't realize the error until later, after you had let me go. Then it was too late, though I waited for a message from you. You should not have trusted an ignorant girl."

He traced a feathery circle around the right nipple, and another creamy droplet oozed out to be caught on the end of his finger and raised to his lips.

"Divine retribution," he chuckled. "To be jealous of the very son I would have given away."

"No, you would not. Jack Silver, perhaps, but not you."

"I *am* Jack Silver, Elizabeth."

"Jack was the angry part of you, the part you dared not show, but he was not all of you."

"And which part did you fall in love with?"

It was the first time she had heard that familiar sarcasm in months, and it brought a smile to her lips. He straightened and would have covered her again, but she clasped her hand around his wrist and held his flesh to hers.

"All of you," she whispered, staring into eyes turned silver in the candlelight and then letting her own gaze travel brazenly downward. When she looked up again, she saw a smile play about his lips and knew that he understood. Still, she would take no chances. If he did not want her, he must say so. "Don't go. Don't lie and tell me you are comfortable in that chair night after night."

"I am not. I have more aches from that chair than I did from Newgate."

"That is nothing to jest about. You nearly died there."

"And I wake feeling as if I had died in that chair." His smile broadened, but with a hint of wistfulness. "Oh, Elizabeth, we are two very frightened fools, hiding behind painful lies because we have forgotten that truth can be sweet and beautiful."

He leaned down to kiss her. She opened her mouth to him readily, even as she tightened her hand around his on her breast. The warm milk trickled over their fingers like some pagan baptism, washing away all that had gone before.

They spoke often of the past, and laughed now and then at the odd tricks fate had played on them. Elizabeth, regaining her strength, did her best not to worry about the future. She was content to watch her son grow, to lie beside her husband at night, to take pleasure in the everyday joys of life.

Still, there were matters that needed attention. The matter of a name for her son, for example.

Her husband did not agree.

"It's too cold to take him to church for christening, and he's too young to need a name for scolding. In a month or two, when he's bigger," he suggested, not looking up from his study of the papers Kaspar Kennicott had brought him that afternoon.

They sat in the parlor, where the light was better for reading and the interminable needlework necessitated by a child who seemed to grow an inch a day.

"He's nearly two weeks old," she said, glancing down at him in his cradle beside her chair. "I can hardly continue referring to him as 'the baby' or 'my son.' I would like him to have a name."

"And what would you do with it? After all, I have three, and you use none of them."

"Perhaps if I knew which of the three you are, I'd know what to call you," she snapped. She pulled the thread through the fabric so sharply it, like her temper, broke. "You admit the John Colfax I *liked* very much was every bit the masquerade Jack Silver was. Jonathan Largent, for all that I married him, was always a stranger, using me, as I used him, for his personal ends.

"So which are you? The noble scholar who read me poetry and made me laugh and told me about a world beyond my own that I never hoped to see? Or are you the gallant rogue who lifted a man's purse on the point of a sword as easily as he kissed a frozen tavern wench in the moonlight? Or are you yet the resolute Jonathan Largent, so busy about your financial affairs from morning till night that you let your servant build a cradle for your son?"

The length of her speech as well as its vehemence

shocked her. Embarrassed, Elizabeth picked up her sewing once again and tried to tie off the broken threads. Her fingers refused to cooperate.

"Which would you like me to be, my love?"

There was no disguise now, no mask, no shadows to hide or distort the familiar features. Yet the mystery of the highwayman remained in the seductive glitter of his eyes and the teasing half-smile.

He laid the papers aside and walked to her chair. After taking the sewing from her, he pulled her gently to her feet and circled her with his arms.

"Elizabeth, my heart, I am all of them—and none of them. Just as you will always have Betsy's laughter and joy and Lizzie's shy determination, I suppose I must always guard against that streak of the rogue in me."

"I rather liked that rogue," she admitted, curling comfortably into this embrace. "Sometimes."

"Only sometimes?"

"Sometimes Jack was very exasperating."

He chuckled and kissed the top of her head, then confessed, "Yes, he was, though he quite often found himself provoked beyond his limits. Does that mean you no longer think of me as Jack Silver?"

Taking a deep breath and letting it out with a long sigh, Elizabeth thought for a moment. She had, she reflected, not taken the time to consider the matter. "No, I don't. It's almost as if some part of me knew, without my being aware of it, that beneath the highwayman's facade lay the man I had loved since the moment I first saw him."

"The bumbling fool who couldn't take his gloves off without dropping them?"

"No, not at all. You told me it took you years to become Jack Silver. It also took you years to become that bumbling fool. When I first met you, you were a melancholy scholar, devastated by loss and grief, yet determined to see everything set right. I admired that John Colfax, impoverished earl of Kilbury though he was."

"And do you still admire him?"

He squeezed her just enough to make her giggle and look up at him.

"Yes, John, I do."

"Good. Then you won't mind if we christen our son John Campbell Colfax III?"

"Not at all, though it may be confusing."

John shook his head. "He will call me Father with filial respect, and I shall call him John with paternal indulgence. And I am certain neither of us will confuse the tone of voice a woman uses when she speaks to her son with the one she uses when she speaks to her husband."

She laughed and tilted her head back in expectation of his kiss. "Ah, yes, the rogue remains."

"You've found nothing?"

John looked down at the pile of papers neatly stacked on Kaspar Kennicott's desk. A month's worth of investigation, all neatly reported and documented with Kennicott's usual attention to detail and efficiency.

"Nothing," the attorney replied. "Bow Street has no record of him. I've checked the prison and court records. If he ever committed a crime, it was under another name. Nor is he listed in any of the London directories. It's as if the man vanished into thin air twenty years ago, exactly as Stanhope said."

"Yet he bought the house, which means he is still alive somewhere. And holding mortgages that would cost me five thousand pounds a year. Damn it, Kaspar, who is he?"

"I have no clue. Have you asked Elizabeth? Might she know him if her father did?"

John shook his head.

"She knows nothing beyond a vague recollection of the name. She said it sounded familiar when I first exploded that he had bought the Waverley Square house, but no more."

There was another route, one that Kaspar, by the grim expression on his face, had not forgotten.

"The payment is due in three days, John," he reminded. "If Thomas cannot make it, take the money yourself. Meet Miner's courier and follow him."

"I can't leave Elizabeth. Damn it, Kaspar, I wanted all this settled. I wanted to take her back to Kilbury and wed her properly and christen my son. Jack Silver's days of haunting the roads and waylaying travelers are over."

"Then your only choice is to let Miner foreclose."

CHAPTER
30

Elizabeth settled the baby in his cradle and pulled the quilts up over him. Even a few minutes out of the warmth of her own bed had her shivering. She quickly pinched out the candle and crawled back between the still-warm sheets. The nights had turned sharply cold, with frost already forming on the windowpanes. The light of a nearly full moon glittered through the crystals.

John wrapped his arms around her and pulled her closer.

"Your teeth are chattering," he whispered in her ear.

"Please, I've not laced up my gown yet."

"Then don't."

He slipped his hands past the tangle of loose ribbons to cup the fullness of her breasts. She felt the sweet tingle of arousal spread from the tightening nipples like slow, liquid lightning sparking along her nerves.

"I begin to think you are determined to make up for the past nine months in a single week," she teased, trying to wriggle out of the gown without letting any cold air into the bed. "You've become as insatiable as Jack Silver."

"It would take the insatiable Jack Silver to tame you, you greedy wench." He twisted her to face him and kissed her hungrily, covering her mouth with his, sliding his tongue against hers with no coy preliminaries. Then, breaking the kiss, he murmured against her throat, "And who wakened whom *last* night, hmm?"

"You weren't asleep."

"I might have been." He stroked skillful hands down her body, finding the secret place that opened only to him. "Ah, Elizabeth, how I've missed you."

There was no shyness in their passion, no hesitation in their delight of each other. Elizabeth welcomed him eagerly with laughter as well as with the soft moans of sensual pleasure.

She found his letter the next morning, propped against the Bible on the shelf beside the fireplace. As she reached for the slip of paper, she felt the fear coil within her, a fear she had almost forgotten.

His words were innocent enough, but even reading them aloud, Elizabeth found herself unable to believe them.

"'I did not want to spoil last night,'" she recited, ignoring Mrs. Davis who was laying out breakfast, "'so I have written to you now, just moments before I leave. I must go to Kilbury but shall return within the week, and if you need anything in the meantime, you have only to send James to Kaspar.' And he dares to sign it 'Your loving husband'!"

She very nearly flung the letter into the fire but at the last moment tucked it into the pocket of her dress. Then she took down the Bible and carried it to the table.

"Here, now, you oughtn't to be carryin' that!" Mrs. Davis scolded, rushing to take the heavy book from her. "An' I'm sure his lairdship meant well."

Elizabeth refused both the assistance and the consolation.

"I am not an invalid, Mrs. Davis. And I'm very tired of being protected all the time. My father did it from the day I was born, and now John's doing it, too." She set the Bible down with a thump that rattled the cups on the table. The sound gave her a deep sense of satisfaction as she strode to the writing desk for quill and ink.

"Before I came to London, I had never been outside my very narrow and sheltered little world," she continued. "I set out on my own, knowing not a soul and hoping only that the man whose name I had found in a book would be able to help me. Alone, carrying a child whose father had abandoned me—and has done so again, damn his soul—I did what I had to do."

"I dinna think he's abandoned you and young John."

Elizabeth sat down and unstoppered the ink, careful even in her anger not to spatter Mrs. Davis's snowy linen.

"And that's another matter," she added. Oh, damn, but she was worried and frightened and yet determined not to give in to tears. Let the anger, over any petty grievance, blot out the fear she could not bear. "He wishes to name the boy after himself, as if I have no say in the matter after enduring twenty-four hours of agony to bring his child into the world." She opened the Bible's cover and dipped her quill into the ink. "Perhaps I will give him a different name. Perhaps I will call him Benjamin, and—"

The lines and words on the page swam before her eyes, blurring and then clearing and blurring again. The pen dropped from her fingers and spread a black stain on the page before it rolled to the tablecloth and left another there.

"Fetch James," she whispered, "at once."

"Is something wrong?"

"Yes, Mrs. Davis, there is something dreadfully wrong."

Elizabeth blinked, and except for the black splotch that marred one corner of the page, it was blank. What she had seen was only a flash of memory from a distant childhood.

She was nearly hysterical by the time she stepped down from the phaeton in front of Kaspar Kennicott's office three hours later. Both James and Mrs. Davis had argued against her decision to see the solicitor in person, pointing out the inadequate protection the phaeton provided against the weather, but Elizabeth had prevailed. Now, with a very wet, hungry, and vocal infant in her arms, she burst into the solicitor's office—and into tears.

Kaspar was at her side in an instant, his arm encircling her shoulders as he led her to his own chair near the glowing coal fire. "Sigwalt, bring us some tea!" he shouted over the baby's wails. "Here, let me take your cloak, my dear. It's all damp from the fog and you'll be—"

Elizabeth shook her head and groaned. "No, please, he's hungry," she whispered, fumbling beneath the cloak to open the front of her dress. She had not expected such pain from breasts swollen with milk; the relief she felt at freeing them from the confines of her clothing overcame any embarrassment.

"Ah, my dear, I have not reached these seventy years without some understanding of the way of the world. Shall I leave you some privacy?"

"There's no time." She leaned forward as the baby began to suckle and the pressure eased. Still, the other breast throbbed and each time his little knees bumped her, she cried out. Unbidden tears trickled down her face. "We've got to stop John or he'll be killed."

The words rushed out so quickly she knew they made no sense, but she could not stop them until

Kaspar halted her with a hand on her shoulder and a cup of steaming tea.

"Whoa, child. Drink this, wait until you're more comfortable, then begin at the beginning. Tell me everything, and we'll see what we must do."

She snaked a hand out from her cloak and took the cup for a single scalding sip. The heat spread some calm through her, enough for her to gasp out the most important news.

"Benjamin Miner is my father, Kaspar."

The midnight air crackled with frost and a wind that cut to the bone. Thin streamers of clouds sped across a moon that had reached its full. The gray stallion stamped and snorted as though the hard run from London had merely whet his appetite for adventure.

John let the horse trot in a tight oval in the middle of the road, thus affording a view in either direction. No one else traveled the road this night as though they knew, even after his long absence, this was a night for Jack Silver.

Though trees encroached on either side of the road, they were thin and leafless, offering little shelter for hunter or quarry. John glanced over his shoulder frequently at each tiny sound and kept one of the primed pistols in his hand. Benjamin Miner could not have selected a more indefensible spot for the rendezvous with his courier.

"That is a fine piece of horseflesh, nephew."

The voice came from behind as though Thomas had been watching and waiting for just such a moment.

"One of Conquest's get, no doubt. A rather expensive mount for a penniless nobleman, wouldn't you say?"

John held the stallion still. Thomas would not have come to an ambush unarmed, but there was a chance he had not seen the weapon already in John's hand.

"He was a gift."

"A gift? From whom? Jack Silver perhaps? Like the twelve hundred pounds you so conveniently produced to meet the interest payment on Mr. Miner's mortgages?" Thomas's laughter cut through the wind. "I think instead it's the other way round, nephew."

He emerged from the trees a few yards up the road. He must have been waiting for hours, almost since John left Kilbury Hall. The big hunter Thomas struggled to control was more horse than an indifferent rider would normally choose but the only one capable of staying with the gray for any distance at all. A clever choice, though not without risks.

"Do you want something, Thomas? You said the courier will not come if he sees more than one person waiting for him."

"Yes, I want something. Do you think I'd be out on a night like this if I didn't? And there's no courier. Not here. He lies a mile down the road."

Reflexively, John turned on the man.

"You killed him?"

With mock innocence Thomas laughed and replied, "Not I, John. Jack Silver will take the blame for the murder as well as the theft of the twelve hundred pounds. After all, he's stolen from Mr. Miner before, and this is such a perfect night for highway robbery."

The clouds shifted again, this time baring the moon and flooding the road with clear luminescence. John saw now that Thomas carried an ancient blunderbuss, its brass furniture dull in the moonlight. At a distance of three or four yards, even Thomas could not miss.

But the pistol, hidden beneath John's cloak, would retaliate.

"You intend to kill me?" he asked.

"Oh, no, not I! Justice is to be served by the courts, not overeager citizens. You'll have your day in the dock, nephew." He laughed again as another streamer of cloud moved across the face of the moon. "And then you'll be hanged, your body hung in chains at the crossroads, where the lovely Elizabeth can see it as I bring her to Kilbury from your quaint little home in London."

The light danced, and so did the brown hunter. Above the rising wind, John heard Thomas talk to the gelding. Under any other circumstances, he would have fired the pistol long ago, but the long barrel of the blunderbuss gave Thomas far more destructive power, even with a bad shot. John refused to take any more unnecessary risks.

He had taken enough already. If he had not been afflicted with overweening pride the past few weeks, he would have contented himself with regaining most of his estate and bringing Elizabeth and his son home to a dilapidated but solvent Kilbury Hall. Instead, he had ignored his better judgment—as well as Kaspar's repeated warnings—and set off to find the elusive Benjamin Miner.

And for what? Never in his life had he been as happy, as complete as in that tiny cottage with Elizabeth, his son, a one-eyed manservant, and a Scots housekeeper who lectured him when he didn't eat his peas. No man in his right mind would risk that against a madman's ambush or the hangman's noose.

Yet he had done it.

And then he saw one of the shadows behind Thomas separate from the rest. If the hunter turned, Thomas was sure to see the figure that crept up on him. John had to keep his uncle's attention.

He knew Thomas loved to brag.

"How did you learn about Elizabeth?" he asked.

"A friend. Hamilton Wilke."

One of the names Elizabeth had remembered in the tower room.

"Edward's associate."

"In a sense. Years ago, Edward suggested I seek out Wilke's partner, a pathetic but greedy fool named

Race, who lent money to your poor father. When Race blew his brains out over a business deal gone sour, Wilke took over the collection of the interest."

The stealthy figure inched closer. Moonlight glinted on the metal of weapon. Thomas noticed nothing.

"For twenty years, Mr. Wilke and I had a very confidential relationship. Until one day a lovely young widow strolled into his office to buy Race's note back, a note no one but he and I—and you, nephew—could know about. Wilke wrote to me about her. In fact, his letter arrived the night you asked me about Benjamin Miner."

John swore involuntarily. He remembered the footman bringing the letter, remembered how he almost took it from him. Another opportunity lost.

As though he had read his nephew's thoughts, Thomas laughed before he continued, "Wilke told me all about this lovely young widow, a very *pregnant* young widow named Largent. Since I already knew a common felon by the same name who had conveniently stepped into your shoes in Newgate, and he wasn't dead, it was easy enough to find you."

"Why didn't you kill me then? Murder is not an uncommon thing in London."

"You misunderstand me, nephew. I don't want to kill you. I want to watch you die. Publicly. Ignominiously. I want to see you stripped of everything you hold dear, from your title and your once-fine estate to your pride and your wife and that bastard son of yours. Just as you and your father took everything from me."

Once again the moon shone clear. For an infinitesimal moment, the wind stilled and the shadows froze. Thomas raised the gun.

"Now!" John yelled at the stalking figure behind Thomas and fired at the same instant he kicked the gray stallion.

He saw the flashes of powder, heard the explosions

as three weapons fired as one. His right arm burned, then went numb but he could not look to see how bad the wound was. Controlling the nervous stallion with his knees, he drew the other pistol.

Thomas slipped soundlessly from the saddle until his body hit the ground with an eerie thud. He lay sprawled in the middle of the road and did not move, even when a stealthy shadow moved out from behind his horse with a pronounced limp and a fowling piece cradled in his arm.

"Is 'e dead?" Harry asked.

John dismounted, aware now of a growing ache somewhere below his right shoulder, and walked to where his uncle lay.

The wound in the center of Thomas's chest stained his shirt with blood that looked like ink in the moonlight. The second shot, from Harry's gun, had taken him in the hip, and the blood was already soaking into the cold dust of the road.

If Thomas lived, he would never walk again. Harry had seen to that.

But he would not live. And he knew it.

There was one question left to be answered.

"Why, Uncle?" John asked. "Why did you do it?"

Thomas laughed, the blood gurgling in his throat. "I loved her," he said, "and she laughed at me. Called me a silly boy and patted me on the head. I was nothing to her."

"Who? Not Elizabeth."

"So beautiful, so cold, so greedy. Lenore only wanted William for his title. I was the better man; she'd have loved me when I finished proving it."

It wasn't true, and John knew it, knew it as surely as he recognized his own mistakes. His parents had loved each other deeply, passionately, just he now worshiped Elizabeth. The knife of his own guilt twisted sharply.

"But Lenore cheated me by dying, and you, you

pampered little bastard who had everything *I* should have had"—he coughed and the blood welled in his mouth—"you put the Kilbury sapphires around her neck as she lay in her coffin and cheated me again. I couldn't let you get away with that."

John choked on the words, disgusted at the very thought, but though it would change nothing, nothing at all, he had to know. "When did you take them from her, Thomas?"

The answering voice was barely a whisper, weak and rough.

"That night, after William buried her, before the earth settled over her, I dug them up. She didn't deserve them, not if she didn't love me. I had to make her pay. And now I will make Elizabeth pay, too."

He closed his eyes but continued to breathe slowly, the death rattle loud in the midnight silence.

The wind stung Elizabeth's eyes and rasped her cheeks raw. Kaspar's curricle, light and pulled by a fresh team, was just beginning the climb to the tree-crowned hilltop when she saw the flashes of what could only be gunpowder. A full heartbeat later, the reports of three shots reached her.

"He'll be all right!" Kaspar shouted above the thunder of racing hooves. "The third shot had to be Harry's, and I've never known Harry to miss."

But Harry could have missed this time, or he could have been too late. She blinked her eyes clear and willed the horses to greater speed.

And then it was she who was running up the last few yards to the top of the hill where John was silhouetted against the moon-silvered sky. He caught her and pulled her to him, nearly crushing the child in her arms between them.

She had already seen the body on the ground at his feet, the blood that covered the front of Thomas's shirt, the dark pool at his side. Even as she buried her face against her husband's shoulder and murmured incoherent prayers of thanks, Thomas laughed. Something vile rose in her throat at the sound, and she would have spat it in his face, but John held her too tightly.

"How touching," the dying man gasped with another choked laugh. "Just like William and Lenore, with their fine son between them."

Elizabeth looked up into the well-loved face now turned to a cold silver mask. "What does he mean?" she asked.

"Nothing. He's dying and he can't hurt us now."

From the corner of her eye she saw him raise his right hand to take the pistol from his left. The sleeve was torn, with a dark stain around the tear.

"You're hurt!"

"It's nothing," he assured her. "Now go, my love. There is nothing you can do here."

Except watch a man die, she thought as she began to move out of John's protective embrace.

He urged her on. "Go back with Kaspar. To the Dower House and—"

She saw everything too clearly in the moonlight. Stepping away from John's outstretched arm, she could not avoid one last glance at the man who had caused them so much pain and who now endured his own last agony. The tortured face twisted into a hideous grimace, and despite his mortal wounds, Thomas raised a hand in farewell. A hand that clasped a silver pistol.

And then she was falling, screaming, pushed out of the way as John lifted his own weapon in defense. Blinded by the flash and deafened by the explosion, she knew nothing else until a heavy body collapsing atop her pressed her into the frost-hardened dirt of the road.

He did not move for a very long second, causing her untold agonies until he whispered, "I should have put him out of his misery long ago. Dear God, Elizabeth, what have I done to you?"

"I believe," she managed to reply above her son's frightened screams, "you have just saved my life."

They left Thomas where he lay, surrounded by the trappings of the man he had set out to destroy: a black silk mask, the pair of silver pistols that had killed him, the pouch containing the twelve hundred pounds he stole from the courier. Someone would find the body and declare Thomas Colfax to have been the notorious Jack Silver, thus laying the legend to rest—and relieving John of the threat of the gallows.

Then they went their separate ways, Kaspar and Harry to take Thomas's horse to the Kilbury stable, John and Elizabeth to the Dower House.

For the first few miles, they rode in silence, as if the treasure of life and reunion were too precious to risk even with words. But as the lights of the ancient Dower House twinkled into view, Elizabeth began the final tale.

"Kaspar told me everything on the journey. How you intended to give Thomas the money to pay the mortgage interest and then follow the courier. I was so worried we'd be too late."

"You have too little faith in Jack Silver."

She turned to look over her shoulder at him. Despite the cold, he had pushed the hood of his cloak back, and the great moon riding high overhead illuminated his features clearly. His smile was as teasing as Jack Silver's had ever been, yet different for the love and fear and relief that no longer had to hide behind the highwayman's mask.

Elizabeth laughed and let him nuzzle her cheek.

"Jack Silver rode into an ambush," she reminded him. "If Kaspar had not insisted we stop first to tell Harry Grove—"

"I wondered why he was there. I thought perhaps he

had simply decided to settle his own score with Thomas."

"Perhaps he did. Kaspar told me, too, how Thomas's efforts to ruin your father nearly killed Harry and cost him his leg." She shuddered uncontrollably; the tightening of her husband's embrace was more than welcome. "He was so cruel! To so many people. And all for a love he knew would never be returned."

"Men have been known to do worse things for lesser motives."

There was much more she wanted to tell him, but something in his voice told her he needed the silence. He needed to come to terms with what he had done. And she had to come to terms with what she would tell him.

The boards were gone from the window, letting moonlight gleam through the frosted panes. Little else, however, was changed. Even the books still rested on the table, *Tom Jones* and *Robinson Crusoe* and even the book of sonnets, along with the needles and thread. Elizabeth set her reticule beside them.

She walked around the room, touching the familiar objects with affectionate hands. The chairs, the wardrobe, the lamp. John pulled a drawer from the wardrobe and set it on the floor at the side of the bed.

"With a blanket, this ought to hold him for the night, don't you think?" he asked, taking the sleeping child from her.

"Hm? Oh, yes, I'm sure it will."

She continued to wander, in aimless circles it seemed, while Peg made a bed for the baby and Ethan hauled in the tub and filled it with hot water. Not until she and John were alone, the door securely closed and latched, did she suddenly feel the weariness and sink onto the chair by the fire. His chair.

"Your bath and your supper are getting cold."

Her eyes snapped open, and she realized she had drifted into a doze.

He took her hands and drew her to her feet, then began methodically stripping her of her clothes. First the cloak, then the ruined dress, petticoats, chemise, shoes, and stockings, everything. And he consigned it all to the fire.

"But, John, I have nothing else!" she protested.

"For tonight, you need nothing else, my lady. Now, step into the tub and let me—"

"Don't," she snapped.

"Don't what?"

"Don't call me your lady. I'm not, you know."

"Ah, I wondered if you had noticed," he said.

With his hands on her naked shoulders, he guided her to the tub where, more out of modesty, she climbed into the water.

"Does it feel good?"

She could not deny the truth. "Yes, it feels wonderful." Even more wonderful when he soaped a thick square of flannel and gently began to scrub the back of her neck. "John, I am quite capable of doing this myself, and your arm must be causing you some pain."

"It does, and it does not matter. Haven't I caused you plenty of pain myself? Stealing your virtue, chasing you off to London with nothing but a satchel of paste jewelry and a baby in your belly?"

"The jewels weren't paste. Kaspar lied to you."

She leaned her head back and looked up at the scowl on John's face.

"Good God, does no one tell the truth any more?"

She did not smile when she said, "I love you, and that *is* the truth. Kaspar thought he was doing you a good turn, making you feel a little more responsible for me. He had no idea I was using you as flagrantly as you were using me."

"When did he tell you this?"

She hesitated and lowered her head, avoiding his gaze. He stroked the lathered cloth over her breasts, then drew it up between them to her chin and tilted her head back once more.

She met his eyes and told him what she knew she must even if it destroyed everything.

"Two days ago, when I told him I knew who Benjamin Miner is."

"You *knew?* And you never—"

The rag fell into the water with a splash.

"Not until the morning you left!" she cried, reaching for him.

But he had walked away from the tub, beyond her grasp, running wet, soapy fingers through his own disheveled hair.

"He's my father, John." She found the rag under the water and ran it quickly over the rest of her body while she told him the tale, learned only that evening from Edward Stanhope himself.

"Benjamin Miner's mother was a governess in the duke of Courtland's household. When their liaison resulted in a child, she was thrown into the streets. He wanted revenge, but he also wanted what he considered his birthright."

"Are you saying I'm no better than he?"

She wanted to assure him she meant nothing of the kind, but her next sentence would only prove that a lie, so she went on without comment.

"He tried to make his fortune in trade, but the money didn't come fast enough, so he stole thousands of pounds from his friends and then disappeared. He changed his name to Stanhope, bought a manor house in Somerset, installed his wife and infant daughter in unexpected luxury, and waited for an opportunity to invest the rest of his stolen money.

"He found it in Thomas Colfax as well as a kindred soul bent on revenge and ruination."

She stepped out of the tub, shivering, and reached

for the towel draped over the back of the chair. Beneath it lay a worn red dressing gown. Drying as quickly as she could, she continued, "My father wanted me to marry you, John. He thought he was helping your father by lending him the money and that eventually he would consent to a wedding. It was his only hope. My mother died when I was two years old, but he was afraid to remarry, for fear someone would learn his secret. Then, when I was five or six, I contracted a simple childhood disease and passed it to him. I only suffered some swelling in my neck and jaw, but it went further with him."

John chuckled with obvious bitterness. "Mumps. I had them, too, about the same time. So he caught them, they went down to his testicles, and he could never father another child."

Elizabeth pulled on the red robe and tied it tightly around her waist. It would not be long before the baby wakened again; already her breasts felt full and tender.

She sat in the chair, not trusting herself to approach the man who stood by the fire and stared into the flames, as if there were answers in them no one else could give.

"He never meant to hurt anyone," she said quietly. "He did his best to make good on the money he stole by lending money at generous rates to the friends he had stolen from, then sending Thomas to them when he mortgaged the Kilbury properties at much higher rates. And he believed that when your father approved our marriage, he would give everything back as a wedding gift."

She reached for her reticule and from it withdrew a sheaf of papers.

"I'm not your wife, my lord, not legally, but here are the mortgages your father gave to Benjamin Miner and Edward Stanhope."

She held them up to him, and one by one he took them from her.

"They're all there. And the deed to the house in Waverley Square. Father planned to live there himself. He said there was nothing left for him here, that he had sacrificed his only child, and if he could—"

"I damn near did the same."

She watched, unable to speak for the sobs held silent in her throat, as he extracted one curled paper from the roll and tossed the others into the fire. That one he laid on the table, beside the books he had brought her from Kilbury's library. Then he took her hands in his, but instead of pulling her to her feet, he knelt at them and bent his head to kiss her upturned palms.

"I asked you the night Jack returned you to the Black Oak why you never married the earl of Kilbury."

Confused, she shook her head and said, "But you drugged me. I remember nothing."

"Not even your answer?"

"Nothing, I swear."

"You said, and *I* remember exactly, 'Because you never asked me.'"

"The note!" she gasped, understanding at last. "John's note! No, no, your note. 'Consider the question asked.' You thought I knew who you were! Oh, damn, but I'm confused."

"Yes, my note, which I realized was far too subtle and so I sent you another, which apparently you never received." He kissed her wrists, running the tip of his tongue across the taut tendons to where her pulse beat. "And you'd best watch that language around Mrs. Davis or she'll have soap in your mouth."

She laughed.

"She will at that, won't she? Oh, John, I *did* receive your note but I never read it. When Jack Silver let me go, I thought I could bring myself to ask you to marry me, to save me from being forced to wed Thomas. But then I realized I had made a mistake, that there *was* a child, and I could not dishonor you, not when I already loved you, too."

Now it was his turn to laugh as he reached up to wipe away the single tear that slid down her cheek.

"Elizabeth, I want you to be my wife not because you are the mother of my son, but because I love you. Because I've loved you since the day I chased those naked boys away to leave us alone so I could read you naughty poetry—"

"Was it naughty?"

"Very naughty, but you were very innocent and I took most unfair advantage. Now stop interrupting me. I want this over because my knees are killing me."

"Then I shall consider the question asked, and the answer is yes."

She leaned forward, forgetting how the red robe gaped open, and kissed him shamelessly. Almost at once his hands were upon her, untying the sash, slipping the soft old garment off her shoulders and arms, pulling her down beside him.

"There is a bed, you know," she said, squirming on the hard floor.

"But I thought you liked adventure. Isn't that why you became Betsy Bunch?"

"I believe, my love, I have had my fill of adventure."

The Entrancing Novel
from the
New York Times
Bestselling
Author of *Perfect*

Until You

by

*Judith
McNaught*

Now Available in
Paperback from

POCKET
STAR
BOOKS

1032-01

KATHRYN

LYNN

DAVIS

The Long-awaited sequel to
the *New York Times* Bestselling Novel
TOO DEEP FOR TEARS

ALL

WE HOLD

DEAR

POCKET BOOKS

Available from Pocket Books Hardcover
mid-April 1995

1081

Pocket Books presents. . .

Everlasting Love

Sparkling new springtime romances from

Jayne Ann Krentz

Linda Lael Miller

Linda Howard

Kasey Michaels

Carla Neggers

Available mid-April 1995

POCKET
B O O K S

1059